MW00353806

A Jenetta Carver® Adventure

A GALAXY UNKNOWN®

A GALAXY UNKNOWN

Book 1

BY

THOMAS DEPRIMA

Vinnia Publishing - U.S.A.

AGU:®

A Galaxy Unknown®

A Galaxy Unknown® series – Book 1
Copyright ©1999 by Thomas J. DePrima
15.c.1

All rights reserved under International Copyright Conventions. The scanning, uploading, downloading, and/or distribution of this book via the Internet or any other means without the permission of the copyright holder is illegal, and punishable by law.

No part of this novel may be reproduced in any form or by any electronic means, including information storage and retrieval systems, without permission in writing from the copyright holder, except by a reviewer who may quote brief passages in a review.

This is a work of fiction. All the characters and events portrayed in this book are fictional, and any resemblance to real people or incidents is purely coincidental.

ISBN: **978-1-61931-000-1**

ISBN-10: **1619310007**

Cover art by: Nicholas Stanton Turner

Appendices containing political and technical data highly pertinent to this series are included at the back of this book.

To contact the author, or see additional information about this and his other novels, visit:

http://www.deprima.com

This novel is dedicated to my good friend Ted King for his invaluable suggestions, proofreading, and encouragement during the creation of this series.

I want to thank Myra Shelley and her team at Independent Author Services for the excellent copyediting and proofreading work they have performed on this and the other books in this series.

This series of novels includes:

A Galaxy Unknown®...

A Galaxy Unknown®
Valor at Vauzlee
The Clones of Mawcett
Trader Vyx
Milor!
Castle Vroman
Against All Odds
Return to Dakistee
Retreat And Adapt
Azula Carver

Other series and novels by the author:

AGU:® Border Patrol...

Citizen X
Clidepp Requital

AGU:® SC Intelligence...

The Star Brotherhood

Colton James novels...

A World Without Secrets
Vengeance Is Personal

When The Spirit...

When The Spirit Moves You
When The Spirit Calls

Table of Contents

Chapter One
~ September 29th, 2256 ~

A montage of red and white splashes radiated from the overhead emergency light, slathering the room and dousing Jenetta Carver's sleeping form without effect. But when the alert-horn's undulating shrieks stabbed at her body and knifed their way to the marrow of her bones, consciousness reclaimed her sleep-anesthetized brain.

At once disoriented and frightened, she realized she was sitting upright in bed. Blinking eyes still thick with sleep, she swiped at each to clear away the vestiges of slumber. A final ripple of mind-numbing din shook the bedroom, then all was quiet— for a full two seconds. An emergency directive, delivered through her implanted cranial transducer, began to reverberate incessantly inside her head at twice-normal volume. At the same instant, the message started emanating from overhead speakers throughout the ship.

She whipped back the lightweight covers and flung herself from the bed, landing lightly on the balls of her feet— a fraction of a second before screaming loudly and crashing solidly to the carpeted deck, arms and legs akimbo like a child's hastily discarded doll.

"Ow, dammit," she muttered, the uncharacteristic oath escaping her lips as she kicked at the ankle-high service boots she had left lying in the middle of the floor; however, the emergency condition of the ship left little time for self-recrimination.

Kneeling on scraped knees, she struggled to pull her night-gown over her head, cursing both its tight embrace and herself for not wearing her usual pajamas this evening.

Once free of a garment that seemed to resist removal, she jumped up and snatched her trousers from the chair where she had left them. Flopping backwards onto her bed, she shoved both feet into the pants legs as she landed, then nimbly leapt back onto the floor. The newly commissioned Space Command officer didn't waste time trying to button her blouse or close her tunic; she simply yanked them on before jamming her feet into her soft, flat-soled boots and grabbing her most prized personal possession from her dresser. With the framed picture of her family tucked safely beneath her arm, she bolted for the door.

A dozen small housekeeping bots were cleaning walls and carpet in a bright corridor devoid of fellow crewmembers as Jenetta burst from her quarters. Except for the flashing emergency lights and horrific message of impending doom being broadcast by the computer throughout the ship, there seemed little amiss until she noticed the soft whooshing sounds generated by the rapid departure of activated escape pods.

"All hands, abandon ship," the computer announced casually in a simulated feminine voice. "This is not a drill. Containment failure is imminent. You have a safety margin of— 218 seconds. All hands abandon ship." Repeating endlessly, only the number of remaining seconds changed. The pleasing sound of the computer's audio interface normally had a calming effect, but the substance of the message belied the delivery. Echoing in Jenetta's CT, it greatly increased an already heightened state of agitation.

Any anticipation of swift departure Jenetta might have had was crushed when she discovered that both escape pods in the nearest tube were already gone. Like a hurdler in a track and field event, she flew over sixty-centimeter-tall housekeeping bots as she frantically raced through the deserted corridors of the quarters' deck, but her search yielded only empty tubes as the computer complacently droned on about the urgency of the situation.

Now fully awake, Jenetta suddenly realized everyone aboard ship, except the skeletal third-watch crew, had probably been snug in their beds at this hour but obviously hadn't squandered precious seconds changing out of nightclothes. The Engineering Section, five decks below, was home to the next largest concentration of escape pods. Breathless, and on the verge of calamitous panic, she jumped into a lift and barked a command that sent the car plummeting to that level.

Her heart seemed ready to burst from her chest when she finally spotted an available escape pod. Its wide-open hatch and inviting interior seemed to scream at her to hurry as the computer announced that only fourteen seconds remained. She hurled herself into the pod and smacked the flashing, over-sized launch button with the bottom of her fist. The action instantly sealed the pod and initiated the emergency launch sequence. G forces pushed her deep into the thick padding of the pod's nose cone. Jenetta fought to fill her lungs as compressed gas jets positioned in the tube walls blasted the diminutive transport out of the main ship.

The capsule's main rocket engine ignited as it cleared the ship and the pod furiously clawed its way through space, desperately seeking to distance itself from its former sanctuary. The noise and vibration from the chemical engine was unlike anything she had ever experienced. Close to blacking out, Jenetta counted off the final seconds in her head, all the time willing the tiny craft to move faster. Since her CT was still functional, she knew that she was too close, much too close.

"...Five, Four, Three..."

The countdown never reached 'Two.' As the *Hokyuu's* long and faithful service to the Galactic Alliance came to an unnervingly violent end, fragments from the ship swatted at the life pod and sent it careening along an erratic trajectory. Automatic gyros and attitude thrusters toiled to stabilize the craft as Jenetta remained helplessly flattened against the capsule's cushioned bulkhead. One of two small portholes flared briefly with a blinding light that brilliantly illuminated the padded compartment as combustible material in the ship ignited. But just as quickly, the porthole darkened again, the oxygen in the *Hokyuu* having been either burnt off or dispersed into the vacuum of space.

The pod's main rocket cut out after completing its programmed sixty-second burn. In the deafening silence that ensued, Jenetta was able to pull herself to a porthole, but an ebony curtain had once again descended over the area. She strained to spot signs of other survivors but, without benefit of a nearby sun, the vast blackness of space that enveloped the pod swallowed hope. The light from distant stars was occasionally broken as nearby objects passed between them and her pod, but she had no way of knowing if the dark, silent shapes were other pods or merely twisted chunks of broken ship radiating outward from the disaster site. Weak, emergency radio beacon signals provided the only testament that others had made it out alive, or at least that other pods had ejected from the ship.

Jenetta was still staring cheerlessly out the porthole when a realization struck her with the force of a micro-asteroid. Her retrorocket hadn't fired! Whirling, she clawed furiously at the thick padding that covered the rear bulkhead and the door to the pod's main compartment. A sensor switch in the doorjamb instantly relayed a signal to the onboard computer as the door opened. Over a sixty-second interval, all pod functions would initiate, including artificial gravity to a full g.

While still literally weightless, Jenetta pushed off from the bulkhead with a powerful thrust of her legs. Intending to reach the onboard computer console on the larboard sidewall, she almost overshot her target, but managed to get a hand on a grab bar and check her trajectory. As she steadied herself in front of the console, she manually entered the command to fire the retrorocket, but the telltale braking that would halt the progress of the life pod and keep it near the original disaster location until rescue ships arrived still didn't occur. The pod continued its pell-mell flight from the last reported position of the *Hokyuu* as artificial gravity slowly exerted its dominance over her and she became firmly rooted on the deck. Jenetta repeatedly sent the command to fire the retrorocket, only to be met with similar negative results after each attempt. She felt an icy hand reach out and clench her heart with a savage grip. "This is bad, Carver," she said ominously in the deathly silent cabin, "you've landed in it deep this time."

Equipped with a low-power communications system, the pod should have been able to contact other life pods from the

Hokyuu. Following the explosion, Jenetta sat at the radio console for hours transmitting, "This is Ensign Carver of the GSC *Hokyuu*, calling anyone. Does anyone copy? Acknowledge please." Although all discernible evidence indicated that the transmitter was working, no one responded to her hails. She had even tried using her cranial transducer, a miniscule electronic component subcutaneously implanted against the exterior skull of every cadet upon entrance to the Academy. Vibrations from the vocal cords, reverberating in the cranium, are picked up by the transducer and piggybacked onto a carrier wave. The devices only function on Space Command vessels and bases properly equipped to provide the carrier, but Jenetta was desperate enough to try nearly anything. Unable to contact any of the other survivors, it appeared almost certain that her com system was malfunctioning. Since the emergency locator beacon was tied to the com system, she feared she might not be transmitting a signal.

The twenty-one-year-old Space Command ensign spent the remainder of her first day aboard the life pod pacing and fretting like a tiger in a cage as she concentrated on the main problem— the retrorocket malfunction. The soft soles of her boots made just a whisper of sound on the medium-blue carpet of the deck as she repeatedly traversed the pod's interior from end to end. The five-foot, four-inch blonde knew that if rescue ships didn't arrive post-haste, she'd be too far away for them to spot the movement of her tiny unpowered pod with their sensors. However, all of her intense concentration on the problem failed to produce the much-desired epiphany.

Having already expended its sixty seconds of fuel propelling the pod away from the ship, the main rocket couldn't be used to stop, or even slow, the pod's travel by flipping the craft and performing a quick burn. A skillful ship's engineer might know of a way to fire the malfunctioning retrorocket, but Jenetta, a young, brilliant astrophysicist, was out of her element. While all Academy cadets must complete rudimentary courses in spacecraft engineering, her limited knowledge of escape pod design and construction didn't permit her to identify what was preventing the rocket from firing, especially since the computer repeatedly verified transmission of the command to fire. The pod's onboard configuration manual showed the electronic connections to be part of a simple fiberoptic wiring harness. After testing the connections to the point where the wires passed through the hull of the pod, she was forced to assume that the problem was external to the craft. With no EVA suit available, there was nothing more she could do.

Admitting defeat with the retrorocket problem, she abandoned the effort and turned her attention to computing the pod's position and course. Four explosive bolts held a small, protective cover over an external sensor array. When she released the cover, Jenetta was able to begin computing position, course, and speed. After performing the necessary analysis and calculations, Jenetta sat back in her chair, stunned. The inadvertent boost received from the explosion of the ship had increased the pod's speed to over thirty-two kps, almost *eight* times the maximum speed that pods are expected to achieve during their short burst. Since departing Earth, the *Hokyuu* had been traveling for ninety-six days, so she knew they were still sixty-three days from their destination, a small SC base on Hyllfoll. Her computations told Jenetta that she'd be over a hundred seventy-five million kilometers from the disaster site when the rescue ship arrived, assuming that it came from the base. Even more depressing, the rescuers would have no way of knowing how many pods had successfully ejected before the explosion.

Not being a bridge officer, Jenetta had no idea how close they'd been to the nearest ship or even if an emergency message had been sent, although the *Hokyuu's* computer should have seen to that automatically once the 'Abandon Ship' order was issued. She only knew that she was now dangerously close to becoming just another miniscule piece of drifting flotsam in the great eternal eddies of space.

The emergency food rations she found in the pod would last Jenetta six months, but she might be able to stretch them to eight or nine. While most of the food was stowed in storage compartments beneath the deck, a lot had simply been stacked and packed in every available space in the passenger section. To open up the living area, Jenetta moved the rations packs during the first hours aboard. The nose cone made an excellent larder. The recycling of water and regeneration of air ensured a nearly inexhaustible supply of the two commodities. Although much too small to contain food synthesis hardware and supplies, each life pod did contain three stasis beds that provided a means to extend the survivable time in a life pod, or to double the pod's capacity for short-term use since stasis-bed occupants would consume none of the food supplies. Once cocooned inside the small, self-contained life support units, the bodily processes were slowed to near death, leaving the user in a coma-like sleep. The beds could theoretically sustain an occupant for years, but, because of the ever-present risk of equipment malfunctions, Jenetta viewed their use strictly as a last resort.

*   *   *

Designed to optimally accommodate no more than three crewmembers, Space Command life pods provide a spacious, although somewhat austere interior encompassing an area roughly six meters in length by three meters in width. Extensive use of polycarbonate mirrors create the impression of a much larger space, while cool, eye-pleasing colors, intended to calm disaster survivors during a time of extreme emotional distress, cover all non-mirrored interior walls and surfaces. A full-wall 3D SimWindow occupies one end of the pod, and pod denizens can select from dozens of different animated views. In tests, the designers found a scene from a tropical island paradise to be the most popular with pod occupants. Tall palm trees leaning drunkenly towards a vast ocean of deep aqua sway gently in the breeze against a medium-blue, almost cloudless sky. While sea birds glide overhead, uttering occasional plaintive cries, and small crabs scurry about silently near the waterline, white-capped rollers crash endlessly on a deserted, white-sand beach. The associated sound track reinforces the image as it plays through hidden speakers in the pod. Although not included in life pods, an optional scent generator can produce the salty smell of sea air.

The second most popular Simage proved to be a full day of images captured at the Northern Hemisphere Space Academy. Shot from a third-floor window in Driscoll Hall, just one of several cadet dormitories, the SimWindow looks out across the parade ground towards the academy chapel. Hundreds of grey-uniformed cadets are seen going about their daily business beneath a pale-blue sky filled with large, puffy clouds. The blue-green grass of the parade ground looks cool and peaceful against the stoic gray granite of the imposing edifice on Solemnity Hill. While the spire of the distant chapel stretches longingly towards the heavens, melodious strains of music from its renowned carillon waft across the campus. The jumbled voices of people engaged in idle conversation as they pass the dorm room's open door to the corridor can be heard in the background.

* * *

After three long months of interminable waiting for rescue, Ensign Jenetta Carver was ready to climb the walls. She had managed to maintain her sanity this long by spending innumerable hours listening to the music selections available on the pod's computer as she partook of the bounty of reading material also contained in its memory. Owing to their acutely insipid nature, she'd only been able to suffer through the plethora of administrative and technical manuals once, but she'd read the few fictional novels several times.

Most of her time in isolation was occupied in studying the dozens of available military tomes. The three-volume masterpiece *On War*, by Karl von Clausewitz, the Prussian general and military theorist who proposed a doctrine of total war, and war as an extension of diplomacy, was definitely the most thought provoking, while the battle strategies of Sun-Tzu, the Chinese general, were the most enlightening. Numerous books written about historical battles, one of which covered major confrontations back as far as the First Punic War in 264 BC, had also been loaded into the computer. As a personal exercise, Jenetta modified a battle simulation program she found in the system so she could change certain strategic variables. She fought historic battles repeatedly, employing different troop strengths, reinforcements, weapons, supplies, terrain, and weather conditions to see how the outcome might have been affected. She was amazed by how many of history's most famous battles could so easily have gone the other way if the defeated commander had possessed marginally better intelligence information with regard to the enemy's position, strength, or movement, better communication with unit commanders, better timing, or, perhaps, just a little better luck. The most successful commanders, such as Sun-Tzu and Alexander the Great, had been those who came to rely on surprising the enemy by always doing the unexpected.

She also whiled away the hours by exercising to stay in shape, or by playing the only game contained on the personal log ring she always wore. Written by an unknown programmer, her game was one of several she had found in an ancient archive of Internet software programs while still in elementary school. Dating back to the days before Earth had made contact with any extraterrestrial species, it assumed all aliens to be vicious, voracious, blood-sucking, flesh-devouring monsters that must be destroyed on sight. Her advanced computer skills had enabled her to adapt it to modern computer systems and it gave her something to occupy her time whenever she became bored.

Jenetta had shared the game— which progressed through four levels of play for the skillful participant— with her computer geek friends at school, but few ever made it beyond level two. The hand-eye coordination required to repel the waves of alien fighter ships, missiles, mines, and torpedoes was extreme. As a result of uncounted hours spent playing the game, Jenetta's skill was unparalleled. Over the past several months she had launched the alien-attack action game whenever she felt a bout of depression coming on. Currently, she was turning to the game for comfort at least a dozen times each day.

* * *

Indisputably headstrong, Jenetta nevertheless knew that when all hope of rescue has evaporated, it made little sense to continue on as if expecting someone to arrive. Her intelligence had always prevented her from sinking into mires of self-delusion and that strength did not desert her now. At two hundred fifty-seven million kilometers from the *Hokyuu's* explosion, she was well outside the area that rescue ships would scour in their search for survivors. If they had picked up her emergency beacon signal, they would have already arrived. Since the craft wasn't under power, there was no energy signature to trigger a rescue ship's sensors. Well clear of the normal shipping lanes in this sector of space, it could conceivably be years before her pod crossed paths with a vessel. With near-term rescue unlikely in the extreme, Jenetta decided to use the only real option left open to her— stasis.

Having made the difficult decision to sleep away the rest of her journey— and her life if rescue never came— Jenetta prepared for a long hibernation. She had been recording a daily log message but, since they were just estimated position reports, they all sounded essentially the same. She knew this one would be very different as she sat down at the pod's console.

Jenetta stared dispassionately into the tiny lens of the camera. Her azure eyes were reminiscent of the deep blue, sometimes purplish colors of Earth's oceans. Sitting ramrod straight, she began her final report in a calm and professional voice.

"Computer, entry to official log of Ensign Jenetta Alicia Carver, GSC serial number 3974A32, Earth date January 1st, 2257. Begin recording. It's now been ninety-three days since the explosion of the *Hokyuu*. As this life pod has continued to move steadily away from the disaster location, it's become abundantly clear that Space Command rescue vessels are not going to find me. I've decided to use one of the onboard stasis chambers, so this will be my final log entry. It has been an honor and a privilege to serve as a Space Command officer. Computer, end message."

Briefly touching the personal log ring that she always wore on the small finger of her left hand to the computer's interface spindle, she said, "Personal log entry. Space Command still hasn't found me; I don't expect that they're still looking. I'm on my own without benefit of spacecraft mobility or com-munications. The isolation is getting to me and I can't take being alone any longer. Rather than waiting until my sanity is gone, or the food supply exhausted, I'm going to take a chance on one of the stasis beds." Glancing pensively towards the chambers, she breathed deeply and released it before saying, almost as an aside, "I hope the bed performs up to specs." Returning her gaze to the camera lens, she continued, "The odds of being found while I'm still alive are probably about a million to one, so I've been thinking for days about what I'll say in a farewell message to my family. There's no easy way to say goodbye, so I'll just keep the message short and to the point. End of entry. Log message."

She deftly keyed in her password and touched the ring to the spindle again to record the entry, then tried to prepare herself for her next task of recording a personal vidMail message to her parents and siblings. A lump began to materialize in her throat as she looked at the framed picture she had been able to grab from her dresser before leaving the *Hokyuu* and she fought back the tears that strained to break free. Composing her attractive face, she did her best to look apathetic about the almost certain fate that confronted her. She hoped she could complete the message before her dam of pent-up emotions broke.

"Computer, personal message to Captain Quinton E. Carver, Galactic Space Command. Begin recording. Hi Dad. Hi Mom. Hi Billy, Richie, Andy and Jimmy, if you're there. If you're seeing this, then I didn't make it. It's New Year's Day, 2257. I hope you all had a wonderful Christmas. A problem with the escape pod retrorocket failed to keep me near the ship's explosion site, so rescue has become— improbable. I'm about to use one of the onboard stasis chambers because I don't know how long it will take Space Command to find me. I still have more than four months of emergency rations left, but it doesn't make sense to stay awake any longer, so I'll just sleep until found. I don't regret my decision to join Space Command and, while I'd hoped for a longer tenure, I'm proud to have served the Galactic Alliance. I want you to know how much I love all you guys, and I—" Jenetta had to pause for a second to swallow the lump in her throat. "—can't wait to be with you again, whether it's here, or— in heaven. Goodbye."

She smiled sadly and kissed the forefinger and middle finger of her right hand, pressing them to the video lens before saying, "Computer, end message."

"Damn," she said with difficulty as she again tried to swallow the lump in her throat. With a trembling hand, she wiped at the tears that had begun to trickle down her face halfway through the message. "I didn't want them to see me cry." She sniffed to clear her sinuses and considered re-taping the message but realized she wouldn't be able to hold back the tears any better on subsequent recordings. In fact, it might be far worse now that she was caught up in the emotion of the moment. It's not easy to say farewell to the people you love.

After initiating the process to lower a stasis chamber from its storage position against the starboard wall, Jenetta removed her clothes and reduced the pod's gravity to one-tenth normal. While also reducing the drain on the pod's power cells, the greatly reduced gravity in the pod would place less stress on her body during stasis. As the bed locked down onto the deck, she wiggled into an elasticized, skintight stasis suit, taking extra care with the plumbing connections so they would perform properly during her sleep. When the fit was right, she raised the cover of the chamber and climbed into the coffin-like enclosure. After connecting the harness that would keep her sleeping form from shifting around inside the chamber should the gravity fail, she connected the suit's electronic sensors to the bed's monitors and its plumbing connections to the polyvinyl hoses that disappeared into the bed's base. With the hookups complete, she pressed the system button to test the plumbing seals. This was the part of the process she dreaded most and she winced as the suction pulled the suit ever tighter between her legs until the green light winked on, indicating the seal was complete. Her final preparation was to insert the mouthpiece and seal the large transparent facial mask to the hood of the stasis suit, then activate the respiration process.

The young GSC ensign sighed, took a sad look around, lay down with the framed picture of her family clutched tightly to her chest, and pressed the button that would close and seal the chamber's transparent cover before beginning the stasis process. An almost imperceptible hissing sound as the color-less gas filled the mask would be the last thing her mind recorded as she slipped into unconsciousness.

Chapter Two
~ June 18th, 2252 ~

Cadet Jenetta Alicia Carver, youngest of Quinton E. and Annette P. Carver's five progeny, entered the Northern Hemisphere Space Academy on Earth in June of 2252. Born into a large family at a time when most couples only sought to complicate their busy lives with one offspring, her young life had been devoted to following in the footsteps of her father and four older brothers, all of whom had graduated from that venerable institution in Missouri, USNA. Their Nordic ancestry patently obvious despite an anglicized name, each of the Carver children aspired to become an officer in the Galactic Space Command like their often-absent father. William, seven years Jenetta's senior, had been the first of the children to enter the Academy, followed by Richard one year later, then Andrew and James, the twins, two years after that.

In fervent pursuit of the academic standards established by her older brothers, Jenetta graduated with top honors in her class at the advanced scientific preparatory school where she had enrolled as an alternative to the regular high school that most children on the Space Command base attended. But graduating with top honors doesn't mean quite as much when older siblings also graduated with top honors. She was so focused on earning even a small degree of respect and admiration from her brothers that she cared little for her academic standing among fellow students; however, being the youngest and smallest of five in a household overflowing with testosterone-pumped energy provided little opportunity for sibling acclaim.

Although her scholastic record virtually assured that she would excel at the space academy, her years there were difficult. People who knew her well traced her problems back to one early, embarrassing incident, but it was actually only the capstone on a juvenile life filled at times with feelings of consummate inadequacy at home.

Before entering NHSA (generally pronounced Noss-sah), Jenetta had never even seen an O'Connell Power-Cell Regeneration Unit. Nevertheless, during their first semester, cadets were expected to partially disassemble and rebuild one without help while encased in an extravehicular activities suit. More commonly referred to as EVA suits, the cumbersome garments allowed people to work and function in a zero gravity, zero atmosphere environment. The O'Connell Power-Cell Regeneration Unit was an integral and critically important part of every spaceship, large and small, and every officer in Space Command must be able to repair one in the event of its failure. A worst-case scenario would have the unit located in a part of the ship that had lost both atmosphere and gravity.

Situated around a single, third-floor classroom, each of the Academy's four, three-story-high zero gravity labs shared a common window with that room, permitting students to watch their fellows perform the lab exercise. After each group of four students had completed an exercise, and had had their work graded, technicians moved in to reset the power units to their former non-functioning condition.

Jenetta was among the final group of four on the day of her test. She had waited nervously all afternoon for her turn to come as one by one the other students suited up and entered one of the four lab chambers. Having studied the OPCR manual intensely for the past month, Jenetta had committed every component of the unit to memory, much as a medical student memorizes the bones of the human body.

When her turn finally arrived, lab assistants helped her into a bulky space suit and then shoved her through the door of the lab. Although the OPCR was visible from the classroom's observation window, coming face to face with it from ground level was a bit overwhelming. The ten-meter-high device loomed ominously above her as she stood looking up at the behemoth from less than a meter away and her task seemed suddenly more daunting. As the gravity in the lab reached zero, Jenetta, trying to sound more confident than she felt, announced that she was ready to begin the exercise. Using the suit's maneuvering jets, she nervously jockeyed into position near the top of the large unit and attached a self-retracting tether strap from her maintenance harness. Special tools clipped to her belt allowed her to begin removing the covers from the unit's control panel. Twice losing her grip on a tool and then having to un-tether and chase it clumsily around the lab until she caught it, she could see her class-mates laughing at her predicament from the third-floor classroom.

When at last the control unit was laid open for mainten-ance access, Jenetta attached the test monitor and proceeded to replace the ruined circuit rods as quickly as possible from the replacement kit strapped to her right leg. She had comple-ted the repairs and was about to close the covers when the five-minute warning timer sounded. In a desperate effort to finish in time, she began furiously bolting the covers into place. With time almost exhausted, she re-connected the power cables and shoved off from the unit. Zipping down to ground level, she was just in time to depress the button on the wall that would stop the clock before time expired. Only two seconds remained.

As technicians restored gravity in the lab, she sank heavily to the deck, breathing a grateful sigh of relief that she had managed to complete the exercise without incurring a time penalty. The same lab assistants who'd helped her don the clumsy suit assisted her in its removal when she exited the lab. Once free of the garment, she hurried along to the class-room where Professor Hubera waited impatiently to grade the last four lab exercises of the day.

Now in his mid-sixties, Hubera had long ago misplaced his sense of humor, if he ever had one, and a permanent scowl defined the pallid face beneath a thick mat of silver-white hair. He preferred that students call him Professor, rather than use his official Space Command rank of Captain.

Moving as a group to each window overlooking a lab, the class watched intently as Hubera remotely applied power to the device just serviced while monitoring its output. During the afternoon, a couple of the units had failed to function and another couple produced only partial power, but no one was prepared for what happened when power was applied to the unit Jenetta had serviced.

As Hubera flipped the power switch, a geyser of sparks spewed from the top of the OPCR! He fumbled anxiously with the control remote and managed to turn off the power, but the unit continued to smolder, filling its lab with a dense cloud of acrid smoke that obscured the view completely. As the class erupted in laughter, Professor Hubera glared silently at Jenetta, his jaw clenched in anger. She turned a bright crimson and prayed for a hole to open up and swallow her as he censured her for confusing the color-coded power cables during the reassembly step and then proceeded to lecture her strongly and loudly at length on the merits of proper dis-assembly and re-assembly in front of her classmates. She naturally received a failing grade for the lab exercise, despite the fact that she had replaced all of the component rods correctly.

For the rest of her years at the Academy, her classmates joked about the day she *smoked* the lab. Fortunately, she led the entire freshman class in math and science coursework, so the incident in the lab didn't result in dismissal from the Academy. However, the embarrassment followed her like an expanding spectre from year to year and she always found herself moving hesitantly during lab exercises, especially during command and control battle simulations in her junior year. So fearful of making a serious mistake that would again make her a laughing stock, she deliberated much too long in every engagement. She either lost her ship within minutes of the danger scenario commencing while acting as captain, or contributed significantly towards its loss by apparent indecis-ion when she occupied some other chair on the bridge. The effects of each loss became cumulative and her performance as a bridge officer declined with each new exercise.

*   *   *

Although all cadets are required to carry the same basic course load during their first year, it changes considerably thereafter. Cadets wishing careers in medicine, engineering, economics, legal, intelligence, or political science are channeled into a heavy concentration of applicable course work. Depending upon the requirements of each field of specialization, they might continue their study at various universities, labs, or hospitals after graduation from the academy. They do not receive their posting until they've completed their studies.

The remaining cadets follow a regimented curriculum of math, science, astronautics, and flight training as they vie for the limited slots that could eventually lead to warship command. At the conclusion of a cadet's third year in the command program, an Evaluation Panel of Space Command officers and instructors make the final career assignments. Cadets not deemed suitable for ship command at that time are redirected into programs of intensive study designed to prepare them for their adjudged apposite postings.

The final postings from among those still under consideration for posting to a warship command slot are made at the completion of their fourth year. Those who have exhibited a pronounced ability for such command are ordered to report to the GSC Warship Command Institute following graduation from the Academy. Successful completion of the two-year intensive command training program will see them advanced to the rank of lieutenant(jg) and posted to the first available command slot on a warship. Those who wash out join the command personnel never offered the opportunity to attend the WCI and, as ensigns, are assigned to quartermaster ships, troop transports, outpost barques, research craft, hydrogen harvesters and tankers, diplomatic corps yachts, or other non-combat vessels.

Jenetta's poor scores in command and control exercises meant her chances of getting into the WCI weren't nearly as good as the survival chances of the proverbial 'snowball in hell.' She was likewise barred from bridge duty aboard the aforementioned support ships, or even a reclamation vessel, leading to the private joke among the more high and mighty of her classmates that she, like all the others dropped from the command program prior to their fourth year, 'wasn't even fit to haul garbage.'

The finding of the Academy's Evaluation Panel had been that Cadet Jenetta Alicia Carver was ideally suited to be a Science Officer. So it was that her fourth year at the Academy was dedicated to concentrated studies in the field of astrophysics. There, she excelled. The lack of ambiguity in her mathematics and science coursework allowed her to enfold herself in her academy endeavors like never before. She even found sufficient time to devote to her other passion—computers.

* * *

Prior to graduation, the soon-to-be ensigns not continuing their studies elsewhere received orders informing them of their postings. Jenetta hesitated briefly before touching the data ring containing her orders to the interface spindle of her computer console. She knew her dream of a life in space was about to be crushed. Her final C&C ranking didn't entitle her to a posting aboard ship. Her best hope now was that her post would be off-world so she'd occasionally have a chance to travel in space as a passenger. She couldn't imagine anything worse than having to spend her entire Space Command career dirt-side.

She took a deep breath and nervously touched the data ring to the spindle, then watched as an image of a Lt. Commander appeared on the screen. As she listened to the recording, her eyes grew wide. She screamed so loud and long that class-mates in the adjoining barracks rooms, sure someone was being attacked, came running to her room.

Cadet Lieutenant Karen Anderson, her closest friend at the Academy, reached her first. Grabbing her to quiet her down and stop her from jumping, Karen shouted, "What's hap-pened?"

So loudly that students at the cadet mess a block away might have heard her, Jenetta screamed, "I got a ship! I got a ship! I'm going into space!"

"You got a ship?" Karen said incredulously as more girls gathered at the door. "That's impossible. Your command and control scores were about the lowest in the class. They were even worse than mine. You have to place in the top seventy-five percent of C&C to be considered for even a support staff posting aboard a ship."

Clutching the data ring containing her orders tightly in her hand and grinning like the Cheshire cat from Alice in Wonderland, Jenetta said more calmly, "Impossible or not, I've got orders to report to the *Hokyuu*. It's moored at Earth Station Three and Ensign Jenetta Alicia Carver is to be the ship's new Science Officer."

Karen just shook her freckle-faced head in disbelief, her collar-length red hair swinging wildly. "You *couldn't* have gotten a ship. Somebody's made a mistake."

"I don't care if it *is* a mistake," Jenetta said lightly as she slid the burnished, white silver data ring onto the small finger of her right hand. Selected as the recording medium only after her Academy file was checked to confirm finger size, it was naturally a perfect fit. "I'm going to report to the ship as ordered. If they don't want me, they'll have to send me back. *I'm* certainly not going to question the assignment."

"It has to be because of your outstanding math and science grades," Maria Torres, a Castilian beauty with blacker than black shoulder-length hair, offered from the doorway. "You're what, the first cadet in seven years to receive the Admiral Matthew Tissdell Award for Excellence in Mathematics? That's what they look for in a shipboard Science Officer. I bet they pushed you up onto the eligibility list solely because of that. After all, it's not as if a science officer is ever going to be in a position of command while any other officer still lives."

Jenetta, nimbly dancing and pirouetting around the room, replied giddily, "I don't care why. I'll be anything and I'll do anything. All that's important right now is that I'm going into space. It's all I've dreamed of since I was a little girl and now I'm going."

"Don't get too excited," Heather Gulvil said casually. "A close friend of my father was posted on the *Hokyuu*. That old bucket is just a quartermaster's supply ship. All you'll be doing is ferrying food and supplies to off-world bases that no one's ever heard of. If you're lucky, you'll get liberty in some *real* port every couple of years."

As Jenetta began pulling Karen around by her hands, trying to get her to join in her celebration, she said lightly, "I still don't care. I'm going into space and that's all that matters. In a few years I might wangle an SO assignment on a re-search ship, or maybe even a destroyer."

"Destroyer, hah. Good luck," Heather said derisively. "They want officers who don't have to think for five minutes before making a decision. You might make it aboard a research vessel, though. You'll fit right in with the other eggheads."

Jenetta stopped dancing and fixed an intense stare upon the tall brunette. "Really? And where are *you* being posted, Heather?"

"I have orders to report to the *destroyer* Vancouver at Earth Station One," she replied haughtily.

"That's only her ride," Maria Torres said, her dark-chocolate eyes twinkling and her smile gleaming brightly. "She's being posted to the Ethridge Space Command Station at Nivella-3 as a Junior Food Service Administrative Officer." A little more cattily, she added, "Maybe you'll be supplying food to *her* off-world base that no one's ever heard of."

Karen started laughing loudly as Heather glowered, turned, and walked sullenly back to her room without saying any-thing further. The rest of the girls grinned before returning to their rooms. The freckle-faced redhead finally surrendered to Jenetta's entreaty to celebrate, smiled widely, and began blithely dancing around the room with Jenetta.

*   *   *

Newly commissioned Ensign Jenetta Carver eagerly reported to the *Hokyuu* at Earth Station Three a few weeks later. Merely a supply ship, the *Hokyuu's* crew complement was incredibly small when compared to that of a warship. Jenetta was to be the only Science Officer on board, but that didn't diminish her excitement at going into space. She spent the better part of fifteen minutes just staring at the gargantuan, six-point-three-million-ton cargo vessel through a viewing port near the airlock before finally proceeding out the docking pier.

The quartermaster ship didn't have a Marine complement and there were no sentries in evidence at the entrance to the ship, just one bored-looking lieutenant(jg). Having the dubious distinction of being the officer of the deck at the forward cargo bay airlock, he accepted her data ring and touched it to his viewpad's spindle interface to confirm that the bright-eyed young officer really was assigned to the ship. When the ship's computer returned her image as confirmation of her posting, he handed the ring back and allowed her entry, telling her to wait just inside the airlock hatchway for an escort.

The ship's fourth officer, Lieutenant Randal Coster, came to the bay when the computer notified him of her arrival. He escorted Jenetta first to her quarters, then to the astrophysics lab. Coster, an eighteen-year Space Command veteran and self-important minor cog in the *Hokyuu's* chain of command, towered over Jenetta. The gold, inverted 'V' insignia of a command officer gleamed brightly on his collar.

"Here you go, Ensign," Coster said. "This is your lab." Glancing scornfully down at the science officer insignia on Jenetta's collar, he said, "You'll spend each first watch here performing whatever it is you people do. Should the computer detect anything abnormal while you're off-duty, you'll immediately report here and determine the nature of the problem. Any questions?"

"Uh, just one, sir. What's our destination?"

Coster had little personal use for science-types, especially recently graduated ensigns who, in his words, 'would probably sit and enjoy the spectacle of a supernova instead of getting the hell away as fast as possible,' and he didn't try to conceal his feelings. His jealousy of people who could master the finer points of quantum physics and spatiotemporal trigonometry was the root cause of his often-derisive comments about science officers. His moderately respectable scores in the command and control lab exercises had allowed him to make the cut for shipboard duty, although his grades and aptitude hadn't been deemed adequate for him to attend the Warship Command Institute.

An officer bypassed during the WCI selection process who later distinguishes himself or herself in action against an enemy can receive a special appointment to the College, but being posted to a quartermaster ship left Coster with little such opportunity. The prospect of serving an entire, potentially mediocre career making 'milk runs' aboard a supply ship while fellow students enjoyed the prestige of serving aboard an active duty ship of the line certainly hadn't improved his temperament.

"It's all in your computer, Ensign," he said in an aggravated tone. "You do know how to use a computer, don't you, *Science Officer?*"

"Yes sir," Jenetta said, her calm voice not revealing a hint of the growing exasperation she was feeling for the string of condescending remarks he had leveled since meeting her at the cargo bay. "I know how to use a computer." She was still too excited to let a disgruntled space weenie like Coster bring down her mood.

"Then carry on, Ensign." Without another word, he turned on his heel and left the lab, overjoyed to have successfully completed the tedious chore of orientation for a new officer.

Jenetta rolled her eyes once and then set about exploring the huge lab, activating the equipment as she went. Some of it was older than the equipment she had trained on at the Academy and all of it had seen a great many more years than she had. Although the equipment was outdated before she was born, the lab contained everything she required for her job. And it was all hers.

* * *

Three months after departure as the tedium of long distance travel between inhabited solar systems and military bases began to catch up with her, Jenetta's enthusiasm had waned somewhat. At the start of each workday, she would sit at the science console and progress through all the motions of astral observation that had been performed tens of thousands of times before in the areas of space through which they were passing. Already containing every bit of information she could possibly record, the computer irritatingly verified back to her that she had done the calculations correctly and that there were no changes from previously reported observations. By exhibiting an interface demeanor even more exasperating than that of Lt. Coster, the shipboard computer system proved it was seriously in need of reprogramming. It took all of Jenetta's willpower to resist an unauthorized hack into the system with the specific goal of performing an 'attitude adjustment.' She thought wryly, with a hint of a smile, that if she were able to hack into Coster's brain and give *him* a new personality, she wouldn't hesitate for an instant.

Although able to complete her entire daily work assignment during the first hour of her watch, Jenetta was required to remain alone in the astrophysics lab until first watch ended. To kill time, she found herself spending long hours playing the ancient video game on her personal log ring. She told herself that the game kept her hand/eye coordination sharp as she destroyed attacking alien fighter craft by the thousands. When that grew tiresome, she recorded messages to home, or exercised. Jenetta was lithesome and every ounce of her hundred eight pounds was properly placed and muscle solid. Like all Space Command officers, exercise was an integral part of her daily existence and it kept her body fit and supple. The last hour of her shift was always devoted to jogging around the large deserted lab.

On what was to be her last evening aboard ship, Jenetta returned to her quarters feeling genuinely depressed. Glancing at the mirror, after slipping into her nightgown and brushing out her collar-length blond hair, she was dismayed to see the bored expression so plainly visible on her normally cheerful face.

A black-anodized picture frame containing an animated image of her family always occupied a prominent position on her dresser and she wondered what her father and brothers were doing as she looked down at the portrait. The other

Carver children had all gone on to attend the Warship Command Institute and then been posted to the bridge of a Space Command warship. At that moment they were probably chasing smugglers or enjoying R&R privileges on some exotic alien world.

"Why can't something exciting happen to break this monotony?" she recorded on her personal log ring just before climbing into bed.

Chapter Three
~ October 18th, 2256 ~

Annette Carver was the first in the family to suspect something was wrong following the horrific accident in space. Lately her daughter had been sending recorded messages every few days. When they suddenly stopped, she was immediately apprehensive. And when two weeks had passed without any response to her messages she could no longer contain her fears. She made her husband promise to investigate despite his assurances that the GSC would have informed them if something had happened. As an active-duty senior officer in the Galactic Space Command, he had a certain amount of access to confidential intelligence information through fellow officers.

Once he began calling friends, it only took Captain Quinton Carver ten minutes to learn that the *Hokyuu* had sent an urgent, automated distress call with a position report and then gone silent. He learned that a rescue ship was on the way, but it would be weeks before it arrived at the *Hokyuu's* last reported position. He also learned that Space Command had scheduled the transmission of a press release for later in the day, announcing that the *Hokyuu* wasn't responding to communications traffic. His own fears for the safety of his only daughter began to increase exponentially.

* * *

Weeks later Captain Quinton Carver received an urgent personal call from a friend in Space Command Intelligence. He nodded silently as he listened to the report filed by the captain of the rescue ship. When the call was over, he put his hands to his face and sobbed in the privacy of his office. He refused all calls after that and left work several hours early.

Arriving in front of the comfortable two-story brick and wood frame house he and his wife had purchased when he was still a lieutenant, Carver dropped the landing pads and let the 'oh-gee' vehicle settle the final quarter-meter to the ground. Currently between off-planet duty tours, the 'opposed gravity' car was about the closest he came to flying these days. At best, it could only achieve twenty meters AGL. To fly higher than that above ground level was a violation of both military and civilian traffic laws for passenger vehicles. Some people removed the factory-installed governors, or incapacitated them, but the fines for doing so were stiff and the penalty for violating airspace above twenty meters AGL without a pilot's license could include jail time if the offender disrupted the legitimate flight path of another craft. Even worse were the penalties for driving outside the permitted traffic lanes, but that never seemed to stop certain immature adolescents whose greatest pleasure in life seemed to be buzzing homes and knocking over satellite dishes on rooftops.

After sitting quietly in his vehicle for a good ten minutes, Captain Carver climbed out and walked to the house.

"Who's there?" he heard his wife say from upstairs as he stepped inside the front door.

"Just me, dear," he called back softly as he did every evening when he arrived home.

Annette Carver came down the stairs smiling. Although three inches shorter than her daughter, her resemblance to Jenetta was remarkable. Her husband lowered his head as she stretched to meet him and they kissed lightly in the habitual greeting of all longtime married couples still in love.

"You're home early, dear," she said, as he lifted his head.

"Yes, I wasn't feeling well," he said, avoiding eye contact with her.

Annette, fifty-three, attractive and slim, scrutinized her husband's face without appearing to. After thirty-two years of marriage, she knew him well. His eyes were a little blood-shot, but she knew he would never come home early simply because he wasn't feeling well. Before *he* left work early, he would almost have to be ill enough to be hospitalized.

"What is it, Quint?" she asked softly. Knowing that only the most serious of news could account for his demeanor, she asked, "Is it about Jenetta?"

He exhaled loudly and grimaced powerfully before closing his deep blue eyes briefly and nodding. His throat had constricted and he couldn't utter the words that he had been practicing all the way home.

"How bad?" she asked, her concern growing immeasurably as she watched his face.

His continued silence and the failure of his red-rimmed eyes to make contact with hers was answer enough. It felt as though someone had plunged a knife through her chest and for a few seconds she had difficulty breathing. As all her strength seemed to leave her body and her knees started to buckle, her husband grabbed her and pulled her to him. Held tightly against his chest, she began to sob, slowly at first, then uncontrollably as images of her only daughter flashed through her mind. Although a grown woman and officer in the Galactic Space Command, Jenetta would always be her baby. She loved each of her sons dearly and would grieve no less if an accident befell one of them, but few relationships are closer than those between mothers and daughters. It wasn't always so during the teenage years, a time when most children begin to assert their individuality and independence, but the bond had redeveloped stronger than ever as Jenetta matured during her Academy years.

Annette had always imagined she would be strong when such news arrived. She'd steeled herself many times when she first heard that a death had occurred aboard a ship to which her husband or one of her children was posted, but it had always been someone else's spouse or someone else's child. Space was a dangerous place and life in the military made it ten times more likely that death or serious injury would occur, but knowing the dangers didn't help when it actually happened.

Quinton held his wife until she was able to stand on her own again, then walked with her to the living room sofa. As they sat together, he tried to comfort her, all the while working to keep his own emotions in check. He felt that he had to remain strong for her sake.

They sat like that for almost twenty minutes as Annette wept. Finally, she was able to ask, between sobs, "What happened?"

"Her ship exploded," he said when he could find his voice. "They either don't yet know why or haven't released that information. A rescue ship picked up all the escape pods, but apparently Jenetta never got out. They searched the area out as far as a pod could have traveled in the event of a retro-rocket malfunction, but they didn't find any sign of her. She's officially listed as 'missing and presumed lost.' The search has been called off."

"My poor baby," Annette sobbed, as she began weeping again.

* * *

Over the following weeks, Annette spent most of her time sitting alone in Jenetta's bedroom looking through the mementos and personal items that her daughter had valued enough to save and, in some cases, prize. There were innumerous scholastic awards, souvenirs of trips and events, and dozens of data rings containing anything and everything about space outside Earth's solar system. There were even a few personal log rings in a small acrylic box marked 'diary,' but Annette couldn't view their contents when she tried them in the computer because Jenetta had encrypted them.

The room was more remarkable for the things that it didn't contain. There wasn't a single skirt or dress in the closet, or a pair of shoes with heels over one and a quarter centimeters, and the contemporary dresser yielded neither stockings nor makeup. Annette had tried to raise her daughter as she'd been raised, but Jenetta had strongly resisted, rejecting anything frilly, delicate, or feminine from an early age. No doubt, the influences from living in a military household with four older brothers were responsible in large part, but it was Jenetta's fascination with outer space that finally defeated Annette's efforts. All of Jenetta's being had been focused towards her goal and she had agreed to put on a dress and short heels for her senior prom only because, if she did, Annette promised never to ask her again.

Annette remembered with fondness the shopping trip to get the prom gown for Jenetta. They must have looked at two hundred dresses before Jenetta found one that she would wear and that Annette would agree to. If it *was* to be the last time Jenetta ever wore a skirt or dress, then Annette was determined that it be a memorable one. After rejecting several similar gowns earlier, Jenetta finally selected a lovely creation of pink silk and taffeta. Either there was something special about this one or Jenetta was simply tired of looking.

After selecting the dress, it was another battle finding appropriate shoes. Jenetta wanted low heels, no more than two centimeters, while her mother wanted eight centimeters to give her daughter added height. Compromising on five centimeters, Jenetta spent hours afterward practicing with the shoes so she could walk, move, and dance gracefully.

On the day of the prom, Jenetta consented to have her hair and nails done at a salon, and even allowed her mother to make up her face before getting dressed. When the computer-science geek friend arrived to escort Jenetta to the prom, he couldn't believe that the vision of loveliness who greeted him was really Jenetta. So radical was the transformation in his mind, he suddenly became tongue-tied when confronted by one of his closest friends. Jenetta blushed three shades of crimson as her date tried to describe how great she looked and Annette insisted that they pose for some pictures before she would allow them to leave for the prom.

Annette kept her promise and an animated enlargement of what she considered the best picture hung in the living room alongside pictures of her sons, each taken on the night of their own senior prom, but the picture of Jenetta in her prom dress was secretly one of her most prized personal possessions.

During the first few days following the death announcement, Annette had been unable to stop the tears that flowed so easily as she repeatedly reviewed the images from Jenetta's prom night. Later, the numerous trinkets Jenetta had valued enough to save stirred a vast reservoir of happy memories and tears flowed again. But life must go on and, whether she was 'cried out,' or had simply come to grips with the death of her only daughter, the tears slackened and Annette finally returned to her normal routine. For now, the bedroom would remain as it was. Annette neither packed up Jenetta's things nor discarded anything. They didn't need the space now that the boys were no longer living at home.

Chapter Four
~ June 6th, 2267 ~

"Captain to the bridge! Captain to the bridge!"

Captain Leopold Lentz glowered at the overhead speaker and cursed under his breath as the message blared in his quarters. Perturbed by the unmistakable tone of extreme urgency in the voice, he hoped it wasn't a ship-wide broadcast. He didn't want his anxious first officer frightening the entire crew again unnecessarily. Already imagining pirates with every distant contact, the captain believed his first officer would fall completely apart when she encountered the real thing.

Leaping from his bed, he jammed his feet into his slippers and ran for the door. Narrowly avoiding a collision with several crewmembers in the corridor as he emerged from his quarters, he never gave his appearance in pajamas a second thought, but he did deliberately slow to a walk and compose his face before entering the ship's bridge. He noted the anxious faces in a quick scan of personnel as he walked to the security station where his first officer stood looking over the shoulder of a crewmember. Both were staring at the forward DeTect monitor. He took a deep breath before speaking so he would appear totally calm. "What is it, Gloria? Why are we stopped?"

"Contact off the larboard fo'c'sle, Captain!" Lieutenant Gloria Sabella said as she turned slightly to look at him with frightened eyes. Her stomach knotted in fear and a slight quiver in her voice, Sabella continued, "The navigation hazard database contains no mention of objects in this area."

She wished she were somewhere else, anywhere else but here. *Why, oh why, did I ever accept this trip contract,* she thought. Hardly pausing for a breath, she added, "Looks like a small craft. It's barely registering on the sensors. It may be a stealth fighter."

Lentz looked sedately into her wild eyes and said softly, "Calm down, Gloria. I'm sure it's nothing. What's our distance to the contact?"

Sabella studied the monitor on the security console for a few seconds. It provided all available sensor information about the contact, including contact dimensions, distance, course, and speed. "Currently about ninety-six million kilometers."

"Is the contact moving?"

"It's not under power, but it's moving. Speed is just over thirty kps. Its path will take it directly across our bow. The collision avoidance system disengaged our Light Speed drive and warns there's an imminent risk."

"Helm, deactivate the collision avoidance control for this contact. Set speed to Sub-Light-100, then slow us to Plus-10 at one thousand km. Any other contacts, Gloria?"

"Negative, sir. The screen is clear. Whoever it is, they're alone."

Roughly a third of the way between the planet Kesserith and its planned destination, Higgins Space Command Base, the ship was essentially out in the middle of nowhere. Contact with any ship in this area of space was cause for concern. The captain's unruffled demeanor helped relieve anxiety on the bridge, but the threat of the unknown still loomed large in everyone's mind.

* * *

Sixteen minutes later, and roughly one thousand km from the contact, the enormous ship slowed to ten kps for their approach to the contact's path. Lentz, now wearing a robe retrieved from his quarters by a crewmember, ordered a CG close-up image of the object put up on the main viewscreen. Rarely a true view of space outside the ship, the images projected on the large monitor that covered the front of the bridge were normally computer-generated representations prepared from sensor data. Optically, contacts are almost invisible in the blackness of space unless there happens to be a star nearby or the ship is able to illuminate it with its outside lighting.

"What is it, Captain?" Sabella asked as she stared at the image. Significantly calmer now that the stalwart strength of her captain was there to fortify her and the bridge crew, she added, "It's definitely not a fighter." The rectangular lines of the target discounted the possibility of it being a naturally occurring celestial object.

Lentz shifted comfortably in his command chair, his own eyes glued to the front view screen as they approached the object. "It could be a loose cargo container, but it looks more like an escape pod to me. Helm, prepare to match the vector and speed of the contact."

"Aye, Captain," the helmsman responded.

"Security, check all known emergency beacon frequencies. See if it's transmitting."

"Aye, Captain. Checking— Captain, the contact *is* emitting an emergency beacon signal on an old GSC frequency, but even at this close range the signal is so weak it's barely recognizable."

"That must account for the DeTect computer's initial failure to recognize it as an escape pod," Gloria said.

"Helm," Lentz said, "let's ease on up to the contact, but be prepared to run if necessary."

"Aye, Captain," the helmsman responded nervously.

As the ship came to a stop relative to the life pod, Lentz gave orders to dispatch a small, robotic tug to retrieve the pod and deliver it to the enormous maintenance bay three kilometers behind the bridge. A dozen anxious cargo handlers and maintenance personnel watched the monitors intently as the automated tug scanned the pod to determine the best way to attach itself. When it was unable to locate any of the recessed annulus fasteners usually found on cargo containers, the tug chose to land on the pod and engage its magnetic skids. Given the wide range of materials used in the construction of pods, it wasn't necessarily the most secure form of attachment, but the automated sensors recorded a solid contact with sufficient traction for the task. The tug immediately began maneuvering its load towards the bay.

After leaving the bridge, Lentz returned to his quarters and quickly changed into his uniform. He hurried out, only to return seconds later to retrieve his stun pistol from his spacechest. When he again emerged from his quarters, the holstered weapon was strapped to his waist.

Lentz hopped onto a maglev sled for travel through the cargo freighter's spine. He arrived at the maintenance link-section just as the bay's large airlock was being re-pressurized. Cargo handlers attached 'oh-gee' blocks to the four corners of the pod, then guided it to a work area. Sensors would first determine if the environment inside the pod was non-toxic and biologically safe. This was a standard pre-caution before opening any container that could potentially threaten the health and safety of ship personnel. The opposed gravity blocks kept the life pod suspended a few centimeters off the deck, making it so simple to maneuver that one worker could have done it easily. Meanwhile, the pod's markings enabled the ship's computer to identify it as having come from a GSC Quartermaster ship named the *Hokyuu*.

"The *Hokyuu* was lost in 2256," the terminal operator read from the portable screen.

"2256?" echoed Lentz absentmindedly as he walked around the pod, noting the severe pitting and scarring of the surface. After almost eleven years in space, the pod showed signs of impact with dozens, perhaps hundreds of small objects such as micrometeorites and space junk. Although not constructed entirely from tritanium, as were the hulls of most Space Command vessels, the pod's shell offered protection equivalent to that of a Space Marine armored personnel carrier. A one-half-centimeter-thick titanium jacket had been bonded to a two-point-five-centimeter-thick tempered steel skin. Although many times heavier than one-fifth-centimeter-thick tritanium hull plating, the three-centimeter-thick hull plating was almost as strong and considerably less expensive to manufacture. A massive length of twisted steel, which might once have been a support truss from a ship, dangled precariously from where it had penetrated the protective heat cone of the main rocket. The portion outside the cone was entangled in a fuel line from the two small tanks, while inside it was partially melted. Obviously, the main rocket was engaged when the truss struck the pod. It was a testament to the builders that the pod hadn't been breached, though it surely could have been if the support had struck the craft in a more vulnerable location.

The terminal operator nodded. "Aye, Captain. All hands recovered except one. According to the accident report, Space Command spent three months searching for their missing crewmember, an Ensign Carver, before abandoning the effort."

"It looks like we may have found him," Lentz said, "for all the good it will do, poor devil. Well, we might as well take a look at the body so we can notify Space Command when we reach Belagresue."

"Interior readings are normal," Operations Chief Rondell said, staring down at the display on the viewpad that he had plugged into the pod's exterior interface coupling. "It's safe to open 'er, Captain."

Lentz nodded at the crew chief who then punched in the 0911 universal emergency code. To everyone's surprise, the pod's hatch-latching mechanism immediately began cycling. The door opened spasmodically, indicative of the weak state of the power cells. Lentz, brandishing his stun pistol, cautiously prepared to step in first as the interior lights flickered on. If this was some kind of trap, he intended to be prepared. The one-tenth gravity inside the pod took him by surprise and he bounced upwards as he crossed the hatch threshold. Immediately releasing his grip on the pistol, he opened his hands wide and stretched out his arms just in time to prevent himself from impacting the overhead with his face. It took him a couple of seconds to stabilize his movements.

A quick check of the austere interior and nose cone showed the escape pod to be empty except for one occupied stasis bed. The transparent cover was fogged over on the inside and the interior of the bed wasn't illuminated, but he could discern the basic outline of what appeared to have once been a human body. Lentz relaxed, picked up his pistol, and holstered it before carefully hopping to the control console to adjust the gravity to a normal, full g. They would have to wait for the ship's doctor to arrive before disturbing the bed's controls because the ship's chief medical officer had sole responsibility for completing death certificates.

* * *

Doctor Rebecca Erikson, carrying a small kit containing her emergency medical equipment and medicines, arrived in the cargo bay about ten minutes later. Captain Lentz escorted her to the escape pod and allowed her to perform an uninterrupted examination of the stasis unit. Once plugged into the bed's interface panel, her medical viewpad displayed a complex assortment of health evaluation graphs and data. The attractive, thirty-six-year-old physician completed her analysis before turning to face the captain.

"The chamber appears to be functioning properly, Captain. The occupant is alive and undamaged. Shall I revive her?"

"Alive? After all these years?" Lentz asked, his face exhibiting the surprise he felt. "Did you say *her*?"

"Yes," the doctor said, grinning, "the bio information indicates that the occupant is female. The fogged cover makes it difficult to see inside the chamber, but the medical readouts indicate that she'll most likely recover. Her small frame no doubt gave you the impression the occupant had perished, especially if you were expecting to see a male Space Command officer."

"I see," he said, nodding. The normally impassive façade had returned to his face by the time he uttered, "Then proceed, Doctor."

The brunette nodded, turned, and pressed several buttons on the chamber's console that would begin reversal of the stasis process. The complete procedure would take several hours, so she pulled a foldaway seat down from the pod's wall and relaxed as she monitored the unit. Everyone else returned to his or her regular duties.

Left alone with her thoughts, Doctor Erikson ruminated about waking up after such a long stasis sleep. Would the rescued woman simply be grateful for being returned to the living, or traumatically disturbed over having lost so many years? The doctor wondered what her own reaction would be should it ever happen to her. She sincerely hoped she never had occasion to find out.

* * *

Ensign Jenetta Carver opened her eyes and blinked several times in reaction to the bar of excessively bright examination lights mounted over the bed in the ship's well-equipped sickbay. Her head throbbed and every muscle in her body seemed to be screaming for relief. But by far the worst sensation was the dryness. She felt a thirst that extended from her throat to her toes. It was as if she'd been picked up and wrung out like a damp towel until every last drop of moisture was extracted. When an indistinct shape appeared next to the bed, she tried to say, "Where am I?" but her first attempt at vocalization was barely audible and totally unintelligible.

"Take it easy, Ensign," the shadowy shape said. "It's going to take a few days for your body to start functioning properly again. You've been asleep for a long time. Here, take a sip of this."

Doctor Erikson gently slid her left hand under Jenetta's head and lifted it to a drinking cup so that a slightly cool and very salty-tasting liquid could more easily be dribbled into her mouth. At this point, a recently awakened sleeper wouldn't even be able to use a straw. Jenetta was barely able to swallow the first small mouthful, but she finally managed. Her parched throat and tongue responded immediately and she felt able to try speaking again as soon as the doctor took the cup away from her mouth. Preparing herself, and trying to talk precisely, her query was still unintelligible, but the doctor thought she understood the word, 'where.'

"Where *are* you?" the doctor offered.

Jenetta strained to nod her head and was successful in moving it a half-centimeter.

"You're on the freighter *Vordoth*. We're in interstellar flight between ports of call. We happened across your pod two days ago, stopped to investigate, and found you asleep inside one of the stasis chambers. The other beds were empty. Did you jettison alone?"

Jenetta struggled to move her tongue and managed a muffled "Yeth."

"Just blink once for 'no' and twice for 'yes.' Your tongue, mouth, and vocal cords will improve slowly over the next 24 hours. All of your muscles have atrophied somewhat from lack of use, but I wanted to wait until you were conscious before beginning rehabilitation. This stasis-recovery bio-bed will feed tiny electrical impulses through your nervous system to stimulate the muscles as we begin the process of rebuilding them. It won't hurt, just tingle a little bit, but it'll be days before you're ready to sit up and perhaps a couple of weeks before you're ready to try standing. Until then, just relax and enjoy the hospitality of the *Vordoth's* sickbay. It'll be nice to have someone to care for. I normally only see cuts, abrasions, and bellyaches." Leaning a little closer and lowering her voice slightly, she added, "Forgive me if I appear to be hovering a bit for the next couple of days, but I'll be staying close since you can't call out or move on your own. Okay?"

Jenetta blinked her eyes twice.

"Good," the doctor said, smiling. "Now take another sip of this drink and I'll activate the bed."

Jenetta took another slow drink from the cup that the doctor held to her mouth. She found it easier to swallow with each mouthful. As she relaxed from straining her neck muscles to help raise her head, she felt the tingling sensations begin. Each sensation was followed by an involuntary muscle twitch somewhere on her body.

Over the next several hours, the doctor returned occasionally to give Jenetta another drink from the sequence of liquids prescribed by her medical journal. Between visits, Jenetta, eager to talk, practiced reciting the letters of the alphabet to exercise the muscles of a mouth and tongue that still felt as if they were made of clay. She was desperate to get some answers and, since she couldn't yet lift her arms to write, she would have to get her voice back.

When she felt ready to try speaking again, she waited until after the doctor had given her a drink and then asked in a hoarse voice, "How long was I floating out there?"

"My God, that was fast!" Doctor Erikson exclaimed, clearly taken aback by this first full sentence. "The medical journal estimates twenty-four to thirty-six hours before you'll be able to articulate a simple sentence. You've hardly been awake more than fifteen."

"How long, *please*?" Jenetta asked again in the most pleading voice she could manage. "What's the date?" The words were slurred, owing to the still-limited flexibility of her tongue and mouth, but recognizable.

The doctor hesitated before answering, knowing the information would come as a shock to her patient. However, the young woman appeared to be resilient and she would have to be told eventually. As a Space Command officer, she had to have passed complex psychological exams that tested her ability to adapt calmly to potentially calamitous situations and outcomes.

"Brace yourself, Ensign. It's now June 7th— 2267." The year was barely audible, as if saying it quietly would make the news more palatable, but Jenetta heard. "The bed controls show that you've been in stasis for ten years, five months, and six days. A new record as I understand it. The previous mark for a deep-space sleep was just a little over five years."

As the words washed over her, a look of shock, then desperation, filled her eyes. "Ten and a half years?" she slurred with barely mobile lips. "It seems like just yesterday that I climbed into the bed. A mirror— please, I want to look at myself."

The doctor retrieved a small hand mirror from a nearby table and held it up so Jenetta could examine her face through eyes still incapable of sharp focus.

"I don't think I look that much different," Jenetta said, puzzled. "Thinner certainly, but definitely not ten years older."

"The gas in a stasis chamber enters your bloodstream quickly and spreads to every part of your body. Within an hour of beginning the process, your heart is pumping just twice each minute and your body's metabolic rate has been reduced to near death. You've really only aged about three months and five days so you shouldn't see any real differences apart from a noticeably dehydrated appearance. The debilitated condition resulting from the non-use of muscles and other bodily functions will disappear as we rebuild your muscles over the next few weeks." The doctor lowered the mirror and placed it on the table beside the bed. "The brain is least affected, and so recovers first, along with heart and respiration. Next will be your voice, as you see, and digestion."

"I feel so weak," Jenetta said. "Like a newborn, not someone who's been asleep for only three months."

"That's because it wasn't normal sleep. A sleeping person will tense and relax their muscles throughout much of the sleep cycle. That simple isometric activity keeps them from experiencing the effects that *total* nonuse brings about. Spacers traveling long distances usually limit each stasis sleep to no more than one year, with adequate time to fully recuperate between sleeps. Six months has proven to be the optimum for long distance freighter operations because the sleeper will only require a single day to achieve a ninety percent recovery. With an accelerated exercise program, he or she can go back into stasis after achieving full recovery within a week; however, it will take weeks of rehabilitation effort for *your* musculature to return to a normal level and possibly months to bring it to the point where you were when you entered the stasis chamber. That will depend on your exercise regimen, of course. As a military officer, I assume that exercise was a normal part of your everyday routine. The sooner you slip back into that habit, the sooner you'll be back in prime condition."

"Thank you, Doctor. I understand. Has Space Command been informed that I've been picked up?"

"I'm afraid you'll have to speak to the Captain about *that*."

"I understand. When can I see him?"

Glancing at the chrono-patch on her left wrist, Doctor Erikson said, "Not for at least seven more hours. He goes to bed at 2200 hours and doesn't come on duty until 0600." Smiling, she added, "Between those hours he'll skin anyone who disturbs him unless it's an emergency."

Not much thicker than a transfer tattoo, and just as flexible, a chrono-patch is powered by a harmless chemical reaction produced when it comes into contact with human skin. It doesn't have timekeeping functions and merely displays the GST date and time being broadcast throughout the ship. The disposable waterproof patches could last several days before needing replacement, but the wearers usually washed them off and replaced them daily using a simple roll-on applicator.

"I didn't realize the hour. Well, I was stuck in that pod for almost eleven years so I guess I can wait a few more hours."

"By now your body should be accustomed to the muscle stimulation current, at least enough that you can sleep while it continues. You should also be feeling generally fatigued from the autonomic muscle responses. Since you have your voice back, I won't need to have someone assigned to stay with you during the night. The computer will keep watch over you and alert me if you call out, or if any of your vital signs vary outside of normal parameters. I'll be sleeping on the daybed in my office if you need me."

"Thank you, Doctor. Can your computer distinguish between sleep and consciousness in case I call out in my sleep? I don't wish to disturb you unnecessarily."

"Yes, the sick bay medical interface will be monitoring you completely, so it will know if you're dreaming or awake. Now take another good healthy swig of this *wonderfully* delicious concoction I whipped up and then try to get some rest."

After swallowing as much of the cool, briny liquid as she could force down, Jenetta said, "Thank you, Doctor. Goodnight."

"Goodnight, Ensign."

Jenetta awoke feeling substantially better than she had the first day. She used her hand to rub the sleep gently from her eyes before remembering that yesterday she couldn't even raise her arm. When she did remember, she was startled to see her hand in front of her face. She tried to squeeze her nose, but found that she didn't yet have the strength to grip it tightly. "No matter," she said lightly to herself. Her strength was definitely increasing and the doctor had provided a timetable for its return.

As she glanced around the sickbay, everything jumped immediately into sharp focus and she caught sight of her framed picture standing on a counter against the wall. She prayed that her family was still intact and that everyone was healthy. Eleven years was a tremendously long time and a lot could have happened.

Doctor Erikson entered the ward with a cheerful smile on her face while Jenetta was still lost in thought.

"Good morning, Ensign. The computer informed me you were awake. Did you have a good sleep?"

"Good morning, Doctor," Jenetta said, with dramatically improved enunciation. "I slept very well and feel much better, thank you. Look, I can move my arm already."

The surprise was evident on Doctor Erikson's face as Jenetta held up her right arm and wiggled her fingers. "That's remarkable. You seem to be way ahead of the projected time-table for recovery. They're going to have to rewrite the manuals once I report your progress."

"Speaking of reporting, would it be possible to see the Captain now?"

"I'll tell him you're awake. He inquired about you several hours ago."

"Several hours ago? What time is it?"

Glancing at her wrist, the doctor said, "It's now 1638 hours, Galactic System Time."

Clearly dismayed, Jenetta said, "1638? I slept seventeen hours?"

"You needed it. Your body is trying to recover."

"But all I've done for the past ten and a half years is sleep."

Doctor Erikson chuckled. "That wasn't normal sleep. That was stasis sleep. The *only* similarity between the two is that you're unconscious. You don't even have dream activity and REM while in stasis because there's limited brain activity."

"Still, it *seems* like I'm sleeping my life away. I want to get up and do something. Anything."

"You will, but first your body has to recover. We're going to start pumping you full of liquids today and we'll have you sitting up soon at the rate you're recuperating."

"I hope so. Uh, Doctor, could you move my picture over to the table by my bed."

"Of course," the doctor said, fetching the framed image.

The 20x30 centimeter black anodized frame with a thin decorative line of gold around the front edge contained an animated photograph of seven smiling people, two women and five men. A man wearing the muted black dress uniform of a Space Command captain and a patrician woman wearing a simple light-blue sheath sat on a curved stone bench in an outdoor park of some sort, while five younger people, none much older than a teenager, arrayed behind them. A meek wind ruffled the heavily leaved bushes in the background and mildly tousled the hair of the men and women. The four younger men, all obviously quite tall, wore the grey uniforms of Space Command Academy cadets. Standing shoulder to shoulder, each had his arms on the backs of the men next to him. At the rightmost side of the back row stood the young woman presently resting on the sickbay bed as she had appeared in her mid-teens. She seemed tiny and insignificant standing there next to the tall, handsome young men. The doctor noted a remarkable resemblance between the teenage girl and the older woman on the bench. For that matter, there was also a close familial resemblance between the young men and the older man on the bench.

The composition of the image seemed a bit odd to the doctor. Normally, a photographer would have attempted to balance the image by putting the young woman in the center of the back row. Wearing a civilian jacket and slacks outfit, and placed by herself off to one side, one could almost get the impression she was being excluded from the group. At least the young man standing next to the girl put his left hand on her right shoulder halfway through the images. The picture played for thirty-seconds and then morphed to the opening frame and began to play again.

"Your family?" Dr. Erickson asked as she placed the framed image on the bedside table and faced it so Jenetta could see it.

"Yes."

"I thought so, from the way you were clutching it in the stasis bed." Smiling, she added, "I thought I'd have to call for one of the cargo handlers to pry it from your hands."

"That picture was taken on the day my oldest brother, Billy, graduated from the Academy. That's him in the center," she said, pointing, "with Andy and Jimmy on the left and Richie next to me. It was the last time we were all together. It's the only thing I had time to grab when the abandon ship alert sounded, but as long as I have that, I don't really care about the other things." Looking at the picture, Jenetta paused for a second, then added, "It's funny..."

"What is?" the doctor asked, wondering if the young woman was going to comment on the composition of the image.

"All my life I've only wanted to get into space, but right now all I can seem to think of is my family and returning to Earth so I can see them and hug them all again."

"That's entirely natural after what you've been through. I'm sure Space Command will arrange for a long survivor's furlough once you report in."

"I hope so."

Smiling again, the doctor said, "I'll go call the Captain. Oh— don't go anywhere."

Jenetta smiled politely at the intentionally preposterous remark. She certainly wasn't going anywhere under her own power today.

Chapter Five

~ June 7th, 2267 ~

Captain Lentz didn't make it down to the sickbay until after his watch ended at 1800. Jenetta had finished eating a late breakfast of mostly liquids with a few pureed items by the time he arrived. She looked up as the door opened and watched as the captain strode in confidently.

"Welcome aboard the *Vordoth*, Ensign," he said as he approached the bed where she lay. "You've been adrift out here for a long time."

Now in his mid-to-late fifties, the short, dense, light-brown hair of his youth still covered the captain's head. While there was no excessive fat on his medium frame, he was getting a little soft around the middle. He had a deeply resonant voice and a face filled with character. Without knowing anything about his background, Jenetta's first guess would have to be that he'd worked his way up through the ranks of the merchant service rather than having received his master's papers after completing the educational requirements at one of the many fine, accredited spacefaring trade schools on Earth or another planet in the Galactic Alliance.

"Thank you for rescuing me, Captain," Jenetta said as she activated the control that would raise the top part of the bed. She wanted to be sitting up as much as possible for the conversation and she was unable to do it on her own.

"You're most welcome. You're lucky your pod happened to be on a collision course with our ship or we might never have spotted you. If you had been more than ten thousand kilometers ahead or back from your actual position, we'd have passed you by at forty-five million kilometers a second without ever knowing you were there. Your emergency beacon was all but dead and in a few more months it probably wouldn't have been sending at all. We're so far out of the normal shipping lanes that you might never have been re-covered." In a flattering manner, he added, "I certainly never expected to find a gorgeous blonde floating around out here."

Jenetta blushed slightly but otherwise didn't acknowledge what she considered a flirtatious remark. She'd never been co-quettish. "Have you notified Space Command that you picked me up, sir?"

"No, we haven't. We can't break radio silence for another month."

"Excuse me? Radio silence?" Jenetta said with a puzzled expression on her face.

"Of course. Our orders require us to maintain strict radio silence while in this area of space. Oh, I forgot," the captain said, as he recalled the length of time Jenetta had spent in the escape pod, "you wouldn't know because you've been asleep for ten years." Lentz took a step closer to the sickbay bed and lowered his voice as if he feared being overheard. "For the past eight years, this region of space has been plagued by space raiders. Emergency calls for help go out, but, when rescue ships arrive weeks or months later, there's nothing left except some minor wreckage to show a ship was attacked. It's like the time of pirates on Earth in the 17th and 18th centuries. Back then, the pirates sank the ships too badly damaged to salvage, with the only evidence of the attack being whatever floated off their decks. Here, the entire ship and crew are just— gone. So far Space Command hasn't been able to find where the Raiders come from, or return to, after the attack. That's why we're so far out of the normal shipping lanes. I selected this course in the hope that we can avoid an encounter with them."

"And if we can't?"

"Then we run. Or, as a last resort, we fight."

"Fight? Do we have an escort, sir?"

"No," Lentz said angrily. "There wasn't another convoy leaving for our destination for four months and the company ordered us to depart as soon as possible. All hands are volunteers receiving double pay, and, as I've said, we're following an unusual course."

"So how do you fight when you can't run?"

"We have phased array lasers mounted every half kilometer along the entire length of the cargo section."

"This ship is armed? But that's a violation of Galactic Alliance law. No merchant or privately owned vessel can mount exterior weapons."

"That *was* the law a decade ago. It was suspended when Space Command finally acknowledged that it was unable to protect freight and passenger traffic."

"I see," Jenetta said, nodding her head slightly. "Uh, what's the size of this— Raider fleet?"

"No one knows. Space Command has encountered them in every part of Galactic Alliance space. And diplomatic missions to other territories have reported hearing of attacks as far away as two thousand light years beyond our borders. The organization must be massive. Estimates of more than a thousand Raider warships have been made by Space Command Supreme HQ."

"A thousand warships?" Jenetta said, her eyes opening wide. "That's five times larger than Space Command! If this group is so big, why have we never heard of them before? They couldn't have grown so large in just ten years."

"The generally accepted theory is that a dozen large crime syndicates combined to form the nucleus of the Raider organization about twelve years ago. They then enticed all the smaller organizations to join them using a rather effective 'join or die' proposal, incorporating them into their own enormous operation. Their intelligence network is incredible. They seem to know the departure time and flight path of every ship in GA space. When the organization grew so huge that they could no longer cling to any hope of anonymity, they apparently decided to make themselves so powerful that even Space Command couldn't stop them. It's worked. Space Command has had its budget increased in each of the past ten years and currently has over three hundred warships in their fleet ranging from light destroyers to battleships, but the Raiders have proven themselves to be far too much for them to control. And their organization seems to get larger, more powerful, and bolder every year."

"This is all too incredible," Jenetta said, looking away while she shook her head a couple of times. Looking back to Lentz, she added, "When I climbed into the stasis chamber, the principal concern of a freighter or passenger liner was the danger from its own power systems, or impact with another ship or object in space. It's like I've awakened in another galaxy— a galaxy unknown to me." Jenetta paused momentarily to take a deep breath. "How long will this ship be in danger, sir?"

"We've been traveling in Raider-controlled space for several days now, but we're back up to our top speed of Light-150 again. With any luck, we'll pass beyond the Belagresue system in four months. There haven't been any attacks beyond that point, so once we get there we'll be able to notify Space Command that you're aboard. Then it's just another month to Vinnia, our final destination. In addition to being the major freight hub in this part of the galaxy, it's also the home of the largest Space Command base in the deca-sector."

"That will be great. Thank you, Captain."

"You're welcome, Ensign. By the way, the doctor tells me you're the new galactic record-holder for survival in a stasis chamber. We'll have to notify the folks at Guinness Galactic when we reach Vinnia."

"It's a distinction that I could happily have lived without, sir. Do you know anything about my ship, the *Hokyuu*?"

"Just what I read in the news dispatches. Lost in 2256, cause eventually blamed on a flawed vacuum restrictor in the antimatter flow. All hands were recovered except one." Lentz paused and smiled. "Correction, all hands have been recovered. *Hokyuu* is a funny name for a supply ship. Someone must have had a belly laugh over that one."

"What do you mean, sir?"

"I'm pretty sure *Hokyuu* means supply in Japanese. So that made you a crewmember of the supply ship 'Supply.'" He chuckled to himself. "As soon as you're fit, I'll arrange a ship's tour, if you wish it."

"I'd like that very much," Jenetta said, smiling.

"Okay, you've got it. I'll see you when you're better."

"Goodnight, Captain."

Jenetta lowered the mattress so her head was elevated barely higher than her feet and relaxed as she considered all the implications of what she had just learned. It seemed impossible that Space Command could have lost control of the territory the way Captain Lenz had said but, for now, she would accept that it was true. And the utter vastness of GA space might make it impossible for Space Command to regain control if they couldn't locate the bases from which the Raiders operated.

* * *

In two more days, Jenetta was sitting up in bed and, in four, she took her first steps with the aid of a walker frame to help support her weight while her legs strengthened. She fell a number of times as she pushed her recovery along at a faster rate than might appear judicious and always refused assistance from the doctor with getting back on her feet.

In seven days she was walking without the walker's support, although some might have described it more as lurching from place to place, and in eleven days she jogged, albeit slowly, for the first time since leaving the *Hokyuu*. Each step on the road of physical recovery was accompanied by great pain as atrophied muscles were stretched, flexed, twisted, and strengthened. Jenetta consistently pushed herself to the limits of her endurance and beyond.

On the twelfth day following her rescue, Jenetta was officially released from the sickbay and assigned quarters on the bridge deck. Of the eight staterooms located in that section, only four were occupied. Having four to choose from, she selected the one closest to the occupied rooms without even looking at the others.

Painted in the same neutral, off-white color as her room aboard the *Hokyuu*, her new quarters were spacious and comfortable. Where her quarters aboard the *Hokyuu* had consisted of a tiny bedroom and miniscule bath, her new quarters were almost the size of the bedroom and bath she'd had at her parent's home on Earth. And she had a moderately-sized sitting room of her own as well. She felt like she had just been promoted to Lt. Commander.

Jenetta's GSC uniform had been found in the pod following her recovery. Taken to the *Vordoth's* supply room, it was scanned by the ship's tailoring computer and the data stored. New clothing was then prepared, including four new uniform tunics bearing a narrow gold bar on each epaulet, the standard rank insignia of an ensign. Made of a comfortable, stretchy fabric comparable to the one used by Space Command, the white blouses fit perfectly, or at least would once she filled out a little. The hip-length tunics and trousers, made of a muted black synthetic fabric almost identical to that used by Space Command, were nearly impossible to distinguish from original SC issue without a close inspection. The sixteen brass buttons on each tunic representing the sixteen planets that were signatories of the original Galactic Alliance Articles provided the only indication that the uniforms were not military issue. And one had to examine the two rows of bas-relief buttons on the front of each new tunic closely to even recognize the difference. Since the tailoring computer didn't have the proper die setups to stamp out the strictly decorative adornments with the Space Command logo, the merchant services logo had been used. The number of buttons also immediately distinguished her uniforms from those of the Merchant Service officers on board because their tunics included just a single row of six functional buttons. After cleaning, her SC-issued uniform was placed into an airtight garment bag to be saved for use when she left the ship. It was her intention to be in 'proper' uniform when she reported for duty.

*   *   *

At 0545 the following morning, Jenetta took breakfast in the officer's mess for the first time, completing her return to a diet of mainly solid foods. A single white laminate table capable of seating twelve officers occupied the center of the spotlessly clean room. The intense brightness reflecting off the white laminate walls seemed powerful enough to force itself in through her pores.

The officer's mess attendant, who identified himself as Anthony, informed her that the first officer was still on duty and that the captain rarely ate breakfast. Jenetta smiled and requested orange juice, corn flakes with milk, sugar, and strawberry or banana slices, and a mug of coffee.

Gaunt in the extreme, Anthony didn't much look like a typical mess attendant, but the slim young man with sandy hair knew his business and his way around his mess kitchen. He brought the juice and coffee first, and Jenetta hadn't even finished her first cup of Colombian before Anthony produced a large bowl of corn flakes with both strawberry *and* banana slices. Of course, the fruit was synthesized and so had the usual wafer-like appearance, but it was the right color, had the proper texture, and, most importantly, it tasted like the real thing.

At 0608 the first officer, Lieutenant Gloria Sabella, who had been relieved by the captain at 0600 hours, stopped in the mess for a light breakfast. She extended her hand across the table as she said, "Good morning, Ensign, and welcome aboard. It's good to see you up and about. Doc tells me you're making remarkable progress with your recovery."

Jenetta stood and shook the proffered hand, saying, "Thank you, ma'am. I'm very happy to be aboard and it's good to be almost fit again."

"You can drop the 'ma'am.' We may wear uniforms similar to Space Command's, but we're a lot more informal in the merchant service than you military folks. Call me Gloria. Only the captain is *always* referred to by rank. The Doctor answers to Doctor, Doc, or Rebecca rather than Lieutenant Commander and the chief engineer would probably slug me if

I called him Lieutenant." With a wide smile and a definite twinkle in her eyes, she added, "He prefers Charley."

Jenetta liked the five-foot nine-inch brunette immediately. Gloria had an athletically trim body, an easy way of carrying herself, and a wonderful smile. It was her smile that made her average face glow, motivating people to elevate their initial impression of her to 'pretty.' Jenetta estimated Gloria's age at between thirty and thirty-two, just a little younger than her own real age, but she couldn't know if Gloria had undergone any stasis sleeps. She just chuckled and said, "Thanks. Call me Jen."

"Okay, Jen. Congratulations on surviving the explosion of the *Hokyuu*— but how— in the hell— did you get all the way out here? We picked you up billions of kilometers from where your ship reportedly exploded."

"I got a heck of a boost when the ship went up. Then the retrorocket on the pod wouldn't fire so I just kept traveling after the main rocket cut out."

"Damn government contractors," Gloria said angrily. "Buying by the lowest bid should be outlawed on life-saving equipment like emergency pods. Government contractors are almost as bad as the damn freight company owners. We shouldn't be out here without a convoy or a private escort."

"I thought this duty was voluntary, with double pay."

"Voluntary? Hah— that's a laugh. In exchange for an astronomical fee, the company committed to an outrageous delivery date on some construction supplies and equipment. Failure to deliver on time imposes a penalty larger than the total fee, so they threatened to fire anyone who refused to go and, for the first time in memory, they were true to their word. Most of the senior staff was turned out. They're probably blacklisted as well, so they'll have trouble getting another decent berth. Charley and Rebecca are the only officers from the original group. The Captain is a new-hire and I was brought over from the *Vordoth's* sister ship, the Kleist. I was offered my choice between a seat on the bridge and a seat in the unemployment section of the union hall. The damn union rep sided with the 'effing' company. I've only been with this hauler for four years, but I'd have had to start over with another freight operation. There have been a dozen times when I wished I told them where they could put this 'effing' job, but there's no guarantee I wouldn't wind up out here anyway if I went to another operation. So here we are, praying that we'll all live long enough to collect our bonuses."

"Speaking strictly selfishly, I'm glad you're here. The captain told me that my pod's power cells were almost dead."

Gloria frowned and nodded sadly. "Too true. Even when equipped with stasis chambers, pods are only designed to last for five to seven years. If you're not picked up in that time, they figure you're space dust anyway. The power cells couldn't have lasted more than another year without a chem recharge."

Jenetta shrugged. "When I climbed into the stasis chamber, I thought my number was up. I knew I'd been too far away from the other pods when the rescue ship arrived and I decided that I'd rather die peacefully in my sleep than go crazy from the isolation, or starve to death when the emergency food packs ran out. I feel like I've returned from the dead— or more aptly as if I've been reborn considering I practically had to learn to move and walk again over the past two weeks. I'm looking upon this as my second life."

"Well," Gloria said, holding up what remained of her orange juice as a toast and smiling widely, "here's to second lives. May we all be forgiven for the inapt missteps of our past and presented with new opportunities to accomplish the things we've dreamed of doing."

Jenetta looked at Gloria strangely for a second, wondering if she knew of Jenetta's difficulties at the Academy. But she immediately realized that wasn't possible and shook herself mentally. Grinning, she raised her coffee mug in unison and said, "Second lives," before taking a sip. After both women shared a chuckle, Jenetta said, "The captain said I might have a tour of the ship."

"Yep, he asked me to show you around. I have to score some rack time right now, but how about 1600 hours? I'll come to your quarters."

"Great," Jenetta said enthusiastically.

"If you're looking for something to do between now and then, why don't you visit the bridge? I'm sure the captain will show you around there, not that you need showing around a bridge. I'm sure your NHSA training included everything you're likely to find aboard the *Vordoth*."

The reference to NHSA made Jenetta pause for a second, as with the toast. She hadn't mentioned she had attended NHSA. She could just as easily have attended SHSA. Then she realized that Gloria might have seen the raised NHSA lettering on her Space Command ring. On the other hand, Gloria might have checked the ship incident files in the computer. Reports on the *Hokyuu* disaster would probably have included a brief biographical synopsis about the only missing crewmember. She smiled and said, "Thanks Gloria, I'll head there after breakfast."

"Okay, I'll see you at 1600, Jen."

"'Til then."

A few minutes before 0700 hours Ensign Jenetta Carver entered the *Vordoth's* bridge, walked to the command chair, and came to attention. Captain Lentz looked up from the report he was reading on one of the chair's attached view-screens and smiled pleasantly.

"Good morning, Ensign," he said. "Stand easy. How are you feeling?"

"Much better, sir," Jenetta said as she relaxed slightly. "Most of the effects of the prolonged sleep are gone. I still need some improvement in my stamina, but it's coming along."

"Good. Very good. What can I do for you today?"

"I'd like permission to look around the bridge, sir," Jenetta said, as she glanced around. The room was about ten meters square. Spaced a meter apart, three independent operator consoles towards the front of the bridge faced a large wall-mounted viewscreen, but only the center console was presently manned. The command chair was in the rear half of the room and located directly behind the center console. On the larboard side of the command chair was a huge work-station in the shape of a semicircle. Several large viewscreens hung above that occupied station. A similar semicircular workstation located on the starboard side of the bridge was also occupied. On the rear bulkhead, facing away from the front viewscreen, were two consoles that Jen immediately recognized as fire control stations. Each had a large view-screen of its own. The Captain was seated far enough back that he could see everyone except the weapons gunners sim-ply by turning his head. "I'd also like to volunteer to help out in any way I can. I thought an extra pair of trained eyes might be of use while we're traversing this area of space."

"Your help and training would be appreciated, Ensign." Using his hands to gesture, Lentz said, "This Bridge has the standard freighter configuration. That's helm control at the center front of the bridge, with the astrogator's console to its left and the science station console to its right. Communica-tion is there on my right. Those two consoles behind me are the weapons stations for the phased array laser weapons and this station to my immediate left is security. The security station is what you would call the tactical station on a war-ship, but, since we don't plot attacks against other ships, our sensors are only used to keep our perimeter secure."

"Is your astrogator on break, sir?"

"No, we're a bit short-handed on this run, but we don't need that station manned most of the time anyway. Once my first or I lay in the course, the computer keeps us there unless it spots something in our path. The helmsman has a readout that shows any deviation from plotted course. We're not very militarily oriented here; we're basically just truck drivers," he said, smiling.

Jenetta smiled back before saying, "A truck that can be ten kilometers long, weighing billions of tons and traveling trillions of kilometers at faster-than-light speeds, unprotected, through hostile territory."

"That makes it a little more— challenging, to be sure. Well, pick your poison, Ensign. Our security station is already being used to search space around us. Would you prefer to watch from the astrogator's console or the science station?"

"I'd prefer the science station for looking around. I think the sensor readouts would be better suited to spotting anything unusual."

The captain smiled and nodded. "That would be my choice as well. Carry on, Ensign," he said as he returned to the report he had been reading.

"Yes sir."

Jenetta took several minutes to wander around the bridge, glancing at the layouts of the various consoles before taking her seat at the science station. Everything looked fairly common, except that the security console included a weapons targeting module. Jenetta decided that it must be set up to function as a backup weapons station if one of the two fire control consoles against the rear bulkhead was damaged.

Like the helmsman, the crewmember manning the security station only wore the rank insignia of petty officer. On a Space Command vessel, a commissioned officer would always man the tactical, helm, and astrogation stations. SC vessels made no provision for a science station on the bridge, using that location for an engineering monitoring console. The science function, as defined in the Space Command operations manual, was far too complex to be properly handled by a few bridge instruments, so the science officer would perform all of his or her work duties only in a fully equipped Astrophysics Lab. The communications station on the *Vordoth* was likewise manned by a petty officer. On SC warships, that post was always manned by two chief petty officers, or by a petty officer with a chief looking over his or her shoulder during the entire duty watch.

She hadn't announced it or let her excitement show, but this was her first time on the bridge of a ship in space. Naturally, she had spent innumerable hours in the bridge simulators at the Academy during command and control exercises, but this was the real deal and it took all her self-control to project a perfectly placid composure. In her three months aboard the *Hokyuu*, she hadn't once been invited to tour the bridge despite several hints to Lt. Coster and the other bridge officers that had been so obvious as to border on being formal requests. Aboard quartermaster ships, science officers were considered about as useful as screen doors for the airlocks.

Over the next five hours, Jenetta used her knowledge and skills acquired at the Academy to search space for anything out of the ordinary. The ship's ACS, or anti-collision system, had the potential to 'see' another vessel that was hours away, even when both ships were proceeding at top speed towards one another, *if* both vessels were transmitting a proper Auto-Tect code, or at least by minutes when only the DeTect grid was active.

Chapter Six
~ June 24th, 2267 ~

A collision between two fully booked passenger ships had the potential to kill tens of thousands and, despite the vastness of space, several deadly collisions actually occurred in the decades following the development of faster-than-light travel. Fortunately, the collisions occurred in solar systems or around space stations where traffic was heaviest and speeds were the lowest. Nevertheless, everyone could see the potential for disasters of great magnitude.

It was decided to restrict ships to specific flight corridors, times, and speeds, but as the volume of travel grew it was recognized that the system would eventually become over-burdened and impossible to manage effectively. The Galactic Alliance decided that an alternate method for travel safety had to be developed. Their solution was to inaugurate a multi-decade R&D project whose mission was to discover a means of identifying other vessels presenting a danger to space-farers. The mechanics of DATFA didn't offer any solutions to the problem, so other avenues were explored. An old discipline, hyperspace, was gloriously resurrected when physicists discovered a way to access it, although only with communication signals.

Following a full-year's test of the new equipment, the Galactic Alliance Council decreed that all ships under power in GA space emit an identification signal within a specific frequency range in the newly established IDS bands for inter-stellar communications. Since Inter-Dimensional Spectrum signals travel at point-zero-five-one-three light-years each minute, this offered more than adequate warning to other ships. Each AutoTect signal, repeated every five minutes, or each time a course correction or change is made, gives the ship's current position, destination, course information, and a GST date/time stamp. Galactic System Time is the current time of day at the Galactic Alliance Council Center on Earth and provides a universal time reference for astrogation in all of Galactic Alliance space. The universal reference time ensures that out-of-date signals are ignored by a ship's Auto-Tect system, while valid signals are processed and passed on to the ACS processor. The ACS processor sorts out all the valid signals and determines which, if any, other ships pose even the remotest possible threat to the safety of the ship, then plots their position and course on a monitor located at the security or tactical station. A moderate threat causes an alarm to be sounded that the entire bridge crew can hear and a serious threat actually shuts down the Light Speed drive, as had happened when Jenetta's life pod was detected and plotted by the *Vordoth's* ACS.

Stiff penalties were established for failure to transmit a proper AutoTect signal. Sentences could range as high as life imprisonment for anyone who either deactivated the equipment or deliberately sabotaged it. Even smugglers understood the value of knowing when another ship traveling faster-than-light was headed directly at their bow. So, while they might alter their signal to mask their true identity, they nonetheless broadcast a signal when underway. That is, they did so until a decade ago, when piracy on the interstellar routes became a way of life.

Since awakening, Jenetta had learned that as law and order devolved, so had travel safety. In areas considered unsafe because of the Raider threat, ships were not only allowed to deactivate their AutoTect equipment but were actually encouraged to do so. The very information that made Auto-Tect so beneficial for safe travel, namely ship identification, course, and schedule, was equally useful to pirates looking to plunder unsuspecting vessels. Once again, hyperspace researchers were called upon to help advance travel safety in outer space. Although the top speeds of military warships were classified, estimates put the fastest ship speeds at three hundred twenty times the speed of light. The top scientists in the field of DATFA calculated that speeds could one day theoretically reach as high as eight hundred sixty-two times the speed of light as improved methods of building temporal envelopes were developed, but most ship designers believed that number to be wishful speculation. A more practical limit seemed to be five hundred twenty-five times the speed of light. Moreover, it was assumed even that speed wouldn't be realized for decades, if ever.

Even so, the goal of the scientists working on detecting approaching objects was to find a method of seeing something traveling at an equivalent speed of one thousand times the speed of light on a reciprocal course and offering sufficient warning time for both to stop, or at least get out of each other's way. They finally found it.

The incredible breakthrough wasn't intended to replace the proven AutoTect system, but to supplement it. It would never be nearly as reliable and foolproof on its own, but, until the AutoTect system could once more be universally employed, their solution provided a suitable alternative that would continue to have significant value when the original system was reinstated to everyday use. To send and receive communication signals in the IDS bands, proper equipment was necessary at both ends, but, like radar, the DeTect system only required equipment at one end. Sent out on a special IDS band in the hyperspace layer closest to normal space, the end of the signal away from the transceiver will actually drop back into normal space for a nanosecond, 'sniff' the electromagnetic properties of space there, and return a value to the sending unit. A computer can then assemble the millions of signals returned each minute.

The DeTect system can provide a four billion kilometer early-warning system with a proven reliability of ninety-nine-point-two percent. At one billion kilometers, the reliability jumps to ninety-nine-point-nine-nine percent. As intended by the designers, two spaceships headed towards one another at one thousand times FTL would have up to six-point-six seconds of warning in which they could alter course or stop until the danger was past. A ship like the *Vordoth*, whose top speed was only one hundred fifty times the speed of light, would have up to twenty-eight-point-two-one seconds to take action if the fastest ship currently in existence was headed directly for its bow on a reciprocal course. Since DeTect signals are tied into the ACS, if one or both of the helmsmen fail to take appropriate action quickly enough, the ACS will shut down their Light Drives.

*   *   *

Scans hadn't disclosed any sign of other vessels within DeTect range during the morning, so at noon Jenetta felt comfortable leaving the bridge to have lunch. The crewmember at the security station would continue to scan until relieved. In the officer's mess just down the corridor from the bridge, both the doctor and a man whom Jenetta assumed to be the chief engineer were already enjoying a bowl of soup when she entered with the captain.

"Ensign," Captain Lentz said as they approached the table, "this is Lieutenant Moresby, our chief engineer."

"Call me Charley," Moresby said, smiling as he stood up and offered his hand, "or 'Chief' if you can't remember my name. I don't like to use my rank in front of my guys."

About forty-years-old and of average height, Charley had rugged good looks and a fit body. The close cut of his jet-black hair would pass a military inspection and he looked fully capable of maintaining his authority over most crew-members under his command without the need to pull rank. Jenetta returned his smile and shook his hand with a firm grip as she said, "I'm pleased to meet you Charley. I'm Jen."

"Hi, Jen. Welcome aboard the *Vordoth*."

"Thanks, Charley. Hi, Doc. How's the soup?"

"Delicious. Our mess attendant, Anthony, has a fine touch on the food synthesizer. He won't tell us what he does, but he always manages to make the food taste better somehow. Today's soup is Petite Marmite."

As they took seats at the table, both Jenetta and the captain ordered Anthony's soup of the day. When delivered to the table, the vegetable consommé smelled heavenly, and tasted even better. Conversation was light as they ate, but the looks passing between Charley and the doctor suggested to Jenetta that there was something more to their relationship than just shipmates and fellow officers.

After lunch, Jenetta resumed scanning the surrounding space while the regular crewmembers were excused in pairs by the captain to grab lunch. Just before 1600, she left to meet Lieutenant Sabella at the door to her quarters for the guided tour.

"Ready to go, Jen?" Gloria asked.

"All set."

"Okay, I'll start with the basics," she said as they turned and started down the wide, well-illuminated corridor. "Unlike the multi-megaton military transport ships used by the Space Command Quartermaster Corps, commercial freighters are not single hull designs. The military looks for better flying characteristics first and utility second. With us, it's the reverse. Like the ancient tractor-trailers that used to ply the highways on Earth, our vessel is composed of separate sections temporarily joined together for the trip. The main ship is like the tractor and naturally provides propulsion and directional maneuvering for the trip. Constructed like a human spine, some flexibility with the cargo section exists, but maneuverability is severely limited compared to that of ruggedly built military vessels.

"The *Vordoth* is almost fifty years old now and most freighters her age went to the reclamation center long ago. But thanks to Charley and several refits, the old girl has a lot of life left in her. Charley says that if she's properly maintained, she'll do another fifty. We have a Benson-Sparr ellipsoidal temporal field generator mounted on the bow to produce our DATFA envelope for Light Speed travel and the rotating larboard and starboard nacelles contain twin McCannes Solarsys II engines that provide our momentum in sub-light. We naturally have numerous deuterium acceleration thrusters within the hull for maneuvering and docking functions. The rest of the ship is devoted to command and control, crew quarters, engineering, and freight operations."

"You have a Benson-Sparr? Are they still in business? They were barely hanging on when I graduated from the Academy in '56."

"The Galactic Alliance Council stepped in to bail them out with a series of interest-free loans and some lucrative contracts, so they've been able to remain in business, but they're still not in the best of shape. According to the maintenance logs, it took more than a year to get the proper replacement parts the last time this ship had a serious problem with its field generator."

"Who's the big kid on the block now?" Jenetta asked.

"Allison-Wilson probably has the most dependable temporal field generator. Several of the company's ships have been retrofitted with their units when it came time for a major overhaul. Our McCannes Solarsys II engines may not be the most elegant available, but they're good, dependable work engines for sub-light travel with enough power to do the job even when we're topped off at ten kilometers of cargo."

"Let's hope that the Benson-Sparr doesn't suddenly develop a problem while we're out here."

"Our spare parts inventory includes most of the vital components, so Charley isn't too concerned. He's the best chief engineer in the company and I trust his judgment."

"That's good enough for me," Jenetta said. "What about the rest of the ship?"

"As many as four individual cargo containers are attached to a Lewiston link frame and then the link is attached to the ship, becoming an integral part once connections are complete. The containers themselves are a standard ten meters wide by forty meters long, but the height may vary because it doesn't affect link loading. They come in five, ten, fifteen, and twenty-meter heights, but since a twenty is the most economical size to ship when calculating volume versus cost, they make up the majority we handle. The next most popular size is the quarter-container, followed by half-containers. We see few three-quarter size. Most containers not designed to handle ore or other bulk cargo are internally divided into multiple levels and sections to protect cargo in transit from being crushed by the weight of other cargo during planetary atmospheric operations, while the ore containers are just one big reinforced box. Placed end to end when inserted into the link-sections, each link becomes one hundred sixty meters wide and increases the ship's length by twelve meters as it's added. The extra two meters come from the framework holding the containers. Each container has two hatches on the top and, with the container secured tightly in the link-section, we potentially have airtight access to every single container while in transit."

"Potentially?" Jenetta queried.

"Certain cargos don't lend themselves to inspection while in transit, such as ore shipments. As I said, those containers have been constructed like one big, reinforced box. If we activated the gravity decking in the container, all you'd see would be the top of the material anyway. And if we didn't activate the grav deck, the material would be in suspension. It takes a pretty hardy individual to climb down into an ore shipment while the ore is in suspension, and then I don't know what you'd see. It would be like swimming in dirt and rocks."

"Is the grav plating usually turned off in the containers?"

"Yeah, to save energy. It doesn't require all that much, but when you multiply it by several thousand containers it adds up. So most containers are no grav, no environment. It really cuts down on the stowaways."

"Stowaways?"

"Not people— vermin. Of course, the irradiation sweep should take care of that problem anyway. No freight hauler wants to be responsible for the kinds of things that happened on Earth when seagoing ships spread pestilence, vermin, and harmful non-indigenous life forms to every port they entered. Every container, except those that have been thoroughly inspected dirt-side by licensed inspectors and granted exemptions, such as for certain fresh foods, medicines, and biological products, is irradiated when it's accepted for shipment by the company. No known carbon-based life form can survive the irradiation process.

"And just like all other freighters, the *Vordoth* itself is sterilized annually, or immediately after it completes a multi-year run. Every person, pet, and potted plant is off-loaded and the ship is irradiated from the bow to the stern. Then everyone and everything is individually decontaminated before re-boarding. At least for a few days, we're as biolog-ically clean as the cleanest 'clean room' in a nanotechnology research facility. The air circulation system continually scrubs the air, but it's possible to bring back something when traveling down to a planet or stopping at a space station so, as a final safeguard, we regularly receive injections to protect us from all known viruses, just like the military."

"I'm afraid my vaccinations are hopelessly out of date."

"If I know Rebecca, you received your vaccination booster before you even awoke in our sickbay so your body would begin to build antibodies immediately. Now, back to the ship. The frame links are like the vertebrae in a human spinal column. They have a hollow core near their center. When connected, they create a tunnel that runs down the ship's length. This provides a fully pressurized passage that extends from the stern of the main ship to the last cargo link-section. The ship can be as long as necessary to transport all of the cargo being shipped in one run, but GA regulations restrict us to ten kilometers for safety reasons. A maintenance link-section is usually attached amidship.

"Since the Raider attacks began, most cargo vessels have carried some form of laser weapon protection and, although they haven't stopped the attacks, at least the crews feel they can do something to fight back. Our phased laser arrays are mounted in special six-meter-wide link-sections inserted every half-kilometer along the entire length of our six thou-sand four hundred eighty meter-long cargo section. The first is the very first section attached to the ship and the last is attached to the stern-most container link. Our total towed length on this run is six thousand, five hundred seventy meters, counting the array sections."

"How many laser weapons in each section?"

"Four. They give us 360-degree fire capability around the center axis of the ship and, once the gun ports are opened and the arrays extended, each array has converging fire overlap at one hundred meters from the ship. They're all controlled from the bridge or can be controlled individually within the section."

"That means you have sixty arrays intermingled with the cargo?"

"Exactly."

"How powerful are your lasers?"

"They're rated at sixty-two megawatts."

Jenetta knew that such low-powered units were normally only used as defensive weapons against torpedoes but could also be used to dispatch most unarmored or lightly armored fighters. They'd be hard pressed to seriously damage the armor of a warship, although the pulses *could* 'chip away' at it until a hole was made. Assuming an armored hardness of twenty kilojoules/cm², the laser would have to remain focused on the exact spot to be pierced for a full four-point-three seconds to punch through. Remaining on one precise spot for four and a half seconds requires a gunner with remarkably steady hands if both ships are stationary and an incredible amount of luck if the ships are moving, even with computer tracking.

"We'll stop by one of the weapon sections later so you can take a look," Gloria added.

"Is that your only armament?"

"Not anymore. This ship was weapons retrofitted just before this trip. Four torpedo tubes were mounted in the bow at that time. The openings are camouflaged and it's supposed to be a closely guarded secret, but everyone on board knows about them, which probably means that everyone we've had contact with recently also knows. The security station on the bridge doubles as the torpedo weapons console. They also mounted four laser arrays on the main ship. Our firepower is probably the only reason we were able to keep sufficient crew for the trip. As it is, we only have enough command officers for two bridge watches."

"Only two?"

"Yes. The Captain has the first watch from 0600 to 1800, and then I take over from 1800 until 0600."

Jenetta nodded. "That explains a lot. I wondered why the first officer had the watch until 0600 and why the Captain was still on the bridge more than eight hours into his watch. There are no other officers on board?"

"Rebecca and Charley are both officers; however, while each is a highly trained professional, they're not command officers. Normally every interstellar freighter has a minimum of four command officers to cover the standard three watches."

"At least you're well armed."

"It might all be window dressing if it comes to a fight."

"What do you mean, 'window dressing'?" Jenetta asked, her puzzlement obvious.

"It's just that we don't have any experienced gunners aboard. In a fight, we may just be providing a light show for the Raiders. The hope is that any Raiders would pass us by if they see our laser array link-sections."

"From the outside you must look like a light destroyer."

"That's the idea. The company asked Space Command to put troops aboard to man the guns, but they said they couldn't post troops to a civilian ship. Against some military regulation or something."

Jenetta nodded. "Probably Article 38 regarding command structure in non-military environments."

"Yeah, I think that was it. Captain Lentz says he argued that it was done on Earth back in World War II when merchant ships were being sunk by Nazi submarines and aircraft, but the SC response was that things have changed considerably since then."

"Space Command would never, ever, agree to place troops under the control of a civilian ship's captain. It would violate Article 38 and a whole bunch of lesser regs."

"Our hard luck if we're attacked. At least it's almost impossible to attack a ship while it's traveling faster-than-light. We just have to be extremely cautious before we drop our envelope. Okay— let's take a tour of Engineering and then we'll take hover sleds through the ship."

Engineering was as pristine as any found in the Space Command fleet. Charley was obviously a disciplined engineer. He wasn't in the Engineering section during the tour, but no one challenged their presence. As they made their way aft for the tour of the cargo section, a door with 'No Admittance' printed in large, red letters caught Jenetta's eye.

"What's that, Gloria?" Jenetta asked.

"That's the starboard torpedo room. Want a look?"

"If it's all right."

"Sure it is. Space Command officers always have access to any part of the ship. A Space Command safety team performed an inspection after the tubes were installed and certified them as 'acceptable.'"

"Just 'acceptable?'"

"Just? I thought it was normal, like being either acceptable or unacceptable."

"Well— it is one step above unacceptable. It means that the equipment passed an operations test and that the birds won't detonate before leaving the tubes."

Gloria looked at Jenetta apprehensively as she placed her hand on a palm print reader and the door slid open noiselessly to reveal an area rarely visited. On either side of the room, five enormous black torpedoes with bright red warheads gleamed ominously in auto-feed racks. When activated, the automatic loading system would gently lower the next of the fourteen-meter-long torpedoes to a conveyor, which would in turn slide it into a tube.

"Now we're talking," Jenetta said as she saw the equipment, then, "Oh— my— God!"

"What?!" Gloria asked anxiously. "What is it?"

"It looks like a Falcon Mark III system."

"That's right, Jen. You certainly know your armament."
Seeing the severe expression on Jenetta's face, her own filled
with concern. "Uh, is there a problem?"

"I thought they stopped making these things a century ago.
There's one in the exhibit hall at the Space Weapons Museum
in Kansas."

"A century ago?" Gloria said with raised eyebrows. "They
looked brand new when they were installed."

"Maybe they'd just been given a fresh coat of paint or
something. I'd say some arms merchant or salvage yard had
these in storage for a long, long time. Apparently they finally
found a suck— uh, purchasing agent or broker to buy them."

"What's wrong with them? I thought a torpedo was a
torpedo was a torpedo."

"The Falcon Mark III system has two major flaws. One,
and the most serious, is that reload takes almost *five minutes*.
The other guy can be pumping a torpedo from every tube
every fifteen seconds while you're sitting on your hands
waiting for yours to be ready. And two, once the torpedoes
are fired, there's absolutely no telemetry and guidance adjustment. They either find the target you initially pointed them at
on their own, or they don't. You have no way to retarget.
Moreover, there have actually been a couple of cases where
Falcon Mark III's lost their intended target and then acquired
their own ship as the target. At least they self-destruct fifteen
minutes after being fired to prevent them from becoming a
hazard to future navigation."

"God! Are there any positives?"

"Just one. You get a full three minutes of controlled flight
time from them before they go ballistic for an additional
twelve minutes."

"But they do explode?" Gloria asked.

"Oh, yeah, they explode. The firing mechanism goes
active three seconds after leaving the ship. The trick is to get
them to explode inside the enemy's hull rather than your own.

And where modern systems give you a choice of several different warheads, nuclear, bomb-pumped laser, or high explosive, the Falcon Mark III's were limited strictly to high explosives. With laser heads, you only have to get fairly close to the target, while with nuclear warheads, you have to get very close. But with high explosives, you have to literally punch through the hull of the target to get the maximum killing effect from concussive force. If you can manage that, they'll do the job nicely."

Gloria took a deep breath as she thought about the damage a torpedo would do to a ship. "Hopefully, we'll never have to use them."

Thinking only about the unreliability of the weapon, Jenetta said, "I'll certainly second that prayer."

The hover-sled ride was a new and exciting experience for Jenetta. Stretching out ahead of them for more than six kilometers, the tunnel had two lanes for sleds with a two-meter-wide walking track between. Overhead conduits carried fiberoptic wiring that linked all sections together for communications, armament control, and life support. Before they entered the tunnel, Gloria recorded Jenetta's name and her own in the terminal near the entrance. Their names immediately appeared on the large wall monitor that listed everyone outside the main ship.

"You put it on the hover track yourself," Lieutenant Sabella said as she took one of the five-centimeter-thick, meter-and-a-half-long sleds down from a storage rack and demonstrated. "It's really lightweight, only weighing about twelve pounds. The larboard lane takes you toward the stern and the starboard lane takes you forward towards the bow. The sleds use maglev to ride about a centimeter above the magnets in the lane."

"Maglev?"

"Yeah. That was the best option when the Lewiston link frame was designed. There are so many hundreds of thousands of link frames in use now that it's unlikely the system will ever change. An independent company introduced an 'oh-gee' sled a few years ago that could be used with the maglev track, but it flopped. It offered improved performance, safety, and comfort, but the old sleds have become so common that they're dirt-cheap. Freight company officials embrace any-thing that's dirt-cheap."

Gloria placed the sled on the larboard lane and raised a piece into position to form a backrest for the rider. Simul-taneously, a T-bar safety bracket lowered into a slot on the track and swiveled. "You sit on the sled, put the heels of your boots against the stops, and grip both handles. When you're ready to move, you squeeze either handle tightly and depress the button by your thumb. The pressure on that handle then determines your speed. To speed up, release your grip a little. The harder you squeeze, the slower you go. You can't manually slow so quickly that you're ejected from the seat, or flip over. When you reach your destination, depress the button again before releasing your hand, remove your sled from the lane, and hang it on a sled rack or on the railing along the walking track. If you fail to slow the sled near the end of the track, the system should slow and stop you automatically to prevent injury."

As Gloria watched, Jenetta sat down on the sled and fidgeted until she felt comfortable. Gripping both handles tightly, she depressed the button by her right thumb and slowly loosened her grip. The sled started moving slowly towards the stern of the ship, picking up speed as she relaxed her grip more and more. Her face broke into a wide smile as the individual link trusses overhead began to blur into one long piece. By the halfway point, she was barely touching the handle and the velocity caused her facial skin to contort and ripple.

As the stern of the ship loomed ever larger, Jenetta gripped the handle, slowly tightening her grasp until she came to a halt just several meters from the end of the track. She had decided not to trust the system to halt her progress. Depress-ing the button, she dismounted, pushed the backrest down, then picked up the sled and hung it on the walking track railing, where she stood until Gloria finally arrived.

"That was fantastic!" Jenetta said raucously when Gloria reached her. "It's better than the Descent into Doom ride at the Old Georgetown Death Thrills Amusement Park. I loved it!"

Gloria grinned and shook her head as she stood up. "Do all Space Command ensigns have a death wish, or only you?"

Jenetta, her face still flushed with excitement said, "What?"

Pointing to the small display on the sled Jenetta had used, Gloria said, "You reached the stern of the ship in just two and a quarter minutes."

"Really?"

"So that means you were traveling what— about a hundred sixty kilometers an hour?"

"It was fantastic! It felt like I was flying!"

"You were flying. And you could have been ejected from the sled if something had happened, like a sudden power loss. There's no seatbelt on these things. Or you could have run up on top of someone going a lot slower."

"Does that happen?" Jenetta asked, her excitement diminishing slightly.

"Well— there are lots of system safeguards built in and I've never heard of it happening, but it *could* theoretically happen."

"But it was so much fun, Gloria! I received pilot training in shuttles at the Academy, which included Free Fall Spin Training, but even that wasn't anything like this. This was so real, so thrilling, so— so— visceral."

Gloria grinned and shook her head again. "Don't take this second life thing too far, Jen. You're not invulnerable, you know."

"I know," she said, then added excitedly, "but it was so much fun!"

"You're just lucky we don't have any flying insects on board or you'd still be picking them out of your teeth."

Jenetta smiled and, picking at her front teeth with a fingernail, said jokingly, "Now that you mention it..."

Due on the bridge at 1800 hours to relieve the captain, Gloria had to cut the tour short, but Jenetta had learned enough so she could travel throughout the ship on her own. They put their sleds down on the other lane and headed back for the main ship, but this time Gloria took the lead and Jenetta was forced to keep a grip on her sled's handle. Even so, their return to the lead link-section took just seven minutes.

Before breakfast the next day, Jenetta began jogging on the walkway in the tunnel. She could only run a half-kilometer the first morning before being forced to return by the limitations of her body, but over the following days she increased the distance as strength returned to her limbs. She would always smile pleasantly and wave when she passed someone traveling the other way on a hover-sled, even though they couldn't raise their hand to respond. She slowly got to know all the faces, even if she didn't know the names. The vitamins, nutrients, and medications provided by the doctor greatly assisted her recovery and, by the end of another week, she managed to jog the entire thirteen-plus kilometers to the ship's stern and back, about a third the distance of a marathon run. Her face had mostly filled out again and, thanks to her punishing exercise regimen, her body was nearing the prime condition it had been in when she leapt into the life pod aboard the *Hokyuu*. Her new uniforms now fit her as if they had been tailored rather than simply being copied from an old uniform.

After working at the science station on the bridge each day scanning space around the ship for any sign of other ships, Jenetta would run or exercise in the gym until she could barely lift her arms and legs. Several crewmembers could usually be found there practicing their kickboxing skills. Jenetta became intrigued and, after watching for a few days, asked them to teach her. It was infinitely different from the standard judo training she had received at the Academy. Her exercise program had redeveloped her quick reflexes, along with strong arms and legs. She proved to be a natural for the contact sport and she picked it up quickly.

Jenetta always tried to wrap up the day with some reading, having almost eleven years of news to catch up on. Although the ship couldn't transmit messages because of the danger of revealing its position, it could pick up vid & text broadcasts from the news services.

*   *   *

At the end of her first month aboard the *Vordoth*, Jenetta was feeling like a regular member of the crew, much more so than she ever had on the *Hokyuu*. She was able to practice with the kick-boxers as if she'd been at it for a year and wore each bruise proudly. The level of her skill improved with every practice session. She had also started getting up an hour earlier each morning so she could surreptitiously take a few high-speed hover sled rides before the first watch reported in. It was the one time of the day when the hover tracks were virtually deserted. Jenetta would laugh and squeal with delight as she flew through the ship at maximum speed.

At dinner one evening, Charley brought up the subject of the escape pod. "I had a chance to examine your pod this morning, Jen. I was curious as to why the retrorocket hadn't fired. I saw that the computer had sent the proper command automatically, followed by a number of manual commands to fire, so I followed the connections up to the rocket and discovered the problem. The line from the fuel tank had been ripped away. It must have happened during the explosion of the ship. There's a two-ton section of steel truss stuck in the heat shield of the main rocket engine. You must have ejected less than ten seconds from the explosion in order to be close enough for that to happen. Also, your com antenna was sheared clean away. No wonder they never picked up your emergency beacon signal."

"I guess that explains how I got here. I'm just glad the stasis chamber exceeded specs. I can't wait until we reach the Belagresue system so I can report in and have them notify my family that I'm still alive."

"Only about 83 more days, I estimate," Gloria said.

Jenetta came instantly awake when the *Vordoth's* alert horn in her quarters began to yelp the following morning. Like its brethren everywhere, it was designed to rattle teeth and 'wake the dead.' Jenetta believed at first that she was experiencing the recurring dream of her final night aboard the *Hokyuu*, but the persistence of the shrieking alarm and flashing red lights made her realize she was awake and that a true emergency existed. Leaping from the bed, she shed her pajamas in two quick movements and had her trousers on before the pajama buttons had even stopped rolling on the deck. No message to abandon ship was being broadcast, so she took a few extra seconds to button her blouse and seal her tunic before racing to the bridge.

Chapter Seven
~ July 9th, 2267 ~

Jenetta knew that command and control aboard ship could collapse during a time of extreme danger, but upon entering the bridge, the word pandemonium most accurately described the situation she discovered. If she hadn't seen it with her own eyes, she wouldn't have believed it. The first and second watch groups were both rushing about screaming orders, or answers, while red emergency lights flickered incessantly.

At the Academy, they screen a preposterously amusing vid for all new cadets showing what *not* to do when an enemy strikes. That worst-case example seemed almost like a piano recital compared to the chaos on the *Vordoth's* bridge. Captain Lentz's presence was conspicuously absent in the bedlam so Jenetta headed towards Gloria, who was concentrating her attention on the astrogator's console to the exclusion of all else.

"What's going on?" Jenetta shouted to Gloria, trying to make herself heard above the din.

"We're under attack by Raiders," Gloria shouted back as her hands tapped furiously at contact points on the console's control panel.

"Where's the captain?"

"We can't locate him!" Gloria shouted without slowing her efforts. "I think he was in the stern-most laser array link when the attack commenced. He came to the bridge about an hour ago and told me that he was going to check out a problem with its weapons control system."

"Why are we traveling sub-light?"

"Our Light Speed drive has been disengaged by the anti-collision system! I'm trying to reengage it, but no matter how many times I reset it and alter our course, it still refuses to build an envelope! When we spotted fighters heading our way, I ordered the sub-light engines to full power. They're on a manual override so the ACS can't shut *those* down."

"What can I do to help?"

"I— I— I don't know. See if you can help out with the weapons fire control."

Without further word, Jenetta wheeled and rushed to the fire control consoles at the rear bulkhead where two crew-members were futilely trying to hit numerous small targets. The tiny ships, a dozen kilometers out, seemed intent on passing the *Vordoth*. Jenetta assumed their goal was to fire on the main ship, but with the *Vordoth* pushing her sub-light engines at maximum acceleration, the fighters were finding it difficult to overtake the ship while flying an erratic course that would help them avoid laser fire.

The weapons consoles were similar to most military weapons training and video game consoles since the twenty-first century. Essentially, they consisted of a simple joystick with a fire button. Additional controls established power settings, readout information displays, and recalibration adjustments, but once the console was set up the gunner could perform his job with one hand.

Several *Vordoth* crewmembers watched in fear and silence while a half dozen others, like spectators at a sporting event, yelled frenzied warnings or shouted advice to the gunners. Several of the Raider fighter craft were in fact occasionally firing on the *Vordoth*. They seemed to be targeting the freighter's laser arrays as they dodged and weaved their way forward, pushing their small craft to the limits of their engines. This was no computer game or simulation.

"Trying to reduce our fire capability, I assume," Jenetta said out loud to no one in particular and it was doubtful that anyone heard her words.

Each of the weapon screens showed the area of fire cover-ed by the laser arrays under the control of that gunner and each of his arrays tracked the target, but the weapons control computer selectively discharged only the array closest to the enemy craft when it received the command to fire. Jenetta watched in stunned silence and amazement as the gunners poured an almost continuous stream of laser pulses towards the six fighters yet never damaged a single craft. She noticed that they consistently divided their fire among all available targets instead of concentrating on one until destroyed. Another failing was that they never waited to get a targeting system lock on the fighters before firing. Without a lock, they might as well have been aiming a spotlight at the fighters.

By focusing all her attention on the attackers, Jenetta felt sure that she saw a pattern to their movements, but her attempts to instruct the undisciplined gunners were seemingly unheard and went unanswered. The gunner on the starboard weapons console was bobbing and weaving like a prize-fighter, as though his movements and 'body English' could somehow make up for a serious deficiency in weapons training. Unable to contain herself any longer, Jenetta finally reached out and grabbed the collar of his tunic during one of his bobs to the right. Using the momentum of his own body, as with a judo move, Jenetta yanked him clear of the chair, sat down, locked onto a target, and fired before the crewmember had even stopped rolling on the deck.

* * *

Arlie 'Vulture' Leggmann grinned wickedly as he fired an intermittent stream of laser pulses into the freighter. He loved his work. While other young boys had dreamed of building things, he'd known that he was born to kill and destroy. The three deadly arson fires he'd set in his own neighborhood before he was even ten years old proved that. The third blaze had been his last though, at least until he reached eighteen. He'd been repeatedly observed chortling and trying to mask his glee while firefighters risked their lives to rescue the people and pets trapped in the homes. A suspicious cop working with arson investigators put the pieces together. Leggmann was arrested. Convicted of seven counts of murder, along with arson charges, he'd been sent to a juvenile facility for rehabilitation. Somewhere along the way, he learned to conceal his psychosis from the psychologists appointed to evaluate his mental condition. Despite the number of deaths, his tender age at the time of the offenses saved him from being remanded to an adult facility to continue the sentences when he reached eighteen. Instead, he was released back into an unsuspecting society.

As soon as he was free, Leggmann took up where he'd left off, but, having been incarcerated once for arson and murder, the cops were quick to identify him as their number one suspect. Leggmann knew he had to clear out or wind up in prison again. Fortunately for him, there were always people who needed a good psychopath on their payroll and Leggmann had no difficulty finding gainful and self-gratifying employment. When the organization for whom he'd been working was absorbed into the giant Raider organization, Leggmann found new opportunities to explore his proclivities. Some of his associates thought his nickname referred to his beak-like nose, but it was in reality a reference to his societal propensities.

Leggmann wasn't trying to do any real damage to the *Vordoth*— yet. In fact, he was under strict orders *not* to cause any serious damage. Captain Goshan wanted the cargo section intact. He'd even ordered that all rockets be removed from the fighters prior to this mission. Leggmann was only trying to panic the freight haulers with a few insipid hits. He reasoned that the more nervous they were, the less likely they were to damage any of his squadron. But in a few more minutes he would reach the main ship and then he would show them what damage really was. If he could punch enough holes to evacuate their atmosphere, the fight would be over before it really began. They couldn't fight when they're sucking vacuum.

"Vulture One to Vulture flock. As soon as we reach the main ship, target their sub-light engines. Then fill the ship with so many holes it'll look like that old dartboard in the ship's canteen. Vulture One out."

Leggmann felt only a slight tickle in his ribs as several powerful pulses of coherent light punctured the unarmored sidewall of the fighter cockpit just below his armpits. He never even knew he was dead. The smirking grin was still on his face as the top half of his body began to topple. His final seconds of thought were devoted to wondering why he seemed to be bending forward. As his upper torso landed at his feet, his detached arms were only slowly beginning to yield their tight grip on the joystick and throttle controls.

*   *   *

Jenetta knew she had scored a kill when the fighter suddenly veered to starboard and corkscrewed away from the freighter. Even the weapons computer acknowledged that it was no longer a serious threat. When the blip representing that target winked out, a loud cheer went up behind her. Jenetta immediately shifted the targeting control towards another blip, tracked the target, got a lock, and fired again. Almost instantly, that blip disappeared from the screen as well, followed by another loud cheer. Her third shot went marginally wide as the small enemy ship zigzagged just as she fired, but her next burst caught it dead center and the blip winked out as a fuel cylinder was breached and the small ship took on the appearance of a diminutive sun for the briefest of seconds. Her new cheering section let out another whoop before turning their attention back to the other gunner.

The remaining three fighters must have realized that the starboard side had suddenly become the more deadly of the two because they limited their flight to the area her arrays couldn't target. They also increased their evasive maneuvers, which thankfully further slowed their forward progress.

Jenetta watched anxiously as the crewmember controlling the larboard weapons failed to get a lock on his targets and just fired randomly as fast as he could pull the trigger. As she rolled her eyes, her gaze flitted across a master switch that swapped control of the guns. Designed to allow either console to take over for the other in the event of an equipment malfunction, the switch offered her an opportunity to supplant the other gunner without again resorting to physical means.

The three remaining fighters were just seconds from the main ship when Jenetta reached up and flipped the switch, giving her control of the larboard weapons. The crewmember at the left station, totally absorbed in his task when the images on the screens swapped, just stared dumbly at the blank screen in front of him trying to figure out what happened to his targets. Meanwhile, Jenetta got a lock on the lead fighter and fired. It took just a few more seconds for her to destroy the other two attacking small craft. All those years of playing the video game she carried on her log ring hadn't been a waste of time after all.

As the last blip winked out on the targeting screens, the bridge erupted in cheers. Jenetta slumped in the chair as the adrenaline began to drain from her system. She only became aware that Gloria was standing directly behind her when she felt hands on her shoulders.

"Great shooting, Jen," Gloria said breathlessly. "Six kills. Thank *God* you were here."

Suddenly remembering the crewmember she had plucked so unceremoniously and ignominiously by the collar, Jenetta looked up at the people surrounding her. Now standing near her right side, the ejected gunner smiled ingenuously at her and gave her a thumbs-up sign. She'd expected to see resentment for her action in his eyes, but she saw nothing but genuine relief. She smiled and returned his sign, then turned to the crewmember in the chair next to her and said, "I'm sorry I took over your console. There wasn't time to ask politely."

"Ensign, I'm just relieved to have survived the attack. I couldn't seem to hit even one of those bastards. I thought we were all dead meat for sure. You can take over for me *anytime*. That was great shooting, by the way. Maybe you could give me some pointers when you have a chance?"

"I'd be happy to," Jenetta said, smiling, with a profound sense of relief that she hadn't destroyed the new friendships she'd been cultivating with the bridge crewmembers.

"Okay, everyone, calm down," Gloria announced, "this isn't over yet. Let's get busy and find out what kind of shape we're in. Someone turn off those damn red lights and, *please*, somebody find the captain and get him up here."

The communications operator called out, "Lieutenant, the chief engineer is waiting to speak with you."

"Put it through to the captain's briefing room. Jen, uh— come with me."

With Sabella leading the way, the two women crossed to the captain's briefing room on the larboard side of the bridge. As the doors quietly slid closed behind them, the alert lights stopped flashing and the horns wailing in the ship's corridors ended their plaintive yowls. The chief engineer's face immediately filled the screen when Gloria raised the cover on the captain's desktop com unit.

"How bad is it, Charley?" Gloria asked.

"The bastards hit us hard, Gloria!" Charley said, his face ablaze with anger. "We lost the last two cargo link-sections and we have some serious damage along the spine. A number of containers were hit. Two are spilling contents. The only way to stop the spill may be to bring the ship to a stop."

"We can't stop, Charley. Engage their grav decking. That will stop the spillage."

"I've already ordered that for all damaged containers. The two still-leaking cargos must have sustained damage to their ship connections or control systems. We have to plug the holes."

"See if you can get me a list of the containers that are spilling so I can see what we're losing. Uh— Charley, is the captain with you? He went out to the aft gun section a while ago."

"He's not with *us*." There was a slight pause and a much calmer and somber Charley said, "I was in the sack when the alert sounded. If the captain was still in the aft link when the fighters struck, then he's gone, along with anyone else that was back there with him."

Following a sharp intake of breath, Gloria leaned heavily on the desk and said, "Thank you, Charley. Keep me informed as you get any new information. Sabella out."

Gloria's face was ashen. The change that had come over her in just seconds was astonishing.

"We're in trouble," Gloria said weakly. "Without the captain, we're doomed."

The utter despair in Gloria's voice was obvious and she had begun to tremble all over.

"You're just giving up?" Jenetta asked. "Without a fight?"

"I'm not a fighter, Jen, I'm a freight hauler. I don't know what to do next. Hell, I didn't know what to do before when the fighters attacked. If I hadn't been needed to work at resetting the ACS, I would probably have run from the bridge. I was that scared."

"Whatever you do," Jenetta said with a calm and steady voice, "don't let the crew see you like this. They have to believe you know exactly what you're doing at all times— even if you don't. Their courage comes from their captain, so you must have enough for everybody."

"Me? Captain?" Gloria said incredulously.

"Yes, you're the first officer. That makes you the captain now that he's gone."

"No," Gloria said, shaking her head vehemently. "No, I can't. I can't. I shouldn't even be out here. I should be aboard some nice large freighter with a full crew, sitting safely in a protected convoy. I was taking on as much as I could chew by being the first officer. Before this trip, I was just a third. I'd never even had the watch before this run. The only reason I'm the first officer is because the senior officers all refused to go and they couldn't find anyone else dumb enough to accept the berth." Gloria had been looking down at the floor while she spoke. Suddenly looking up, she said eagerly, "You! You could do it. You're a trained Space Command officer. You've been trained to command a ship and crew in battle. You can get us through this. You'll have to take over for the captain."

Gloria was trembling more visibly now. Jenetta had heard it was like that with some people. After the shooting was over and the realization of what had just happened dawned, they came down with the shakes. It wasn't something typically seen following battle simulations because subconsciously everyone knew their lives weren't on the line regardless of how realistic the simulation appeared.

Out here though, lives depended on the captain's ability to make the right decisions at the right instant and it was obvious Gloria wouldn't be the effective leader that was needed right now. Nor did Jenetta think that either the Doctor or Charley would want to accept command since neither was particularly qualified to step in despite their tenure and rank. Fortunately, Gloria had displayed a brave front to the crew during the action and there was no one else in the briefing room to see her deteriorating condition; however, the Raiders could return at any time. Nobody knew how many there were and the group that had attacked might have been only an advance party.

"Gloria, I'm just an ensign," Jenetta said in protest. "I've never commanded a ship. I'm a science officer, an astro-physicist."

"But you've received training for ship command, haven't you? And participated in battle simulations as the command-ing officer?"

"Well, yes, I've received the standard three-year NHSA command officer training. But I've never actually been in a battle before."

"Neither have I. And I haven't had three years of training for it either. You're our only hope."

As a very young girl, Jenetta had dreamed of traveling through space as the captain of a powerful warship. But being the smallest and weakest participant in a seemingly never-ending round of fiercely competitive games while growing up, it was rare when she was able to top her four brothers. She had become quite used to being cast in a supporting role, perhaps even comfortably so, rather than as the leader. Her outstanding scholastic achievements had done little to erase diffidence in her adequacy for command.

Without any real responsibility, her days as a member of the *Vordoth* crew had been some of the most wonderful times in her life. She no more desired to take command now than she wished to become infected with a three-month bout of

Kuwloon Flu. In fact, the mere thought of becoming captain made her stomach roil. But with Captain Lentz gone and Gloria seemingly unable to assume full command, there was no one else. Meek surrender to the Raiders was not an option.

Whether at sea or in space, a ship's captain was the final authority on everything. Ships, even civilian ships, were not democracies; they were the ultimate in stratocracies. Jenetta knew some of the crew might object to her promotion to Captain, but having the full support of Gloria behind her meant they would be guilty of mutiny if they refused to follow her orders. She swallowed hard and made her decision.

"Okay— if that's what you really want," Jenetta said. She expected to feel sicker when she said it, but she actually felt better. "But I need you to get a grip on yourself. I'll need a good first officer and you're it. Now take a few deep breaths and stop shaking."

Gloria's face registered shock as she looked down at her hands. Until then she hadn't realized she *was* shaking. Clasping her hands together tightly, she took several deep breaths, seeming to calm a bit more with each now that the question of command had been settled.

"Good," Jenetta said. "That's better. Now put on as confident a face as you can and go out onto the bridge. You're presently the senior officer of this ship. You'll have to inform the crew that I'm accepting command at your request."

Gloria nodded. Taking one more deep breath, she composed her face, then led the way out of the office and over to the crewmember that was manning the communications station. "I have an announcement for the entire crew," she said assertively. "Put me on all shipboard speakers."

"Aye, Lieutenant." The crewmember said, before tapping some points on the communications console and handing her a tiny wireless microphone. "Whenever you're ready, Lieutenant."

"Attention all crewmembers, this is Lieutenant Sabella. First the good news. The six Raider fighters that attacked us have been destroyed and there's no sign of others at this moment." She paused for a couple of seconds, allowing a little time for celebration. "I also have some terrible news to convey. It appears that Captain Lentz has been lost, along with whoever might have been with him in the aft laser section when the Raiders struck. We all mourn this loss and we will carry on with the certain knowledge that he would have been proud of us. We are fortunate to have Ensign Carver aboard. It was she who saved our skins by shooting down all six attacking Raider fighters. As you know, Ensign Carver is a Space Command officer trained at NHSA. Her military training includes ship command under battle conditions and I've decided that makes her the best candidate to assume command of this ship. She has consented to become our Captain. Captain Carver?"

Jenetta had been silently rehearsing what she would say. Taking the small microphone, she forced her voice to sound clear, calm, and confident. "This is Carver." She wasn't yet willing to use the title of captain. "Until we're out of danger, we'll operate as if this is a military ship. We need complete damage reports as quickly as possible. And if there are any former military people with gunnery experience aboard, report to me on the bridge. Carry on. Carver out."

She had an overwhelming urge to take a deep breath, but she knew it might conflict with the image she was attempting to convey. She calmly handed the mike back to the com operator and turned to the crewmember manning the security station, "Any sign of other vessels?"

"Negative, Ens— Captain. The plot is clear."

Turning to the crewmember at the science console, she asked, "What's our distance to the objects responsible for disengaging the Light Speed drive?"

"They're gone, Captain. The contacts disappeared right after the six fighters were destroyed."

"Disappeared? Completely?"

"Aye, Captain. One second a seemingly solid barrier of obstructions stretched for thousands of kilometers across our bow and the next they were gone. There's no trace of them left."

Jenetta stared at the large front viewscreen as she thought, then said to the communications crewmember, "Any reports yet from damage control parties?"

Holding out a portable viewpad, the female crewmember said, "Here's everything so far, Captain."

Jenetta scrolled down through the list of reported damages. Items were still coming in and the list was being updated as she watched, but, so far, the most serious ship damage seemed to be the loss of the aft laser array section and two cargo link-sections. Two crewmembers, Deitrich and Higgiby, were unaccounted for in addition to the captain, and two others were injured, but not critically.

As soon as the new 'captain' called for former military people with gunnery experience, Chief Rondell headed for the bridge. He stepped in front of her while she was still scanning the data on the viewpad. She was so absorbed in what she reading that she didn't immediately acknowledge his presence. Although he hadn't talked to her previously, he'd been in the maintenance bay the day she came aboard and he'd seen her jogging in the spine tunnel a number of times. He also knew of her kickboxing training and that she'd shown she wasn't afraid to mix it up with people whose skill level was far above her own in order to learn and improve. And once, when he hadn't been able to get back to sleep after waking too early, he'd caught sight of her flying down the maglev sled track at top speed. There was only one thing about her that bothered him; she looked like a 'snot nosed' Academy cadet. The facts proved there was more in that diminutive package than outside appearances indicated, but if she hadn't just shot down all six fighters that had attacked the ship, he still might have found it difficult to take orders from her.

As Jenetta finished reading the list and lowered the viewpad, she realized a crewmember was standing in front of her.

Bracing to attention, he said, "Senior Freight Operations Chief Rondell, Captain. Thirty-eight years in the Galactic Space Marine Corps. Most of that as a Master Gunnery Sergeant."

Standing about six-foot four-inches tall with close-cropped hair, Gunny Rondell looked exactly like one would expect a Space Marine gunnery sergeant to look. And despite the early signs of a budding beer-gut at fifty-six, he was still able to handle any three ordinary men stupid enough to take him on.

Once commissioned, officers who had satisfied the service requirements of their Academy education remained in the service until they either resigned their commission or retired, but enlistment and reenlistment tours for Space Command and Space Marine NCOs and crewmen ran ten years, so it was unusual to find someone with thirty-eight years of service. Jenetta reasoned that although he looked healthy enough now, he might have been injured and separated with partial disability. But it was also possible he took advantage of an 'early out' provision that allowed a one-percent-pay per year of service retirement at age fifty-five if the applicant had at least thirty-five years in. A third possibility was that he'd been dishonorably discharged for some crime or infraction. Whatever the reason, Jenetta would overlook almost any fault if he could help the situation.

"Okay, Gunny, at ease. I need you to take command of weapons control and give eight crewmembers a crash course in gunnery. I'll leave the crew selection up to you, but we must be prepared for the next attack."

"Aye, Captain. If they'll give me twelve hours for training, we'll be ready for 'em."

"Carry on, Gunny. Gloria, let's talk in the briefing room."

"Aye, Captain, I'm right behind you."

As he watched her walk away, the edges of Gunny Rondell's mouth curled ever so slightly upward, though certainly not enough to be obvious. Carver might not look much like a ship's captain, but she certainly sounded like one.

There'd been no hesitation or doubt in her voice as she issued her orders. He'd begun to worry when he heard the captain was lost because he knew Lt. Sabella was far too 'green' for command. But Captain *Carver* appeared to be something else again.

Chapter Eight

~ July 9th, 2267 ~

As the doors whispered closed, Jenetta turned and asked, "Did you get a look at the battle damage list?"

"I studied it while you were speaking with Chief Rondell."

"I'd like to hear your assessment before I send a message to Space Command."

"But we're under strict radio silence!" Gloria said aghast. "You *can't* call Space Command."

"Gloria, there's no reason to observe radio silence anymore. I can't imagine that the Raiders don't know precisely where we are. Their fighters would certainly have transmitted our position before they commenced their attack run."

"Oh— oh, yes, of course. How foolish of me. Well, we're holding together so far. We're leaking unprocessed bastnasite ore and we've lost a couple of small wine casks from the Sebastian colony." As she was talking, Gloria moved over to the large viewscreen on the wall and activated the display. "Computer, display the reports from the damage control parties on the wall monitor."

The screen lit up with the text Jenetta had been reading from the handheld display. Waving her hand lightly above the optical sensor on the desk, Jenetta scrolled down until they reached the reports she hadn't seen yet. Charley had reported that he was attempting to patch the hole where the wine casks had slipped out, but didn't think anything could be done about the dribbling ore unless they went outside. As if aware of their contemplations, Charley called on the com system.

"We've managed to rig an inside patch in the container holding the wine casks, but we'll definitely have to go outside to plug the ore container."

"How long will it take?" Jenetta asked.

"We'll have to slow the ship to at least Plus-50 to secure the patch. I estimate two hours for the work and then another hour to build the envelope and get up to our top speed because we don't want to put too much strain on the cargo spine until we're sure of the structural condition."

"Okay, Charley, we'll slow to Plus-50 in five minutes. Be ready."

"Aye, Captain. Charley out."

"You can't seriously intend to slow the ship?" Gloria asked.

"We have to. Leaking unprocessed bastnasite is like leaving a trail of radioactive breadcrumbs. If we alter course they'll only find us again by following the trail with their sensors."

"Oh— right. Guess I'm still not thinking like a military person."

"It'll come," Jenetta said gently, as she raised the cover of the communications unit on the desk and touched the Space Command ring on her right hand to the spindle in the console's media drawer. Received at graduation from NHSA, the decorative band replaced the cadet ring she had worn for four years. It contained Space Command's latest encryption codes at that time and should prevent anyone from listening in as long as the ten-year old codes were still secure and could still be decrypted by Space Command vessels. Selecting the newest code from the list that came up on the screen, Jenetta pressed the start button and spoke directly at the display so the com unit's camera would record her image.

"Message to any Space Command vessel in or near deca-sector 8667-3855, with a copy to Higgins Space Command Base.

"This is Jenetta Alicia Carver, ensign, GSC serial number 3974A32, originally posted to the GSC quartermaster supply ship, *Hokyuu*. The commercial freighter *Vordoth* picked up my life pod thirty days ago. I'm well, and had expected to report for duty as soon as the ship reached Higgins Space Command Base at Vinnia. Unfortunately, Raiders attacked the *Vordoth* in sector 8667-3855-1642.3817 post-median 0072. The captain is missing and presumed lost. The first officer has asked me to take command in light of my military training and I am now acting as the *Vordoth's* captain. We've lost three crewmembers, including the captain, and have two injured. We managed to destroy the six Raider fighters that attacked us, but we lost a small part of the ship's cargo section during their assault. We need assistance from any Galactic Space Command vessel in the area. We're slowing to make external repairs and expect to resume our top Light Speed within one-eight-zero minutes. In light of the imminent danger, I ask that my family not yet be notified that I'm alive.

"Captain Jenetta Carver, aboard the *Vordoth*, message complete."

Pushing the stop button, Jenetta logged the message for immediate wide-spectrum transmission on the emergency IDS bands. Although traveling at point-zero-five-one-three light-years per minute, it still might take hours for the IDS band transmission to reach a Space Command vessel and many more hours for a reply.

"Gloria, take over on the bridge. Have the helmsman slow to Plus-50. I'm going back to take a personal look at the damage. Call me immediately if anything shows up on the sensors."

"Aye, Captain."

As she exited the briefing room, Jenetta observed that Sergeant Rondell was already working with the group of gunnery trainees he'd selected. The weapons fire control stations were set to simulation mode and she heard him bellow as loudly and gruffly as any Marine Drill Instructor with a handful of raw recruits, "No, no, no! I keep telling you that you have to get a lock on the target before you fire! If you don't have a lock, it means the light energy isn't focused. And if it isn't properly focused, the pulse won't slice through butter, much less steel or titanium. Remember— the targeting circle will change from yellow to red when you have a focus lock."

As the hover-sled glided silently through the tunnel, Jenetta's right hand gripped the throttle handle tightly to keep her travel down to a respectable speed of no more than twenty kph. She longed to open it up, but restrained herself, awareness that there could be possible damage to the track ahead tempering her hunger for a speed that would push her current situation from the forefront of her thoughts if only for a few minutes. The full realization of her commitment kept rolling over her like thunder during a violent storm. She was now responsible for every person on board, not to mention the ship and billions of credits in cargo. Such liability is supposed to come gradually, after years of service and steadily increasing responsibility. It's not supposed to be thrust upon someone who graduated from the Academy just six months ago. As she'd slept in stasis for most of her time since graduation, that was a fair, if inaccurate, description of the past eleven years.

Several engineering crewmen were working to raise a fallen support truss blocking the lane just beyond the five-kilometer point, so Jenetta picked up the sled and ducked through a shower of cutting torch sparks before placing it down again on the other side of the fallen beam to continue her trip. Charley was supervising another work party five hundred meters beyond the blockage while devoting half his attention to a work monitor temporarily clamped to the railing beside the walking track.

"How's it going, Charley?"

"As soon as we slowed to fifty kps I sent out the space tugs," he said distractedly as he watched the repair efforts via live image feed from a camera mounted on one of the tugs. Pointing to the monitor, he added, "They have prefab sections to weld over the holes as soon as they cut away the obstructions. With luck, they'll be back within ninety minutes. Without luck, it could take two hours or more."

"Very good," she said, nodding as she shared his view of the repair effort. "Charley?"

"Yes, Captain?"

"How many link-sections do we have after the last laser array section and what's the cargo?"

Turning to look at her as he rubbed his chin, he said, "Let's see, we were sixty-four-meters over six and a half kilometers, so we added an extra laser array link at the end. With that gone, and two cargo sections with it, that would leave three cargo link-sections following the last weapons section now. The last kilometer of cargo is all unprocessed bastnasite ore from the mines of Kesserith intended for delivery to the orbiting foundry factories around Lazziter."

"How difficult would it be to separate the last three sections while we're traveling at top speed?"

"Not difficult at all. The tug jockeys normally handle single section separations. As a space tug locks onto a section, the airtight doors in the prior section automatically close to prevent the tunnel from losing atmosphere unless someone in the link section activates an emergency override. Once the sensors indicate the doors are sealed, the tug pilot can remotely release the section's locks and it floats free of the ship. But we can detach single sections without a tug being involved. For longer section removals, the designated separation point can only be unlocked from either the bridge or engineering. That's to allow us an opportunity to ensure that the entire section is empty of personnel."

"What happened when the last couple of sections were cut away by the Raiders?"

"The tunnel automatically sealed all airtight doors as soon as a pressure drop was detected. But anyone within three or four link-sections could have been sucked out before the doors closed completely. There's also the chance that someone can get caught by a closing door and be cut in half, but we didn't find any body parts when we re-pressurized and opened all doors except the last."

"Would separating at FTL do any damage to the cargo section separated or the rest of the ship?"

"No. Temporal envelopes stretch slightly at first, but as the new envelopes form, they exclude the detached section once the gap exceeds fifteen-point-two-eight centimeters. Without an envelope to surround the section, it's immediately back in normal space at a dead stop. Why just the last three sections?"

"Two reasons. One, the absence of the sections will allow the last laser array link greater coverage. Once the sections are gone, the turrets can swing around to fire straight back. Right now, the three sections are a handicap because they create a blind spot for the gunners. A fighter could *conceivably* come up behind us and sit in complete safety as he fires his laser weapon into the spine. Even if we closed all the link-section doors, he'd eventually be able to cut through everything and evacuate the atmosphere in the ship."

"I see. You said two reasons?"

"Yes, I did," she said, grinning. "The other one is a little nastier. As you said, when the envelope has decayed around the detached link-section it will immediately be at a dead stop in space. If someone gets a little too close and we can't get them off our six, we'll just release one of the link-sections. Contact with thirty-two thousand cubic meters of bastnasite ore sheathed in a reinforced steel cargo container sitting at a dead stop will end all their problems quick."

"Ouch!" Charley said, and then grinned. "Any fighter that hit that would wind up looking like one of the grease spots on the wall at Harry Hardy's Hotdog & Hamburger Haven back home in Cinci. Do they teach sneaky stuff like that at the Academy?"

Jenetta returned his grin. "No, I had to become sneaky just to have a chance of beating my brothers at the games we played when we were young. They had all the size and strength, so I had to be devious one."

"Gottcha. Okay, as soon as my crews return we'll work on the connections."

"Place a tracking transponder in each of the link-sections. It'll enable us to locate the sections later so the cargo won't be permanently lost if we have to detach them. After completing the work, seal all the airtight doors between the last three sections. We want to make sure no one wanders into that area in case we have to detach from the link sections in a hurry. How's the rest of the ship?"

"Not nearly as bad as I originally thought. The Raiders never reached the main ship and they didn't score very many solid hits on the spine." Grinning, he said, "I guess they were too busy dodging your laser fire. Anyway, one section was weakened by a substantial hit, but we reinforced it to better than new and my people are now busy repairing and reinforcing the other damage points. By tomorrow we'll be as solid as any ship plying the lanes, unless we get clobbered again."

"Then we'll just have to make sure we don't get clobbered again. Say Charley," Jenetta asked thoughtfully, "how fast are your tugs?"

"Space tugs are mostly power-plant, Captain. They have to be if they're going to generate the opposed gravity forces necessary to lift huge loads from the surface of planets and control the mass contained in huge sections of fully loaded cargo links while in space. Our speed in N-space is really only limited by rate of acceleration, time, fuel quantity, and the physical laws of relativity. Since space tugs are constructed with an eye towards towing merchantmen and passenger liners that become disabled in deep space, most have temporal field generators for FTL. I'd guess that ours are like most and can achieve Light-75, although the *Vordoth* has never had a situation arise that required any of our tugs to use faster-than-light speeds. With no armament, no crew quarters, and no long range sensors other than AutoTect and DeTect, our tugs have no business wandering very far from the ship."

"Thank you. Carry on, Charley."

"Aye, Captain."

Only three hours had passed since being awakened by the attack, but it felt much longer. As Jenetta returned to the main ship, she stopped in the officer's mess to grab a cup of coffee before continuing on to the bridge. The caffeine would help keep her alert. Anthony, the mess attendant, greeted her as

'Captain' and, guessing her reason for being there, hurried to fetch a mug of coffee.

"I heard you did some mighty good shooting this morning, Captain," he said as he handed her the mug. "I'm sure glad you're on board."

"Thank you, Anthony. I'll just take this to go. I want to get back to the bridge."

"Okay, Captain. If you want more, just call and I'll bring you a fresh pot."

On the bridge, things had returned to normal except for Gunny Rondell's intensive class in gunnery. Within thirty minutes of her return, the crewmember at the communications console said, "The Chief Engineer reports that the stopgap repairs are complete, the space tugs are back aboard, the ship is sealed, and we can resume FTL whenever you wish, Captain."

Jenetta leaned forward in the command chair and said, "Very well. Helm, start building our envelope and take us up to full speed, slowly, as you resume the programmed course."

"Aye, Captain."

Turning towards the crewmember manning the science station, Jenetta said, "Science, scan the area behind us and see if we're leaving any kind of a trail as we increase speed."

"Aye, Captain."

Jenetta leaned back in the command chair to relax and sip her coffee as she watched the front viewscreen.

Formation of the envelope took just two minutes, but it was another sixty before they were back up to Light-150 as the ship built up speed gradually to ensure that the temporary repairs would hold. Although a ship essentially remains stationary within its envelope during FTL travel and disassociation with normal space eliminates all sensation of movement, there is some stress on the ship's frame as new envelopes form and pull the vessel ahead into the new position.

When the science station crewmember reported nothing was being trailed except a normal residual ion stream that dissipated fairly quickly, Jenetta moved to the astrogator's station and entered a course change. It would add a few hours to the trip, but might foil the Raiders if they were waiting somewhere ahead in ambush. The computer would advise the helmsman of the necessary course corrections in easy increments designed to prevent too much stress on the ship's structural integrity.

Just before noon, a reply to Jenetta's message arrived from the Space Command destroyer *Brasilia*. She watched the communication in her briefing room with just Gloria in attendance. As the message began playing, the face of a senior Space Command Captain who appeared to be near mandatory retirement age appeared on the monitor.

"To Jenetta Carver, Acting Captain aboard the *Vordoth*, from Robert Aubrey, Captain of the Space Command destroyer *Brasilia*, GSC-D1240.

"I regret to inform you that neither the *Brasilia* nor any other GSC vessel can come to your aid at this time. All ships within a thirty-day travel time are presently responding to other declared emergencies. The nearest available ship, the destroyer Kiev, is a full thirty-eight days from your location and it makes little sense to divert from its present patrol since you allege you've destroyed the Raiders and are about to resume Light Speed travel.

"I suggest you rebuild your envelope and do not again foolishly drop out of FTL speed until you reach Higgins. If you learned anything at all at the Academy, Ensign, it should have been that you can't be attacked while traveling FTL.

"As to the matter of your separation from service, I'm sure a copy of your broadcast message will reach Higgins. They are the proper authority in this deca-sector.

"Robert Aubrey, Captain, Space Command destroyer *Brasilia*, message complete."

"He thinks we *chose* to stop?" Gloria said, her eyes as large as saucers. "He believes we had some kind of choice in the matter?"

"Apparently," Jenetta said, not wishing to verbalize the negative opinion she was feeling towards a myopic officer and senior captain whom she had never met or even heard of before. "In any event, we're clearly on our own out here."

Their sensors hadn't detected the presence of any other vessels since the attack, so Jenetta and Gloria felt comfortable walking to the officer's mess to have lunch. It seemed to be the only meal where most of the officers were present in the wardroom at the same time. Both the Doctor and Charley had just arrived.

"How are the injured men doing, Doctor?" Jenetta asked as they took their seats.

"Quite well, Captain. Injuries were mostly limited to superficial cuts and bruises, but one crewmember has a broken finger and another has a slight concussion. The crewman with the broken finger has already returned to duty and the other man should be okay in a couple of days."

"Excellent. Charley, how's everything in engineering?"

"Returning to normal," Charley said, then scowled as he added, "except Rondell's recruited six of my best men to function as gunners."

Jenetta smiled. "Do your best to get by without them while they train. We need them more as gunners right now."

"Aye, Captain."

"Is it possible to set up additional gunnery stations? We'll have eight gunners soon and only two stations on the bridge."

"Sure. Each of the four laser arrays on the main ship has its own console in the turret. When unmanned, control automatically passes to the console covering the adjacent space, or to the bridge fire control stations. The only icons that show up on each operator's console are for the targets that fall within the area covered by that operator's guns."

"That'll give us six stations. Could we do the same with the two stations in the laser array section immediately behind the main ship?"

"Yes. Those consoles are almost identical to the others."

"Okay, you have your project for this afternoon, Charley. Divide all laser arrays into larboard and starboard functions and then further sub-divide them into four groups. Gunny Rondell can assign his new gunners where he sees fit."

"Aye, Captain."

After lunch, Jenetta told Gloria to go get some sleep. She'd been up for more than twenty hours, much of it during an extremely stressful time. Jenetta, having had four hour's sleep before the Raiders hit, returned to the bridge. Gloria would relieve her at 2000 hours.

* * *

Gunny Rondell got his hoped-for twelve hours. After that, each gunner was assigned a weapons station. If a new gunner was injured or away from his station during an attack, control would pass to the first manned console in a prioritized list.

The *Vordoth's* crew spent the next day waiting for an attack that never came, but Gunny Rondell didn't waste the time. Throughout the morning and afternoon, he had the new gunners practice with the sim systems for a half-hour, take a half-hour break, and then practice for another half-hour during their entire watch. At the end of the day, he declared them as good as any newly trained gunnery squad in the Space Marines and cancelled further mandatory training exercises, but he authorized them to practice on their own if they wished and all took advantage of the opportunity to better their new skills. They were well motivated to be prepared for the next attack if it should come.

Settled comfortably onto a course parallel to their original track, but offset by five hundred billion kilometers, the ship would never be observed on the sensors of any Raider ship lying in wait for them along their previous route. Jenetta managed to get eight hours sleep when Gloria relieved her and she reentered the bridge refreshed and alert after a simple breakfast the following morning. Each shoulder now sported the four wide gold bars that visually proclaimed her the ship's captain. Most likely Gloria, or at least someone operating on Gloria's instructions, had taken all four of Jenetta's new uniforms while she slept and changed the rank insignia. As Jenetta settled into the command chair to enjoy the fresh cup of coffee she had carried from the officer's mess, Gloria left to have breakfast.

Rested, and with the ship repaired and out of immediate danger, Jenetta reviewed the facts of the Raider attack in her mind. Six fighters had assaulted the ship, but fighters were short-range ships and she wasn't aware of any habitable planets nearby. The attackers had to have come from either a base or a ship since it was impossible for them to have been that deep in space on their own.

Upon assuming command Jenetta had quickly discovered that there was an untapped wealth of skills aboard the ship. Gunny Rondell had been just one of many. If Captain Lentz had read the personnel files as Jenetta had done within hours of her ascendancy, Rondell would already have been assigned to the fire control battery. Jenetta had also found four cargo handlers who'd had bridge experience and she immediately reassigned them to duties on the bridge.

Approaching the now constantly manned astrogation console, Jenetta said, "Show me the chart for this area, every-thing within say— five-trillion kilometers from the point where we were attacked."

"Aye, Captain," the crewmember conscripted to function as an astrogator said as he keyed in the parameters to meet the request. "Here it is, ma'am."

"There's nothing here," Jenetta muttered as she examined the chart displayed on the viewscreen. "Where's the nearest planet or moon that could properly support a base? A breathable atmosphere isn't necessary."

The crewmember punched in the parameters and the image of an off-white planet popped up on the screen. Informational text filled the foreground of the image. "Regoserth-Five, Captain," the crewmember said, interpreting the compendious data. "It's at the extreme edge of a system that doesn't have a decent planet in the lot. Its star is about one and a half light-years from where we were attacked, roughly fourteen-trillion kilometers."

"Thank you."

"Aye, Captain."

Moving to the security station console where a crewmember was busy scanning space for any sign of other ships, she asked, "Are you picking up any sign of activity?"

"No contact, Captain."

Looking over the crewmember's shoulder, she asked, "How come your stern DeTect screen looks so clear? How far out are you scanning?"

"Since there's no danger of colliding with something in our wake, Captain Lentz had us scan only to a billion kilometers. The next setting is full scan and the screen becomes cluttered with noise from DeTect signal dropouts, making it much more difficult to spot the movement of someone overtaking us. At the present setting, any movement jumps out at you."

"Change to full scan, please. It's a little harder on the eyes, but you get used to it after a while and the computer will help alert you to movement when you use the higher setting."

"Aye, Captain," the crewmember said as he adjusted the viewing controls. His screen lit up with white dots that continuously appeared and disappeared. Some were quite large but most were miniscule.

Standing behind the crewmember, Jenetta watched the screens for several minutes. She had spent many hours staring at such displays while aboard the *Hokyuu*. Pointing to a steady dot in the dead center of the stern image monitor, she asked, "Does it seem strange to you that there should be a steady image on the course that we've just followed? We would have had to fly right through it, whatever it is. What do you think?"

"I don't know, Captain. Let me see what the computer thinks of it." The crewmember touched the dot with a stylus and then tapped a few keys. After a few seconds, the computer responded. "According to the computer our distance from the contact isn't increasing, so it's either a sensor ghost or a ship that's matching our course within one degree. That's the best we can get at this distance."

"What's the calculated distance to the contact?"

"The computer says one billion, ten million kilometers."

"Just outside the range we'd normally be scanning. And since the distance is so great and the course nonreciprocal, the DeTect system wouldn't warn of a possible danger from collision. Hmmm, have the computer keep an eye on it and plot its course."

"Aye, Captain."

Jenetta turned and walked into her briefing room as disquieting thoughts about the dot of light on the screen tugged at her mind. After pacing around the room for the better part of ten minutes, she called the officer's mess. Anthony's image appeared on her screen.

"How may I help you, Captain?"

"Are any officers there?"

"Yes, Captain. Lieutenant Sabella, Charley, and the doctor are all here."

"Please convey to Lieutenant Sabella and Charley that I'd like them to come to my briefing room as soon as they finish breakfast. And please bring a thermal carafe of coffee when you have a chance."

"Aye, Captain."

* * *

Jenetta was studying an overview of the ship on the large wall monitor when Gloria and Charley arrived at the briefing room. Charley was carrying the insulated decanter of fresh coffee that she'd requested of Anthony.

"You sent for us, Captain?" Gloria asked.

"Yes, I believe we're being followed. We've spotted what appears to be a ship matching our speed and course. It's one billion, ten million kilometers behind us, which happens to be just ten million km beyond the scan range that Captain Lentz had ordered. If someone knew of his appointment as Captain aboard this ship and was familiar with his habits, it makes sense that they would pick that distance to tail us. Of course, it *could* be a sensor ghost reflection, but I doubt it. I suspect it might be the ship that launched the fighters. They were too far out to have been there on their own."

"Do you think they intend to attack us?" Gloria asked, apprehension creeping into her voice. Her face paled appreciably as she spoke.

"No, they've had plenty of opportunity if that was their intention," Jenetta said calmly, aware of the effect her words would have on Gloria. "I think they're either waiting for reinforcements or, more likely, just reporting our position so a trap can be set up ahead of us. It's probable they've been following you since you left Kesserith. It's the only way they could have known precisely what your course would be and so been in position to spring a trap that would shut down the FTL drive. Since they can't attack while we're traveling faster than light, they'll most likely try to fool our ACS into shutting down our Light Speed Drive again. Charlie, is it possible to disengage the ACS on this ship?"

"No, ma'am. We can ignore the ACS feed and go full power with the Sub-Light engines, but we can never override the ACS to engage the FTL drive. The GAC penalties for doing that are so stiff that most freight companies have made it impossible to tamper with the envelope generator controller. We can engage or disengage the AutoTect but never the ACS."

Jenetta sighed. "Too bad. They might not be able to stop us if we could ignore whatever it is they used before."

"Then we should change course, Captain," Charley said.

"They'd only move the trap. No, we have to find a way to get them permanently off our six before we set a new course."

"Our six, ma'am?" Gloria said.

"Sorry, it's an old military term dating back to when chronographs had hands to indicate the time instead of displaying digital readouts. It means our six o'clock position or, more simply, 'our tail.' I'm sure we won't be able to outrun them, so we have to incapacitate them— or destroy them."

"*Incapacitate them?!*" Gloria exclaimed incredulously. "*Destroy them?!*" Taking a deep breath and calming her voice a little, she continued with, "How can we possibly do that? This isn't a warship. We only have tugs, not fighters, and our weapons are strictly defensive. If the Raiders don't move in, we can't even fire on them."

"There are two possibilities I can think of," Jenetta said tranquilly, apparently unperturbed by Gloria's emotional outburst. "We could rig a space mine that would detonate with a proximity trigger or we could attack them directly with the ship. Charley, do we have the components needed to put together some space mines?"

"Not really. We *might* be able to rig something with a couple of torpedoes, but it'd be tricky and we might blow ourselves up just trying to prepare it. We lost our best chance for building such a bomb when the Raiders first attacked us and the last two link-sections broke away."

"What do you mean?"

"The stern-most link-section, the one right next to the gun section, was loaded with Dithulene-35. It's the catalyst for Corplastizine, the plasticized explosive used by miners. We had enough of the two compounds to destroy a small moon. A minute explosive charge, mounted on a vial of Dithulene-35 and then strapped to a brick of Corplastizine, is all you need to make a serious bomb."

"Too bad we don't have any Corplastizine now. We could use it."

"But we do. We have about eight hundred metric tons in the link-section nearest the main ship."

"You mean," Jenetta said, shocked by what she had just learned, "we were sitting on an eight-hundred-metric-ton bomb when the Raiders attacked?"

"Not at all, Captain," Charley said evenly. "The Corplastizine was sited in the front cargo link-section, while the catalyst was intentionally located in the very last. Being separated by more than six kilometers of other cargo made it all but impossible for them to come into contact with each other. And if we did experience a problem, we could just jettison the link containing the catalyst."

"That would be perfect then. What else can we use to detonate it?"

"Not much. That's what makes Corplastizine so safe to transport, store, handle, and use. Its stability has been embraced by most mining operations so it's come into widespread use during the past decade. Unlike other forms of plastic-bonded explosives such as C-4 and Semtex developed back in the twentieth century, it doesn't require a blasting cap to initiate detonation, nor can fire or explosion detonate it. Only by vaporizing the proper catalyst against the Corplastizine can a cascading detonation effect be produced. If we had the Dithulene-35, we'd have instant destruction on a scale you have to see to believe. One kilo of Corplastizine can produce the equivalent explosive effect of a kiloton of TNT."

"That means we have the equivalent of an eight-hundred-megaton bomb aboard. That's certainly enough to do the job. Can you reproduce some Dithulene-35?"

"No, it's an extremely complex compound and can only be fabricated in a proper lab. I can synthesize a substitute catalyst, but it won't initiate the cascading effect. It will only ignite the surface material. Unless the Raider ship happens to come into direct contact with it just as it explodes, it won't do anything more than get their attention for a few seconds. In fact, in the vacuum of space, any high-explosive yield will only give you a bright flash unless you can get the explosion to occur while the bomb is in almost direct contact with their hull."

"Yes, and that's unlikely to occur without either a proximity trigger or contact trigger. I guess the only option is to attack them with the ship and use our torpedoes."

"Captain," Gloria said, "the *Vordoth* can't possibly maneuver well enough to attack another ship effectively. Besides, they'd see us coming and avoid us. If they are, in fact, a Raider warship, their acceleration and speed has to be substantially greater than ours and they can easily remain out of range."

"Maybe— and then again— maybe not. Charley, have you prepared the three sections as we discussed? I'd like to drop one off and see how the Raiders react."

"They're ready whenever you are, Captain."

"Okay," Jenetta said thoughtfully. "We'll detach the rearmost section first, then release two more, one at a time on my command. Also, ready the foremost connection so we can detach the entire cargo section as one unit. I want three tugs standing by ready to launch as soon as we drop our envelope. They're to lock onto the main cargo section and engage their engines to full power, maximum speed Sub-Light-50, following the ship's original course. Are the four torpedo tubes loaded, Gloria?"

"Loaded and ready to fire, Captain," Gloria said. "We just have to disengage the safeties."

"Okay," Jenetta said, clapping her hands once, "let's get rigged for action. Clear the cargo section of all nonessential personnel and seal the ship."

Chapter Nine

~ July 13th, 2267 ~

While Gloria and Charley hurried out to perform their assigned tasks, Jenetta climbed into the command chair on the bridge to contemplate the upcoming action. Gloria rejoined her after unlocking the torpedo autoload system, removing the trigger safeties and visually checking their state of readiness. Almost another twenty minutes elapsed before Charley returned to the bridge. He announced that the tugs were manned and ready to launch, the cargo section was clear of all other personnel, and all airtight doors had been closed.

"I have an announcement for the crew," Jenetta said, and accepted the small wireless mike Charley passed to her from the com operator.

"You're on, Captain," the com operator said.

Jenetta took a deep breath and released it slowly before saying, "Attention crew of the *Vordoth*. This is the captain. By now most of you know something is up. It is my belief that we're being followed by a Raider warship. I suspect it was the source of the fighters that attacked us and is currently relaying our position and course so their forces ahead of us can prepare another trap. We cannot elude the ship behind us, so we must disable it. We've cleared the cargo section and closed all airtight doors. I intend to separate from our cargo and use the main ship to engage the Raiders while several tugs continue on with our freight. Gunners should be at their posts. All others should find a secure location, settle in, and hang on. Captain out."

From his post at the security station, Gunny Rondell watched Jenetta solemnly. She had given him his instructions for the attack while they were waiting for Charley to clear the cargo section. Her proposed maneuver had to be the most audacious battle tactic he'd ever heard. Old freighters have no business attacking modern warships. But— it might not be too late to stop it. He could refuse to comply and then attempt to take command of the ship. If they abandoned the cargo, perhaps the Raiders would let them escape. He glanced around the bridge trying to decide how many, and which, crewmembers would side with him in a mutiny. The First Officer and the Chief Engineer seemed committed, or at least resigned, to the plan. That made a successful takeover more doubtful. If one of them showed the slightest lack of support for Carver, he might pull it off. Damn, there wasn't enough time to speak to the other bridge personnel surreptitiously and determine whose support he could count on. If he'd thought she'd pull anything as crazy as this, he would have begun plotting a takeover the first day. He wondered if he should risk it anyway. The merchant services didn't impose the death penalty for mutiny but, unless the action could be defended and adjudged appropriate, incarceration was sure. Still, incarceration was better than death. But if he didn't get some support from other bridge team members, a takeover would fail immediately. He decided to play along for now but would be ready if an opportunity presented itself.

Without rising from her chair, Jenetta looked in Rondell's direction and nodded. He needed no further instruction and released the first cargo section. All eyes turned towards the huge viewscreen at the front of the bridge as it presented a CG image from sensor data. At first, the bond between the ship and cargo section seemed unbroken, but then the unseen temporal field that enveloped the ship at FTL speeds reformed without it. As normal space and time reasserted its control over the single cargo link, it fell away behind the freighter so quickly that it just seemed to disappear.

When the distance from the cargo container passed just beyond a billion km, Gunny Rondell said, "The contact has slowed, Captain."

"He's curious," Jenetta said quietly to Gloria. "He wants to know why we lost it."

The distance between pursuer and pursued widened beyond the DeTect range of their equipment and the image that had seemed like a sensor ghost disappeared from the screens temporarily. When it suddenly reappeared, Gunny Rondell said, "He's back, Captain. The contact is moving considerably faster than we are now. The computer estimates their speed at Light-211."

"They must be trying to close the gap," Gloria remarked. "It'll take them almost four minutes at that speed."

Once the contact reached a point one billion, ten million kilometers behind the *Vordoth*, it slowed to Light-150 to maintain that distance.

"Well, there's no longer any doubt that he's tailing us and also no doubt that we can't outrun him," Jenetta said before lapsing into silence to ponder the situation further while Charley and Gloria hovered near the security station and kept a close eye on the sensor data.

Jenetta waited another twenty minutes before telling Gunny to release the next container. This time the tailing ship didn't slow its forward motion as it bypassed the container.

"Okay, it looks like he's accepted that we're breaking up," Jenetta said. "I imagine they're attributing it to damage from the earlier attack. Let's take it to the next level."

"What *is* the next level?" Gloria asked. "So far all we've done is turn over cargo containers full of valuable ore. They may believe that we're breaking up, but they haven't moved in for the kill."

"I never assumed they would. We're going to have to take the battle to them. That should be something they'll *never* expect if they're a Raider warship. I doubt any warship captain would anticipate an offensive attack from an old freighter in transit. Helm, drop our envelope. Gunny, release the third rearmost section and then detach the main section from the ship."

Acknowledgments flowed back to Jenetta from both the helmsman and Gunny.

"Charley, send out the tugs. Helm, using maneuvering thrusters only, drop us down under the cargo body, then turn us 180 degrees and move us back to a position just behind the cargo section we detached. I want that single cargo section to stay between us and the ship that's following us until they close to within a million kilometers. Don't use the sub-light engines unless I tell you to. We don't want to light up their sensor grids."

"Aye, Captain."

"We're not going to fool them, Captain," Gloria said. "The returned blip on their scanners will be much larger than the one returned from the containers they passed before."

"I'm hoping they'll just think a larger section has broken off. There will still be a six-kilometer-long section moving away from us on our former flight path and that has to be returning a *major* blip on their screens."

"But they'll see that the main cargo section has slowed."

"The logical action for us to take if we really were losing link-sections would be to drop our envelope and investigate. They'll think we're doing that. I just hope they're so bored with following us that they won't question why we've engaged our sub-light engines instead of merely stopping to resolve the problem. Perhaps they'll believe we want to continue putting as much distance as possible between ourselves and wherever those fighters came from. Anyway, if they don't question it, they'll drop their envelope to maintain their distance from the main cargo section."

The underbelly of the cargo section could be seen on the large monitor at the front of the bridge as the tugs locked onto it and began to accelerate away. One tug hauled from the front while the other two locked onto the top of the steel link framework with the electromagnets in their landing skids. Once they attained fifty thousand kps, they would hold that speed until they received additional orders. The helmsman brought the freighter to a stop just short of the container left behind and then raised up behind it. Only a close up view of the back side of that single cargo link-section, with its four cargo containers locked solidly in place, showed on the front monitor. With the ship in position, the bridge grew deathly quiet. It was almost as if everyone was afraid to make the slightest noise out of fear that the trailing ship would hear him or her and detect the ambush.

* * *

"Helm, all stop!" the tactical officer screamed when an alarm sounded on his console aboard the Raider destroyer *Satan's Own.*

Captain Garth Goshan twisted his bulk to look at his tactical officer and ask calmly, "What is it now?"

"It's the freighter, sir. She's dropped her envelope and engaged her sub-light engines."

"Match her speed."

"Aye, Captain," the helmsman said as he keyed in the changes.

Captain Goshan stared at the enhanced image on the front viewscreen. The ship seemed to have lost another cargo section. She must have slowed to check out the problem. "A reasonable action," he mumbled to himself, "but why has she engaged her sub-lights? No matter. We can return and retrieve all the separated containers once we take the freighter at the new ambush point."

* * *

The crew spent the anxious minutes staring either at the large front viewscreen or at their new captain. Jenetta's heart was racing like never before, but she forced herself to look perfectly calm as she relaxed in the command chair and sipped from a mug of coffee while glancing up occasionally to the large screen at the front of the bridge. She knew the appearance of imperturbability would help keep the crew calm and focused.

As Gunny Rondell gazed at Jenetta, he wondered if her equanimity was real or show. She seemed as cool as any commander he'd ever served under and he wondered if she realized just how dangerous the situation was. He'd missed his opportunity to stop this earlier and now had to follow through as though he believed they really had a chance of surviving. The others on the bridge showed sensible signs of fear but managed to remain calm as they concentrated on their tasks.

After numerous anxious minutes, the crewmember at the science station said nervously, "Captain, the Raider ship is nearing a point one million kilometers aft of us. It's slowed to match the speed of the main cargo section, but it's closing fast on our position here."

"He's so sure we're not a threat, he's ignoring the inconsistency," Jenetta said to Gloria with a grim smile.

"Sensors indicate it's about the size of a GSC destroyer," the science station crewmember said.

"Very good," Jenetta said calmly. "Gunny?"

"Confirmed, Captain. I have them on the plot."

"Helm, using thrusters only, gently nudge us lower than the link-section, just enough so Gunny has a clear shot with the torpedo tubes. Gunny, as soon as you get a lock on that ship, fire torpedoes one and three. They'll have torpedoes also and a lot more tubes than we have, so we need to get them before they can figure out where we are and get a lock on us."

Both men said, "Aye, Captain."

As the *Vordoth* sank slowly behind the cargo section, Jenetta watched the front viewscreen intently. Gunny Rondell amplified the view to maximum sensor magnification and a CG image of the approaching ship leapt onto the viewscreen. The image lacked sharp definition at this distance, but it was definitely a destroyer and it bristled with armament. Announcing from the security console that he had a lock on the target, Gunny Rondell lightly depressed two illuminated contact switches. The heat trails from the torpedoes were clearly visible on the forward viewscreen's enhanced image as the deadly missiles left the *Vordoth* and accelerated rapidly towards the approaching ship.

"One and three away!" Gunny announced.

* * *

The sudden shriek of the imminent threat warning alarm on the bridge of *Satan's Own* caused Captain Goshan to sit up straight in his chair and look anxiously towards his tactical officer.

"What is it?!" he asked, slurring the words in his eagerness to get them out.

"Torpedoes, Captain. Someone's locked onto us and fired. There are two of 'em."

"From where?"

"They're approaching from dead ahead."

"Eject counter measures. Helm, hard to port. Full power."

"Aye, Captain," the young helmsman managed to squeak out as he twisted the joystick and punched in the speed variable. His eyes were wide with fear and he had trouble swallowing over the enormous lump that had suddenly materialized in his throat.

* * *

The Raider ship didn't seem to spot the two torpedoes until they had traveled over three-quarters of a million kilometers and were closing rapidly on its position. But then it altered course violently to larboard and expelled counter measures designed to confuse the targeting systems of the torpedoes. Jenetta's eyes widened and she re-swallowed her heart as both torpedoes lost their lock on the escaping ship and began flying in circles around the zigzagging counter measures. The torpedoes were still trying to kill the counter measures as the Raider ship disappeared from view. The bridge crew of the *Vordoth* watched in horror as the counter measures went cold and the torpedoes lost track of even *them*.

"Damn Falcon Mark III's," Jenetta muttered.

"What do we do now, Captain?" Gloria asked.

"That depends on our friend out there. We've had our only free shot. It'll be tough to sucker him again. Gunny, any sign of that destroyer?" Jenetta asked.

"He's still headed directly away from his previous track," Gunny said, watching the plot screen on the security console. "No wait, he's turning around, Captain. He's reversing course and accelerating rapidly back."

"I guess we're not through here yet. Prepare to fire torpedoes two and four, Gunny."

"Aye, Captain, I'm ready."

* * *

"Tactical," Captain Goshan said calmly, "Do you have a location on those torpedoes?"

"They're off the plot, sir. I didn't record any explosions so they must have exhausted their fuel and gone ballistic after being distracted by our counter measures."

"Where the devil did they come from?"

"It's almost a certainty that they came from the freighter we're following, sir. Our intelligence data does state they have four bow tubes."

"Bow tubes? How could they fire torpedoes at us from bow tubes? Unless..."

"Sir?"

"Give me maximum sensor magnification on that cargo link-section that's fallen away. Put it up on the front view-screen."

"Ready, sir."

Captain Goshan stared at the image. "There," he announced as he pointed to the image. "Look at the lower edge of the link-section. Does that look like a ship to you?"

"It isn't part of a cargo link section, that's for sure."

As *Satan's Own* continued on a course perpendicular to its original track, Goshan grinned evilly and mumbled to himself, "So, our young captain is more clever than the commandant believed. She distracted us by sending her cargo section on ahead and preparing an ambush. But she's not commanding a warship, just an old freighter." Raising his voice he said, "Tactical, target that ship and fire tubes seven and eight."

"Aye, Captain."

Goshan leaned his bulk back into his bridge chair as the torpedoes left his ship. He was supremely confident in his ability to destroy the freighter and he had a grudge to settle. Despite assurances from the commandant that the freighter's crew was incapable of putting up a fight, they'd somehow destroyed the six fighters he'd sent out. Six fighters? He would have sent six squadrons, but on their last mission Leggmann had done serious damage to the ship he was sent to seize, so this time they had been under strict orders that specifically limited the size of the force Goshan could send out. But now that the freighter had separated from the cargo section, she was fair game. He could use whatever force he wished. And since that ship out there was only a freighter, two torpedoes with high-explosive warheads should split it open like an overripe melon.

* * *

"Captain," Gunny said calmly, "the Raider has fired torpedoes. They're presently bearing down on us at— 36,178 kps and still accelerating. Estimated time to impact is— one-niner seconds."

"Gunny, fire two and four," Jenetta said quickly, trying to remain calm but unable to remain totally unperturbed in the face of this new development.

Anticipating her order, Gunny had been targeting the destroyer. He immediately depressed the two switches that would send the missiles on their deadly errand. "Aye, Captain. Two and four away!"

"Helm, get us back up behind our cover. Quick."

The *Vordoth's* ascent seemed agonizingly slow as tiny thrusters struggled to raise the mass of the ship into position. All that could be seen on the viewscreen was the rear of the cargo link-section until Gunny locked in the targeting sensors. Suddenly, it was as if the cargo section wasn't there at all. As Gunny counted down the seconds, everyone on the bridge watched in stunned silence as the torpedoes raced menacingly towards them. The crewmember at the science station began whimpering until she realized those around her were hearing the noise. She clamped both hands over her mouth and nose. Two seconds before impact Gunny changed the view back to regular sensor data.

The four ten-meter-deep by twenty-meter-high containers filled to the brim with unprocessed ore took the full force of the two Raider torpedoes. Jenetta watched in silence as the mass of thirty-two thousand cubic meters of rock completely absorbed the energy of the torpedoes. Since the torpedoes didn't penetrate the cargo containers, the explosive force discharged almost harmlessly against their surface in the vacuum of space. The link-section held together, but the force from the accelerated mass of the torpedoes bent the hundred-sixty-meter-wide link-section inward and drove it towards the ship hiding behind it.

"Helm," Jenetta said, "full reverse."

The *Vordoth* responded to the order from the helm and immediately began to back away. The sub-light engines strained mightily to push it back from the approaching cargo link-section. Within seconds, it had matched the velocity of the link-section, ensuring that the damaged cargo unit couldn't catch and damage the ship.

"Helm, disengage sub-light," Jen said. "Keep us hidden behind the cargo link-section using thrusters."

Gunny locked in the targeting sensors again and the bridge crew was able to watch as the latest counter measures from *Satan's Own* died and the *Vordoth's* second pair of torpedoes shut down as well.

"Where's that destroyer, Gunny?" Jenetta asked anxiously.

"It crossed our original track and continued on, but it's turning again, Captain. He's headed back."

*   *   *

"Did we get them, tactical?" Captain Goshan asked.

"I don't know sir. The explosions blinded my sensors for a couple of seconds. Immediately after detonation, I got a reading as if they fired up their sub-light engines."

"Which way did they go?"

"They didn't go anywhere. The sub-light engines cut out after just a few seconds. Here's the image of the link-section at maximum magnification, sir."

Goshan studied the two-dimensional CG image carefully. He saw no sign of the ship and the link-section appeared intact. "We got the little bitch," he announced with a confident smile. "We must have blown them to pieces. At sub-light, they couldn't have cleared the area in a few seconds, certainly not far enough to avoid power signature detection. The explosion must have shorted out their control systems and ignited the sub-light engines briefly." His rubbed his chin for a second and then added, "But— helm, let's maintain this position until we're absolutely sure."

"Aye, Captain," the helmsman said, as he brought the ship to a halt. The lump in his throat had begun to shrink appreciably.

Chapter Ten

~ July 13th, 2267 ~

"Gunny, are tubes one and three loaded yet?"

"Not yet, Captain. They'll be available in— forty-two seconds."

"Unfortunately, we may not have forty-two seconds," she said calmly. "If that Raider sees we're still intact, he'll try to finish the job. What's his position?"

"He's holding at— eight hundred eighty-two thousand kilometers from us, almost the precise position when he first altered course to avoid our torpedoes. His helmsman must be some kind of perfectionist."

"How long until we can fire again?"

"Tubes one and three should be ready in— thirty-one sec... Damn!" Gunny stopped talking, peered more intently at the console and then stabbed a finger at the console interface pad.

"What is it, Gunny?" Jenetta asked, with just a touch of anxiety in her voice.

"Look, Captain," Gunny said, pointing to the image that he had just put up on the front viewscreen. It was a greatly magnified view of the Raider destroyer as provided by the targeting sensors. Counter measures were erupting from the warship like seeds from a fluffy dandelion seed ball caught in a powerful Terran gust of wind. At the same instant, laser weapon gunners began to fill space with pulses of coherent light as they opened up on seemingly invisible targets. A second later, an explosion white'd out the *Vordoth's* viewscreen. Another explosion immediately followed the first.

The two explosions opened great holes amidship in the destroyer, wiping out bulkhead walls and exposing large sections of the ship to open space.

As the bridge crew of the *Vordoth* looked on in surprise, two additional explosions rocked the heavily damaged Raider ship on the opposite side, finishing the job so effectively begun by the first blasts. The destroyer, already severely weakened, broke apart, leaving two large halves and clouds of detritus tumbling and spreading through the coldness of the cosmos.

"What happened?" Jenetta asked, her jaw hanging slightly open.

"*Captain* Jenetta Carver happened," Gunny said, grinning. "Those explosions were from the four torpedoes you ordered fired."

"But they were dead."

"Apparently they weren't quite as dead as we thought, ma'am. They suddenly came back online and reacquired their original target. My sensors picked them up as they reignited and accelerated towards the freighter."

"But how?"

"I don't know ma'am— but I'm not complaining."

The danger past, Jenetta smiled lightheartedly at him, leaned back in her chair, and stared at the image. "I'm not either, Gunny," she said after breathing a silent sigh of relief.

A delayed cheer went up on the *Vordoth's* bridge as the crewmembers realized the threat was gone. Everyone was suddenly smiling, laughing, crying, clapping, slapping one another on the back, or shaking hands. Jenetta just sat in the command chair and breathed another silent sigh of relief, letting the tension drain from her body and the exhilaration wash over her while doing her best to maintain a staid exterior.

Gloria, white-faced and visibly shaken, leaned over to say, excitedly, "Congratulations, Captain. It was brilliant how you used the ore containers to protect the ship! With a full load of ore, they were better than the toughest and thickest battleship armor ever made."

Drawing in a deep breath, Jenetta expelled it slowly. Smiling, she said quietly, "I thought I would have a heart attack when the first two torpedoes lost their target. Space Command torpedoes aren't confused by counter measures once they've locked onto a ship's mass and shape. And usually a guidance specialist is in constant contact, directing them to the weakest location of the hull. I certainly wasn't expecting yours to behave quite so— unpredictably as they did. And I still don't understand how they came to life again."

"What I don't understand is why the ship returned to fight after you fired the first two torpedoes. If all they wanted to do was watch us, they could have easily stayed out of range."

"I suppose they were so stunned to see a freighter take the offensive that they weren't thinking clearly. And can you imagine the embarrassment if word leaked out, and it would have, that they ran from a shootout with an old freighter. Their captain would probably get the sack, or worse. I suppose he also looked upon it as an easy opportunity to grab our cargo now rather than later."

"You should make an announcement to the crew about our incredible victory, Captain."

Standing up, Jenetta straightened her tunic. "You're right. But first let's see if this link-section is salvageable and then we'll have to catch the rest of our cargo. Charley?"

"Aye, Captain, I'm on it," Charley said from the security station where he and Gunny were using the imaging equipment to view the link-section. "The link is too badly damaged to couple with the cargo section, but I'll send a bot out to see if any of the containers can be salvaged. Congratulations on a successful attack, Captain."

"Thank you." To Gunny Rondell, Jenetta said, "Excellent shooting, Gunny. If we'd had anything to shoot but those screwy old Mark III torpedoes, you'd have taken him out with your first shots."

"Thank you, Captain," he said, beaming proudly. A new admiration began to fill his eyes as he looked at his commanding officer while a profound sense of relief that he hadn't attempted to take over the ship flooded his abdomen.

A robot tug was dispatched to perform a close examination of the damaged cargo containers as Jenetta walked to the communications console. "Please put me on ship-wide speakers," she said to the com operator.

"Ready, Captain."

"This is the captain speaking. We have just successfully destroyed the Raider warship that was tailing us. We'll now recover our cargo section and resume our trip along a different route to Higgins. Thank you for your fine work today."

The bridge erupted briefly in applause again. Jenetta smiled and nodded at everyone before turning to Gunny and Charley at the security station. They were busy examining the images being relayed from the service bot. "What's the story with the four containers?"

"Those two Raider torpedoes did a real number on them," Charley said. "They're far too badly damaged to be transferred to another link-section. We'll have to leave them as they are and use a space tug to tow the link-section along until we reach port. It can follow along behind the ship and we can change the personnel once each day."

"No, we can't do that, unfortunately. The tug would cut our speed in half. Other Raider vessels may already be on their way here. We have to be out of DeTect range before they arrive. I'm sorry, but we'll have to leave it. Bring the service bot back in and let's go get the main cargo section."

"What about the other two sections that we released first?"

"We don't have time to recover them either, or to look for survivors in the Raider ship. We know where the link-sections are and they have tracking transponders in them. If the company wants them, they can have them picked up on the next run through this area."

"Aye, Captain."

*   *   *

Charley's gaze lingered for just an instant upon the large wall monitor in the captain's briefing room as he entered a short time later. Gloria was there already, studying the projected illustration with keen interest.

"The cargo section has been reattached and the three tugs are safely back aboard, Captain," he said.

"Thank you, Charley," Jenetta said. Gesturing towards the monitor, she asked, "How long would it take to reconfigure the cargo section like this?"

Studying the diagram intently before answering, he said, "With maximum effort I'd say that we could do it in about an hour. Are you sure that you want to consolidate all the gun sections together like this behind the main ship?"

"Yes. In the event of another attack, we'll drop the cargo section and fight with just the main ship. Right now, the guns are too far apart to give us really concentrated fire and we completely lose their firepower if we separate from the cargo section to improve our maneuvering capability. With the guns remaining attached to the main ship after the cargo section is released, we'll come close to the maneuverability and armament of a Galactic Space Command light destroyer, although our lasers are comparatively lightweight and we still lack its armor and greater FTL speed."

"Okay, you're the captain. I'll get right on it."

"Thanks, Charley."

Every tug in the *Vordoth* was pressed into service to separate the cargo section into dozens of pieces. Then, like a giant jigsaw puzzle, it was reassembled. As promised, Charley had the new configuration ready in an hour. For the first time since the initial attack, Jenetta felt good about their chances of getting through. The crew had been under fire and had performed well. The ship was fairly well armed for an old freighter and the gunners now knew their job. The weapons system had been reprogrammed and all laser arrays that locked onto a target would now fire instead of just the one closest to the object, filling the immediate area around any target point with pulses of coherent light energy. Most importantly, Jenetta was settling into her new role and gaining confidence with each passing day.

In a little over a month's time, Jenetta would be back with Space Command and, perhaps in six or seven months, she might be able to get home to see her family. For now, she had the framed picture in her quarters to keep the memories fresh.

*   *   *

Things calmed down over the next several days, but the bridge crew never relaxed their vigilance. Everyone was on maximum alert as crewmembers took turns scanning the surrounding space for signs of Raider activity. Jenetta began to notice a real change in the attitudes and behavior of the crew, who were acting more as if they were on a military ship with each new day. On the fifth day following the destruction of the large Raider ship, Jenetta was brought up short by a loud announcement of, "Captain on the bridge," when she arrived in the morning to relieve Gloria. All crewmembers not at stations came to immediate attention and held their position until Jenetta thought to say, "As you were."

Jenetta turned to Gloria with narrowed eyes and said, "Could I see you in my briefing room before you leave for breakfast?"

"Of course, Captain," Gloria said, as she moved to follow Jenetta.

As the briefing room door slid closed behind Gloria with just the slightest whisper, Jenetta turned. Gloria stopped and braced to attention.

"Okay, what's going on?" Jenetta asked.

"What do you mean, ma'am."

"Knock it off, Gloria. You know damn well what I mean. What's with the formal military recognition of a commanding officer's arrival?"

The corners of Gloria's mouth turned up almost imperceptibly. "The crew is just showing their respect for you as captain of this ship. Gunny Rondell has been schooling those of us who were never in the military and refreshing the rules of military conduct for those who have been out for a long time."

Jenetta's nostrils flared for a second. "That's not right. I don't want him forcing people to feign military conduct."

"Force? Captain, you don't *force* freighter crews to modify their behavior about *anything*. They do it only if they want to, and they *do* want to. They requested that he teach them. They know you saved this ship and everyone on it, twice now, and someone suggested it might please you if, until we reach Higgins, we simulated the kind of atmosphere you're most familiar with and which you've been away from for so long. By the time we reach port they'll probably be able to pass inspection in a review parade."

"They *requested* that he teach them formal military conduct? Really?"

"Yes, ma'am. And if there was anyone aboard who might have been reluctant to follow your orders when you first accepted command, I can guarantee you that isn't the case anymore. There isn't a crewmember aboard who would hesitate to follow any order you give now. And I'm talking about orders well above and beyond those that most freighter captains could ever hope to have obeyed."

Jenetta was stunned into silence by the revelation. The irritation she'd been feeling evaporated and was instantly replaced by astonishment. "That's extraordinary," she finally said. "And I'm truly honored. But this isn't a Space Command vessel and I'm just an *acting* captain. I have no right to ask for the kind of unquestioning obedience expected by the commanding officer aboard a military ship."

"You don't have to ask for it, Captain; you already have it. Ever since our last Raider encounter, this crew will do *anything* you ask of it. Over the past decade, we've all lost friends and, in some cases, loved ones to Raider attacks. This is the very first time that a freighter has not only *escaped* almost unscathed from a Raider attack but actually *bested the attacker*. Everyone is simply busting with pride that they were a part of it. And you did say 'until we're out of danger, we'll operate as if this is a military ship' when you accepted command."

Jenetta frowned, remembering her perhaps ill-chosen words. "Yes, I did, didn't I? But I never meant that to extend to formal military conduct." Scowling, she said, "Gloria, you don't have to stand at attention and, when we're alone, call me Jen." When Gloria didn't change her position, Jenetta sighed and added, "At ease, Lieutenant."

Gloria relaxed. "No ma'am, I can't call you anything except Captain. I might slip when we're not alone and I only want to set a good example for the rest of the crew. They're trying really hard to adapt."

Jenetta sighed. "Very well. Ask Anthony to send me a pot of coffee when you go to breakfast, please."

"Yes, Captain."

Jenetta walked around her desk and sat down. Looking up, she was surprised to see Gloria still standing there. "Was there something else you wanted to discuss?"

"No ma'am. Gunny Rondell told me that in the military you never leave the commanding officer's presence until you're clearly dismissed."

Jenetta groaned inwardly to herself. "You're dismissed, Lieutenant."

"Aye, Captain." Gloria came to attention, turned on her heel, and left the briefing room.

Jenetta knew from her military training that nothing inspired such intense loyalty in a crew like success in a military campaign and no one could deny the outstanding success of their attack on the Raider ship, even if luck did play a significant role. But she wasn't at all happy about the new military formality. Knowing Gloria wouldn't use her given name, even though they had become friends before she'd assumed command, made her feel the first traces of loneliness that always come with senior level positions. She knew she couldn't ask the ship's company to stop the formality because it was a special gift to her rather than a duty, and she couldn't possibly reject such an unprecedented gift from an entire crew.

Touching her log ring to the spindle of the desk's media drawer so she could make a daily entry to her personal log, she started by expressing her personal unhappiness with the new military protocol on the ship. She had just finished articulating her thoughts when Anthony arrived with the pot of coffee she'd requested. She said, "Log update," to record the new entries on her ring, touched it to the spindle again, and then said, "Come." Anthony entered when the door opened and set the tray down on her desk to pour a mug for her.

"Nice and fresh, Captain. I just made it."

"Thank you, Anthony." When he continued to stand there, she smiled and added, "You're dismissed."

Anthony returned her smile and said "Aye, Captain," before turning and leaving.

Well, at least he didn't come to attention, she thought.

Jenetta spent the rest of the morning reading the technical manuals related to the ship's construction and performance. A search of the database turned up an engineering manual on the installed Falcon Mark III system and she devoted a couple of hours to a cover-to-cover study of the weapon system materials. "Ah ha! Mystery solved!" she said aloud as she read an addendum of system upgrades. Although the basic weapon system still had most of the shortcomings which led to the military ceasing installation in new warships, the missiles themselves had been upgraded. They were still dumber than a housekeeping bot, but the single propulsion stage had been replaced with two smaller stages. The modification was intended to increase its effective range by sacrificing higher velocity. Instead of accelerating towards the target for one hundred eighty seconds and then going ballistic, at which point the torpedo lost all ability to maneuver, the two-stage design accelerated for only one hundred twenty seconds, then went ballistic. It would travel that way for up to twelve minutes unless it first lost the target and then reacquired it. Reacquisition of a lost target would cause the second stage to immediately ignite. Since its velocity after the first stage burned out could be something along the lines of 42,500 kps, sixty seconds of renewed acceleration and maneuverability when it neared its target was a significant improvement.

Based on her interpretation of the upgrade, the *Vordoth's* torpedoes must have exhausted the fuel in stage one while chasing the destroyer's counter measures. They had dumped all their acceleration in changing directions so, when the counter measures died, the torpedoes went ballistic in whatever direction they were headed but were moving only slowly. When proximity to their original quarry suddenly retriggered the targeting system, the second stage ignited and the rest was history. Jenetta smiled as she remembered the eruption of counter measures from the Raider ship a second before the first torpedo struck. That must have been one very surprised tactical officer when the alarms went off and he realized four torpedoes were just seconds away, converging from four different directions.

Still engaged in reading a little before noon, she had just picked up her mug to take a sip of coffee when the crewmember manning the communications station buzzed her com unit.

"Captain," the crewmember said when she lifted the cover of her com unit, "I'm picking up a distress call by a freighter under attack."

"Verify that it's being recorded and pipe it through to my console."

"Aye, Captain."

Almost immediately, an excited voice began to emanate from the speaker on her com unit. "...repeat, this is the freighter *Jouraklihest*. We're under attack by Raiders. We need help from any GSC ship in or near sector 8667-3855-1653.5682 post-median 0071. Please respond. Two of our escort ships have already been destroyed. We're on a mercy mission, carrying vital food and medicine for the colonists on Obotymot. They won't survive without these supplies. Please, we urgently need assistance!"

Jumping up from her desk, Jenetta hurried to the door still holding her coffee mug. Before the doors opened, she reminded herself that she must appear unruffled before the crew. Composing herself, she stopped and took a deep breath.

"Sound GQ," Jenetta ordered as she stepped calmly out onto the bridge. "It seems the Raiders are at it again." Turning to the astrogator, she asked, "How far are we from sub-sector 1653.5682 post-median 0071?"

Before the astrogator could respond, the alert lights throughout the ship began pulsing and the sound of wailing alarms emanated from the corridors.

"About forty billion kilometers, Captain."

"Do you know anything about this— Obotymot?"

"I know that it's an Earth-class planet. I heard it was hit by a meteor about two years ago and dirt in the upper atmosphere has partially blocked out their sun. Most of the existing vegetation has withered and disappeared, new crops fail, and most of the domestic animals and wildlife have died or been slaughtered for food. A massive first supply effort several months ago was intercepted by Raiders and never reached the colonists. I imagine things are pretty desperate there by now."

The corridor door slid open, temporarily flooding the bridge with mournful yowls as Gloria, still buttoning her tunic, rushed nervously onto the bridge. Jenetta's cool composure immediately reassured her that everything was under control.

"What is it, Captain? Raiders?" Gloria asked. "How close are they?"

The door opened again before Jenetta could answer and Charley, followed by Dr. Rebecca Erikson, hurried to where Jenetta was standing with Gloria.

"The Raiders are less than fifteen minutes away at our top speed of Light-150," Jenetta said, "but we don't seem to be the focus of their attention. Presumably, they're attacking a freighter named the *Jouraklihest* that's carrying food and medicine for desperate colonists on a planet called Obotymot."

"Presumably?" Gloria questioned.

"We have to face the possibility that this might be a trap. The Raiders know they've lost track of us and may be trying to get us back into their gun sights while we're still in the area."

"The situation on Obotymot is real, Captain," Charley said, "and I know the *Jouraklihest* is a real freighter. It's of Nordakian registry and Obotymot is a Nordakian colony. I can't know if the freighter is really in trouble, but we're not far from the shipping lanes they'd use for sending a convoy to the planet."

"Nordakian?" Jenetta echoed. She was unfamiliar with any race by that name.

"Yes, we only made official first contact with them about ten years ago. They've had space travel capability for centuries but not FTL. It seems their priests have done every-thing possible to keep the planet isolated, even to forbidding planetary communication transmissions that might be picked up by extra-world travelers. Anyway, some enterprising spaceship captain stumbled across their out-of-the-way planet some twenty-five years ago and, in exchange for a king's ransom of precious metals and gems, he gave them the secrets of DATFA technology. When they were discovered by an official GA survey vessel, they had already developed a small fleet of interstellar freighters and colonized Obotymot for agricultural development. Encounters with Raiders had forced them to begin developing warships for home system pro-tection. They're members of the Galactic Alliance now so Space Command has an obligation to defend them."

"But we're not Space Command, Charley. This is a private freighter engaged in commercial enterprise. I can't ask this crew to risk their lives fighting someone else's battle."

"This is *our* battle as well," Rebecca said. "They're fellow freight haulers, Captain, and they're in trouble. We can't leave them to the mercies of the Raiders, not when we can help. I'm sure the entire crew would want to do this and we don't have time for a vote."

"Yes, Captain," Gloria said, "we have to assist them. We can't just run away. Only by sticking together will we ever have a hope of defeating these pirates."

As they'd talked, the bridge had filled with personnel trying to ascertain the reason for the alert. Jenetta surveyed their faces and was stunned by the resolve she saw in their eyes. They obviously agreed with the bellicose attitude being exhibited by their officers. But fighting to defend yourself was one thing; voluntarily entering a battle zone to fight an offensive action for someone else was quite another.

Having accepted command, Jenetta was now legally, morally, and ethically responsible for the safety of the ship and the lives of the crew. She was torn between that obligation and her Space Command duty to help anyone in peril. More than anything else she feared seeing someone under her command permanently injured, or possibly even killed. She was again filled with thoughts of how this was not a decision a young ensign essentially fresh from the Academy should ever have to make. She wished desperately for the counsel of a senior officer with decades of experience, but there was none with whom she could consult and each second's delay might mean that additional Nordakian lives were being lost.

Chapter Eleven
~ July 16th, 2267 ~

Jenetta sighed silently at the looks of grim determination on the faces of her officers, then said almost abjectly, "Well— maybe we can confuse things a bit and buy some time for the Nordakians to get their ships back to FTL while we make our own getaway."

A number of heads began to nod in vigorous agreement.

"Okay, let's get rigged for action," Jenetta said loudly. "Turn off the alert horns and lights. Helm, take us to 1653.5682 post-median 0071 at maximum speed. Security, get us a directional fix on their position and feed it to astrogation…"

Gunny Rondell, now standing at the security console, interrupted with, "We've got a clear emergency squawk on the AutoTect grid, Captain. Should I feed that to the astrogator?"

"She's squawking her position?"

The crewmember who had been manning the security station when the distress call came in, said, "It just started a couple of minutes ago, Captain. About the same time that we received the distress call."

The freighter had nothing to lose once the Raiders attacked. Jenetta realized she'd want to have her position clearly established in case help was near.

"Okay, Gunny, send the data to astrogation. Astrogator, plot the most direct course and feed it to the helm. Charley, prepare us for separation from the cargo section. Get all personnel into the main ship and button us up. We'll separate from our cargo at four-point-five billion kilometers from the target to make our DeTect reflection as small as possible when we come into their range. Gloria, make sure all torpedo tubes are loaded and ready and that all safeties have been removed. Okay, let's do this."

Gloria and Charley acknowledged with an "Aye, Captain," and sprang into action. In accordance with Jenetta's standing orders since becoming captain, the cargo section evacuation should have begun as soon as the alert was sounded, but Charley ran from the bridge to ensure, personally, that everyone was out. Only three names should still appear on the monitor once the cargo section was emptied— Captain Lentz and crewmembers Deitrich and Higgiby, lost during the initial Raider attack and left posted for the present as a sort of memorial.

Meanwhile, Gloria hurried down to the torpedo rooms to visually check the systems and remove the safeties. The two bridge gunners sat down at their consoles to prepare their stations as Gunny Rondell officially relieved the crewmember at the security station. Jenetta calmly walked to the com station and made a ship-wide announcement that all gunners should prepare for action. They should have immediately gone to their stations when the alert sounded, so the announcement was as much for the rest of the crew as it was for them. With the preparations complete, Jenetta climbed into her command chair, then stared at the front viewscreen as if in a mild trance while she formulated her battle plan.

Within three minutes, Charley confirmed that the cargo section was clear of personnel and was ready to separate. Jenetta reiterated her order to Gunny to separate at four-point-five-billion kilometers from the estimated battle location. She then instructed the helmsman to reduce speed to Light-2 at twelve million kilometers in order to allow twenty seconds in which to size up the situation while they traveled the final distance.

Gloria, her face slightly flushed with physical exertion, returned from her task of readying the ship's weapons and crossed the bridge to stand by the left arm of Jenetta's command chair. "What's the plan, Captain?" she asked. Though an anxious look swathed her face, there was unmistakable resoluteness in her voice.

Jenetta breathed in deeply and then released it before answering in a voice lowered so that it only carried to her XO. "We're going to have to slash and burn," she replied.

"Slash and burn?" Gloria questioned, equally sotto voce.

"We don't yet know what we're facing, so we can't prepare anything tactically sophisticated. We certainly won't be able to arrange for a convenient artificial mountain as cover this time, and it's a given that whatever Raider ships we're about to face are considerably better armed than we are. So— surprise will perforce serve as our main weapon. I intend to slash our way in with as much speed as practical, dump our envelope, and then burn down any enemy ships we encounter before they can do the same to us."

"That's it?" Gloria asked, wide-eyed. "That's your whole plan? Shoot them before they shoot us?"

"That's a time-honored military objective," Jenetta said, with a hint of a smile. Then more soberly, she added, "As I said, we can't prepare anything tactically sophisticated. Our options are too limited. We're one ship against a force of unknown numbers and strengths. We can't contact the Nordakians and query them for information about the situation because our communications would have to be in the clear. It would alert the Raider ships and we'd lose whatever element of surprise we might presently have. And we need that desperately if we're to have any chance of pulling this off." Jenetta paused to suck in another breath and release it. "If we assume the Raider intelligence network is even half as absolute as Captain Lentz seemed to believe, then they'll know as well as we do that there are presently no Space Command vessels within a month of their ambush point. That factor *could* make them sloppy if the battle with the Nordakians is going in their favor."

"*Could?*"

Jenetta shrugged her shoulders. "I very much regret that conjecture and supposition is all I have to work with. And, of course, the possibility that this is a trap still remains. Or even that the enemy forces might be too overwhelming for us to engage."

"What do we do if they are?"

"Punt."

"Huh?"

Jenetta grinned slightly. "It's an old joke from my Academy days. When a football team is getting its butt kicked and has its back against the end zone, punting the ball downfield changes the situation tremendously. You lose possession of the ball, but your opponent has to change his focus, strategy, and player assignments. If we recognize that we've flown into a trap, or that the odds preclude our having a chance of surviving, we'll turn tail and get out of there at full power. A calculated risk is one thing, but I won't throw away everyone's life if I believe we don't have a chance of helping and still surviving."

The final minutes seem to drag on forever. Most of the bridge crew was again experiencing dry mouths and sweaty palms. They'd had time to think about what they were flying into and a couple were beginning to have second thoughts about their decision to support this action, but they were committed now. Jenetta just sat in her command chair looking calm and supremely confident.

Gunny's face was far more calm and composed than at any time since he'd first reported to her. She'd seen the doubt in his eyes prior to and during the last operation. She'd even thought he might resist following her orders and she was prepared to replace him at the security station if he did. But that look was gone now, replaced with the same look of firm resolve she'd seen in the faces of the others before she'd made her decision. And when he acknowledged her orders now, there was no hint of hesitation in his voice.

When Gunny announced separation from the cargo section at four-point-five-billion kilometers, everyone knew the stage was set. The eyes of all bridge personnel not otherwise engaged were on the large viewscreen at the front of the bridge as the armed freighter, sans cargo, moved towards the battle area at six hundred thousand kps.

They were still more than twenty million kilometers out when Gunny announced, "The convoy seems to be dead ahead, but there's a large stationary blip some two million kilometers closer, Captain, a thousand km off our larboard bow."

Jenetta knew that no freighter from the convoy would simply be hanging around to watch unless it had been disabled. And if it wasn't a freighter, it might be a Raider command ship. She decided to proceed on that assumption. Since their course would take them a thousand km from the contact, its DeTect equipment wouldn't have alerted the tac officer about a possible collision. And if everyone's attention was on the battle, they might still be unaware of the *Vordoth's* approach. That would change as soon as they changed course and the DeTect system sounded the alarm. "Helm, continue on this course. At one million kilometers from the new contact, dump the envelope and accelerate with maximum sub-light power. When we achieve Sub-Light-10, turn us directly towards them. Gunny, be prepared to fire torpedoes as soon as we close to within a hundred thousand km."

Gunny smiled. "How many, Captain?"

"At least two, but let's see exactly what we're going up against before we fire our first volley. Can you provide any better information on the target?"

"Not yet, Captain."

"Inform me as soon as you have some."

"Aye, Captain."

A second later Gunny said, "I have some new data on the target, Captain. It appears to be about the same tonnage as a GSC medium cruiser."

A medium cruiser? Jenetta thought nervously. *Good God, I hope this works!* In a calm and confident voice she said, "Better fire all four torpedoes, Gunny. Two by two."

"Aye, Captain."

Gunny Rondell focused every bit of his attention on the targeting screen in front of him. As the envelope dissolved, oversized sub-light engines powerful enough to haul and control billions of tons of cargo in sub-light were engaged. A slight lurch was felt as the engines kicked the *Vordoth* in the sides and the enormous horsepower rocketed the ship ahead in N-space. The gravitative inertial compensators kept everyone from being splattered against the rear bulkhead as the ship accelerated like it had been shot from a powerful cannon.

* * *

When the 'unidentified contact' warning buzzer sounded at the tactical station aboard the Raider medium cruiser *Mara's Marauder*, the tactical officer simply reached over and reset the device without ever fully taking his eyes off the main viewscreen at the front of the bridge. A CG representation of the fighter attack on the convoy was playing up on the large monitor and the chatter between fighters was playing through the bridge speakers.

"What is it, Tac?" Captain Lester Hodges asked, turning his head towards the tactical officer.

"Just one of our fighters returning, sir. Bandit Leader Four has informed me he's suffered serious damage and that his avionics are intermittent. Each time the system momentarily loses his ID, it will identify him as a bogey."

The captain grimaced and turned his attention back to the main viewscreen, along with everyone else on the bridge.

* * *

"One and three away," Gunny said, as he stabbed at the two buttons on his console. A second later he added, "Two and four away."

"Helm," Jenetta said, "veer off and head for the action, Sub-Light-10."

"First torpedoes released at roughly eight-niner-thousand kilometers," Gunny said. "Current time to target for the first pair, seven seconds."

"Gunny, are your people ready?"

"Ready and waiting, Captain."

Everyone on the *Vordoth's* bridge watched as the targeting sensors provided an image of the four heat trails converging on the Raider cruiser.

* * *

The tactical officer continued to watch the fighter action and ignore the 'unidentified contact' buzzer until the imminent threat alarm also sounded. He finally tore his eyes away from the action to study his plot screen. An icon representing the *Vordoth* was bearing down on the cruiser at ten thousand kps. His hand flew first to the GQ button and then to the console button that would produce a scan of the unexpected ship.

* * *

Surprise was almost complete. Everyone aboard the Raider ship who had access to a viewscreen was busy watching the attack on the convoy and cheering on the fighters. The senior officers knew there were no Space Command ships in the sector and therefore no chance in hell they would be attacked. The cruiser didn't even scan the freighter until the first torpedoes were mere seconds away from impact. Neither counter measures nor torpedoes emerged from the cruiser and only one laser weapon gunner on the cruiser even managed to fire at the approaching missiles. In his haste, he missed.

The first two torpedoes slammed into the starboard hull of the Raider cruiser at nearly the same instant. Separated by a mere one hundred meters, one torpedo impacted almost exactly amidship, with the other just slightly aft. The speed of the *Vordoth*, coupled with their own acceleration, had boosted their velocity to 12,026 kps by the time they reached the cruiser. Hardened casings surrounding warheads packed with high explosives allowed the torpedoes to smash through the steel-and-titanium-armored hull and bore deep into the ship's bowels in the fraction of a second before they denoted. They exploded with blinding light as everyone and everything in the vicinity of the warhead was instantly vaporized. The large viewscreen on the *Vordoth* momentarily white'd out until the sensors recovered and adjusted.

As the Raider ship bucked and twisted, balls of flame belched from two enormous holes that suddenly appeared amidship on the larboard side. Bulkheads bent and support trusses twisted and collapsed as the force of the blasts drove through the enormous warship. Crewmembers not strapped into seats were suddenly flung like rag dolls against whatever stationary equipment or bulkheads were nearby. Many died without an inkling of what had happened.

Then the second pair of torpedoes plowed through the hardened armor of the forward hull as if it was mere aluminum. Although they had been crafted in a different century and fired from an old freighter, the retrofitted dual-stage torpedoes were military grade ordnance all the way. Again, the immense warship bucked and rolled from the one-two punch of massive explosions that blew through to the other side of the ship. As oxygen and combustible material ignited, tentacles of fire raced snakelike through ship corridors. Crewmembers might have burned to death if the lack of oxygen hadn't instantly smothered the flames, along with their lives. The cruiser actually seemed to writhe like a wounded leviathan, but it still lived.

Jenetta knew she couldn't leave such a powerful warship at her back, even a seriously damaged one. She was about to order the *Vordoth* to swing around for another torpedo run when an immense secondary explosion ripped through the massive ship. The explosive damage from the *Vordoth's* torpedoes might have fortuitously reached an armory, or perhaps an antimatter container or nuclear fusion plant had been damaged during the carnage. But, whatever the cause, the great ship suddenly erupted into a gigantic ball of plasma that burned as hot as a sun for several seconds. The faces of the crew on the *Vordoth's* bridge were wide-eyed and stunned as they witnessed the death of the warship and all aboard. Jenetta forced her own features to remain completely impassive. She wanted the crew to see only the mask of calm professional resolve she believed a senior military person should wear during battle.

As broken and twisted pieces of the cruiser tumbled slowly away from the explosion area, Jenetta forced her attention from the spectacle on the small viewscreen mounted on the left arm of her chair to the front viewscreen where the fight ahead was looming ever larger as the *Vordoth* raced on.

Nearing the four-ship convoy, the *Vordoth* passed the wreckage of two warships with unusual configurations. Most Space Command ships, as well as the Raider ships Jenetta had seen, could almost be considered 'boxy' by comparison. Those two small ships appeared to have been designed with specific aerodynamic considerations in mind. The sleek design allowed for much less useful interior space.

"Nordakian stealth destroyers," Gloria said. "The Raiders must have surprised them, like we surprised the Raiders."

"Not completely," Jenetta said. "I see what looks like dozens of fighter hulls floating near the destroyers."

"Ah, yes," said Charley, who had returned to the bridge just in time to see the destruction of the mother ship. "The Nordakian destroyers got a little satisfaction of their own before their guns were silenced."

"How long has the Galactic Alliance permitted GA worlds to operate their own warships outside their home system?"

"About six years, Captain," Gloria replied. "Every system can maintain a home guard force of up to twenty warships. Until the situation with the Raiders is resolved, they can operate up to fifteen of those warships as convoy escorts or for diplomatic transport."

"Com, signal the *Jouraklihest*. Inform them that we've destroyed the cruiser mother ship and we're coming to help with the fighters. Tell them not to fire on us."

"Aye, Captain." After sending the message, the com operator said, "Message received and acknowledged. They witnessed the explosion of the cruiser and convey their appreciation."

"Helm, slow to Plus-10 as we reach the battle and take us directly under the center of the action. Then turn to starboard and take us in a wide circle around the perimeter. We don't want to give those fighters a stationary target on which to lock their weapons."

"Aye, Captain."

As the *Vordoth* approached the battle, several fighters broke off their attack and turned to face the new threat. Anxious gunners aboard the *Vordoth* opened fire much too early, causing Gunny to bellow into his headset to hold their fire. It seemed that the ship was almost on top of the action when he finally gave the order to open up. Blips on the weapons fire control screens immediately began to wink out. The *Vordoth's* fifty-six phased array lasers unleashed a deadly barrage as the newly trained gunners locked onto their targets and fired. Coherent beams of light punched through cockpits, killing the pilots or destroying their control systems. Some ships exploded in small fireballs as beams of energy sliced through fuel lines or tanks. The other attackers appeared to panic as they witnessed their comrades quick destruction and forgot all about the convoy of freighters, but their uncoordinated attack on the *Vordoth* was doomed to failure before it began.

Passing beneath the battle area had given the gunners on both larboard and starboard sides an opportunity to fire at Raider fighters, and the first pass dispatched almost half the small craft. After passing all ships, the helmsman turned the freighter to starboard and took the *Vordoth* in a clockwise circular path around the battle area. The starboard gunners picked off the fighters that continued to fight, while the larboard gunners concentrated on those that broke off engagement and tried to flee.

The *Vordoth* came to a stop relative to the convoy ships once the shooting ended and Jenetta breathed a silent sigh of relief. She'd taken a tremendous risk, but it had apparently paid off. The cruiser had died without getting a torpedo off and the fighters either never had missiles or they'd exhausted their supply before the *Vordoth* arrived. The fighters had targeted the *Vordoth* with their laser weapons, but the shooting was over almost before it began. She hoped casualties aboard ship were light.

Only now that the battle was over did Jenetta realize that one of the ships she originally thought to be a single-hulled transport was actually another Nordakian destroyer. It had a more conventional configuration than the stealth destroyers and probably much more protective armor as well. Still, it was so thoroughly damaged from missiles and energy weapons that she doubted it would ever again move under its own power. Huge gaping holes peppered the hull. It would be remarkable if an appreciable number of crewmembers had survived.

"Collect damage reports, please," Jenetta said to the com operator.

"Reports are coming in now, Captain. No severe damage reported. We suffered a few hits but all are in non-essential areas and will be easily repaired."

Jenetta could hardly believe their good fortune. "Really? That's astonishing— and wonderful!" Realizing she was letting emotion show through, she forced herself to resume a stoic façade. "Can you get me the officer in charge of the *Jouraklihest*?"

The com operator nodded and a minute later announced that he had the captain of the *Jouraklihest* on a video link.

Jenetta stood in front of her command chair, tugged on her tunic to straighten it, and said, "Put it on the forward monitor, please."

The large viewscreen immediately lit up with the image of the Nordakian captain. Essentially Hominidae in appearance, the captain had a wide, flattened nose but no hair or external ears.

Jenetta said, "Greetings, I'm Captain Jenetta Carver of the freighter *Vordoth*."

"I'm Captain Phuth Yuixotical. Uh— your uniform appears to be GSC, Captain."

"You're very observant, Captain. It's true that I'm a Galactic Space Command officer."

"But you're on a commercial freighter? Or at least what I understood to be a commercial freighter from your communication messages." Glancing down at a small monitor mounted on the right arm of his chair, Captain Yuixotical said, "It looks more like a light destroyer now that I look at the external configuration more closely. Is it a decoy gunship?"

"No, it's a freighter as you first understood. We detached from our cargo four and a half billion kilometers from here in order to come to your assistance. What's your condition, Captain?"

"We have a great deal of serious damage from the attack. But wait— I'm forgetting my manners; I haven't thanked you for saving my ships and my people. Without you, we would surely have been lost. On behalf of myself, my crews, and all the peoples of Nordakia and Obotymot, I thank you and your brave crew."

"We're glad we were close enough to assist. We were attacked ourselves just a few days ago."

"Yet you obviously were successful in defending yourselves."

"Yes, but it was a much smaller force— just a destroyer mother-ship and half a dozen fighters."

"And you defeated them by yourself?"

"Yes, but as you've observed, we're carrying a lot of firepower. They never knew what hit them."

"We had a three-destroyer escort and yet, without your one small ship, we would now either be dead or imprisoned by the Raiders. I suspect your GSC training made the difference." Sitting up a little straighter, Captain Yuixotical stated proudly, "Our planet presently has two dozen cadets attending the academies on Earth."

"They'll get the best education available, Captain. I'm a graduate of NHSA, class of '56. Do you need further assistance from us?"

"Yes, most certainly! My early damage reports indicate that one freighter is incapable of propulsion, another will only be able to achieve fifty-five percent power, and this ship has extensive damage to sensors and life support systems. It will take a week or more just to get my convoy marginally operational again. We'll need protection until then."

"Then I suggest that you come over to the *Vordoth* so we can discuss our options. While we talk, my crew can retrieve our cargo section and bring it back here."

"Very well, Captain Carver. I'll notify the other captains to join me there. Where should we dock?"

Jenetta turned to Charley, who said, "Bay Two has sufficient room for three Nordakian tugs, Captain."

Turning back to the viewscreen, Jenetta said, "My chief engineer tells me that we can accommodate your three tugs in Bay Two."

"Thank you, Captain. We'll be there shortly."

The viewscreen reverted to an exterior view and Jenetta turned to Gloria. "They look a lot like us."

"When they wish to."

"What do you mean?"

"Just that the Nordakian captain expected to be talking to a Terran, so he prepared himself."

"They can change their shape?"

"Not as far as I know."

"Don't keep me guessing, Gloria," Jenetta said, grinning. "What did you mean when you said he prepared himself?"

"If they have the ability to alter their shape, I've never heard about it. And I'm unsure if their physiology is as close to ours as it appears, but I do know they can change their chromaticity at will like some of the species on Earth, such as the cuttlefish or chameleons that use their coloration abilities for warnings, hiding, or stealthy hunting."

"Really? That's interesting."

"I understand their normal color is a medium shade of aqua and they can only maintain an adopted color while awake. The females are supposed to be much lighter in shade than the males, but any of them can appear however light or dark they wish while awake. When they're attempting to be sociable with Terrans, they try to simulate the coloration of their host or the emissary. When they wish to exhibit displeasure without actually saying something, they adopt their true color. And if you get one riled or excited, his colors will vary. They can ripple across his form either slowly, almost ponderously, or so quickly that you almost get a headache from trying to focus on what appears to be a wildly gyrating piñata. I've heard that when they get angry, their color flashes mostly in shades of red or orange, sort of like a warning to stay away. If they're excited, happy excited, the colors lean more towards blues and greens."

"That's even more interesting. Talk about wearing your heart on your sleeve. Do you know what they eat and drink?"

"Not offhand. I'll check the computer, Captain."

"Thank you, Lieutenant. Join me in Bay Two after you arrange for the food with Anthony."

"Aye, Captain."

Jenetta walked to the com station and asked the operator to put her on ship-wide speakers.

Handing her a microphone, he said, "Go ahead, Captain."

"This is the Captain speaking. We've destroyed a Raider medium cruiser and thirty-four fighters while not suffering a single casualty or taking a single serious hit ourselves. Very well done, everyone." She paused for a few seconds as the bridge and probably every other section of the ship erupted in celebration. "The captains of the convoy freighters are coming aboard shortly to discuss their situation. Their ships have suffered extensive damage and we'll have to decide how best to get them operational again. Our visitors are Nordakians and I'm sure you'll be on your best behavior in front of our guests. Captain out."

Jenetta walked quickly to her quarters to put on a fresh tunic and brush her hair, and was waiting in the bay observation area near the airlock when the three tugs arrived. She was eagerly looking forward to her first meeting with members of the alien race. Gloria joined her as the outer doors closed and sealed, and air pressure in the bay began to rise.

"Anthony is trying to synthesize some Nordakian beverages and snacks," Gloria said. "Here's a translator, Captain."

Jenetta accepted the small flat box that could be worn on a belt or hooked onto a uniform button. It was capable of translating dozens of different languages, including Dakis, the principal language on Nordakia.

"Thank you, Gloria," she said as she held the device over her cupped left hand and depressed the button on the back that would both activate the device and release the small plastic receiver from its storage cavity.

"You're welcome, Captain."

"It's Jen," she said, as she fit the wireless receiver into her left ear.

"Yes, Captain."

Jenetta groaned silently. *Maybe it's just something she has to work through,* she thought.

As the air pressure gauges moved into the green, the locking mechanism in the airtight doors to the bay began to grumble loudly. The doors parted to the accompaniment of a whooshing sound as pressure instantly equalized between the bay and the corridor. Sliding in and up, the hatchway cover on each of the tugs opened to reveal an empty airlock chamber. A ramp quickly extended down to the flight bay deck from the opening as the inside airlock doors parted, allowing the occupants to pass through without performing a cycling procedure. Jenetta masked her surprise upon seeing the height of the aliens emerging from each of the ships. Nothing in her conversation with Captain Yuixotical had disclosed the fact that most Nordakian males are over seven-foot tall. In most other respects, the Nordakians didn't appear very different from Terrans. In fact, each of the emerging aliens exhibited a light skin color close to Jenetta's.

Following introductions, Jenetta led the way to the lift. Gunny Rondell would escort the pilots to the crew mess where beverages and snacks were available.

Although Amer had become the defacto standard language in Galactic Alliance space, the development of translation devices that almost rivaled the abilities of a live translator had obviated the need for everyone to speak or understand it, however, the nuances of body language and facial express- ions still dictated that live translators always be used in diplo- matic and business negotiations, as well as for other formal discussions. Of the three captains, only Captain Yuixotical spoke Amer well enough to forego a translation device. Since the red and gold uniform tunics of the Nordakian Merchant Service offered neither buttons nor belts, the other two captains wore a translation device suspended from cords around their necks with a connecting earpiece placed in one of their auditory orifices.

As the lift rose towards the bridge deck, Captain Phuth Yuixotical said to Jenetta, "I know earthlings are normally shorter than most of our race, but you seem smaller than other Terrans I've met, most of whom have been GSC officers. I don't mean any offense."

"You're correct, Captain. I am shorter than most GSC officers and no offense is taken. I think many senior GSC officers are taller because some Terrans are of the opinion that physical height is important in order to command respect. There was an infamous general on Earth whom historians have so mocked because of his physical stature that many people believed him to have been a dwarf. Napoleon Bonaparte was a brilliant tactician who conquered vast territories before being defeated himself and exiled. At five- foot seven-inches, he was about three inches taller than me. Perhaps things have changed during the past four and half centuries because I can honestly say I've had few problems because of my height since I received my commission."

"Forgive me also for saying, but you don't look as old as your years. I would never have guessed that you graduated from NHSA more than ten years ago."

Smiling, Jenetta said, "A woman is never offended when you tell her she looks younger than her years, even ship captains." She had decided this was not the appropriate time to tell the Nordakian she was just an ensign who had slept for more than ten years in a stasis bed. Better that he simply believe she availed herself of the medical techniques employed to make people appear younger.

As the group entered the bridge on their way to the captain's briefing room, someone said loudly, "Captain on the bridge," and everyone came to rigid attention. Jenetta said, "As you were," and continued leading the way to her office.

Once inside, Captain Yuixotical said, "I take advantage of every opportunity to practice my Amer, but I realize that I still make errors. Perhaps I misunderstood the facts in our earlier conversation. I thought you said this *wasn't* a GSC ship."

"It isn't."

"No? Forgive me, but it's more than a bit unusual to find military protocol aboard a commercial freighter. If you didn't tell me otherwise, I'd guess this was an undercover operation of GSC surreptitiously sent here to fight the Raiders that have been plaguing this area of space by acting as a decoy. But don't worry, your secret is safe with us, Captain. If you wish, none of my people will tell anyone of the freighter with the firepower of a light destroyer which drops its cargo and comes to the rescue of other freighters."

Jenetta was trying to determine how best to set the record straight while not offending the Nordakians when the door-chime sounded. The computer opened the briefing room doors when she said, "Come."

Anthony entered carrying a tray of beverage carafes and mugs, followed by another crewmember carrying a tray of snacks. As they set the trays down on the desk, Anthony gestured towards the four hot beverage decanters and said, "Coffee, Tea, Rathiger, and Vesipoa, Captain."

"Thank you, Anthony. Dismissed."

"Aye, Captain."

After preparing their beverages, the captains and Gloria took their seats around Jenetta's desk. Only two of the freighter captains selected a snack.

"Excellent Vesipoa, Captain, and the Frincizi cakes smell delicious," Captain Yuixotical said, "but unfortunately I have to watch my weight now that I'm getting older."

"You're the first Nordakians I've met, but you look like a young man to me, Captain." The other Nordakian captains, both of whom appeared considerably older, smiled and exchanged knowing glances.

"I'm about thirty-five, in Terran years, but my level of activity has dropped off somewhat in recent years and it would be all too easy to lose control of my waistline."

"I understand. I'm careful about my weight also, but I can never resist a good cup of coffee. Tell me, Captain, what were you doing stopped in open space?"

"Our collision avoidance systems shut down our Light Speed drive and we stopped to investigate. At first, we thought that two freighters might have collided and broken apart. Since we're unable to use our AutoTect systems, the risk of collision is always of grave concern. We sent out space tugs to gather the cargo containers and clear a path, only to learn that there were just a few actual containers. We discovered they were filled with electronic equipment sending out false contact information in a sort of a fishnet of electronic signals that made our collision avoidance system believe there were hard contacts ahead. That's when we were attacked. Our warships engaged the cruiser to screen our escape in sub-light, but the Raider cruiser managed to severely damage two of our escorts with torpedoes in the first few minutes of battle. The third destroyer, originally posted as rear guard, moved to engage a group of fighters that suddenly appeared in front of us. They made a valiant effort and destroyed a dozen squadrons armed with missiles, but there were just too many of them. Weapons fire from her ceased just before you arrived."

The com system on the desk buzzed before Jenetta could respond. Lifting the com screen panel to answer, she watched as an image of Charley filled the screen.

"We're about to complete the linkup with our cargo section, Captain."

"Carry on, Chief, and return us to the Nordakian ships as soon as you've completed the link procedure."

"Aye, Captain."

"You run a taut ship here, Captain," Captain Yuixotical said as Jenetta pushed the com screen back down.

"It's easy when you have a top crew. They make me look good. Now, how soon do you think you can be underway?"

"My latest information is that we'll need at least a week to make repairs to the *Klidestru*. She's the most severely damaged."

"I don't believe we can afford to remain here a minute longer than necessary. The Raiders may already have additional ships on the way and they'll come in greater force this time. Your three fully laden ships have to be too tempting a target for them not to try again. I'm frankly surprised they sent only one cruiser for the assault. I was expecting to face a small task force as we moved in."

"We can't possibly leave any of our ships. The situation on Obotymot is dire and these supplies are too vital to our people there. Many die each day. Although the dust in the upper atmosphere has finally started to settle, it might be decades before the environment on the planet allows it to be totally self-sustaining again. Part of our cargo is new equipment for the establishment of hydroponics cultivation processes in converted grain warehouses."

"There's an old Earth saying," Jenetta said. "'Half a loaf is better than none.'"

"Ah! We have a similar saying on our world, derived from a popular apologue. We say, 'Tis better to dine with a dalinnar than sip sulp soup.'"

In response to Jenetta's questioning look, Captain Yuixotical said, "A dalinnar is a rodent who eats tullibers, but they only eat the centers where the seeds are located. You must carefully cut away any part of the tulliber where the dalinnar has gnawed because its saliva is mildly toxic and ingesting it can make you quite ill. Usually, only half of the tuber winds up being edible. Sulp is a kind of grass that grows in fresh water near the shore. It's slightly bitter-tasting and provides no nutritional content to Nordakians, but it can be used to fill the belly when food is unavailable, merely as a means of chasing away hunger pangs."

"Ahh, I understand."

"But despite our mutual sayings, we still can't leave a single ship. You have to help us, Captain. Perhaps you can get reinforcements from GSC."

"The nearest GSC warships are at least a month away— far too distant to assist us. We're on our own, I'm afraid. Can your ship, the one capable of only fifty-five percent power, exceed Light-75?"

"Just barely— I believe."

"Good. We'll let it proceed under its own power then, instead of towing it." Jenetta stood and crossed to the large display screen on the wall. "Computer, display the star chart for this section." When the chart appeared, Jenetta stared it for a few minutes. Extending her hand, she touched a spot on the viewscreen and said, "Computer, voice on, identify."

"Asteroid ring around the star Zighesta. No planets exist in this solar system."

"Time at Light-75?"

"Fourteen hours, six minutes, thirteen seconds."

"Computer, identify," Jenetta said as she touched another spot.

"A small absorption nebula commonly known as Periseras. Approximately three thousand kilometers across, the cloud is densely composed of interstellar gas and dust."

"Time at Light-75?"

"Seven hours, fifty-five minutes, twenty-two seconds."

"Computer, voice off."

Turning to face the captains, Jenetta said, "We're much too vulnerable here and our options are limited. The asteroid belt would give us excellent cover while you make repairs and it's only fourteen hours away, but I think the space dust cloud, Periseras, would be a better choice. It will shield us from the

Raider's electronic sensors while concealing us visually. It's only eight hours away and it's marginally better aligned with the route to Obotymot."

"We still have the problem of the *Klidestru*, Captain. The engines are off-line and can't be restarted without a major repair effort. If we tow it, the entire convoy will be limited to Light-75."

"Perhaps the *Vordoth* can take it to the cloud. Are our container locking systems compatible?"

"No. Our newest freighters and cargo link-sections are built with the Lewiston container locking system that you employ because it's become the standard system in this quadrant of space, but, until all our ships are converted and link-sections replaced, we're employing adapter links for coupling the incompatible sections. They don't provide internal tunnel access to the containers, but they're secure. All Nordakian ships carry at least one adapter link in case we need it. It should be a relatively simple matter to connect with your ship, but you already have a cargo. How long are you?"

"Just over six kilometers."

"The *Klidestru*, like our other two ships, is maxed out at ten kilometers, the maximum safe length permitted by Galactic Alliance regulations. Your ship may not be able to handle the load and control may be impossible."

"I believe it would be less dangerous than remaining here to face Raiders who are no doubt aware of the battle location. Someone is definitely going to be looking for the cruiser we just destroyed."

Captain Yuixotical sighed, making a strange nasal sound. "You're right, of course."

"Our first priority, after searching your destroyers for survivors, must be to patch all holes so we're not leaving a trail the Raiders can follow. Then we'll get underway."

"Search and Rescue teams left the ships at the same time we did. By now they're working their way through the destroyers to see if anyone is still alive. Others are at work sealing the holes in the cargo containers. The cargo is too precious to let any escape."

Jenetta lifted the com system screen, punched a button, and said, "What's our position?"

The helmsman replied, "We're at rest relative to the convoy ships, Captain, five kilometers off the stern of the *Jouraklihest*."

Jenetta lowered the com screen and looked at the Nordakian captains, saying, "If we're in agreement, I suggest we get to work."

The three visiting captains stood, thanked Jenetta profusely for her help and hospitality, and turned to leave. Since none of the visitors had changed their hue while in her presence, she felt they were satisfied with the arrangements.

Gloria escorted the Nordakians to Bay Two so they could return to their ships and then returned to the bridge where Jenetta was sitting in her command chair watching the activity on the large viewscreen. All exterior lights on the freighters were illuminated and Nordakian crewmen and space tugs were busy everywhere, performing emergency repairs to the freighters.

"It looks like we're going to be delayed again, Captain," Gloria said.

"We saved them, so I guess that makes us sort of responsible for them until they reach Obotymot. We certainly can't just leave them here without a destroyer escort. As soon as the tugs are clear, move us into position to attach the *Klidestru* and have Charley link us up."

"Aye, Captain."

Chapter Twelve
~ July 17th, 2267 ~

Unsightly is far too kind a word to describe the emergency patches to the three freighters. If anyone was disposed towards making light of the situation, they might have said the patches made the ships look far worse than the actual damage. However, they weren't leaving a trail anyone could follow when the small convoy of ships finally got underway for Periseras three hours later. The Nordakians had used pieces of hull from the fighters, destroyers, and even the Raider cruiser to complete their repairs as expeditiously as possible. Aboard the *Vordoth*, the gunners had remained at their weapons consoles the entire time while the bridge crew spent the hours scanning space for Raider ships, fearful that reinforcement vessels might appear at any time. They didn't.

It took almost seventeen hours to reach the dust cloud instead of the predicted eight because the freighter with the partially damaged power system couldn't maintain Light-75. Her Nordakian captain reported early on that the ship was in danger of shaking apart because of power fluctuations from their temporal envelope generator. At Light-40, the generator power was stable enough to continue. Space tugs could have been used to tow the ship at Light-75, but 40 c was certainly adequate for a successful evacuation of the battle zone and Jenetta didn't want to stop to make the changeover once they were finally underway.

Upon reaching Periseras, the convoy proceeded cautiously, moving just far enough inside to ensure that the sensors of anyone looking for them would be confused by the murky background, but not so far in as to have their own sensors rendered completely ineffective. Separating from the *Klidestru*, the *Vordoth* moved off a short distance to give the Nordakians unimpeded access to their ship. Space tugs immediately took control of their damaged vessel and pushed it into position next to the other Nordakian freighters. As round-the-clock repairs began, Charley initiated a mainten-ance program of his own to tidy up the emergency repairs made after the initial attack on the *Vordoth*. Since the *Vordoth* had to stand by anyway, he would use the time to best advantage, also assisting the Nordakians wherever possible.

On the second day following their arrival at the Periseras nebula, Crewman Pieter Johnson had been hunched over the science station console for more than ten minutes muttering to himself and punching contact points on the keyboard. Finally he said to Jenetta, "Captain, there's something strange here. Two of the three cargo containers we left behind seem to be moving."

Jenetta rose from her command chair and moved to look over his shoulder.

"See, Captain," Johnson said, pointing to the monitor, "the tracking transponders are sending clear signals, although they're a little weak at this distance, and they're a long way from where we left them. This plot shows you how far the two undamaged link-sections have traveled since we dropped them off. They've almost reached the damaged link. They have to be traveling FTL."

"Excellent job, Mr. Johnson. Keep an eye on them and continue to plot their course."

"Aye, Captain," he said, beaming proudly from the compliment.

Climbing back into her chair, Jenetta appeared to be watching the front viewscreen, but she was actually thinking about the movement of those cargo containers. She knew it had to be either the Raiders or salvagers and, since this area of space was clearly dominated by Raider forces, it seemed illogical to presume that independent salvagers might be operating here. More likely, the Raiders were cleaning up the mess to hide evidence of their operations. The unprocessed ore in the containers had a respectable value, but its sale could leave a trail back to the Raiders unless they had covert access to a processing facility.

Being able to track the cargo containers offered a unique opportunity to find out where the Raiders were taking their loot. Unfortunately, having successfully slipped away from the Raiders, Jenetta couldn't report the information to Space Command until they were clear of Raider space, and by the time GSC ships got here, as much as four months might have passed. The ore cargo would be long gone by then, possibly even processed and moving through distribution pipelines.

Jenetta waited almost an hour before checking with crewman Johnson at the science station again. She learned that the transponders had definitely moved some distance from their previously reported locations.

It was almost noon when Jenetta walked to the officer's mess. Gloria, the Doctor, and Charley were seated at the large white table enjoying the noon repast served up by Anthony. They started to stand up as Jenetta entered the room.

"As you were," Jenetta said quickly. It had become an automatic reaction by now. Everyone jumped when she entered a room and then she, in turn, told them to sit back down. She had concluded that this must be why so many GSC captains took their meals in the small, private dining room that usually adjoined their quarters, or in their briefing rooms. Hurrying over to see what Jenetta wanted for lunch, Anthony took her order and then rushed away to prepare the food.

During a lull in the conversation at the table, Jenetta said, "There's a new development. The containers that we were forced to leave behind are moving."

"Moving? They can't be," Charley said. "The braking thrusters would prevent that from happening."

"We've tracked them for over an hour since we first detected their movement just to be sure. Also," Jenetta paused for effect, "they're all moving in the same direction at FTL speeds."

No one spoke for several seconds. Everyone realized the implications of the statement without further elaboration. Finally, Gloria ventured rhetorically, "Raiders."

"That would be my guess. Now that their attack has failed, I think they're cleaning up and salvaging what they can. The question is, where are they taking the containers? To their base, a processing plant, or just a storage area?"

"I'd sure love to know," Charley said.

"So would I— that's why I've decided to follow them."

"What?" Gloria said excitedly. "You want us to track them to their base? That would be suicide!"

"Yes, it might be," Jenetta said calmly. "That's why I've decided to go alone. I'll take a space tug."

"*Alone?*" Charley said. "You can't go alone, Captain. I'll go with you."

"Me too," Gloria said.

Jenetta grinned at Gloria. "But didn't you just say it would be suicide?"

"And I still think that, but you can't go alone. And maybe you won't take as many chances if you have to think about the lives of others."

"I need you to stay here, Lieutenant. It'll be your job to get the freighters to their destinations if I don't make it back. And the same goes for you Charley. I need you here to keep things running. I do appreciate the offers though, especially in light of the possible danger. I've given this a great deal of thought during the past hour. Captain Lentz told me Space Command doesn't have a clue where the Raiders hide between attacks. This intelligence information could be vitally important. It might even provide a means of reducing the pirate activities in this deca-sector. I can't afford not to go, but I also can't risk your lives any further."

"You *can't* go alone, Captain," Charley said. "If we can't join you, how about asking for a couple of volunteers from among the crew?"

Jenetta grinned. "You don't think I can pilot a space tug?"

"There's more to handling a tug than you might think. It's *not* just a significantly more powerful shuttle. If you get into a situation where there are other tugs, you have to know both the written and the unwritten rules of space tug operations in order to avoid detection and you don't have time to learn them all right now. The signal from that tiny transmitter will be getting weaker by the minute as it moves further away at FTL. If you're determined to do this, you'll have to leave almost immediately."

"You're right about my not knowing space tug operation protocols, but I hesitate to put anyone else's life in jeopardy again. I've already asked too much of this crew."

"The crew has come to believe that you live a charmed life. After the last fight where we destroyed a medium cruiser and almost three dozen fighters without taking a single serious hit ourselves they'd follow you down the cone of an active volcano on Io."

"We were lucky, Charley. That cruiser's crew obviously wasn't properly disciplined. They were most likely aware that there are no GSC ships in the sector and were watching the battle instead of their sensors and rear viewscreens. I was counting heavily on just that lack of attention when we attacked, but I was just as surprised as everyone else that they never even ejected counter measures. Like the Raiders aboard the destroyer, they probably never contemplated being attacked by a freighter. If they'd been more alert, we could easily have been on the receiving end of a couple of torpedoes. And I never expected us to actually destroy such a large and powerful vessel. Initially I was only hoping our torpedoes would sufficiently damage whatever ships we encountered so we could help the Nordakians escape while the Raiders were handling their emergency repairs. As to the fighters, the gunners get all the credit for that. The excellent training Gunny Rondell gave them kept them intensely focused on their job, while the fighter pilots panicked when their ship was destroyed and paid the price."

"Oh, Captain, it's a lot more than just luck. It's your training, intelligence, and— temerity. But that doesn't change the fact that you still need help for this job."

As they talked, Anthony brought her food and Jenetta ate. She used her napkin to wipe her mouth when she was done, pushed her plate away, stood up, and walked over to the com panel on the wall. Picking up the receiver she said, "Com? This is the captain. Put me on ship-wide broadcast."

"Go ahead, Captain," the com operator said.

"Attention crew of the *Vordoth*. This is the Captain speaking. I've decided to undertake a mission that may provide the GSC with vital and invaluable information about Raider operations in this deca-sector. I'd like two volunteers to accompany me in a space tug. This is an extremely dangerous mission and, if discovered, we may not be returning. There's no shame involved for anyone who doesn't volunteer. Anyone interested in participating should be in Bay Two in ten minutes. Carver out."

To the others in the wardroom, Jenetta said, "Well, that gives me enough time to enjoy another cup of Anthony's delicious coffee."

Anthony grinned and hurried over to fill Jenetta's cup as she sat back down.

"Charley, I'd like you to prepare the last cargo link section for separation from the ship. I'll be taking that with me as a cover. Have some bots remove any signs that identify the contents. No, better yet, alter them to indicate that they contain only empty Argon gas canisters."

"But Captain, the last section is the one containing the Corplastizine. You had us put it there when you reconfigured the cargo and gun placements."

"Yes, I know, that's why I need the hazard warning signs removed. Please synthesize whatever catalyst you can. I realize the yield will be abysmally low without the dithulene-35, so I'd also like you to place a torpedo in two of the containers. They should provide some extra boost to the detonation. If we get into a bind, it might provide us with enough of a diversion to make our escape. Rig a detonation switch on the console of the tug and another on the command chair console of the *Vordoth's* bridge. If I'm not back by the time repairs are complete, I probably won't be coming back. We can smite the Raiders one more time just before you leave this area if I've successfully placed the cargo container where it might do some good. At the very least, it will keep the Corplastizine from being used by the Raiders. Gloria, what say we drop down to Bay Two to see if there are any other suicidal fools on board?"

"Aye, Captain," Lt. Sabella said glumly.

Jenetta was awestruck as she and Gloria entered the bay, but she managed to keep herself in check and swallow the enormous lump that suddenly materialized in her throat. It appeared as if everyone on board was volunteering to accompany her on the dangerous mission. If they didn't have some intestinal fortitude, they wouldn't be freight haulers in the first place and if they didn't have more than the average hauler they wouldn't be on this particular ship for this run, but this display of courage was more than she ever expected. The group that was assembled in the bay lined up in formation and came to attention as Jenetta approached.

"At ease," Jenetta said loudly, and everyone in the bay relaxed but remained in formation.

Prominent in the front row was Gunny Rondell. "I haven't thanked you for the excellent job you did in preparing the gunners for our last fight," Jenetta said as she stopped in front of him. "Well done, Gunny, and thank you."

The early doubts he'd had about Jenetta's ability to command had been dispelled with their first action. After the second action, he couldn't believe he'd ever seriously entertained thoughts about wresting control of the ship. Things had definitely gone their way in both engagements, but Gunny had been in the Corps long enough to recognize superior intelligence and leadership when he saw it. She might still look like a snot-nosed cadet, but she'd been as cool under fire as any battle-hardened veteran Gunny had ever fought alongside or even known.

Bracing to attention, Rondell said, "It's been an honor to serve under your command, Captain. I hope you'll pick me for this mission. The Raiders have been killing my fellow haulers for years; a lot of them have been close friends and I'll do anything I can to put a crimp in the Raider operations."

"Do you have a family, Gunny?"

"Just the Corps, and now the brotherhood of freight haulers, Captain."

Jenetta looked up at fierce steel-gray eyes that stared straight ahead. His vibrant black hair had not yet begun to grey even slightly. "I can't think of anyone I'd rather have along," she said.

"Thank you, Captain. I won't let you down."

"I know you won't, Gunny," Jenetta said aloud. To herself, she said, *I hope I won't let you down.*

Stepping out of line to fall in behind Jenetta, Rondell said, "Captain, almost everyone on board wants to go, but those on duty can't leave their posts so, if you don't select a second here, there are still others to choose from."

"Thank you, Gunny, but with so many excellent crewmen to choose from, we'll easily find someone here." To the group, she said, "Thank you all for volunteering. You don't know how good it makes me feel to see this expression of your confidence in me, but this is an extremely dangerous mission. Someone has already described it as suicidal. Considering the danger, I'd like to ask that anyone with at least one dependant family member step out of line."

There was some murmuring and about three-quarters of the group stepped out of line and reassembled off to the side in front of a space tug. The eight remaining volunteers moved together to form a single line. She would have been happy with any of them, but she needed to limit her selection to only one more. After looking them over, Jenetta said, "Anyone with military service, take a step forward." Three of the eight moved towards her. Two were men and one was a woman.

Stepping in front of the first volunteer, a tall man of about forty with medium-brown hair, she said, "What was your job in the military, Clarey?"

"Motorpool, Captain. If it runs with a motor, I can fix it."

Jenetta nodded and said, "Thank you," and moved to the woman volunteer. She was also about forty, physically fit, and stood perhaps two inches taller than Jenetta. She had often seen the brunette working out in the gym and had even sparred with her a few times. "What was your job in the military, Harris?"

"I was a supply clerk in the quartermaster corps, Captain."

"Thank you." Moving to the last man, who appeared to be about fifty, she asked, "What was your job, Browne?"

"Ship's engineering tech, Captain," he said. His soft-spoken reply, enunciated clearly and crisply, immediately gave one an impression of marked intelligence.

Browne's jet-black hair was graying slightly at the temples and he had a narrow shock of white near his forehead. With his hair combed back, the white patch formed a streak that extended almost from front to back. Another prominent distinguishing feature was a long scar that ran from his right cheekbone to his jaw line before cutting back slowly towards his ear to form the letter 'J.' She had seen him around but had only spoken to him briefly before today. Although Browne, at five-foot eleven and about a hundred ninety pounds, was shorter and lighter than Gunny, he looked fully capable of holding his own in most situations. His dark complexion, indicative of his Caribbean ancestry, was in stark contrast to Rondell's, whose progenitors were French European.

Jenetta nodded, said "Thank you," and then paced back and forth in front of the line a couple of times. When she had made her selection, she addressed the entire group.

"Thank you all for volunteering. With so many excellent candidates to choose from, it's been difficult to decide. I'd love to have each and every one of you with me but, given the danger and knowing how vitally important you are to the *Vordoth* if this ship and the Nordakians are to safely make port, I can't. You're the finest group of people I've ever worked with and it's been my great privilege to be your captain. I wanted to say that now in case we don't make it back. Those who weren't chosen have nothing to be ashamed of. My selections are Gunny Rondell and crewman Browne. Everyone else is dismissed and thank you again."

The bay emptied slowly, many people stopping to congratulate Rondell and Browne on being chosen and wish them luck. When everyone else was gone, Jenetta briefed the two men and instructed them to be ready to leave in two hours. That was the time Charley said would be needed to prepare the diversionary explosive charge. Both men appeared outwardly calm, but they knew the inherent danger the mission entailed.

Jenetta's personal preparations included a brief trip to her office on the bridge to record messages for Space Command and her family. Removing her personal log ring and Space Command ring from her fingers, she dropped them into an envelope, sealed it, and placed it on the desk. A simple note on the outside instructed that if she failed to return, the pre-recorded messages in the outgoing queue should be sent when the ship reached safe space, and the envelope should be forwarded to her family.

All preparations for departure were complete when Jenetta returned to Bay Two. Rondell and Browne were already in the tug, running through the operations checklist. Charley, Rebecca, and Gloria were naturally on hand to see them off. After shaking hands with Jenetta, all three officers came to attention and saluted her. Jenetta smiled enigmatically and returned their salutes before climbing into the tug.

The roomy cockpit of the tug had seats for a pilot and copilot at the front of the craft, with rearward facing jump seats that could accommodate two passengers. Unlike the main ship, which didn't have a single viewing port anywhere in the hull, the tug had thick polycarbonate panes in the bow for the pilots. Anyone occupying a jump seat could activate a monitor on a positional arm mounted to the bulkhead to get a forward-looking view of space outside the craft. All occupants of the tug could access any of the views available from a dozen perimeter cameras mounted in the hull. Rondell was flying left seat with Browne in the right, so Jenetta took the jump seat behind Gunny. As soon as she was belted in, she swung the monitor out in front of her.

Jenetta took a deep breath and released it slowly. "Okay, Gunny, let's do this."

"Aye, Captain," Rondell said as he flipped the switch that would close and lock the hatch. When the console indicated the small vessel was sealed, he signaled the control room that they were ready to depart. As the bay was cleared and depressurized, the outer door was opened and gravity reduced to zero. Gunny Rondell disengaged the electromagnetic skids, then expertly flew the tug out of the ship and along the length of the cargo section. Backing the tug against the last cargo link, he slowly maneuvered it until the hubs were properly positioned, then flipped the switch to lock the tug to the cargo section. The tunnel door had been secured, so the tug immediately floated free of the ship with its hundred-sixty-meter-wide link-section attached.

Rondell advanced the tug slowly forward until well clear of the ship, then engaged the navigation computer. A course had already been plotted and piloting instructions popped up on the helm monitor. It would direct them to a point where they would intercept the containers they intended to tail.

There were no crew quarters on the tug, but they had stocked sufficient emergency food packs for 30 days. Water and air were recycled, so the supply was almost inexhaustible unless vented to the outside. Thin gravity-shielding cloth, like that used in gel-comfort beds, could be rolled out on the deck for sleeping. Suspended between twelve and twenty centimeters above the cloth where the normal gravity field from the deck plating in the tug curved over the cloth and again took hold, the crewmember could rest in complete comfort. If they didn't reach their destination in 15 days, they would turn around and return to the *Vordoth*.

With a top speed of Light-75, it took the tug a little over twelve hours to close with the Raider tugs moving the abandoned cargo container sections. Gunny fell in line behind them and matched their speed to maintain a separation distance of ten thousand kilometers.

They had been following along for several hours when Rondell said, "Captain, we have other contacts converging with our course."

"How many, Gunny?"

"A lot. They're too congested to get a precise count at this distance, but I'd say at least twenty."

"It might be another raiding party. Can you determine their point of origin?"

"We'll need at least five minutes of plots to get an accurate positional map. I'll get the computer chewing on it."

Five minutes later, Gunny said, "I have the plotted information now, Captain. The computer indicates that their course has them coming directly from the site of our last battle. The Raiders are probably mopping up and salvaging everything usable."

"How long before they join the others?"

"They won't actually meet the others. They'll fall into line a few thousand kilometers behind us unless we alter course."

Jenetta sat back in her chair and considered the options. In order to guarantee an unchallenged escape, they should pull out now before the new group got any closer. On the other hand, this might be their only opportunity to get a precise fix on the Raider base.

"Gunny, start moving up slowly to close the distance with the tugs ahead. Let's try to blend in with the salvage parties."

"Aye, Captain."

Eight hours later, they were only a hundred kilometers behind the last tug in the first group, and the second group had moved to within a thousand kilometers behind them. So far, no hint of an alarm had been raised, but Gunny was ready to drop the cargo link and push the throttle to the stops if Jenetta ordered it. Dropping the cargo wouldn't give them any greater speed, but it would make them appear immeasurably smaller and therefore more difficult to discern on DeTect screens.

"We seem to be headed towards that asteroid belt, Captain."

Jenetta had been following their progress on the jump seat's viewscreen and she agreed. Apparently, she wasn't the only one who had thought about hiding in the asteroid belt around the star Zighesta. Thank God she had led the freighters to the cloud instead or they would have been trying to repair their ships right in the Raider's backyard. "It certainly looks that way, Gunny. Let's close up a little so we look more like a part of the front group."

"Aye, Captain."

The Raider salvage group continued to move towards the asteroid belt over the next hour, leaving little doubt of their destination.

"The base must be located on that large, black asteroid near the outside edge of the belt," Gunny Rondell said. "We should break off now while we can still get away clean. Space Command can come in and clean house."

"I want to be absolutely certain of our facts before we leave. If that asteroid *is* a base, we need to learn how they hide their vessels. A large contingent of Raider warships circling an asteroid couldn't be missed by patrolling Space Command vessels. Have the Raiders developed some kind of cloaking method, or do they move their ships somewhere else when Space Command is patrolling in this sector? We have to know. And we should also leave this little present we brought along. It might look suspicious if we leave with the link-section still attached. Just keep following the other tugs, Gunny."

"Aye, Captain," Gunny said, without the slightest hint of reproach in his voice.

As they moved ever closer to the two-hundred-kilometer-long asteroid, Gunny said, "There's something strange here, Captain. Nobody's slowing down to set up an orbital entry approach and the gravitational pull from the asteroid is minimal even though the sensors indicate its probable composition is principally nickel and iron."

"That's impossible, Gunny."

"Yes ma'am."

Thoughts raced furiously through Jenetta's mind as she analyzed the available information. "Do you think it could be hollow?"

"Hollow? Uh— I've never heard of anything that massive being hollow."

The leading tugs finally dropped their envelopes and engaged their sub-light engines but never altered their path as they headed directly for the center of the asteroid at Plus-10. All three sleuths spotted the orifice at the same time when navigation lighting suddenly illuminated and a small ship emerged from the asteroid, speeding away.

"Look at that opening in the asteroid. It's enormous," Jenetta said.

"Aye, Captain, it looks to be about a thousand meters across and that's where everyone is headed. You must be right about the asteroid being hollow."

Jenetta's heart quickened as the tugs ahead of them dropped their speed to Plus-0.02 for their entrance into the mammoth aperture. To leave the convoy now would draw too much attention their way, so they timorously followed along, trying not to alert anyone of their growing apprehension.

At the greatly reduced convoy speed of 72 kph, it took over seven minutes just to traverse the tunnel leading into the asteroid. By Gunny's measurement, the tunnel was six kilometers in length, but that incredible fact became inconsequential when they emerged in a cavern that took their breath away.

Gunny's initial response was to whistle softly before saying, "Holy S— will you look at this place. It's at least sixty or seventy kilometers deep and thirty to forty kilometers wide. It's enormous."

"It's the perfect place to hide," Jenetta said in a reverent tone not much louder than a whisper. "Who would look for a Raider hideout inside a hollow asteroid when everyone knows there isn't any such thing?" Raising her voice slightly she said, "Better start the onboard cameras."

"Cameras rolling," Browne said. "This can't be a naturally occurring cavern, Captain. It must have taken a year to hollow it out."

"Or longer. But they wouldn't have had to carry the debris very far to conceal it," Jenetta stated. "They probably just released it into the asteroid belt. Or they might have taken it to a smelter and processed it. Nickel and iron aren't rare elements, but, if they had to mine it anyway, the return could have helped offset the cost of construction. Have you noticed the surrounding walls? They appear unusually smooth."

"That looks like plasticrete," Gunny said, nodding. "Could they have covered the *entire* inside surface with pre-stressed plasticrete panels like they do with the vacuum tunnels used by transcontinental tube trains on Earth?"

"The expense would be incredible," Jenetta said, "but anything's possible, and it would help ensure the integrity of the walls, especially if they then pumped vacuum plasticrete between the erected panels and the rough excavation surfaces during construction."

The tugs ahead of them had a specific destination and Gunny Rondell followed along, then stood off and watched as first one, then the other, attached their cargo link-section to rows of others in an area that already contained thousands. The other tugs left as soon as they had separated from their container sections, permitting Gunny Rondell to back the link-section against another with the same Lewiston locking system and engage the locking hubs. Once it was secured in place, he released the tug.

"Gunny, as innocently as possible, fly around the entire center of this thing. I'd like the cameras to get a good look at this place and every ship in here so we can identify them all later if they show up in lawful ports."

"Will do, Captain."

New tugs continued to arrive at the base with pieces of ships from the Nordakian battle site. As they were brought in, they were delivered to an area apparently dedicated to salvage operations. Hundreds of workers in EVA suits swarmed aboard the new salvage and began cutting up the damaged ships after they had removed anything of value. Thousands of small 'assist' bots zipped around ferrying the materials to storage locations. In some places the Raiders were rebuilding damaged fighters and ships, but the latest fighting had left the salvaged ships beyond hope of repair and the fighters that weren't in pieces were almost as bad. Rondell used the industrious activity to screen their movements as he flew the small craft to every section in the enormous asteroid port.

Jenetta's eyes widened appreciably when they rounded the stern of an enormous passenger ship and found two, brand new GSC battleships floating side by side at adjoining airlock piers. At nineteen hundred seventy meters in length and with a beam of two hundred ninety-two meters, the sleek, powerful-looking battleships were the largest GSC warships Jenetta had ever seen. She was sure the identical vessels must each mass close to a million tons. The natural bright bronze coloration of their tritanium skin glistened through a clear stealth material coating in the dim lighting of the cavern.

While the ship designers had strictly followed the rule of practicality first and esthetics second, the ships had bold, clean lines. There was naturally no need for aerodynamic shaping since it was unlikely that either ship would ever enter the atmosphere of any planet, but the requirements of stealth capability ensured that the ships had certain streamlined characteristics. The special stealth material that covered every exposed plate of the massive ship would make it appear no larger than a shuttle on DeTect screens and the styling

ensured that the effectiveness of radar and lidar detection
equipment was suitably diminished.

Closed hatches, no doubt concealing torpedo tubes and
energy weapons, were visible on the sides and stern. The
three even rows of oversized hatches that lined each side of
the massive vessel had to be covering phased laser arrays.
Jenetta counted forty-three on the larboard side alone, so,
assuming an equal number on the starboard side and adding
topside, bow, and keel arrays, the total had to be in the
neighborhood of one hundred twelve of the deadly weapons.
While still at the Academy, she'd overheard two officers
discussing the development effort for a hundred-gigawatt
array and the hurdles that faced the Weapons Research &
Development Section working to make it a reality. The major
problem at that time was the same one always encountered in
laser weapon development— the dissipation of excess heat.
She assumed that by now they had successfully completed the
R&D work and put the weapon into production in time for
inclusion in this ship's armament. Although energy weapons
were principally intended for defense against torpedoes, a
hundred-gigawatt laser would add a new dimension to
offensive efforts. The thickness and composition of the hull
armor on an enemy ship would naturally be the final
determining factor in the ability of the beam to punch through
quickly, but she assumed the battleship would make mince-
meat of most anything that came under its weapons.

Since the ships were docked bow in, the number of bow
torpedo tubes couldn't be ascertained, but Jenetta estimated
them to be in the range of between fourteen and twenty,
giving the ship a total of between forty-two and forty-eight
tubes. With a reload time of fifteen seconds, the firing rate
had to be prodigious. If any battleships ever deserved the title
of dreadnaught, it was these. Few enemy ships would survive
for long once they began to take incoming fire from these
battleships. The fact that the Raiders had somehow acquired
them frightened Jenetta more than she cared to admit, even to
herself.

"What do you suppose they're doing here, Captain?"
Gunny said.

"I don't know, but there's not a mark on them so they weren't taken in battle. They already have all their exterior markings, so I would guess the Raiders seized them from a shipyard just before the ships were to be turned over to the GSC. They'd *never* have gotten them away from a base once they were manned. I sure wouldn't want to go into battle against them." Sighing lightly, she added, "They're beautiful, aren't they?"

Perhaps only a military person would view battleships as 'beautiful.' They did have pleasing lines for a battleship, but the overall appearance would still have to be described as 'somewhat boxy' when compared to the sleek styling of a fighter craft whose lines were dictated by the aerodynamic requirements of atmospheric operations.

"Aye, Captain. Perhaps someday you'll command one like them."

Jenetta sighed again, knowing she'd be extremely lucky to ever serve in even a minor staff position aboard a light destroyer once she got back to Space Command. Her only response to Rondell's comment was, "It's nice to dream about."

As the three infiltrators finished their filming and turned to leave, they were confronted by several small security patrol ships. When a message came over the com demanding their assignment number and supervisor contact, Gunny punched the throttle and zipped behind a large passenger cruiser. The security ships immediately began close pursuit. Intending to head for the asteroid opening, the three sleuths were shocked to discover it wasn't there. As they had been working to record the data about the ships inside the asteroid, giant doors had closed over the opening, effectively cutting off their escape route.

Gunny took the tug on a crazy tour around ships, cargo container farms, and junkyards looking for another way out, but there didn't seem to be any other openings.

"It looks like we're trapped, Captain."

"I think you're right, Gunny. There doesn't seem to be any way out. I'm sorry for getting you and Browne into this."

Gunny chuckled. "I wouldn't have missed this party for anything, ma'am. What do we do? Surrender?"

"Let's play our hole card and blow the Corplastizine. Maybe an opportunity will present itself."

As Gunny triggered the device, a crushing blast crashed into the tug and the interior of the small ship glowed momentarily with a bright blue light. The infiltrators awoke a minute later, dazed and aching. If they hadn't been strapped into their seats, they would surely have been flung about the cabin.

"That was some blast, Gunny," Jenetta said, rubbing her forehead where it had impacted with her seat's viewing monitor. "I thought we were too far away to be affected. Let's see if we can find a way out in the confusion."

"That wasn't our blast, Captain. We were hit by something. All power is gone and we seem to be drifting toward an open maintenance bay."

The monitor she'd been watching was dead. Jenetta was required to release her seatbelt so she could stand up to see out the forward windows. "I don't think we're drifting. I think we're being guided in, probably by another tug."

Gunny Rondell unbuckled his own seatbelt and floated free of his seat. Without power, the gravity plating on the deck couldn't maintain the one g field. Pushing off from his seat, he swam to the back of the cabin where he opened a cabinet and removed two laser pistols. After a quick examination, he said, "Both pistols are dead. Whatever they used, it drained every bit of energy on board. Even my chrono-patch has stopped functioning."

The tug rocked slightly as it settled to the decking in the bay when the bay's gravity field was reestablished. Everything in suspension in the tug suddenly dropped to the deck, including Rondell, who grumbled a curse as he picked himself up. A slight vibration in the ship indicated the bay's entrance door was closing. They knew the next steps would be to pressurize the bay and then assault the tug.

"I may not have a pistol," Gunny said, "but I'm not giving up without a fight." Taking a large spanner from the tool closet, he stood behind the hatchway door with the wrench held over his head.

It was several minutes before they heard the torch cutting through the hatch lock. As the door started to move, Gunny tensed with the spanner while Browne stood opposite with a hammer. Jenetta crouched down on the pilot's chair as the door was pushed open a dozen centimeters. But instead of immediately entering the tug, the Raider security forces tossed in a stun grenade. The first Raider to enter the tug found three unconscious bodies.

Chapter Thirteen
~ July 20th, 2267 ~

It could be worse, she thought. Her head throbbed incessantly and her mouth was as dry as cotton, but she was still alive— at least her mind was telling her she was, in direct contradiction to the way she felt. *No*, she decided, *I'm definitely alive. No one who'd died could feel as god awful as I do right now.*

The small room in which she'd awakened was dark, but there was little doubt it was a jail cell. A three-centimeter-wide band, glowing dimly near the ceiling, circled the entire room. Like a night light, it only provided sufficient illumination to discern the outline of objects in the cell. Sluggishly swinging her legs over the edge of the wall-mounted cot, she labored to stand. The room tipped and rocked as she pushed herself upright, but her equilibrium returned slowly and her head started to clear as she stood on wobbly legs. Until then she hadn't realized that except for her underwear, she was naked!

Full consciousness also brought awareness of the wide, flat bracelets on each wrist and ankle. Similar bands hugged her waist and neck. Her first reaction was an attempt at removal of the thick composite bands, but they were solid and hardly flexed when she tugged on them. Although not loose, they thankfully didn't pinch. They actually seemed custom made because of their precise fit. Without knowledge of how the apparently seamless bands had been affixed, she had no idea of how to remove them.

The three-meter by four-meter room contained only the cot and a single-piece stainless steel toilet, also mounted in suspended fashion on a wall. Jenetta moved to the solid door and pounded on it with her fists, but the sound failed to produce any response and sore hands were the only reward for her efforts. Returning to the cot, she plopped down onto the thin mattress in disgust— disgust with herself. She knew she'd recklessly endangered their lives by insisting they continue on to the Raider base to verify the location and gather more information. Her only hope was that Gunny and Browne were still alive and unharmed. Lying back down on the miserable excuse for a mattress, she tossed and turned for a while, but eventually drifted off to sleep.

Awakened hours later by a sound she could only describe as a soft 'bong,' she wondered if there had been more than the six she recalled hearing. Illumination in the cell increased considerably after the last bong, so she deduced it must be some kind of wake-up call. Sitting on the edge of the bare mattress, waiting for someone, anyone, to come to the cell, she wished she had a blanket, towel, or anything with which to cover herself, but she knew from her psychology training that nudity and semi-nudity were one of the procedures used to break down a prisoner's resistance. For women especially, the near total lack of clothing in a hostile environment made them feel more vulnerable.

It seemed forever, but it was actually only about twenty minutes before a small viewing port in the otherwise solid metal-alloy door slid open to reveal a pair of squinty eyes. A gravelly, disembodied voice said loudly, "Prisoner, stand on the large black circle two-meters in front of the door."

Jenetta glanced down and saw a painted circle a half-meter in diameter which she hadn't spotted in the near-darkness. She stood up and stepped onto the blackened area, facing the door.

"Put your feet together, touch your wristbands to the belt around your waist, and hold them there," the voice instructed.

Shifting her weight, she brought her feet together. She lifted her arms and heard a soft metallic click as the bands on her wrists touched the waistband. A human hand holding a small remote control device appeared briefly at the window slot and she felt her ankles pulled together at the same time her wrists were pulled tighter against her waist. She immediately realized that what appeared to be simple bracelets were in fact some form of electromagnetic prisoner restraints. As the hand disappeared, the eyes appeared at the slot again. Satisfied that Jenetta was secure, the guard unlocked the cell door and pushed it open, then carried in a covered food tray that he set on the floor just beyond the swing arc of the meter-wide door.

A large, aquiline nose protruding prominently from a sinister face only a mother could love preceded the guard into the cell. Two days of brown beard growth surrounded a mouth shaped in a permanent sneer. As he straightened up, he said testily, "Okay, here's the drill, doll. You get fed twice a day. Ten bongs precede each meal so you can get ready. You must be standing on the circle when the guard looks in or you get shocked. You don't *have* to put your feet together or your wrists against the belt if you don't want to but they'll wind up there anyway. This way you don't get hurt when the EM field kicks in. I saw someone get their arm broken about a year ago when they tried to keep it from being pulled to the belt."

Jenetta started to say, 'I want to see someone in charge' but only managed the first two words before the world turned inside out and landed on her. She found herself sitting on the floor as she recovered from an unexpected electrical charge that had stunned her from her toes to the top of her head. Through barely focused eyes, she could see the guard's mocking grin as he lowered the handheld controller.

"What you want has no relevance and prisoners are not permitted to talk unless asked a direct question," he said. "Besides, I always like to get the first shock out of the way so the prisoner knows what to expect for improper behavior. That was a level one shock. A level five leaves you dazed for more than a day and maybe permanently. For really serious violations of the rules, such as escape attempts, the detention center supervisor can tighten your neckband enough to cut off your air, crush your windpipe, or squeeze until your head pops off your shoulders. I'll be around to collect the tray in an hour. One bong is sounded when I start collecting the trays.

Get on the circle when you hear the single bong or you get a level two shock. Your next meal will be in twelve hours."

The guard turned and left, locking the cell door behind him. Dazed and recovering from the electric shock, Jenetta sat on the floor until she could focus her eyes properly again. But when she tried to put her hand down on the floor, she realized that her wrists were still attached tightly to her waistband. She uttered a few choice remarks that called into question the pedigree of her jailer as she struggled for several minutes, but she couldn't move her arms away from her waist even a fraction of a millimeter, nor pull her ankles apart. Not having eaten in almost a full day, the aroma of food was so overpowering that she stopped struggling, swung her legs around to the side, and rolled over to the tray where she lifted the cover off with her mouth.

"Hmmm, today's breakfast selection is some kind of lukewarm mushy cereal, runny eggs, and watered-down tea," Jenetta muttered aloud to herself. "Well, only one way to get to the food." Jenetta positioned her face over the cereal and lowered her head until she was able to suck it up with her mouth. The entire lower part of her face became coated with milk but she was able to eat practically everything that wasn't stuck to her face. When she was finished, she rolled over to the cot and struggled for several minutes to scale the raised platform. Unable to reach the cot without damaging herself, she finally accepted the futility of the effort and simply lay on the floor next to it.

When Jenetta heard the single bong, she rolled around until her feet were on the black circle. The door slot was pulled back a short time later and the guard looked in.

"You're supposed to be *standing* on the circle, prisoner," he said.

"I can't get up."

"Why not?"

"I don't have the use of my arms or legs."

The guard looked down and saw the mess on the tray and on Jenetta's face. "Okay, I'll give you a break this time. I musta forgot to release you." He opened the door, removed the tray, and locked the door again. Then he aimed the controller at Jenetta and pressed a button. Instantly, she was released and the door slot clanged noisily closed.

Her first action was to stretch her arms out and the next was to wash her face using the water in the toilet after having flushed it a couple of times to make sure that it was reasonably clean. With her hunger sated for the present, Jenetta sat on the cot and reviewed her situation. While not hopeless, she would be the first to admit it was bleak. She would just have to wait until someone told her what they intended to do with her because she certainly wasn't going to risk talking to the guard again, especially since it was unlikely he would answer her even if she managed to get the entire question out before he lit up her nervous system.

A small control panel she hadn't noticed in the pre-breakfast darkness caught her eye as she sat on the cot. She moved to the head-high, twelve-centimeter-square electronic device on the wall opposite her bunk and began pushing the flat contact spots in various sequences but none of the six had any effect that she could discern.

She spent the rest of the time until dinner pacing around the cell while chastising herself for her hubris. Three quick and decisive victories over Raider attackers had made her reckless enough to believe she could find the Raider base and return safely with the information. She had gambled with the lives of two people who trusted her, and lost. She wasn't a great military leader. She was just somebody who had been lucky a few times. And now her luck had run out.

* * *

An hour after breakfast on her third day of captivity, a pair of eyes appeared at the door slot and a voice ordered Jenetta to stand on the circle. She complied immediately and her wrists and ankles were secured before the guard entered the cell. Once inside, he moved quickly around behind her, grabbed her hair, and savagely pulled her head back. She tried to scream, but the thick rubber gag suddenly thrust into her mouth with practiced ease cancelled all sounds. An elastic-like band attached to the gag was stretched out and slipped over her head, then solidified in that position when the guard pressed a button on his controller. Jenetta now understood how the bands on her neck, waist, wrists and ankles seemed like they were custom made without any visible seams, but the knowledge hardly seemed worth the price at the time.

Thus silenced, only Jenetta's legs were released by the guard so she could be shoved out the door and prodded along an empty corridor lined with cell doors until they emerged from the cellblock. Jenetta found herself in a large, circular room with ten doors evenly spaced around the off-white walls. One door had no markings and one was marked 'Head,' while the others were sequentially marked 'A' through 'H.' Like the door to her cell, all other doors here seemed to depend upon old-fashioned hinges and locks for opening and closure. It meant that no one could manage an escape by circumventing electronic locks and could only move around in the detention center with access to one of the heavy ancient keys the guards carried. Her superior computer skills would be of no use to her here.

Propelled to an empty area against the wall between doors 'D' and 'E,' Jenetta's ankles were re-secured before her arms were released. After ordering her to raise her arms over the bar suspended above her head, with one arm on either side, the guard pressed a button on the controller that pulled her wrists together. She had foreseen what was intended so the sudden movement didn't catch her by surprise, but the next action did. The guard depressed one of two buttons on the wall and the bar rose until Jenetta was standing on the balls of her feet. As her arms began to protest the sudden distention, her guard smirked at her and released the button before taking a seat in an 'oh-gee' chair at one of the four desks in the center of the room.

Jenetta hadn't seen this guard before, but he was cut from the same cloth as the others. About six-foot tall and weighing roughly two hundred twenty pounds, he had the look of someone who enjoyed inflicting pain on others. His unkempt brown hair and unshaven face complemented his rumpled uniform. It was only a few hours into the new watch and he already appeared as if he had been on duty for days without a break. Like the hawk-faced guard who had shocked Jenetta with a Level-1 on the first day, his lips were curled into a permanent sneer. Jenetta nicknamed him Big Ugly.

Pulling the stun pistol from his holster, BU dropped it into a drawer of the desk before taking his seat and removing a holo-magazine cylinder from a different drawer. Twice as long as the holo-tubes used for data lists, the three-centimeter-thick holo-magazine cylinders were extremely sturdy, light-weight, and offered better image resolution. Even at twenty-centimeters length, the composite-material tubes were comfortably portable and could be updated in seconds by downloading different issues of magazines or newspapers contained in the central computer.

Placing the narrow tube on the desk in front of him, BU pressed the recessed button to activate it and watched as a page of text and images rose up along the length of the cylinder. He twisted the end of the cylinder slowly until he found the page he was looking for, then picked up the cylinder, leaned back in the chair, and began reading. He glanced over at Jenetta's gagged, helpless, and suspended form every few minutes.

Over the next forty-eight minutes, Jenetta's arms screamed for release as a number of security people came and went from the detention center, most taking time to ogle her body with lust-filled eyes. Jenetta visually ascertained that the doors with the letters were cellblocks and the unmarked door was the entryway to the center. A chronometer on the wall maddeningly ticked off the seconds and confirmed that she'd been in the detention center for three days.

When a giant of a man dressed in the white clothes of a medical attendant and smelling of antiseptic entered the center pushing an 'oh-gee' chair, BU jumped up and glowered at him. There was no mistaking the acrimony in his voice as he said, "It's about damn time you got here. I got a call telling me to prepare her almost an hour ago. I can't even go to the can when one of my prisoners is in the anteroom."

Easily six-foot-nine, the blasé attitude of the newly arrived man seemed to irk BU even more. Despite BU's menacing posture, the medical attendant remained insouciant. "Don't blame me, I got held up at medical stores. I needed a restraint chair and the clerk wasn't around. He finally showed up with some lame excuse about having to deliver something."

"Restraint chair? For her? She's so small you could just throw her over your shoulder."

"The last time I did that I threw my back out and was laid up for a week. Now I use a restraint chair for *all* prisoner transports. Release her."

As BU aimed a controller at Jenetta, her arms and legs were instantly released. She ached all over from having been suspended from the bar and immediately rubbed the sore muscles in her shoulders.

"Into the chair, bitch," BU said impatiently.

Reaching up, Jenetta tugged at the gag, to the amused delight of a smirking BU. When the band remained inflexibly solid, she reluctantly climbed into the waiting chair. As she settled in, she felt the EM field engage. Her arms were pulled tightly to the chair's arms and her ankles were anchored to the chair's footrest. The attendant touched something to her neck and she felt herself sinking into a pool of warm liquid as darkness smothered her.

* * *

Jenetta awoke back in her cell, feeling as if she'd been beaten up and left for dead in an alleyway after an all night drinking binge. She ached everywhere and her stomach was trying to do things no respectable stomach had a moral right to be doing. She rolled off the cot and crawled to the toilet, but nothing came up as her stomach tried to heave imaginary contents into the bowl. After hanging limply onto the stainless steel receptacle for a good ten minutes, she crawled back to her cot and climbed up, a string of spittle still dangling from her mouth. She was thankfully asleep again in minutes.

When she awoke hours later, she sat up and looked around. Her stomach felt a little better but her chest was throbbing with pain. Peering down, she discovered that she'd been tattooed. In seven-centimeter-high letters just above her breasts, was imprinted the word 'SLAVE.' Beneath that, in four-centimeter letters was written 'PS89726.'

"Those miserable bastards," she muttered aloud with fire in her eyes. In those first moments, Jenetta was angrier than she had ever been at any time in her young life, angry enough even to kill, and she swore an oath to herself that whoever was responsible for the tattoo would regret his or her actions to their dying day, which couldn't come soon enough.

* * *

Removed from her cell again the next morning by BU, Jenetta was once again suspended in the anteroom. As she balanced herself on the balls of her feet in an effort to relieve the painful distention of her arms, she glanced up at the wall chronometer. If not for the gag that filled her mouth, she wouldn't have been able to suppress an emotional outburst. According to the date display, a full eight days had passed since her last session here. She could only recall one. She couldn't account for the discrepancy and wondered if the guards were playing with her head.

On this occasion, she was only made to dangle like a sprig of mistletoe for a short time before an attendant arrived with a restraint chair to pick her up. There was no mistaking the fact that the medical attendant wasn't the same as for her last trip. Although also wearing hospital 'whites,' he couldn't be much more diametrically different in appearance. No taller than Jenetta, he had just a few precious tussocks of carefully combed-over white hair left on his aged, liver-spotted head. When Jenetta was freed from the bar, he just motioned feebly to the chair and then secured her when she sat down.

Not being sedated for this excursion through the corridors presented Jenetta with an opportunity to see a little of the station as she was taken to the medical department and what she saw impressed her. The sophisticated design of the multi-tiered structure corresponded favorably with the amazing feat of coring and lining the asteroid. The trip took her through an impressive medical facility and past numerous research labs.

Moved from the restraint chair to a special recliner in a small lab, straps were used to secure her to the arms of the chair before an adhesive strip with attached wires was applied to her head. Soothing strains of classical music were the last thing she remembered until she awoke in the 'oh-gee' chair as she was being taken back to the cellblock. At least the chronometer in the anteroom indicated it was still the same day.

Expecting to be returned directly to her cell, she was surprised when the guard in the anteroom put her on the holding bar. She was forced to stand there in her underwear as dinner was served to the prisoners in each of the eight cellblocks. She observed that there seemed to be four guards working to feed the prisoners, in addition to the one in the anteroom, so surely they could have taken her to her cell if they wished.

A guard who had finished his feeding duties early returned to the anteroom to relax. Definitely the smallest of the jailers Jenetta had seen in the center, he stood no more than two-inches taller than herself and weighed perhaps only one hundred thirty pounds. At roughly twenty-five years old, he also appeared to be the youngest. As he sat down at the desk next to the other guard, the sandy-haired turnkey nodded towards Jenetta and said, "What's she doing out here?"

The anteroom guard who had put her on the bar said, "Bellis is still feeding the prisoners in her cellblock. You know the rules. No prisoners can be transferred during mealtime."

"I'm sick of all the ridiculous rules around here. With the electronic collars on them, these prisoners are as docile as sheep. And when their EM bands are secured, they're even more helpless than baby lambs. There's no good reason why we can't have more than one cell door in a block open at the same time."

"If you wanna avoid the shit details you follow the rules, all of them, and you keep your big mouth shut."

"Yeah, yeah, yeah," the small guard said as he gazed salaciously at Jenetta. "I thought you might have some ideas about doing a little diddling. She wouldn't be bad looking if you cleaned her up a bit. I like them young and sweet. How about it, honey," he said, raising his voice slightly, "are you sweet?"

If Jenetta hadn't been gagged, she would have given him explicit instructions on where he could put the stun baton he was abstractedly fondling as if it was an erect extension of his body. It might even have been worth the electric shock she would certainly receive.

"Put your tool away, Romeo. If you mess with a female prisoner, they'll throw you out an airlock without a spacesuit."

"Yeah," he said, grinning at Jenetta with lust-filled eyes, "but only if we get caught."

The first guard scoffed, "Any guard here would turn you in for the reward in a heartbeat. A week's stay, all expenses paid, at the pleasure hotel on Timerius Prime ain't easy to ignore. The company is serious about guards not messing with their new slaves."

Romeo suddenly growled angrily and turned away from Jenetta. "I have to work off this frustration. I'm going up to the mess hall for a pie."

Glancing up at the chronometer, the first guard said, "The cell block is already locked down for the night. Opening the door before 0500 will set off alarms all the way up to the commandant's quarters. Five patrol groups and a supervisor will be down here before you get halfway to the lifts. You're really anxious to take a vacuum stroll without a suit, aren't you?"

"I won't set off any alarms. I'm not going out the main door."

"Then just how the hell do you intend to get the pie?" the first guard asked, chuckling.

"I'll use the food elevator."

"You're nuts! You can't survive the sterilization sweep unless you're enclosed in a food container, and you're about five-foot too tall for that."

"I've done it before."

"Liar!" the first guard practically spit out.

"I'll prove it to you, right now," Romeo said confidently. "Key in 'ORSTR156.'"

"Oh, I've heard about that— but it doesn't work. The guy you replaced tried it and got fried. It was okay going up, but when he tried to come back down, the sweep got him. All we found was his clothes, a small pile of dust, and an empty dessert pan."

"Yeah, I heard about that also, so I looked into it. I know a guy in the computer center. My buddy says the defaults are automatically reset at the top of every hour. The guy who got dusted made it to the kitchen but wasted too much time up there. It was ten seconds after the new hour when he tried to come back down and the sterilization sweep process had defaulted back in. I still have twenty minutes before the hour, so punch in the code."

"It's *your* neck," the first guard said as he punched the code into the terminal.

"Detention center food elevator sterilization sweep process disabled," the computer announced in an androgynous mechanical voice.

Jumping to his feet, the guard that Jenetta now associated with the name Romeo said, "I'm off."

"Bring me back an apple pie."

"Get your own, Rosewood."

With a malicious grin on his face, Rosewood gave Romeo a sideways glance and said, "How about if I reengage the sterilization sweep procedure while you're on the way up?"

Romeo hesitated for a second, knowing that he had been outmaneuvered. Smiling balefully, he said, "Okay, *two* apple pies coming up, or rather down."

Romeo used his jailer key to initiate the operation of the food elevator. As the door opened, Jenetta observed that the car was about a meter wide and two-meters deep, but only a meter and a half high. Even Romeo, with his short stature, had to squat as he entered. He pressed the single button on the wall outside the elevator and yanked his arm in as the door slammed close. Jenetta saw the 'in service' lamp illuminate and remain lit for about 60 seconds.

At four minutes before the hour, the 'in service' light lit up again. When the door opened a minute later, Romeo stepped out carrying two pies. Jenetta's stomach began rumbling loudly as the sugary sweet aroma of freshly baked apple pie assailed her nostrils.

Romeo glanced over at her and said, "Yeah, I know you'd like some, but you know what? You ain't gonna get any, bitch." He laughed cruelly as he cut his pie into pieces and started stuffing his face.

Rosewood, still sitting at the desk, said, "You cut that awfully close, kid. You only had three minutes left."

"I ran into a guy I know as I was taking the pies off the bakery cart and we shot the bull for a while. I still had time to get back."

As the two guards greedily attacked their pies, Bellis emerged from the cellblock where Jenetta was housed. "Hey, pie. Save a piece for me."

"Get your own," Romeo said.

"We're in nighttime lockdown or I would."

"Too bad. That's your problem. Besides you still have a prisoner to put away."

Bellis looked over at Jenetta, scowled, and pulled his controller from a side pocket to release her hands. She dropped them to her belt, was re-secured, and then her ankles were released. Bellis grabbed her arm roughly and pulled her into cellblock C, repeatedly muttering, "Miserable goddamn bastards," under his breath as they walked. Opening the cell door, he shoved her in, secured her legs, and removed the gag. She expected some lecherous remark, but he was still so upset with the other guards that he stepped out of the cell, locked the door, and released her without uttering a word.

Jenetta worked her mouth and rubbed her arms before reaching down to pick up the food tray that had been left in her cell. As expected, there wasn't any apple pie, just a large portion of the usual overcooked vegetables and a small dish of plain white rice. "The pie is probably as poorly prepared as the vegetables anyway," she grumbled as she started to eat.

*   *   *

During each of the next two days Jenetta was taken to the medical lab, but on the day following she received a visitor in her cell. Verifying that she was secured before unlocking the door, Rosewood pushed the door open wide and respectfully stepped back out of the way. A man bearing an uncanny resemblance to Captain Lentz entered the cell. As he pushed the unlocked door closed behind him, Jenetta just stood there staring with her mouth partly open as she examined his face.

"Hello, Angel, how are they treating you?"

Although the face was slightly different, there was no mistaking that voice.

"Captain Lentz?" Jenetta asked hesitantly.

"Yes and no," the man replied with a grin.

Chapter Fourteen
~ August 4th, 2267 ~

"My real name is Mikel Arneu," he said. "I looked enough like Lentz that some minor cosmetic surgery allowed me to take his place. After we disposed of his body, I reported to the *Vordoth* as its new captain. My involvement became necessary when the previous captain refused to make the trip without GSC convoy protection. The double we'd prepared to take his place looked nothing like Lentz. We needed the Corplastizine that the *Vordoth* was carrying for the creation of our newest spaceport, not to mention wanting the rest of its six kilometers of valuable cargo. My face was returned to my original appearance after the mission was over."

"What? You're with the Raiders?"

"Better than that, Angel— I'm the commandant of this base. We call it Raider-One because it was the first of our hidden bases and one of our most ambitious undertakings up until that time. It took several years to hollow out this asteroid, fully line the interior, and construct the habitat. The cost was staggering, but over the past eight years it's paid for itself many times over." He chuckled as he said, "Do you know we operated from here for almost *two years* before people realized Raiders were behind all the mysterious ship disappearances in this sector? After that, we didn't even bother jamming the IDS bands when taking ships. We had grown so strong that I decided they could scream all they want. It wouldn't make any difference."

"If you're with the Raiders, why didn't you just stay with the *Vordoth* and surrender it?"

"Simple. There's always some blasted fool who wants to make a fight of it, especially in situations where prisoners are never released. Some people figure they don't have anything left to lose by fighting to the death. I couldn't risk being hurt, or possibly killed, so, after stunning the two crewmen who were with me, I just separated part of the cargo section and gently drifted away with the Dithulene-35 as the fighters approached to await pickup by one of our tugs. I had already done everything I could to make the takeover as easy as possible. I made sure that my first officer was a young, inexperienced, and extremely insecure lieutenant, and that none of the gunners I appointed could expect to hit a small moon, much less a moving fighter. It should have been a simple takeover, so simple I ordered that just one squadron be used and that they not carry missiles. I didn't want to risk destroying the cargo. But— there was a fly in the ointment. I suspect that fly was you. The uniform you were wearing when they brought you in here had captain's bars on it. Tell me, at what point did you seize command?"

"I didn't. Gloria *requested* that I take command. She didn't feel qualified because of the Raider threat."

A grin appeared on Arneu's face and slowly spread until it widened to a smile. And then he laughed out loud, slapping his hand to his thigh. "Damn! I didn't think she had the brains to do that. I'd have bet a month's pay that her own insecurities would *never* have allowed her to promote you, a mere ensign, to captain." Arneu sighed at his lack of prospicience in the matter before continuing. "I suppose you were responsible for shooting down my fighters?"

"I got lucky."

"With all six?"

Jenetta just shrugged her shoulders.

"What about our destroyer, *Satan's Own*, that was tailing the *Vordoth* and providing position updates?"

"I got lucky."

A serious expression replaced the grin that Arneu was wearing. "I don't think so. There's more than luck involved when an old freighter beats a modern warship. I think I seriously underestimated you. I assume you were also responsible for destroying *Mara's Marauder*."

"Mara's what?"

Arneu grinned. "Don't get shy *now*, Angel. I know it was you. One of our fighters radioed that they were under attack by a heavily armed Terran freighter with a configuration identical to that of the *Vordoth*. We know the ship was still somewhere in that area at the time. I also know no freighter captain would ever rush to the aid of a convoy under attack by my forces. Only a softheaded Spacc officer with delusions of grandeur would even seriously consider it. You were the only Spacc officer in command of a ship in that area. Ipso facto, it was you." Arneu took a deep breath and then released it slowly, as if he was trying to remain calm. "One minute we had the situation under complete control and were about to finish off the Nordakians, and the next, one of our best battle cruisers is destroyed and a top notch fighter group wiped out. That damn fool of a cruiser captain was *so* confident the Nordakian convoy presented no challenge that he sent his two escort destroyers off to search for *you* when *Satan's Own* failed to report in. I'm sure you were responsible for the attack that resulted in the destruction of my cruiser, but I know you didn't shoot down dozens of fighters by yourself."

"I didn't," Jenetta said nonchalantly. "And I wasn't being shy, I just didn't know the name of the cruiser. As for shooting down your fighters, I merely saw to it that the right people got the intensive training they needed to become proficient gunners."

"Ahh! I suspected as much. And where's the *Vordoth* now?"

"On its way to Higgins, I imagine. That's the order I issued to Gloria before I left."

"Is that so? And just how did you expect to reach a base from here in that small tug?"

"We stocked enough food aboard the tug for a month and I'd planned to contact Space Command as soon as I got far enough away from this base. They'd have come double quick, in force, when I reported that I'd discovered the location of a hidden Raider base filled with warships."

Arneu shook his head. "You've given us more trouble than all the fools at Mars when we used a work barge to infiltrate the shipyard and steal the two recently completed battleships. The pictures you took of them were outstanding, by the way. I'm thinking of having one enlarged so it can be mounted in my office. What do you think?"

"A picture may be the only way you can look at them soon. Space Command will track you down and take them back. The Galactic Alliance will destroy you and your entire organization."

"Spare me the jingoisms, Angel. The Spacc high command structure couldn't spot its own arse if they were naked in a hall of mirrors, so they'll never find this base in a million years. We're too well hidden and they're not imaginative enough to look for a hollowed asteroid. Our next big mission will show them just how powerful we've become when we employ the firepower they've enjoyed for so long."

"Don't underestimate Space Command; *I* was able to find you."

"Yes, you did, didn't you? How did you, by the way?"

"I just asked myself where I'd cower between attacks on innocent and almost defenseless civilians if I was the lowest scum in the galaxy, and— here you are."

Arneu chuckled and grinned malevolently. "I suspect you just hid near the last battle site and followed our recovery operation ships back here when we cleaned up. We'll be more careful about that in the future. I could get the truth out of you in the psych lab, but that might damage you and you're much too valuable to allow that to happen."

"What do you mean?"

"Surely you've noticed your chest?"

"I have," Jenetta said, not even trying to conceal the anger boiling up inside her, "and I'm no slave. Slavery isn't even legal in this part of the galaxy. As soon as I'm out of here, I'm having this damn tattoo removed."

"It's not a tattoo, Angel. The pigmentation of the skin has been permanently altered, so— it's like a birthmark. The only way to eliminate it is to have all the skin permanently removed, which of course isn't much of a solution."

"Then I'll have replacement skin grafted over it."

Arneu shook his head and grinned. "That'd only be a very temporary solution. You see, you've been given two great gifts, Angel. Our research lab here has been making all kinds of wonderful breakthroughs in age prolongation and DNA manipulation."

"Human DNA manipulation research has been outlawed for hundreds of years."

Arneu laughed loudly. "You're priceless, Angel. Do you really think we care anything about Earth illegalities out here? Just because the people there got upset over human cloning efforts back in the early 21st century and pressed their lawmakers to pass one ridiculous feel-good law after another doesn't mean the research ever stopped. It just went underground— first to countries that would look the other way after payoffs to corrupt leaders who provided prisoners for research, then into space when private companies started moving among the stars. Mainly through my efforts, we have one of the best research labs in the galaxy right here on Raider-One. You see, I want to live forever."

Jenetta's face reflected the shock she was feeling. "You're insane!"

Arneu laughed again. "Am I? To want to live more than the hundred and thirty odd years that medical science provides these days for most people? If that's insanity, then go ahead and call me crazy."

"Not crazy to want it, just crazy to expect it."

"Really? Just because it hasn't been available until now?"

"You know as well as I what would happen if everyone could live forever. The population would explode and the planets couldn't support them. Look what happened on Earth in the 20th century when major diseases were all but eradicated. The population grew faster than the ability to feed them and millions starved annually in third world nations where charitable organizations had moved in and vaccinated the population without first educating them about birth control. Once most of their children weren't dying before age five, the populations doubled every ten years. The wars and genocide on the African continent were the only things that kept it from going the way of India and the Middle East. Then, when nano-particulate medicine was approved for general use and the average age of humans began to increase dramatically, moving into space became not just a dream but a necessity so we could disperse a burgeoning population."

"I'm not suggesting that everyone be given immortality, just those who can afford to pay for it or those who are worth preserving, such as yourself."

"I'm flattered you think I'm worth *preserving*."

"Don't be. I only plan to preserve your body, not your mind. You've cost us a lot of money, Angel. The loss of two fully equipped warships and their personnel has put a huge hole in my annual budget. And that doesn't include the profit I expected from the thirty-six kilometers of cargo the *Vordoth* and the Nordakians were carrying. We have to recoup that somehow. So, your body is now the property of Resorts Intergalactic and your slave number is officially registered with the twenty-three occupied star systems in that part of the galaxy where they respect the property rights of legitimate slave owners. You're going to make a lot of money for us over the next several hundred years."

"Several hundred years?"

"Oh, I guess I didn't finish telling you that part. You've been the recipient of those 'age prolongation' and 'recombinant deoxyribonucleic acid' procedures I mentioned."

"Recombinant DNA? What are you talking about?"

"Our brilliant doctors here at the base have developed a procedure that can totally rewrite a person's DNA."

"That's impossible," Jenetta scoffed. "A person's unique DNA makeup is imprinted in every cell of their body."

"True. But every cell in the human body eventually dies and is replaced. In fact, our bodies are constantly at work making new cells to replace the dead ones. Normally, new cell creation occurs through cellular mitosis so new cells have the same DNA as the old cells, but with our process cells adopt the new encoding and eventually your entire body is changed. It will take years, perhaps as many as ten, for the process to be complete. I don't pretend to understand it all. In fact, I begin to get a headache whenever the scientists become excited and get carried away with their detailed explanations of cells, glands, secretions, hormones, and all the rest. But I know it works. It takes a week of very painful injections to start the process rolling. The metabolous action of the body and the uncontrollable muscle spasms are enough to drive the patient mad, so you were kept unconscious for the whole time. That's why you have no memory of it."

"You bastard! You've used me in one of your illegal experiments?"

"Oh, no, Angel, you got the real deal, the proven formulas. You're actually the second recipient of the tested and proven cocktails my scientists have whipped up; I was the first. Of course, hundreds of *test* subjects have gone before us, most of whom died or were so horribly disfigured they had to be euthanized. And once we got the processes locked down, I required all my researchers here to take it as well. Sort of like a reward— and a security measure at the same time."

"You took it?"

"Of course. Naturally, I was mainly interested in the Age Prolongation process. I told you I want to live forever."

"We're going to live forever?" Jenetta said sarcastically. "Right."

"No, not forever, Angel, at least not yet. Nano-technology research has brought Terran physiology forward to a point where we can expect a life double that of twentieth century man, and estimates are that the technology will continue to carry mankind forward until we can one day expect a lifetime of perhaps two hundred years. But that's not nearly long enough to suit me, and the only kind of research that will offer the human body longer life is, as you've said, illegal. So if we don't do it here, who will?

"We really don't know how many additional years the present prolongation process will provide. You see, they can create computer models and run simulations all day, but the only real way to know for sure is to monitor the process in real time. Of course, that means I'd have died of old age before they knew for sure that it would extend life as predicted. We do know the procedure changes the body so that it essentially stops visible aging. My researchers are still looking for a way to reverse the signs of middle age and restore youth, but so far that's eluded them. However, the scientist in charge promises me I'll live to at least 350 years and the computer models predict I'll have ten times that or more. I'm willing to settle for a lifespan triple that of most people, if that's all I get, but who knows, even without improvement the formula might give us thousands of years of extended life."

"You mean I might live to be 3,500 years old?"

"You received the procedure at a much younger age than me. Doctor Willetti tells me the computer model predicts *you'll* live to be at least five thousand years old."

Jenetta smirked. "And live for four thousand, eight hundred years as a wrinkled prune? I think I'd rather die when God intended."

"No, not a prune, Angel. In fact, the doctors say we won't show *any* sign of aging until the last few years and then it will be incredibly rapid."

Jenetta's face mirrored the shock she was beginning to feel as she started to believe that Arneu was in complete earnest. "You're serious? You're saying that I'm going to have a greatly extended life? And that I'm always going to look like I'm twenty-one?"

"Except for the last few years, yes." Arneu smiled. "Now you can see why you're so valuable to us. You'll be making money for us for hundreds, maybe thousands, of years. And people will be falling over themselves to be with you once the transformation is complete."

"What transformation?"

"I just told you, Angel. Pay attention. Your DNA is also being rewritten."

"I heard that part. But why would people be falling over themselves to be with *me*? I don't labor under any delusion that I look like a goddess."

"But you will!" Arneu's smile changed into an expression of delight that covered his entire face. "You're being transformed into exactly that, a *goddess*. You're attractive now, but as you've said, you *aren't* a goddess. However, by the time the changes are complete, you'll have grown another six inches, or maybe a little more, and your body will have men salivating when they just *imagine* touching it. In fact, your body will be nearly perfect and your metabolism will be programmed to maintain it like that. In a few years, even your own mother may not recognize you.

"As part of our reconfigurations, we'll have incredible healing powers. Our bodies will repair themselves ten times faster than ordinary humans without requiring surgical nano-bots, and you'll be able to drink any ordinary man under the table and never even feel the effects. That's important at a resort where liquor sells for a hundred times normal retail and part of your job is to get the customers to buy you drinks."

Jenetta's anger, largely held in check until now, finally began to erupt as she said, "I won't do it! I'm not a slave and I won't do it!"

"You don't have any say in the matter, Angel. If you look down at your identification number, you'll see that the first two letters are 'PS.' They stand for 'Pleasure *Slave*.' For the past three days, you've been undergoing radical psycho-therapy. You don't realize it yet, but much of what you'll need to know for your *new* profession is already implanted in your mind."

The news that she was being brainwashed in preparation for becoming a whore was more than Jenetta could stand. She could restrain her temper no longer. "You bastard! You no good, lousy, murdering pimp! You're a…"

Her words turned to a scream as Arneu stepped behind her and viciously yanked her head back by pulling on her hair with his right hand. Ramming a gag into her mouth, he pulled the connecting band over her head so she couldn't push it out with her tongue. His now-free hand reached quickly into his pocket and produced a controller that he used to solidify the band. Jenetta tried to scream a profanity but only a muffled gurgle broke the silence of the room.

"There now, that's better, isn't it?" he said calmly. "I haven't finished telling you about your new life and you really should know better than to interrupt. Your therapy will take care of that and you'll learn your proper place. The final step will be to wipe out all your old memories. You won't be able to read or write, but you'll know every trick ever learned about pleasuring men— and women."

Jenetta glared at him as he strutted around her in the cell with his hands clasped behind his back.

"You know, I toyed with the idea of trying to recruit you to our side when we captured you. As soon as I saw your altered uniform, I realized immediately you were the one responsible for our two recent defeats. And it takes a lot of guts to enter an enemy camp in an unarmed space tug. So I called my doctors in to find out how we should proceed, but they said they couldn't ensure your loyalty without destroying the very abilities that make you worth converting in the first place. It's a pity because we would have made a hell of a team, Angel. My work here should give me the boost I need to make it onto the Lower Council; then it's just a matter of time before I rise to the Upper Council and then eventually to the Chairmanship of the company." Arneu laughed as he said, "If nothing else, I'll simply outlive all the other council members." Turning serious again, he added, "With you at my right arm, we would have ruled the galaxy for eons."

Arneu stopped directly in front of Jenetta with his face just centimeters from hers as he stared down into her eyes. "A pity. It would have been so much more satisfying a life for you. Now, instead of wielding more power than you can imagine, you'll spend your days and nights getting hot and sweaty between the sheets with people you probably wouldn't have given a second glance before." Arneu grinned again. "It's not going to be all bad, though. The doctors tell me they'll be implanting thoughts in your mind to ensure you'll really enjoy yourself. It's important that you enjoy your life if you're to spend the rest of your days satisfying other people with absolutely no conscious thought for yourself."

Arneu bent slightly and kissed Jenetta gently on the forehead. His face was barely ten centimeters from hers as he said softly, "Goodbye, Angel. The next time we meet, you won't know me. Enjoy immortality as a mindless hotel whore."

Arneu moved to give her forehead a parting kiss, but she pulled away. He thought she was just trying to distance herself from him and grinned malevolently, but then, without the slightest regard for damage to herself, she brought her head forward as hard and fast as she could. The move caught Arneu totally unaware, with his head where hers had been until she pulled back. He was so unprepared for any sort of attack that he never moved until her forehead connected solidly with the bridge of his nose. Jenetta heard the crack of cartilage and bone, immediately seeing bright flashes of light and feeling extreme pain. She wondered if she had cracked her own skull on his. Arneu, meanwhile, was falling backwards to the floor, screaming in agony, his hands going to his face where blood was already gushing from a mutilated nose.

Simultaneously screaming and groaning in great pain, Arneu rocked from side to side for minutes before finally calming himself enough to sit up. Jenetta looked on dispassionately. She would have grinned if the gag hadn't prevented it. Arneu had, after all, admitted to being responsible for the slave imprint on her chest.

Clumsily fumbling for a handkerchief in the side pocket of his coat, Arneu yanked it out and held it against his face for several minutes before attempting to stagger to his feet. His face was a contorted mask of pain and suffering as he approached Jenetta, blood dripping onto a white shirt already heavily tainted crimson. When he balled his right fist and cocked his arm to punch her, Jenetta closed her eyes and braced herself for an impact that never came. After a few seconds, she opened one eye, then the other. Arneu was still standing in front of her, although out of head-butt range.

"No, I'm not going to strike you, Angel," he mumbled through the pain that continued to wash over him in waves. "Maybe I even had this coming for the life I've sentenced you to. One of these days I'll look you up at the resort. You won't know me, of course, but you'll pretend you love me like no other. I'll laugh so hard you'll wonder what I could possibly find so amusing and that'll make me laugh all the more. Goodbye, Angel."

Arneu turned and wobbled drunkenly out of the cell, leaving the door open and unlocked. But Jenetta couldn't take advantage of it with her wrists and ankles still secured. A few minutes later Rosewood came in and removed the gag, never taking his eyes off Jenetta for a second and never getting closer than necessary.

"You are one crazy bitch to head-butt the commandant of the station. He could have you killed in an instant and no one would question it. I wouldn't want to be in your shoes for all the gold in the freaking universe."

Rosewood backed out of the cell without removing his eyes from Jenetta's hate-filled face. He locked the door, then opened the viewing slot to release her. The first thing she did was rub her forehead where it had come into contact with Arneu's skull. As her rage slowly subsided, waves of depression replaced it. She thought about the many things Arneu had said as she made her way over to her cot. An extended life as a mindless nymph in a pleasure resort was about as far from the future she'd planned as could be. Her head drooped as she sat down and stared silently at the floor. But in the depths of her despair, she became aware that something wasn't right in the cell; something seemed out of place. Spotting an unknown object on the floor near where Arneu had fallen, Jenetta hurried over to pick it up. Unlike the blue controllers carried by the guards, this one was black. She knew it must be Arneu's, having fallen from his pocket when he'd yanked out his handkerchief. It had wound up against the wall, pushed there when the door was opened wide.

Jenetta immediately realized the significance of her find and that it wouldn't be long before Arneu realized he'd dropped it. She also knew they'd come to her cell first. She looked around for some place to hide it but the cell was so austere that it provided no place where it might be concealed. She might secret it in the thin mattress if she could cut the material somehow, but she didn't have anything sharp enough. In desperation bordering on panic, she began searching every corner of the room for anything she could use to rip the fabric. She even felt up under the wall-mounted stainless steel toilet, but all the surfaces were filed smooth. She knew she couldn't hide the controller in the bowl because the water would destroy the electronics. She was still sitting on the floor next to the commode when she had an inspiration. She took the controller and wedged it up underneath the back of the toilet between the curvature of the bowl and the wall. The fit was tight and perfect. She tested it by getting up and jumping on the toilet. The controller stayed in place.

Suddenly things weren't quite as bad as they had seemed just minutes ago. Possession of the controller offered a glimmer of hope for escape. Jenetta lay down on her cot and immediately began formulating a plan. Arneu had said she would be almost immortal. Well, she could live with that if it was true. He'd also said she would eventually be five-foot, ten-inches tall, or maybe a little more. That wasn't so bad either. She'd always wanted to be a little taller. Her brothers were all over six-foot tall like her father, while she had definitely taken after her five-foot, one-inch mother. Looking twenty-one for most of the rest of her life was going to be a problem though. Would she ever be taken seriously by anyone in Space Command if she always looked like a newly graduated ensign? Well, first things first.

Her jailers didn't return to 'toss' the cell for almost three hours. It probably took that long for Arneu to get medical attention and have the painkillers kick in before he realized he had lost the controller. Jenetta was lying on the cot when Rosewood opened the viewing slot on the door and ordered her to get on the circle. Once there she was secured. Then he and Hawkface entered with stun pistols drawn and searched the cell.

Rosewood, the first guard in, said, "Nothing here."

"Yeah," Hawkface said, "but let's swap the mattress anyway. We'll check it again in the corridor."

After they had removed the mattress and brought in a replacement, Rosewood said, "He probably lost it while he was tossing down brandies in the bar."

"He had good reason. Did you see the size of the bandage on his face? His nose must be the size of a grapefruit."

Rosewood chuckled. "Better him than me. Let's get out of here. I don't trust this crazy little bitch."

The guards left, releasing Jenetta after locking the door. When the viewing slot had closed, Jenetta took her first full breath since Rosewood and Hawkface had arrived. She arranged the thin replacement mattress which had been left half hanging off the wall-mounted platform and lay down to continue her planning. She was trying to recall every single thing she had seen or heard since arriving here, especially anything that might be important for her escape.

* * *

Jenetta's trips to the medical lab resumed the next day. She hoped she could put her plan into action before they totally brainwashed her or wiped her memory, but there were a few critical answers she still needed before attempting an escape. For now she preferred not to dwell on the fact that once she'd removed the bands from her wrists, ankles, waist, and neck, she would still be locked inside her cell, locked inside a cellblock, locked inside a detention center with armed guards blocking the only exit, and trapped in the bowels of a station with thousands, perhaps tens of thousands, of Raider personnel between her and a useable ship.

"One step at a time," she said resolutely.

Chapter Fifteen
~ August 9th, 2267 ~

On the fifth morning following Jenetta's highly successful and eminently satisfying assault on Arneu, Bellis came to her cell and ordered her to the circle before securing her. Expecting to be taken to the medical lab once again, she was surprised when a woman dressed like a stereotypical prostitute was escorted into the cell and the door locked behind her. Red leather ankle-strap shoes with heels that must have added five inches to her already remarkable height had the visitor quite literally towering over Jenetta. A knee-length dress of shimmering crimson silk so taut across her thighs that they appeared fused, surely didn't make walking in the towering heels any easier, but it certainly contributed to the desired effect on any male observer. Bellis was panting like a marathon runner near the end of a race when he pulled the cell door closed.

Jenetta stared at the curvaceous woman warily. About twenty-seven-years-old, she simply oozed allure. Her attractive face was a bit too heavily made up and her waist-length raven locks glistened more than seemed possible in the diffused light of the cell. Jenetta didn't miss the fact that the woman was wearing a restraint collar, but not the rest of the restraint bands that Jenetta had seen on all other prisoners.

Smiling pleasantly, the woman greeted Jenetta with, "Hi, honey, I'm 721."

"721?" Jenetta echoed.

"Well, actually I'm PS89721, but I shortened it and the guards don't seem to mind."

"I'm Jenetta Carver."

The expression on the woman's face immediately turned to one of shock and fear. She leaned in close and whispered loudly, "Hon, never, and I mean never, use your old name. From today on, they'll hit you with a level two if they hear you utter it. Your only name is PS89726, or you can use 726 if you want."

Jenetta's indignation was obvious as she said, "I am not— a number!"

Straightening back up, her visitor said softly, "Then you'd better become one fast, hon, unless you enjoy living in perpetual pain. Besides, we'll be getting our new names soon enough. I heard we're being shipped off to a resort in the Uthlaro Dominion in about two weeks. We'll be put into stasis for the five-year trip. They don't want us to have any memories of this place or the trip, so once we reach the resort they'll blank our minds."

"Doesn't that also wipe out the new stuff they've implanted?"

The woman looked bewildered for a moment. "Apparently not, since they take the time to put everyone through the training. Now, what's your name?"

Jenetta sighed and said wearily, "726."

"Good." 721 smiled and took a couple of steps backward before aiming a small controller at Jenetta. As she pushed a button on its face, Jenetta was suddenly unsecured.

"You have a controller?" Jenetta said incredulously.

"Yes, I'm a trustee." She held out her hand and showed the small red unit to Jenetta. "It's only a trustee controller, though, so it can't administer a shock. I wish I could remove this damned collar, but it doesn't work on them either. You need a green or black one for that."

"Right now I'd be satisfied just to get the rest of them off, like you."

"Ta-da, your wish is granted."

"What?"

"I've already unlocked them. All you have to do is slip them off, hon."

Jenetta looked into her eyes for a second to see if she was kidding, then used her right hand to reach for the band on her left wrist. As she pulled, the lightweight band stretched as if made of elastic. In seconds, she had stripped the bands off her wrists, ankles, and waist. She even tried the neckband but it was still solid.

Giggling at the attempt, 721 said, "I tried the first time too, just in case. How about taking a shower?" Wrinkling her nose, she added, "Your hair is pretty grungy. And you could use some clean clothes."

"Are you kidding? I'd kill for a shower," Jenetta said facetiously. "I've been bathing in the toilet until now. I've also been washing my bra and panties in it every night after lights out, and then getting dressed after I hear the first bong in the morning."

"Let's open your bathroom," 721 said cheerfully as she moved to the small control panel on the wall.

"Bathroom? What bathroom? That control panel doesn't work. I tried it the first day I was here."

"You simply have to have the right touch," 721 said, pushing the top left button. A small section of the wall just wide enough to be a doorway slid up to reveal a bathroom with a sink and shower stall.

Jenetta just stood there with her mouth open for a couple of seconds. "Why didn't that open for me?"

"Just one of the guards' little jokes. They don't activate the switches for the first few days and then take bets to see how long it takes you to find out they're working. Prisoners are always gagged when they leave the cell so they can't pass on the information to anyone else."

"Those lousy, sadistic bastards. Uh, I didn't notice any camera monitors in the anteroom. How do they know when we find the bathroom for the first time?"

"I don't know. I guess they can determine when and how often the buttons are depressed from computer records or something. I do know why they don't have cameras in the detention center. One of the guards told me after I became a trustee and was finally permitted to talk."

"Okay, I'll bite. Why don't they have cameras in here?"

"The guards used to spend all their time ogling the mostly naked female prisoners in their cells and they'd work themselves up until, out of total sexual frustration, they'd rape the women or go beat up on the male prisoners. Since the prisoner population is so easy to control without constant monitoring, the base commandant finally ordered that all security cameras be removed from the cells. The commandant also offers huge incentives to any guard that rats out another who abuses a prisoner, sexually or physically." Smiling pitilessly, 721 said, "The stoolpigeon gets an all-expense-paid vacation and the abusive guard gets a no-expense trip out an airlock without a suit. That keeps them all faithfully toeing the mark, at least as far as touching the women or beating up the men is concerned. Now they work out their frustrations with sadistic games, gambling on the results."

Jenetta nodded her head towards the control panel. "What do the other switches do?"

"This one turns on the lights in the bathroom," 721 said as she pressed it. "I'll show you the others after you clean up."

Following 721 into the heretofore hidden room, Jenetta looked into a mirror for the first time in almost three weeks. She was a mess— correction, a full-blown disaster. Her eyes were sunken and her face was sallow. Her shoulder-length hair had the appearance of a rat's nest and she looked like a wild thing fresh from a jungle. The weeks of captivity, medical procedures, and worry had left her looking terribly shabby and worn down. *Beaten down is a more appropriate description*, she thought, *but that stops now. I know how to remove the restraints and I have the means. I'm getting out of here very soon— one way or another.*

"Strip and put these on, hon," 721 said as she removed a pair of what looked like opaque swimming goggles and a shower cap made of a soft silver fabric from a hook next to the mirror. "Press the large silver buttons on both sides of the mirror once, simultaneously, when you're ready. Make certain all your hair is covered by the cap— every single strand. And don't press the buttons until you have the goggles securely in place; the light can destroy your eyes in a nanosecond. Even closing the lids won't protect them completely. The ray should work now that I've been assigned to show you the ropes."

"What light? What does it do?"

"It cleanses your body by killing any harmful parasites that might be on you. The shampoo on the shelf in the shower stall will do the same for your head and hair when you shower."

Jenetta donned the cap and made sure that every strand of hair was tucked neatly beneath it. Then she positioned the goggles carefully and pressed the buttons. For just a fraction of a second she was bathed in a blinding light so brilliant that she could see clearly through the blackened glass of the goggles.

From outside the bathroom where the light couldn't directly reach her, 721 said, "Okay, you can take the goggles and cap off now. Enjoy your shower, hon."

All other thoughts faded as Jenetta savored her first shower in weeks. She used the shampoo from the shelf, cleansing her hair three times before treating it with the conditioner, then soaped and rinsed her body four times using the bar of sweet, fragrant soap she found in the stall. After that, she just stood under the hot spray until the skin on her fingers started to wrinkle, as if the water alone could wash away the days of misery she'd endured since her capture.

As Jenetta toweled off, she realized she was totally hairless from the cheekbones down. The stubble had gotten quite bad on her legs during the past few weeks, but now they were as smooth as a baby's bottom. After toweling herself dry with an incredibly soft towel smelling of lilacs and wild-flowers, Jenetta wrapped a fresh towel around her body and left the bathroom. When 721 smiled, so did Jenetta, for the first time in weeks.

"I bet you feel a hundred percent better."

"A thousand percent, at least. I seem to be missing some hair, though."

Giggling, 721 said, "The ray is responsible for that. It sure beats shaving, even with the laser razors that partially damage the follicles to keep hair from regrowing for months. The goggles protect your eyebrows and eyelashes, as well as your eyes, so you still have to pluck your eyebrows manually."

"But I'm missing hair on— an area where I usually let it grow."

"Oh— don't worry about that. I've been told men like it better this way."

"Really? Then let them do it. What's this?" Jenetta asked, pointing to a pile of clothes lying on the cot.

"Your clothes. From your closet."

"I have a closet?"

"The button immediately below the bathroom door button opens your closet. Here's a clean pair of panties."

"Is that what they are?" Jenetta asked flippantly. "There's so little material, how can you tell?"

"Would you rather wear your old, dirty cotton ones?"

"No— I guess not," Jenetta said as she pulled on the lace-edged panties and then dropped the towel as she put on the matching bra that 721 tossed to her. When 721 walked over to the wall and pressed the third button on the top row, another door panel slid up to reveal a makeup table and chair.

"Come sit down, hon," 721 said as she pulled out the chair, "and I'll try to do *something* with that hair."

It took a good hour, but 721 was able to comb all the tangles out of Jenetta's hair and fashion it into reasonable hairdo.

"Okay, put these on," 721 said as she held a pair of charcoal-tinted stockings out to Jenetta.

"No way! I never wear stockings!"

"You do now. They insist."

"No!"

After sighing in exasperation, 721 said, "Hon, they'll just shock you repeatedly until you comply. You can't possibly win while you wear that damn collar around your neck. We're like a herd of cattle, but what can we do?"

Jenetta hesitated, then reluctantly took the stockings and put them on.

"Good, now stand up."

As Jenetta rose, 721 pulled a heavy piece of black fabric around her middle and fastened it. It extended from her bust to her hips and had a strange composite metal closure in the front.

"What's this?" Jenetta asked.

"It's a waist-cincher, what was commonly called a corset hundreds of years ago."

"A corset? You're kidding. Women don't wear corsets anymore. They're unhealthy and extremely uncomfortable."

"But the company's pleasure slaves all do. That means you and I do, along with every other woman in this detention center. It's part of the required uniform and you won't fit into your new clothes if you don't wear it."

Jenetta bit the inside of her lip. She could put up with all the nonsense until her escape attempt and then she was going to get out of here, or die trying. There was one thing she knew for sure— she would *never* set foot in any pleasure resort as a slave.

After picking up a white controller from the makeup table, 721 held it against Jenetta. It only had two large buttons. "Okay, hon," 721 said, "take a full breath and then expel as much as possible."

As she released her breath, Jenetta felt the corset material constrict wherever 721 touched the white controller to her body. By moving the controller up and down, 721 could sculpt a new figure for Jenetta.

"STOP!" Jenetta managed to shriek as 721 attempted to simulate more of the fabled wasp waist than Jenetta's muscled torso could easily permit.

"Not yet, hon. Just a little more off your waist."

By the time 721 stopped, Jenetta felt like she was being cut in half. With minimal body fat to work with, the corset was reshaping muscle mass and realigning internal organs.

"You're killing me," Jenetta groaned. "I thought hanging in the anteroom was torture."

"Oh, don't be silly; you're fine. You just have to get used to it. After a few hours you'll feel naked without it. Here's your garter belt."

"I don't need that," Jenetta groaned.

"Of course you do. For some strange reason, this silly little piece of material turns men into simpering, drooling fools. The company requires that all pleasure slaves wear one when dressed." After hooking the belt in back and then connecting the four suspender straps to Jenetta's stockings, 721 said, "Okay, hon, sit down and give me your left leg."

As Jenetta complied, 721 put a shoe on her foot that caused Jenetta's eyes to open wide.

"That heel has to be at least twelve centimeters. Can't I start with something smaller? I've never worn heels higher than five centimeters, and not even those since my high school prom."

"Neither had I until I got here. I'm just over six feet tall so I've always done my level best to appear smaller than I was. It's difficult to find a guy taller than you when you're as tall as I am. And now I have to wear shoes that make me look like I'm six and a half feet tall. How many guys want a freak? Anyway, this is the lowest pair of heels in your closet," she said as she let go of Jenetta's foot. "Okay, that one's buckled. Give me your other foot."

With both shoes fastened, 721 helped Jenetta stand and walk around the cell. After a few minutes, 721 released her and had Jenetta walk around by herself for about five minutes.

"Okay, you're doing great, 726. Here, put this slip on."

As the slip settled over Jenetta's body, 721 held a dress out for her to step into.

"The slip is riding up with the dress," Jenetta said, as 721 raised the ultra-tight garment.

"I'll get it, hon," 721 said, and reached up under the dress.

Jenetta squirmed her legs and shifted her hips to get into the dress as 721 maintained a tight grip on the bottom of the slip. Finally, the dress was all the way up, but when 721 tried to close the full-length zipper, it wouldn't budge. "Suck in, hon," Jenetta heard at about the same time the corset started to constrict again. A second later, the zipper easily moved all the way to the top of the dress.

"I can't breathe," Jenetta wheezed.

"Sure you can. Maybe not the full breaths you're used to, but you can breathe. Just— take smaller breaths. Now, come over to your makeup table and sit down."

Over the next two hours, 721 taught Jenetta the basic tricks of makeup application. Having always been something of a tomboy, Jenetta learned much that she'd been unwilling to learn from her mother and friends while a teen. The use of makeup was forbidden at the Academy.

"Okay," 721 said, "time to finish getting dressed."

"I am dressed."

"Not yet you aren't. Here, put on your gloves. Slaves must always wear their gloves. Some guests are funny that way, I guess, because I have more pairs of gloves than dresses and shoes combined. The guards tell me they make me look even sexier," 721 said, giggling.

Jenetta had no desire to look sexier for the guards but pulled on the opera-length gloves 721 handed her. They reached almost to her armpits.

"Now put your restraints back on."

"I thought we were done with them?"

"Not hardly! Until you become a trustee, you're only allowed to remove them while you're getting dressed, undressed, or bathing. And everyone must wear them from night bong to morning bong, even trustees. M girls normally wear special restraints with attachment rings. You'll probably get your new set when they wipe our minds."

Jenetta replaced the restraints, telling herself, *Just for a little longer.*

"You have a beautiful face, 726. You'll probably be a duration girl."

"A what?"

"A duration girl. You know, at the resort. There're three different types of girls— hourly, daily, and duration. Hourly girls are available to any client on an hourly basis. The daily girls stay with the same client for a full day and duration girls remain with the same client for the duration of their stay. They're the most costly and they're treated the best. They get the nicest clothes, jewelry, and food, and also the most rest."

"How do you know all this?"

"From my trainer. She knew someone who had been there as a client many years ago and he told her all about it."

"You don't sound all that upset about going there."

"I'm not upset— *anymore.* Oh, I admit that I was at first. I've always been pretty strong-minded and independent, so I naturally rebelled, but I got shocked so many times that I lost count. Then slowly I just seemed to get used to the idea. They'll feed me and clothe me, and all I have to do is lie around and look pretty. And it will be so great to get out of this hole."

"Are you kidding? You'll still be a slave. Even if you don't have any work to do, they'll still tell you what to eat and when you can eat it, when to sleep and when to get up, what to wear and who you can be with. Is that a life?"

"It's not so bad. It could be worse; at least I'm going to be a regular."

"A regular? A regular what?"

"Regular sex. No serious kink, dominatrix, or masochism stuff?"

"Umm, what am I supposed to be?"

A pained expression came over 721's face and she hesitated for a second before saying, "I'm sorry, hon. You're going to be an M girl."

"An M girl? You used that term before. What's an M girl?"

"The big M, like in Sado-Masochism."

Jenetta felt her abdomen constrict. "How do you know?"

"Look in your closet."

Jenetta's eyes flicked to the closet and she hobbled over to examine the clothes.

"What? I see a lot of black leather, but that doesn't mean anything. They're trying to turn us into whores. Isn't this what whores typically wear?"

Moving behind Jenetta, 721 put her hands on her shoulders to comfort the seemingly younger woman. "Not exactly, hon. Look at this dress here," she said, pointing to one on the rack. "The sleeves are stitched solidly together in the back from the elbow down. When it's pulled up, your arms are trapped behind you. Once the front zipper is pulled up, even a Houdini couldn't get out of it on her own. And look at your boots. Twelve-centimeter heels every one, and they lace right up to the top of the thigh with rings attached every dozen centimeters on the inside surface so your legs can be easily secured. And although the company likes tight dresses, you don't have a single one that you can walk in. Look what it took for you just to get over to your closet. The company doesn't expect you to be walking very much because M girls spend most of their time tied to beds or suspended in restraints. I understand that the M girl rooms are outfitted like mini torture dungeons. The guest can do anything to you except brand you, cut you, or kill you. If they accidentally kill you, or even permanently disfigure you, they have to give the company the amount you would have earned in ten years of service. If the guest can't pay up, and I would bet the charges would be astronomically high, they become slaves themselves. Brandings or scarring from cuts are prorated depending on the amount of damage."

"I don't believe it! Arneu said I'd be too valuable, for too long. They wouldn't risk me getting killed or damaged and only receive the equivalent of ten years of service."

"The clothes in your closet say different, 726. My trainer told me that M girls fetch a considerably higher premium than regular girls. Probably because they need time to heal between customers."

Jenetta didn't respond for several seconds and then said quietly, "This has to be Arneu's revenge for me attacking him. And he did tell me they had performed DNA changes on me that would make me heal much faster than other people."

"There you go then. They probably also implanted thoughts that will make you love the pain. Pain will make you feel euphoric and you'll crave more. My trainer told me that M girls can't get enough, which is why so many are injured so badly. They keep goading their tormentors to hurt them."

"I'll feel better when I'm subjected to pain?" Jenetta said incredulously.

"That's what my trainer told me." Attempting to change the mood, 721 said brightly, "Now come on, let me see you put your face on again."

With 721 watching, Jenetta removed all the makeup she was wearing and applied new. As she worked, 721 taught her a few more small secrets about proper application. They continued talking afterwards about clothes and fashion until Bellis arrived to take 721 back to her cell.

"Wait, how do I get undressed?" Jenetta asked quickly as 721 started to leave. "I'm still wearing the restraints."

"Oh, the guard will release your restraints an hour before lights out. There's a timer built into your makeup table that begins when you're released. You'll have 30 minutes to undress and get ready for bed. You have to have the restraints back on when he returns or you get a level two shock. After they pick up your breakfast tray in the morning, you'll be released again and you'll have one hour to bathe and dress. You must have the restraints on again when the guard returns." Putting her hand lightly on Jenetta's arm, she said, "Good night, 726."

"Goodnight, 721. Thanks."

"You're welcome, hon. See ya."

Romeo came by her cell and released her restraints an hour before lights out as 721 had apprised. Just as he had done when he delivered her food, and again when he picked up her tray, he made a number of lewd comments and suggestive remarks concerning the way she looked. Jenetta had always ignored such flirtatious comments from men, but now she discovered they excited her. It had to be the result of the conditioning she was being subjected to. She silently vowed that Romeo would never suspect she was being affected in the slightest.

With her restraints released, Jenetta was able to undress, but she pressed the wrong button on the white controller and the corset started to tighten when she touched it against her body. She quickly pressed the other button because she didn't want the pain to set her off. She would need to remain completely in control if she was to escape from the detention center.

Quickly stripping off the clothes and putting on a teddy she found in the closet, she put the restraints back on before sitting down to remove the makeup. When Romeo returned, she hopped onto the circle and he solidified the bands. Her closet yielded a pillow, sheets, and a soft, thin blanket, and, for the first time since she'd been captured, she slept peacefully. The cot still wasn't anything like the temperature and firmness-controlled beds she'd always had on Earth and aboard ship, but the bedclothes made a world of difference.

*   *   *

After retrieving her breakfast tray the next morning, Hawkface released Jenetta's restraints. She peeled them off, removed the teddy, and gleefully hurried to the shower where she spent fifteen delightful minutes in the hot spray, then toweled off quickly. Once dry, she pulled on the panties and bra she had brought into the bathroom and went out to her cell to finish getting dressed.

Jenetta meticulously examined every outfit in the closet before selecting a black leather skirt with matching vest. For footwear, she chose a pair of knee-high black leather boots.

As with the shoes she had worn yesterday, the stiletto heels were at least twelve centimeters.

She began getting dressed by putting on the corset, but only tightened it a little at first. As she rolled her stockings on, she found that she had started to enjoy the sensuous caress of the gossamer material on her legs. She again wondered how many of the new sensations she was experiencing lately were the result of the 'therapy' she'd received so far. After attaching the garter belt and putting on the boots, she tightened the corset until her breathing became labored. Next came a black half-slip and then she wrapped the leather skirt around her. With a rear zipper that ran from the waist down to the bottom hem, she didn't have any trouble getting the zipper started because she only had to adjust the corset, but getting the zipper down over her tush and closing the skirt around her thighs was difficult. Once zipped, she could barely walk, but she found that by swinging her hips, she could take tiny steps.

The vest-like top did little to cover her natural attributes. As with all the clothes in the closet, her chest was prominently displayed, with her 'slave' identification clearly visible. After pulling on the required opera length gloves, she finished dressing by replacing the restraints.

There was still some time left, so she sat down to brush her hair and put on some makeup. She didn't apply it as heavily as 721 had, but it was much more pronounced than she would ever have considered before, and, when Hawkface came back to solidify her restraints, he actually entered the cell after he had secured her. He circled her twice as she stood stone-faced on the black position mark.

From behind her, he said, "Wow, you sure clean up nice." She felt the warmth of his breath as he put his head near hers and sniffed the sweet fragrances left in her hair and on her skin by the shampoo and soap. Then he extended his tongue and licked her neck from the top of her vest to her hairline in one slow motion. "You are *one hot chick*," he said breathlessly, as he finished.

Jenetta could hear the silent plea in his voice but kept her eyes focused straight ahead. She suddenly flinched her head a few centimeters and Hawkface jumped back a full meter. Naturally, he knew of her effective attack technique and her willingness to use it. Arneu hadn't been seen since the incident and the current rumor was that he was holed up in his rooms because his nose was the size of a cantaloupe.

Stepping close again, with his head to one side, Hawkface wrapped his arms around her and began massaging her breasts. In a voice dripping with lust and desire, he asked, "How do you like this, honey? What say we get it on? I could be real nice to you if you were nice to me."

Jenetta felt her pulse quickening and knew she was becoming aroused by the physical contact. As she struggled to keep her breathing regular, she asked evenly, "Are you looking to get tossed out an airlock without a spacesuit?"

Hawkface stopped, then looked at her with a saturnine expression. His lips twisted with contempt as he stormed from the cell and locked the door. Jenetta was afraid he was going to leave her secured, but after a minute the slot opened and she was released. Once the slot had closed again, she allowed herself a little shudder and took several deep breaths to shake off the sparks of passion that were coursing through her. Hawkface held absolutely no appeal for her so the undesired response *must* be the result of the conditioning.

Knowing she must make good her escape before they were taken to the transport ship and placed in stasis sleep, Jenetta spent most of the morning pacing around her cell, working on her plan. She felt she had solved the problem of how she would get out of her cell, but there was still so much she needed to know with little chance of learning it while she was stuck in the detention center. The success of the escape would depend upon having information about the layout of the base, as well as coming up with a plan for commandeering a tug, or at least a shuttle. Her chances were slim enough without wandering aimlessly about the base trying to find usable, unmanned, and unguarded transportation. Then there was the matter of food and water. She knew GA regulations required space tugs and shuttles to carry a week's worth of emergency rations for a crew of four, but the Raiders made their own rules. She had no way of knowing if they subscribed to the basic rules of ship safety that everyone else was *required* to follow. As it happened, part of the information she needed would come to her in a most unexpected way.

A little before noon, Hawkface returned to her cell. She was secured, gagged, and then taken to the anteroom where she was fastened to the overhead bar before it was raised so high she was barely able to touch the deck with the tips of her boots.

"What's she doing here?" one of the other guards asked.

"She gave me some lip earlier and I thought I'd let her watch us eat lunch so she could see what's she's missing. Also, it gives us something to look at. She's a looker when she's fixed up. What a body! Look at that skirt. It's so tight I thought I'd have to carry her up here. She can't move her legs more than a dozen centimeters at a time, even when she swivels her hips."

"You're a fool," the other guard hissed. "You're coming damn close to crossing the line regarding abuse of prisoners."

"I'm not abusing her. I'm not even touching her. I'm just teaching her that she shouldn't give lip to the guards. Call it an educational session."

The first guard seemed about to argue, but the food elevator arrived with their lunch. In minutes, the four guards on duty had collected in the anteroom to attack the fried chicken, mashed potatoes with gravy, and corn on the cob. Dessert was lemon meringue pie, and, when Jenetta's stomach starting rumbling loud enough to be heard over the sounds of the gourmandizing, a couple of the guards laughed heartily.

As the guards were finishing lunch, another entered the cellblock from the outside corridor.

"Hey, you guys didn't leave me much," the newcomer said.

"Run up to the kitchen and get some more," Hawkface said. "We didn't think you were coming back before the shift ended."

"Ah, I got roped into working security at an operations briefing. There's something really big going down. Most every single ship that operates out of this port is here and the ship's officers are all attending meetings in the conference center."

"What's up?" another guard said.

"I don't know exactly, but I heard that every warship in good fighting condition is being readied to leave the day after tomorrow, including the two new ships at airlocks 1-Sierra and 1-Tango."

"The battleships?"

"Yup, the ones we stole from right under the noses of the stupid Spaccs. The word is that they're space ready, provisioned, and fully armed."

Jenetta's ears had picked up every word and she knew immediately that this was the final piece of information she needed. Everything would be in confusion as last minute preparations for ship departures were being wrapped up. Most people would be exhausted from overwork while others would be having parties tonight since key personnel probably wouldn't be allowed to imbibe alcohol on the night before leaving port. With a major operation in the works, other raids would have been canceled, so the tugs and small ships necessary for the support of ancillary and cleanup operations should be sitting empty and idle. The situation was ready-made for an escape attempt.

* * *

An hour before dinner, as the first shift was preparing to go off duty, Jenetta was finally returned to her cell. After the guard had locked the door and released her, she worked her jaw and arms to remove the stiffness. She had gotten sufficiently used to the skirt after wearing it all day that she paid little attention to the peculiar way it forced her to walk as she hobbled around the cell working out the details of her escape and planning the timing. Although she could have raised the rear zipper to give herself more freedom, leaving the skirt looking more like a tourniquet than a garment was an integral part of her plan.

When she heard the dinner bong, Jenetta moved immediately to the circle. Shortly, a guard opened the viewing slot
in her cell door, looked in, then put his hand to the window
and secured her before unlocking the cell door and carrying in
her meal. Since the head-butting incident, they'd normally just
backed out and released her, but this time the guard circled
her several times. It was Romeo, the small guard who had
used the food elevator to get the two apple pies, then called
her a bitch and laughed about her not getting any. Her boots
made her inches taller.

"I heard about this outfit— and about you spending the
afternoon in the anteroom. I'm real sorry to have missed that.
They let you down just before we came on duty. Say, how
would you like some fresh apple pie tonight? All you have to
do is drop to your knees, pull down my pants, and give me
some relief." He snickered as he flicked a finger against the
tautness of her skirt where it covered her thighs. "That is, if
you can even get down on your knees with that skirt on."
When no answer came, he said, "No?"

Jenetta kept her face composed and stared straight ahead.
Failing to get a rise from her, Romeo patted her ass a couple
of times and then left, locking the door behind him.

Looking in the viewing slot, he said, "I should leave you
secured and make you eat while lying on the floor. That
would take you down a peg, Miss High and Mighty." His
eyes pulled away from the slot to be replaced by his hand
with the controller; then the slot slammed shut.

Released, Jenetta bent over, picked up the tray, and carried
it to her cot. The meal was just rice and vegetables but she ate
it greedily. She'd been famished ever since she'd watched the
guards gobble down the veritable banquet that was their
normal lunchtime fare.

When she had finished the meager repast, Jenetta very
precisely placed the tray in front of the door. She'd been
calculating exactly where it needed to be for each guard since
they all picked up the trays differently. Satisfied, she retrieved the controller from beneath the toilet bowl and tested it by
changing the bands from solid to flexible. It still worked! She

next unzipped her skirt all the way to her waist to remove the half-slip. Letting it drop to the floor, she kicked the slip into the closet and re-solidified her restraint bands.

For the next fifteen minutes, she practiced securing and releasing herself while standing on the circle with the controller concealed in her right hand. The small black controller, hidden as much as possible in her black-gloved hand while being held against her skirt and vest, should go unnoticed if Romeo followed his normal routine. She hoped he wouldn't get amorous again. That could wreck her entire plan.

Hearing the single bong indicating Romeo would be starting to collect the trays, Jenetta's heart started pounding in her chest so loudly that she thought he would surely hear it. This was an all or nothing plan—a chance for freedom, or a life of slavery, sexual abasement, and servitude as a mindless nympho. Luck had been on her side before and she hoped she had just a little bit left.

Romeo finally reached her cell after some fifteen minutes and looked in. Jenetta was standing on the circle with her wrists against the belt. Concealed in her right hand was the small controller. Both hands were carefully positioned against her skirt to hold it tight against her. With a cursory glance, it should appear to be zipped even though it was open to the waistband in the back. Romeo's face disappeared from the viewing window and his hand appeared with the controller just before Jenetta felt her restraints lock. As the hand with the controller retracted from the slot and the slot was closed, Jenetta used her own controller to release herself. She held her hands where they were and waited patiently.

Romeo unlocked the door and shoved it open unceremoniously. Apparently, her earlier disinterest had hurt his ego enough to ensure that he wouldn't make any new overtures tonight. He simply bent over to get the tray.

Chapter Sixteen
~ August 10th, 2267 ~

Regardless of what else Jenetta might have thought about Romeo, she couldn't fault his reflexes. She had shifted her weight to her left leg as the cell door began to open and then stood motionless until his hands touched the tray. Her leg was a blur as she drew it back for the kick, but he saw the movement and tried to straighten up. As quick as he was, he just wasn't quite quick enough, and his upward movement only served to help Jenetta. Her booted foot caught him under the chin with a force that surprised even her. Combined with the momentum from his own effort to rise, he lifted completely into the air, flipped over, and came down obliquely on his head and neck. Jenetta heard the sickening sound of vertebrae shattering, but Romeo also grunted as he landed, so Jenetta jumped over to him, prepared to put the stiletto heel of her boot through his throat if he moved. He didn't. After a few anxious seconds, she pulled back her leg and bent to feel for a pulse. Romeo's days of fondling his baton were over.

The flip had sent Romeo sprawling partway into the corridor so Jenetta swiftly dragged him back into the cell. She removed the thick brass key from the outer lock, checked the corridor, then closed the door quietly. She pulled his stun pistol from his holster and set it on the floor where she could get to it quickly before removing her restraints, skirt, vest, corset, and boots. She would need unrestricted movement for the rest of the night and her company-provided clothes were definitely designed with the opposite objective in mind. The only loose garments available to her were those belonging to Romeo.

As Jenetta stared down at the guard's unmoving body, the horrific, albeit necessary act she had just perpetrated replayed in her head, but time was limited so she shook herself mentally and bent to unbuckle Romeo's belt and unzip his trousers. The mind will sometimes employ black humor as a defensive mechanism, so as she worked, Jenetta quipped, "I hope you're happy, Romeo. You finally got me to pull down your pants."

After stripping the guard to his undershorts, Jenetta began pulling the uniform on. Fortunately, Romeo was among the shortest guards in the detail, being only a couple of inches taller than Jenetta. His shoes were several sizes too large, but she shoved his socks up into the toes and they were usable. She had to roll the bottom of the trouser legs up, but luckily the belt was the adjustable kind so she was able to tighten it down to fit her smaller waist. The final uniform adjustment was the shirtsleeves and rolling the cuffs several times proved adequate.

Removal of the slave collar was her final task and, as she examined the black controller, she located a small flap that concealed two buttons marked lock and constrict. She aimed it at herself, pressed the lock button, then reached up and tugged on the collar. To her almost unrestrained delight, it stretched easily. Pulling it out, up, and over her head, she was free! At least partially.

Eager to begin the next phase of her escape, Jenetta picked up the stun pistol, moved to the cell door, and cautiously peered out. Nothing was moving in the part of the corridor she could see and no noises could be heard. She pulled the door open quickly and stepped out, pistol at the ready. All the cell doors appeared to be locked. She hadn't really expected to see anyone else here since regulations prohibited having more than one cell in a cellblock open at any one time. Still, she breathed a slight sigh of relief for having reached this point and was invigorated with new energy to proceed.

Taking a deep breath and then releasing it, she hurried quietly to the door that led to the anteroom. The door made no sound as she unlocked it and opened it sufficiently to peer out. She had expected to find at least one guard lounging there, but the room was empty. That had to mean they were either in the other cellblock corridors or the head. There wasn't any light coming from under the door to the privy, so that narrowed the choices to the cellblocks, unless someone had reason to sit in the dark. She checked the small lavatory just to be sure it was clear before proceeding. It was empty, as she'd expected, but she couldn't afford to depend on simple deduction and assumption. She couldn't afford any surprises at her back.

She'd been housed in cellblock C, so she walked now to the door leading to cellblock A. She was going to have to open every door eventually and this was as good a place to start as any. Taking two deep breaths, she pushed open the door.

The guard for the block was just backing out of a cell with a tray. He never even knew what hit him as Jenetta fired the pistol. He pitched forward, back into the cell, the tray and dishware clattering loudly to the deck. His unmoving legs protruded into the corridor so Jenetta figured he was down for the count. She hoped the stun pistols were as effective as the ones used by Space Command. A full blast from one of them would knock a person out for anywhere from four to eight hours. She half expected the prisoner in the cell to cry out, but, since everyone was punished whenever they spoke, the silence was entirely understandable. The prisoner was no doubt secured and unsure of what was going on, but Jenetta couldn't take the time to investigate further at that moment.

"It would be nice to know how many guards are on duty," she said to herself, very quietly, as she moved to the cellblock B door. Her best estimate on the number of guards was four or possibly five. It was best to estimate conservatively, she knew. "Two down and three to go," she said before quickly pushing open the door to peer in. There was no sign of any movement in B and the cell doors were all closed, so she gently let the door close again and moved to cellblock D.

She could definitely hear noises coming from the cellblock as she readied herself and then pushed the door open. Rosewood was walking towards her pushing a cart and he spotted her immediately but didn't realize at first glance that she wasn't another guard since she was wearing a uniform. As Jenetta brought her pistol up, he froze for an instant, then started to back away, tugging desperately at the pistol in his holster. Jenetta's shot hit him dead center and he collapsed backwards into a seemingly lifeless pile. She closed the door silently, muttering to herself, "Three down, two to go."

Cellblock E was clear, so Jenetta moved to the door of cellblock F. Just as she began to push open the door, the doors to cellblocks G and H both opened and guards pushing food carts emerged. Jenetta's heart couldn't possibly have beat any faster or harder as she crouched down against the partially open door leading to F block, trying to make herself as small as possible while she waited for both guards to present themselves as clear targets. The guard from cellblock G spotted her first and she fired into his chest. As he was falling, she swung the pistol to fire at the guard coming from cellblock H. He was turning to sprint for the cover of the cellblock so the blast hit him in the middle of his back and he dropped like a meteor caught in a gravity well.

"And that's five," Jenetta muttered as she slumped weakly against the doorframe of cellblock F. The adrenaline that had sustained her since the arrival of Romeo in her cell was beginning to drain from her system. With the guards unconscious, she could now move onto the next phase of her plan—freeing the other prisoners.

She was still collapsed against the doorframe a half-minute later when the door was suddenly pulled wide open. As her support disappeared, she spilled onto her back into the cellblock entranceway and found herself looking up at the guard named Bellis! He was as surprised as she for a second but then began to reach for her. Her response was to raise the pistol, but he was fast. He halted his movement, shifted his weight, and aimed a kick at her hand. The pistol went flying towards the other side of the anteroom but not before she'd managed to get off her shot. He seemed to totter for a second and then fell, unconscious, atop her. She grunted as his full weight landed on her prone body and she lay there for a few seconds to get her wind back before pushing him off and getting up.

"And that's six," she said as she shook her hand to relieve the stinging sensation cause by the force of his kick. "I sure hope he's the last."

After retrieving the pistol that Bellis had kicked from her hand, she quickly checked each of the cellblock corridors again to make sure there were no other guards still feeding prisoners. The cellblocks appeared clear. To ensure that no guards were enjoying the services of a female captive eager for better food or treatment, she checked every cell door in blocks B through H. All were locked. Lastly, she rechecked each of the downed guards except the one in cellblock A; she already knew she had a potential problem there. All appeared to be sleeping soundly, except, of course, for the one in her cell.

"Okay, Carver," she said aloud to herself, "let's see just what kind of trouble we're going to have in cellblock A."

Pushing open the door to the block cautiously, she peered in. The guard's legs were still sticking out of the cell, just as she had left him. Staying as close as possible to the wall on that side, Jenetta moved down the corridor, checking each cell door as she went until she was adjacent to the cell opening.

Moving her head just far enough to see that the guard's stun pistol was now missing from his holster, Jenetta's mind started racing. She knew she couldn't enter the cell and risk being shot and she couldn't just leave because her escape plan included bringing all of the prisoners with her. She pulled back and said in a loud, commanding voice, "This is Jenetta Carver of Galactic Space Command. Throw out the stun pistol and you'll be released."

She was hugging the wall with her pistol at the ready when she heard a familiar voice call out from the cell, "Captain?"

"Gunny?" Jenetta said in genuine surprise.

"Aye, Captain. It's me."

Jenetta released her breath and peered slowly into the cell. Gunny Rondell was lying on his side, aiming the stun pistol at the doorway, the full weight of his upper torso crushing the unconscious guard's face and head into the rough stippled surface of the plasticrete deck. His restraints were still engaged so his ankles were locked together and his wrists were pinned to his waist. His only garment was his boxer shorts. He appeared clean, but weeks of beard growth covered his normally clean-shaven face. His limited mobility had allowed him to reach the stun pistol, but he hadn't yet been able to get to the guard's controller and free himself.

Jenetta holstered her pistol as Gunny relaxed his hand. Just knowing that he was still alive buoyed her spirits immeasurably and seeing his familiar face made her heart soar with delight. Similar feelings of relief were coursing through Gunny at that moment.

"That looks like a very uncomfortable position, Gunny," Jenetta said casually as she moved into the doorway and leaned against the frame, folding her arms in front of her.

"Aye, Captain, it is, but at least I've found myself a nice cushion to rest on. Sorry that I can't come to attention."

"You're also out of uniform," she chided facetiously.

"Yes ma'am. Sorry, ma'am. I seem to have misplaced mine somewhere. May I say that yours is quite attractive, although your tailor seems to have gotten the measurements wrong."

"Really?" Jenetta said, dropping her arms and looking down at her clothing in mock seriousness as she pulled the abundant material in the trousers outwards. She grinned as she glanced down at Gunny. "He told me this was the new look." Jenetta reached into a pocket and pulled out her controller. Aiming it at Gunny, she released his restraints and then made them flexible.

Gunny stretched his arms and, as he stood up, he said, "Thank you, Captain."

"One more step, Gunny."

Aiming the controller at him again, she pushed the lock button that would make the collar flexible.

"All set, Gunny, you can remove all the bands now."

"Really?" His hands went to the collar first and he pulled it over his head. As he rubbed at the red discoloration on his neck where the collar had been, he said, "Ah, it feels so good to have that off. I thought I'd go crazy if they shocked me one more time."

"I know what you mean. The pain is incredible."

Gunny removed the rest of the bands before asking, "Has Space Command taken over the station, Captain?"

"No, I've just decided we've visited here long enough. Have you noticed that their hospitality leaves so *much* to be desired?"

Gunny smiled for the first time in weeks. "Aye, Captain. And the food makes you long for ice-cold Marine field rations. How many in the escape party, ma'am?"

"So far, just you and me. But I want to take every captive with us, at least those that will go."

"You think some will want to stay in this miserable hell-hole?"

Jenetta took a deep breath and then released it slowly. "I don't know, Gunny. I do know they've been brainwashing the women and some are already resigned to becoming pleasure slaves at resorts in the Uthlaro Dominion. They may refuse to leave with us."

"Well, I'm ready to leave as soon as you give the order, ma'am."

"First I need you to collect all the sleeping guards, strip them to their shorts, and lock them in this cell. I'm sure one of their uniforms will fit you, but I don't know how long they'll be unconscious, so lock them up before you start trying on clothes."

"Aye, Captain. Should I put my restraints on this one?"

"No, it's possible we'll need all the restraints later. Make sure you account for every controller and jail key the guards are carrying and hang onto them personally."

"Aye, Captain."

While Gunny was rounding up the guards, Jenetta sat down at the computer console in the anteroom. Calling up a list of prisoners, she found that Crewman Browne was in block H, cell 4. Entering that cellblock, she peered in the window slot of the cell. She confirmed that there was a man in the cell, but she wasn't sure if it was Browne since he was lying on the cot with his back to her. Deciding not to just enter the cell because he might get up and swing at her before he realized who it was, she put her mouth to the slot and said, "Prisoner, move onto the circle."

Getting up slowly, the man moved onto the circle as instructed. Jenetta aimed the controller into the window and secured his restraints before unlocking the door and stepping in. The man was wearing weeks of scraggly beard growth, but there was no mistaking the streak of white hair that extended from his forehead. Browne looked terrible and smelled even worse. Much worse than she had before she had taken her first shower, if that was possible. Obviously, he hadn't learned that his bathroom was available after three days.

"Crewman Browne, if you've had quite enough of this hedonistic lifestyle, I'm ready to return to the *Vordoth*. I expect you to accompany me. Of course, you're free to return here afterwards if you wish."

"Captain?" he asked cautiously.

"Yes," she said, grinning.

"How…?"

"It's not important right now. I'm going to release you and then we're getting out of here." Jenetta unlocked the restraints and made them flexible, then did the same for the collar. "Okay, you're a free man once again. You can remove all the bands."

The first one to go was the collar. "They'll never get one of those on me again," he said as he rubbed his neck. "I'll kill myself first. What about Gunny?"

"I've already freed him. He's carrying the unconscious guards into the cell where he was housed. Why don't you give him a hand and then pick out a uniform for yourself. He's in cellblock A."

"Aye, Captain. Um— is it a problem if the guards wake up with some bruises?"

"It's certainly not a problem with me."

"I mean some seriously *bad* bruises?"

"I'd be quite disappointed if they didn't, Mr. Browne. Just don't hurt yourself. I need you and Gunny healthy."

Browne smiled dangerously. "Aye, Captain, I'll be *most* careful."

While Browne helped Gunny, Jenetta returned to the computer console in the anteroom and downloaded a list of all the prisoners into a holo-magazine cylinder she found. Then she started hunting through the computer's menu screens. There was a wealth of information there, but security blocks prevented her from accessing most of it, so she resorted to hacking tricks and worked her way into the database files. She could get the raw data files, but it would take a computer to reassemble them into usable form. She recalled that while restrained in the anteroom, she'd seen a small box of data rings on the desk. Looking through the drawers now, she found it, but the eight rings in the box were of the low-density variety so they wouldn't hold much data. She touched one to the media drawer spindle and saw that it contained only music. Checking another, she found it also contained only music. Without checking further, she began overwriting the music tracks with gigabytes of database information. As each ring reached its capacity, she replaced it with another. While the files were being downloaded, Jenetta added the general floor plans for the station to the holo-magazine cylinder. In a station this large, people could get lost easily so the floor layouts weren't password protected.

Jenetta was slipping the tiny box of data-laden rings into a side pocket when Gunny and Browne returned to the anteroom carrying the extra clothes, stun pistols, and personal items of the guards. Each had outfitted himself with a uniform after completing their task. There were three complete uniforms among the things placed on a side table.

"All the guards are locked up in my old cell, Captain," Gunny said, "except the one in cellblock C. There didn't seem to be much point in locking him in."

"Yes, I had to take him out without benefit of a stun pistol. I guess I hit him a little too hard."

Browne's eyebrows rose in surprise and he said, with a grin on his face and admiration in his voice, "You did that, Captain?"

"Yes, I needed his stun pistol to effect my escape. Once I had that, the others were easy. Only Bellis, the one that was lying in the doorway of cellblock F, managed to put up a fight. I thought the prisoner in cellblock A where the guard had fallen into the cell might give me a problem, so I was relieved to learn the prisoner was Gunny."

"Shouldn't we get moving before someone comes in, Captain?" Gunny said.

"No, we have to stay here for a few more hours yet. I've learned it's highly unusual for anyone to come down here after the dinner hour. And, given the current operational status of the station, it's unlikely anyone will be bringing in any new prisoners. I want to study the station floor plans for a few minutes and then we'll start releasing prisoners. Gunny, why don't you look through the desk drawers in here to see if there's anything we can use? Mr. Browne, may I suggest you take a quick shower?"

"Shower? I'd love to," he said smiling.

"Speaking for Gunny and myself, we'd greatly appreciate it also. Gunny can show you how to open the bathroom door in my old cell. Be sure to don the shower cap and goggles before activating the parasite removal ray."

"Parasite removal ray?" Gunny echoed.

"The ray activated by the buttons next to the mirror."

"There weren't any buttons next to the mirror in my cell."

"Oh—," Jenetta said. "Well, maybe that's good. The ray can destroy your eyes in a heartbeat if you don't know that you have to wear the goggles. Mr. Browne, the shower cap and goggles are hanging on the hook next to the mirror.

Cover your hair completely, and make sure your eyes are well sealed by the goggles, then simultaneously depress the buttons once. It only takes a second. The shampoo in the shower stall will clean any parasites from your hair."

"Okay, Captain."

As Browne showered, Gunny went through all the desks, finding half a dozen stun batons to add to their assembled arsenal. Jenetta had plenty of time to study all the floor layouts and plan their escape route.

When Browne emerged from the cellblock, he was squeaky clean and devoid of beard, but obvious distress shrouded his face. Gunny asked what was wrong and Browne leaned in to whisper something. Gunny immediately guffawed. Browne's facial expression became even more pained.

"You look much better with all that hair off your face, Mr. Browne," Jenetta said.

Browne smiled sheepishly. "Yes, captain. I feel a bit naked though. Down below I mean."

Jenetta understood exactly what he meant. She smiled and nodded knowingly, but then couldn't resist a bit of teasing. "I was informed that men prefer it that way," she said.

When Browne's eyes widened and his jaw dropped, Jen grinned and said, "Don't worry. It'll all grow out again, very quickly."

"Yes ma'am. I'm just thinking about what I'll tell folks— about my bare chest, underarms, and legs I mean."

Still smiling, she said, "The truth, or a close approximation, would probably be the best response. Simply tell them it was removed as part of the Raider delousing procedures while you were their prisoner."

When Jenetta was ready to start releasing the prisoners, she posted Browne at the main entrance to the detention center.

"Don't let anyone get past you. Shoot them if necessary. If that door is opened even a millimeter, the station's security alarms will go off and we'll be neck deep in security people within minutes."

"Aye, Captain. No one will get past me." Browne's face reflected his determination. He adopted a stance with his arms crossed and the stun pistol in a slightly raised position, aimed at the ceiling, to show everyone he meant business.

Starting with the women prisoners, Jenetta made each move to the circle before locking their restraints and entering their cell. The first captive to be freed was 721.

"Hi, Leah," Jenetta said to her, softly.

The woman just stared at her intently without saying a word. Jenetta wondered if she still remembered her real name.

"It's me, Jenetta Carver." Jenetta pulled down the zipper of the uniform so 721 could see her number. Leah stared down at the imprint, then looked up at Jen's face.

"Is it you, 726?"

"Yes, but I prefer Jenetta— Jen to my friends."

"You're a guard?" she said, puzzled.

"No, never. We just— borrowed— these uniforms for our escape," Jenetta said as she unlocked 721's restraints.

"Escape?" A look of fear came over Leah's face.

"Yes, some of us are leaving this place and I'd like you to come with us."

"No. There is no escape," she said quietly. "They're everywhere."

"Listen to me, Leah," Jenetta said a little more forcefully. "We're going home and I want you to come with us. Will you come?"

"Home?" Leah's voice made the concept sound so foreign.

"Yes, will you come?"

The woman put her hand to her throat and stroked the collar as she began shaking her head. "I can't. I belong here. I belong to them. They own me. They won't let me leave."

"Please come. I— I need you to help me with my makeup and clothing."

"Oh— okay 726. I'll help you."

As Jenetta reached up and removed the collar, Leah began to tremble and sob. The life she had grown to embrace as her immutable future was crumbling too quickly. She needed something to replace the concept of the stable, albeit horrific, future.

"It's okay, Leah," Jenetta said in a soothing voice. "You're going to be just fine. We'll be leaving very soon. I can't wait to introduce you to all my wonderful friends on the *Vordoth*. You'll love it there. We just need to speak to a few more people here, first. Come out into the anteroom with us."

That was how it went with most of the women. All had been there much longer than Jenetta and they had accepted their fate, mainly as a result of the psychotherapy. Having abandoned all hope of a life other than as a pleasure slave, the prospect of leaving actually terrified them. Jenetta suspected it might take years for the full damage to be undone.

The situation with the men was completely different. The company hadn't wasted any time conditioning them because most were destined for hard labor or dangerous jobs and the company wanted them strong of mind, knowing the collars would control their rebellious nature. Jenetta secured each prisoner in his cell before entering to explain that she had organized an escape. She told him that she would take him with them if he agreed to follow her orders without question until they were safely out of Raider space and back at a Space Command base. Facing the prospect of a life of slavery other-wise, all agreed immediately. They were then released and sent to join the others in the anteroom.

Two of the prisoners turned out to be the men who had gone missing during the initial attack on the *Vordoth* because they had been assisting Captain Lentz during his 'exam-ination' of the stern-most laser section. Gunny, working with Jenetta as she released prisoners, had an ebullient reunion with each man. On Jenetta's orders, he immediately took crewmen Deitrich and Higgiby out to outfit them with guard uniforms.

In determining the order of release, Jenetta had used the list downloaded into the holo-magazine cylinder. She knew the more dominant personalities would be the most difficult to control, so she'd left the ship's officers for last. When all prisoners had been freed, she joined them in the anteroom. The male prisoners were standing around in small clusters and all were giving a scowling Browne, who stood defiantly in front of the entrance door with pistol still raised, a wide berth. The women were huddled in one large group near the door to cellblock D, quietly seeking support from one another as they tried to cope with the situation.

The eight cellblocks, with their combined 160 cells, had yielded 53 captives, including Jenetta. A stealthy exit would be difficult for a group that large, so timing and coordination would be imperative. Jenetta climbed up onto the desk closest to the main entrance to address the group. From there she could see everyone in the room.

"As I've already told you, I'm Captain Jenetta Carver. I'm a Space Command officer and I've had just about enough of this place, so I'm getting out, tonight. You've all agreed to follow my orders without question, so I'm willing to take you with me. I warn you now that I won't tolerate any dissension before we're clear of Raider space and reach a Space Command base. After that, you'll be free to go your own way. We're currently imprisoned deep in a Raider stronghold and for this escape to be successful you must do what I say when I say it. Is that clear?"

In response, one of the men near the door to cellblock F spoke up. "If you're a Space Command Officer, what are you doing here?"

"I was on a reconnaissance of this installation. We managed to infiltrate the port and had just completed a camera sweep of the asteroid's interior when we were detected and imprisoned."

"Then it sounds like you're not much of an officer if you allowed yourself to be captured."

Staring at the man, Jenetta said, "You're Captain Starnos of the freighter Nova Dawn, aren't you?"

"Aye, that's my name and ship."

"And you allowed *yourself* to be captured, didn't you?"

Starnos let anger dictate his response when he realized she had turned his own question into an accusation of *his* abilities. "We were outnumbered and outgunned by Raiders! It was either surrender or die!"

"Meaning that being captured isn't *really* a good measurement of leadership skills after all?"

Gunny Rondell shouted out, "Captain Carver has been my captain during two ship engagements with the Raiders. In both instances, we were outsized and outgunned. But when the space dust settled, the Raider ship had been destroyed, the Raiders were all dead, and we suffered no loss of life."

Gunny's outburst seemed to infuriate Starnos further, but the rest of the group was quiet for a few seconds and then started speaking among themselves. Jenetta let them talk. It was better that the issue of command be resolved now rather than after they left the detention center. After perhaps twenty seconds, one of the men said, "I'll follow you, Captain. Just tell me what you want me to do."

A chorus of voices began to agree with the man who had just spoken, but then Starnos shouted from the back, "Now hold on just a minute, girly. Why should we follow *your* orders? We appreciate that you freed us from our cells and all, but if it's all the same to you, my first mate and I will find our own way from here on out." To the assemblage at-large he said obstreperously, "Anyone here is welcome to join *my* group. *I* can get you out safely."

The group parted as people tried to distance themselves from the obvious imminent confrontation.

"It's not all the same to me," Jenetta said calmly. "We can't have multiple escape groups running around. If one gets spotted, this entire space station will go on alert and that would jeopardize all our chances."

"I'm not following any orders given by a child," Starnos said haughtily. "Especially not any from a little girl."

"You agreed before I released you to follow my orders without question."

Captain Starnos scowled as he and his first mate moved towards Jenetta. The overweight officer looked a ridiculous sight with his large stomach protruding over the waistband of his boxer shorts, but Jenetta knew just how dangerous the situation was.

Chapter Seventeen

~ August 11th, 2267 ~

Starnos and his first mate continued to advance towards Jenetta until they were within two meters of her. "That was then and I was wearing that damned collar. Things look a lot different now and I'm sure I can do better on my own."

Jenetta knew Starnos would never adhere to previous promises. In just the time it takes to blink, she raised the pistol she'd been holding hidden in her right hand behind the folds of the overly large uniform pants and shot him in the chest. Before his body had even begun to fall, she shifted the pistol and fired into the chest of the first mate. Both men fell backward to the deck and lay there unmoving. The room had been quiet before the shooting, but not even normal respiratory sounds could be heard afterward. It was as if everyone feared to breathe lest they become a target.

"Captain Starnos and his first mate will not be joining us on our trip tonight," Jenetta announced in a chilling voice after a few seconds. Enunciating each word loudly and clearly, she added, "Does anyone else expect to have a problem following my orders— to— the— letter?"

None of the wide-eyed throng said a word.

"Good," Jenetta said after a few more seconds of complete silence. "Gunny, take a couple of men and put Starnos and his mate back into cells and lock them in. They can sleep off the effects of the stun and try their own escape some other day."

A soft murmur of whispering voices slowly filled the void of silence caused by the shooting. Jenetta waited until Gunny and the others had returned before starting again.

"Okay, listen up everyone. We haven't been rushing yet because we have a secure location with little fear of discovery before 0500— but once we leave here, things will have to move along at a rapid pace. We can't afford to sit for too long in any one place and we can't afford to be seen. If we are seen, we have to treat that individual as a threat and neutralize him or her, whether that means using a stun weapon or— more lethal means.

"I want the men to divide into three groups. First, over on my right, I want every male who has had military service. In the middle, I want male non-military ship's officers, engineers, astrogators or bridge personnel, and cargo handlers. All other males move over to my left. The women should remain where they are."

Over the next hour, Jenetta spoke to each of the men, learning his experiences and skills. She knew the women would be undependable until their conditioning had been reversed. She set up teams for special functions and handed out the remaining uniform and weapons. Each team understood its function and the overall plan. The restraints had been collected as they were removed and put into pillowcases. Two people were made responsible for seeing that the lightweight restraints were brought along with the escaping captives.

"We're almost ready to go," Jenetta finally announced. "We can only fit four to six people in the food elevator at one time so it'll take a number of trips. Mr. Jergen, you're in charge of the elevator loading. You understand that everyone *must* be transported within fifty-six minutes or the sterilization process will kill everyone after that time. We don't have time to waste. Everyone has been assigned a position number for his or her elevator trip. If anyone balks, load the next one instead. When you get to the end, if someone you had to skip still refuses to go, stun them and leave them here. We don't have time to wait for them to screw up their courage. Understand?"

Jergen nodded. "Yes, Captain. Do I have to stun them?"

"Yes. If they're just left here and they manage to open the regular exit door, they'll set off security alarms and put the entire base on alert. Although there are no cameras in the detention center, the same is not true of the corridors on this level. I've seen plenty of them when I've been taken to the medical section, so the food elevator is the only possible escape route."

"I understand, Captain."

Addressing the entire group, Jenetta said, "The choices are to come with us or be stunned and remain here. Once we leave this room, I won't have time for questions or discussions. Anyone failing to follow orders immediately will be stunned and left behind. The stun effects should wear off after four to six hours. We'll all be long gone by then, free, and well on our way to a Space Command base, but if you awaken before the security people find you and imprison you again, you can follow whatever escape plan you wish. Everyone understand?"

A lot of people nodded, and some said, "Yes, Captain."

"Okay, as soon as everyone is upstairs, we'll move to the locker room down the corridor from the kitchen. Hopefully, we'll be able to find enough clothes for each person. Remember, once we enter the elevator there is to be no more talking except for absolutely essential communications. And that includes whispering as well. Make no unnecessary sounds. Our lives depend on maintaining absolute silence.

"It's now midnight and I expect the majority of station personnel will be asleep, although there will probably be a small staff working in the kitchen operating the automated equipment that prepares foods such as bread and bakery items. There will also be at least some people eating meals since a station like this naturally operates on a twenty-four-hour basis. We have just five hours to get clear of this base because at 0500 the next shift's security personnel come to this detention center."

At one minute past midnight, Jenetta entered the code to disable the sterilization process in the elevator. Gunny had found a slab of ham steak on one of the guard's dinner trays and it was put onto the floor of the elevator against the rear wall. As long as that remained there, intact, Jergen would know it was safe to continue sending people up. Jenetta assigned Deitrich to relieve Browne at the detention center entrance.

Gunny and Browne took the front two positions in the elevator, with Jenetta and an officer from a freighter, Lieutenant Commander Hugh Michaels, just behind them. Michaels, whose jet-black hair was turning prematurely gray at the temples, was a former Space Command officer. Two years earlier he had taken a job with a freight-hauling company after retiring with twenty years service. He had been first officer aboard a ship captured several months ago. Most of the crew had been killed during the takeover and he was anxious for some payback, but his training would keep him in check. His two years of separation from active service hadn't led to any sloppy habits and he was still fit and trim. Deep brown eyes stared out from a handsome face chiseled from stone as he stooped to squeeze his six-foot, two-inch frame into the food elevator.

The sixty-second ride up to the kitchen seemed to take forever. Knowing they could wind up as a pile of dust on the elevator floor if Jenetta's information about disabling the sterilization sweep was incorrect kept each of them sweating, despite their calm appearance. But they made it without a problem and the elevator door opened to reveal a wide corridor with dozens of large, empty food carts lining one wall. The wall with the elevator opening contained several other elevator doors as well, each bearing a sign indicating what section of the habitat it serviced. There wasn't anyone in sight, but they heard a lot of noise coming from their right.

"That's the kitchen, obviously," Jenetta said in a whisper, looking at the floor plan she had downloaded. "We want to go to the left."

Closing the elevator door, Gunny sent it back down. Less than three minutes later the next group appeared. After that, another four or five people arrived near the kitchen every three minutes. When they had a sufficient force at the elevator opening, Jenetta and Gunny went to scout ahead, easily finding the locker room. Not encountering any lingering staff, they returned to the elevator.

By then there were more than twenty-five people in the corridor by the elevator, most of them clad in only their underwear, so Jenetta and Gunny escorted all but Michaels and Browne to the locker room.

"Find something that fits as quickly as you can," Jenetta whispered loudly, once they were inside. "A uniform would be better, but kitchen clothing will do."

Jenetta and Gunny made two more trips to the elevator to escort people to the locker room. Miraculously, no one happened by while they were transporting people from the cell-block level and the trips were completed in just forty-six minutes. When everyone was in the locker room Jenetta noticed that Jergen was tightly hugging a young woman who was shaking so badly that the flab on Jergen's chubby arms was vibrating noticeably.

"Any problems, Jergen?"

"Just her, Captain. She was scared to death of getting into that tiny elevator. I'm sorry, ma'am, but I couldn't just stun her and leave her behind. I grabbed her and pulled her in as I closed the door. I think she'll be okay now."

Jenetta looked at the girl, barely seventeen or eighteen judging from her appearance. She'd been totally uncommunicative when Jenetta had released her from her cell, but had seemed to come along willingly enough at that time.

"What happened to your hand, Mr. Jergen," Jenetta asked when she noticed he was bleeding.

"It's just the tip of my middle finger," Jergen said, holding up the digit. "I was a bit slow getting my arm into the elevator after I boarded. Those doors close pretty fast and I was struggling a little with Delilah. The poor kid was frightened half to death."

"You did an excellent job, Mr. Jergen. Take care of her."

"Will do, Captain," he said, smiling proudly.

There were plenty of clothes in the locker room, although the women had difficulty finding things that were small enough. Only a half dozen full uniforms were pieced together, but that was enough for Jenetta's plan. The rest of the people put together whatever they could, most winding up in white kitchen clothes and grey work shoes with red rubber soles. It took just nine minutes to get everyone dressed and ready to move.

Gunny, standing guard at the door, suddenly made a hissing noise as a signal to get Jenetta's attention. He held up two fingers to indicate that two people were coming. Jenetta snapped her fingers to get everyone's attention, put her finger to her lips, and used her arms to motion that everyone should head for the back of the locker room. In less than five noiseless seconds, everyone had melted from view. Gunny joined Jenetta and Browne in the penultimate locker row.

The doors to the corridor opened less than thirty seconds later and two jaded security guards dressed in the standard light-grey uniforms of the Raider Security personnel sauntered into the locker room. Each carried a stun pistol in a flap-style black leather holster.

"Doesn't look like anyone's here," one said, glancing around. "Rarely is at this hour."

"Good, let's grab some shuteye. I'm beat. I've been on duty for twelve hours without a break."

"Yeah, me too. I don't know what the big deal is. So there's a major operation coming up. So what? We've seen lots of big operations and there's never been a security problem here on the station. They're acting like we have to be ready for a commando attack or something. I'm sick to death of it and I know everyone else is too. This base is the most secure place in the deca-sector. Outside of the company, no one even knows it exists."

"It's the damn brass. They've been edgy ever since that lone space tug got in and filmed every ship in the port. Now they're seeing spies in every corner, for Christ's sake. One dumb little bitch and a couple of old tug jockeys wander in and they keep us on alert for a month."

"Did you hear what the bitch did to the Commandant? She was in her cell, fully restrained, and he went in to talk to her. Somehow, she managed to attack him, smashed his nose flat to his face and knocked him to the floor."

"While she was restrained in EM bands?"

"Yeah! If she'd been free, she probably would have killed him before the guard could stop her. I hear that Arneu's nose swelled up like a watermelon."

"What is she, some kind of freak superwoman?"

"No, that's just it— she's just a little bitty thing. Can't be much more than twenty years old, nor weigh much more than 100 pounds soaking wet. She's a real looker too, according to the detention center guys. She has a face like an angel and a body to kill for. I heard the guys downstairs hung her up in the anteroom all day yesterday just so they could stare at her while they were on duty."

"Man, that's playing with fire. If the commandant hears about that, those guys will find themselves in one of the cells. The brass doesn't like guards messing with the company's pleasure slaves."

"Yeah— but I'd still like to meet her sometime."

"Me too, but right now it's time to call in."

Holding his gloved hand to his lips, the guard said, "Com link on. This is patrol Sierra 124. All quiet in sector November-Niner-Tango. Com link off." Dropping his hand, he said, "Okay, we've got an hour. Let's grab 40 winks down in the back. Set your chrono alarm for fifty-five minutes."

The guards started moving towards the back of the locker room for their midnight siesta, but, as they reached the next to last row of lockers, they pulled up short. Jenetta stood there facing them, with Gunny and Browne behind her. Both pairs of eyes traveled down to the stun pistol in her hand. As they calculated whether they could un-flap their holsters and draw their weapons before she fired, their faces reflected the fear gripping their chests. She couldn't kill them with the weapon she was holding, but she could easily manage that after they were unconscious. One swallowed hard.

"What's the matter, guys," Jenetta said smiling, "you just said you wanted to meet me sometime. Now, as a friend said to me recently, your wish is granted."

Neither guard tried for his radio. Both grabbed instead for their pistols, fumbling with the locked down holster flaps as Jenetta fired twice, so quickly that it appeared she had two weapons. The guards crumpled noiselessly to the floor.

Not having heard about the attack on Arneu until now, Gunny Rondell and crewman Browne exchanged glances and grinned knowingly. When their gaze again rested on Jenetta, it was with even greater respect.

"We have two more guard uniforms and pistols," Jenetta said. "Strip these fools and dump them in one of those laundry hampers over there. Pile some dirty laundry on top to hide them. They'll have a nice soft bed for their early morning siesta."

Two men about the same size as the sleeping guards were selected to receive the new uniforms. When they had dressed, Jenetta called everyone together.

"We're more than halfway there. We're on the docking level and our next step is to get to a ship. Everyone is to remain here and keep absolutely quiet while our experienced cargo handlers go find some transportation for us. Gunny, it's two minutes past 0100, your team *must* be back in thirty minutes."

"Aye, Captain, we'll be back."

Jenetta took up a position near the door as Gunny led his group out of the locker room.

*   *   *

The minutes seemed to pass like hours and, at half past one, the group assigned to secure transportation still hadn't returned. The guards had been stunned twenty-eight minutes earlier and in thirty-two minutes they were supposed to report in. If they weren't heard from, alarms might be sounded. A search would definitely be conducted, starting with this area since it was their last reported location. The size of the escape group ruled out a tug or shuttle, so Jenetta had earlier decided they'd require a slightly larger vessel. But if an alarm was sounded, it would become almost impossible to board a ship at any of the airlock piers. Jenetta had naturally developed contingency plans, but hesitated to implement one until forced to assume that the transportation group had been captured. She couldn't know how long it would take for the base's security force to make one of the transportation group reveal the whereabouts of the escapees, but she knew the persuasive power of the collars. Jenetta sighed to herself and asked for everyone's attention so she could address the group.

"If the transportation group doesn't return in two minutes, we'll have to move out and attempt to get to a ship, any ship, by foot. When we leave, we'll stick to the shadows as much as possible. Walk single file and remain silent. Remember that your fate and the fate of everyone around you will be determined by how you act over the next hour. Okay, make your preparations to leave."

Jenetta motioned to the group and led them out of the locker room when the allotted two minutes were up. Just twenty meters down the corridor was a door that led to the kitchen's loading dock where food was delivered from the warehouses. There wasn't anyone in sight, so she led the group across the dock, down the three steps, and out into what looked like a deserted city street with a twenty-five-meter-high ceiling. Most likely because of the time of day the area was only dimly illuminated. A seventeen-meter-wide aisle that appeared to be used like a two-lane road ran along the walls to the left and right. After verifying the direction on the floor layout map, Jenetta led the group to the left. She hoped there were no security cameras in this area because a line of forty people moving towards the docked ships would be impossible for even a half blind security man to miss.

They had only gone about twenty meters when a cargo truck came gliding along on a cushion of 'oh-gee' waves. Jenetta hid her hand containing the stun pistol behind her right pants leg as the truck slowed, then stopped just two meters from her. The darkened roadway didn't allow Jenetta to see inside the cab, but it was a familiar voice that said, "Taxi, ma'am?"

Jenetta released her breath and said in a loud whisper, "Dammit Gunny, you scared the stuffing out of me."

"Somehow I doubt that, Captain, but I'm glad I caught you before you got out of sight." He jumped down from the cab and hurried around the back. After lowering the tailgate, he began to help people climb into the vehicle.

"Only one truck, Gunny? It's not big enough to hold everybody."

"The others will be along in a minute. I wanted to get back before you did something really dumb, like trying to walk to a ship."

"I thought you might have been caught. I couldn't wait any longer."

"I know, Captain. Sorry it took us so long. We needed trucks with covered rear cargo areas and I figured we should have some cargo-handler coveralls for the drivers when we get to the ship."

"Good thinking, Gunny. What's the delay?"

"The other boys had to strip the coveralls off the fellahs that we stunned and then they had to get dressed in them. Here they come now."

Three more trucks floated to a halt behind the first and there was now more capacity than needed. Browne was wearing cargo-handler coveralls over his uniform so Jenetta told him to take the lead truck. She gave him some quick instructions, including directions to the airlock piers, and the trucks moved out as soon as she had climbed into the rear.

Arriving at the designated pier which extended out alongside the ship, Browne's eyes opened wide, but he quickly concealed his anxiety. There was an armed guard at the docking ramp entrance and another at the other end where it disappeared into the ship's forward cargo bay. He pulled up next to the first guard and said calmly, "Got a load of food provisions for you."

"This ship's already been fully loaded. We're not expecting any more deliveries."

"Yeah, well, there was some kind of screwup. This will be the last shipment unless those dillweeds find something else they missed."

"Let me see your shipping manifest."

"Sure," Browne said as he made a production of looking for the viewpad in the cab. "Shit, it's not here. I musta left it in the back of the truck."

"Stay in the cab," the guard said nonchalantly. "I'll get it."

The guard sauntered around to the back of the truck and was momentarily out of sight of the other guard. As he flipped open the rear canvas flap, Jenetta shot him point blank with her stun pistol and he crumpled silently to the ground.

"Mr. Deitrich, you're about the same size. Take his place here and don't come into the ship until you're called or security teams approach with weapons drawn."

"Aye, Captain."

Deitrich jumped down and lifted the sleeping guard into the back of the truck. He picked up the guard's white helmet and electronic clipboard and sauntered slowly around to the cab.

"Okay, Mr. Browne," Deitrich said, "you're cleared to drive in."

"Thank you, Mr. Deitrich," he said, grinning.

Deitrich waved to the other guard as the trucks drove out the enclosed airlock ramp leading into the ship. When they reached the second guard, a big brutish-looking dolt, he held up a giant paw to stop them.

"Waz goin on? Why waz you passed tru? We waz told this ship waz fully loaded except for crew."

"Last minute food delivery," Browne said. "The officers must've wanted more fresh fruit and meat. Can't say I blame them; there isn't a food synthesizer made that can make a decent apple. You know what I mean? Applesauce yes, apples no."

The guard's simple mind was completely confused by the talk about apples and applesauce. To regain control of the discussion he said, "Lemme see your shippin pad."

"Sure thing, pal. Here."

Browne lifted his stun pistol and fired just as the barrel cleared the bottom of the window opening. The huge guard crumpled to the ground as noiselessly as the first. On Jenetta's orders, another former captive dressed in a security guard uniform hopped out of the back and managed to drag the sleeping guard behind some stacked crates before putting on his white helmet and taking his place. The trucks immediately drove the rest of the way into the cargo bay and discharged the teams that would take the ship.

Assembled into the three groups Jenetta had arranged while still in the detention center, they made their final preparations to begin the assault. Led by Jenetta, the first group would race to the bridge. Browne would lead the second group to Engineering while the third group, led by Gunny, would head for the crew quarters. All would stun any crewmen they encountered on their way and the guard in the cargo bay would stun any new crewmen reporting aboard during the takeover.

Checking the cheap wristwatch she had picked up from among the personal items stripped from the guards in the detention center, Jenetta said, "We have just fifteen minutes before the guards we left in the locker room are supposed to report in. If their 0100 nap habit is known among their comrades, someone in security will probably go looking for them before a general alarm goes out. So at best, we have perhaps a forty-five-minute window. Let's do this!"

The three groups raced off in different directions to complete their missions. Deck layout images in the 'you are here' style were mounted on the walls in the corridors so crewmembers could find their way around the ship and that made it easy for the assault groups to find their destinations. As they proceeded to their objectives, they encountered people walking in the corridors, but they were past each one before the crewmember had even finished sliding, unconscious, to the deck.

Reaching the bridge, Jenetta's assault team paused for thirty seconds to catch their breath.

"We'll rush in as soon as the doors are open," Jenetta told them. "Try not to shoot. We may need these people to operate the ship until we learn the controls. Ready?"

Lt. Commander Hugh Michaels said, "Ready, Captain."

The others all nodded and Jenetta stepped into the area where movement was monitored by the door-opening mechanism. As the two doors slid noiselessly open, Jenetta's group thundered into the room.

"Everyone freeze!" Jenetta yelled.

The only two officers on the bridge, a young ensign and a lieutenant, froze as Jenetta and her team of seven quickly surrounded them. After relieving them of their weapons, a full set of restraints was put onto each young Raider officer and then activated. Team members who checked the captain's briefing room found it empty. One man was then assigned to watch the prisoners and another the corridor door while the rest checked out the ship's controls. Everyone was breathing a little easier.

"Everything is straight forward, Captain," Lt. Commander Michaels said. "Two men, a helmsman and astrogator, can operate this ship well enough to take it out. We don't need these Raider officers. The ship is ready to go."

Jenetta looked over at the two young officers. They had overheard the comment about not being needed and fear was evident on their faces. They believed they were about to be killed.

"Don't worry," she said to them, "you won't be harmed unless you offer resistance. Sit down."

Both men, their arms held tightly against their waists and their ankles locked together, bent at the waist and knees and fell backwards to the deck. Jenetta walked over to them and pointed her controller at one to release his arms while the man assigned to guard them covered them with his pistol.

"Put your left arm through his right and then put it against your waist again."

When the ensign had complied, Jenetta secured his arms again. Both men were now linked together in addition to being completely secured. They could offer almost no resistance.

Jenetta bent over the lieutenant and said, "Do you know what this is?" She held out her pistol.

"Of course. It's a stun pistol."

"And do you know how it works?"

"You aim it and pull the trigger?"

"And do you know what happens when you're hit?"

"It knocks you out for about six hours and you wake up with a hell of a headache. But you won't need that. We won't offer any resistance."

"I'm glad to hear that. For the first offense you get stunned. For the second offense you get stunned and tossed out an airlock. There are no third offenses. Understand?"

The lieutenant swallowed hard and said, "I understand, Captain."

"Good. Keep it uppermost in your mind and relay that information to your fellow prisoners— when they wake up."

Jenetta looked at her watch. The bridge takeover had required just seven minutes. They had eight minutes left before the guards were supposed to report in. Better yet, she had confirmed the strength of the stun pistol. Even the hardiest individual, such as the huge guard at the airlock, should be out for at least four or five hours.

As she dropped her arm, Gunny entered the bridge. Eight pistols swung in his direction until he was recognized. He paused until the pistols were lowered, then walked over to Jenetta.

Coming to attention, he said, "The ship is secured, Captain. We've stunned everyone we could find below.

Browne has Engineering under control and my boys are roaming the decks looking for strays, but almost everyone on board was in the sack at this hour so it was too easy. The idiot crewman in the armory opened the outer door without challenging me when I buzzed and then just stared at me in surprise as I stunned him and his partner. We'll have to find someone who can unlock the cage door before they come to. And I guess they hadn't assigned quarters security codes yet because none of the doors were locked. We can seal the ship and leave as soon as you give the order."

"At ease, Gunny. Well done. It took you just eight minutes in an unfamiliar ship."

"Thirty-eight years in the service, ma'am," Gunny said as he relaxed. "I've been aboard a lot of ships. This one isn't so different, Just a bit bigger than the other Space Command battleships I've served on."

"Tell me, Gunny. Could you do it again?"

"Again, Captain?"

"There's a second, identical battleship right next to this one. Remember?"

Lt. Commander Michaels exclaimed, "You *can't* be serious, Captain! We have to get out of here before they find out their detention center is empty or their security patrol is missing. We can't start another operation now."

Chapter Eighteen
~ August 11th, 2267 ~

"Commander," Jenetta said, "if we don't take that other ship, it'll be on our six before we've gone a billion kilometers. And, since a warship's temporal field generator is retracted into the hull when not in use, we can't simply blast theirs as we leave to prevent them from following us. We know we can't outrun it and we can't put up much of a fight with our limited crew, so we either have to take it or disable it. We don't have time to figure out how to disable it without first taking control of it and I would prefer to take it anyway. Besides, having two battleships facing them might give pause to anyone considering pursuit."

Lt. Commander Michaels grimaced but couldn't offer any response that would annul the logic of Jenetta's argument. Gunny would do whatever Jenetta said without question.

"Gunny, get below and round up your men. Leave three on mop up and the two at the airlock. Have Mr. Browne leave two men from his team in Engineering. Everyone else should be in the trucks so we can take our 'food provisions' to the other ship."

"Aye, Captain," Gunny said, grinning as he ran for the door.

"Captain Yates, you were a Lieutenant and a command officer in Space Command before becoming a freighter captain. Do you think that you can handle this ship?"

"Aye, Captain. I believe so."

"Good. I'm putting you in command here. I'll leave Farrencroft and Lyons with you, in addition to the seven men below deck. Monitor commercial frequency 25932.5 while you're waiting. As soon as we take the other ship, I'll send you a communication that we're ready to leave. The coded message will be 'Carver to Yates. Proceed.' At that time you call in Mr. Deitrich, seal the ship, and prepare to get under way. As soon as you see the other ship begin to move, follow us. If the other ship hasn't moved in twenty-five minutes, get out of here and get to the nearest Space Command base as best you can."

"Aye, Captain. We'll be monitoring commercial frequency 25932.5."

"Good luck, Captain."

"You too, Captain."

"Commander Michaels, are you ready?"

Lt. Commander Michaels, wearing a wry grin, exhaled loudly and said, "About as ready as I'm ever going to be, Captain."

"Good, let's do this. Kellogg, Ito, Newman, you're with us."

Jenetta ran from the bridge with the four men hard on her heels. They reached the forward cargo bay as Gunny, Browne, and their teams arrived.

"Everyone into the trucks," Jenetta shouted, "we have one more job and then we're out of here. Mr. Browne, you take the lead truck again. Same procedure."

As Jenetta climbed into the rear of the lead truck, she immediately noticed the fear-filled faces of the women captives. She had forgotten about them as her mind raced with the details of the still-unfolding plan to take the other ship. Doubts began to surface that she might again be pushing things too far, as when she had given orders to enter the spaceport instead of dropping their cargo and making a run for it. But it was too late to make arrangements for leaving them here now. She sat down on the bed of the truck as it started to move.

No alarm had yet sounded, so the guards at the other ship's docking ramp and airlock weren't any more alert than the first two. They were easy prey for the now-practiced assault team. Once again Jenetta posted two men at the cargo bay's airlock entrance and the rest separated into squads, although smaller now. Jenetta's team was comprised of only four plus herself. Checking her watch, she saw that time had run out. The security guards were supposed to be reporting in right then, instead of sleeping peacefully in laundry wagons.

"Okay," she said, "we're out of time and I'm anxious to get the hell out of here. Let's do this."

The three teams raced off as before, but this time they knew where they were going and didn't need to check the deck maps on the bulkheads. Jenetta's team stunned four Raider crewmen on their way to the bridge and, upon reaching the bridge, Jenetta allowed just fifteen seconds to catch their breath before giving the signal to enter.

"Everyone freeze," Jenetta shouted as the team stormed onto the bridge of this second ship.

Four men, all standing at the tactical station, were discussing something on the main plot monitor. They stopped what they were doing and calmly turned to face the five intruders. One, wearing the three wide gold bars of a full commander on his epaulets, said in an arrogant voice, "What's the meaning of this?" His stance and expression showed that he was used to being in command and having people jump when he spoke. His curly black hair, protruding ears, and dark bushy eyebrows gave the forty-something-year-old a slightly comical appearance.

"Galactic Space Command," Jenetta said forcefully. "We're taking this ship back. Everyone drop your weapons very carefully, using just two fingers, and then move to the rear bulkhead."

She saw the disbelief in their eyes, but they were hardly in a position to deny that five pistols were pointed in their direction. While not as lethal or messy as the lattice pistol that each of the four Raider officers carried, the stun pistols would be just as effective at enforcing the takeover.

Lattice pistols had long ago been outlawed by the Galactic Alliance, but the extremely lethal weapons remained the favored personal weapon of Raider officers because they could be fired aboard ship with the certain knowledge that the projectile couldn't puncture a titanium hull. Like laser pistols, they used energy in place of chemical propellants, but they fired an actual object rather than an energy beam. Each fifty-millimeter-long projectile consisted of four narrow pieces of formed spring steel. Loaded under great pressure into hundred-round magazines, each projectile was stored in a flattened, compressed form. When pulled into the chamber, it instantly expanded to become a twelve-millimeter-diameter latticework tube. Three tubes were always loaded into the chamber, ready to be fired instantly. With a leading edge as sharp as any straight-edge razor, and spun by a rifled chamber, the fired projectile performed like the narrow blade of a filleting knife, slicing its way through whatever it struck. Since it wasn't attempting to push its way through the matter as a lead projectile would, it didn't require nearly the mass. And where a laser pistol sealed the wound as it made it, the lattice pistol left large, gaping holes that allowed a person's life force to bleed out in minutes from wounds in what would otherwise be non-vital areas.

The commander and two of the others carefully removed their pistols and dropped them to the carpeted deck, but one officer, a lieutenant(jg), tried to make a fight of it. Jenetta saw the movement and fired as she threw herself to the left, narrowly escaping a three-round burst from his lattice pistol. The projectiles bored large, nasty holes in the fabric and padding of the first officer's chair and didn't stop cutting until they reached the hard surface of the backrest's main support, while the lieutenant crumbled to the floor from the stun blast Jenetta fired.

In an attempt to use the distraction, the other Raider officers bent to retrieve their dropped weapons, but Lt. Commander Michaels shouted, "*Not* a good idea, boys!"

Newman collected the weapons as the three officers straightened back up, but Jenetta remained lying on the floor, holding her left arm.

"Are you all right, Captain?" Lt. Commander Michaels asked, concern evident in his tone.

"I'm fine. I think I broke my arm though."

Moving to her side, Mr. Kellogg helped her get to her feet.

"Can you continue on, Captain?"

"Yes, I'm great. Thanks to our jailers, pain actually makes me feel good. I'm beginning to feel quite wonderful right now. Who's got the bag of restraints? Let's show our new friends here what we've been enjoying for so long."

The Raider commander, still confident that the takeover would fail, said, "You're all escaped prisoners, aren't you?"

"Bingo," Jenetta said.

"You! You're the one who broke the Commandant's nose?"

"Two for two," Jenetta said, feeling a little light-headed and giddy. A warm feeling was spreading through her thorax and abdomen.

Each of the four men was fitted with restraint bands and Jenetta locked them on using the controller that had belonged to Arneu. Then she secured their wrists to the belts.

"Great feeling, isn't it?" Jenetta said, grinning at the three officers. "What's your name?" Jenetta asked the senior officer.

"I'm Commander Levande Pretorious," he said, smirking, "and you'll never get away with this."

"Ohhhh, I think we will. Commander Michaels, would you and the others care to prepare the ship for departure? I'll watch our friends."

"Aye, Captain."

The assault group, all experienced bridge personnel, immediately turned to the control consoles.

"Captain, the controls are locked out on this ship," Lt. Commander Michaels said from the helm console. "We can't move."

Jenetta looked over at the still smirking face of Commander Pretorious. She knew from his expression that he had no intention of giving her the lockout code. She would have to take it from him by force. She knew she had to pretend to be just as cruel and hard as her jailers had been with her. She had to make Pretorious believe his life meant absolutely nothing to her and that she wouldn't hesitate to torture him, or even kill him, to get the code.

"Would you care to give me the authorization code without the pain, Commander?"

"I'm not giving you anything," he said smugly.

Jenetta masked her face with a malevolent grin and said lightly, "Okay, contestant number one, you've selected the pain category for yourself and your companions. I'll remind you all that you can end this round of the game at any time by giving us the proper lockout code."

Jenetta suppressed a grin as she saw the frightened expressions on the faces of the two other officers. Her act probably had them believing she had lost her grip on reality. If they knew the code, they would already be shouting it out. Perhaps Pretorious wasn't aware of the effectiveness of the EM collars. If so, he was about to learn the hard way. She pushed the button that locked the ankles of the officers. The commander managed to keep his feet because his ankles were already quite close together, but the two junior officers fell as their legs, like those of the unconscious officer, were pulled together.

"Is that your idea of pain?" the commander asked her.

"No, I'm just warming up. My idea of pain is what I did to Arneu. I really enjoyed that. How would you like to have your nose smashed flat against your face? The pain is almost unbearable, I've heard."

"You don't frighten me," Pretorious said smugly. "I think you're all talk."

Jenetta nodded. "I suppose you could ask my jailer if I'm all talk. Unfortunately, he won't be able to answer. You see, I snapped his neck just after dinner last night." From the corner of her right eye, Jenetta saw Lt. Commander Michael start and his eyes go wide at the pronouncement. He had already heard about her attack on Arneu when the guards entered the locker room earlier in the escape attempt. She knew the assaults he was learning about, those he had witnessed, and the violent nature she was exhibiting now were totally inconsistent with her appearance. She suppressed the grin she was feeling and continued, never having taken her eyes off Pretorious. "I don't think he suffered though— *unfortunately.* He was dead in seconds. But I digress; let me show you what they did to us in the detention center. I think you'll find it most interesting. Here's a level one. I received this on my first day merely as a warning of things to come."

Jenetta pressed the button that sent a level one shock and all four officers went into a mild convulsion. The commander struggled to remain on his feet, but with his feet placed so closely together he wound up joining his comrades on the floor almost immediately. Jenetta stood watching dispassionately until they stopped convulsing. The release of the monoamine neurotransmitter in her brain continued to push her into a more euphoric state.

"As I mentioned, that was just a level one," Jenetta said. "Would you care to try a level two?"

"I'm still not telling you anything," Pretorious grunted through clenched teeth.

"Beeep! Oh, too bad, another wrong answer."

Jenetta pressed the level two button. The three conscious officers began whimpering loudly and writhing all over the floor while the fourth just convulsed. Again, Jenetta waited until they stopped moving.

"Interesting sensation, isn't it, Commander?" she asked coldly.

"You little bitch," the commander croaked.

"Is that a request for level three? I have to admit I've never felt this one. *I* was smart enough to avoid it. I understand a lot of people go mad, so they normally only use level two in the detention center. No. Tell you what. I'm not going to use level three. Instead, I'll just zap you every minute with a level two.

This will be more amusing to watch. Are you ready, contestants?"

Jenetta grinned malevolently again and pressed the button. Forty-five seconds later she pressed it again. And forty seconds later she pressed it again. It was now ten minutes past the security guards' reporting time.

During the first few zaps, the officers had been able to keep from screaming, but after that they couldn't contain themselves anymore and screamed openly. Jenetta's bridge assault team looked on objectively. They had all been subjected to the effects of the collars for months and weren't distressed to see the Raiders getting it in the neck now.

Jenetta didn't even ask the officers for the code anymore, she just continued to zap them every thirty seconds. She must have zapped them ten times before the commander croaked out, "Enough!"

"Tell me the code or I keep going. I can keep this up for hours. It's even more amusing that I expected."

"Alpha Hotel Tango Three Five Niner November Kilo," Commander Pretorious hissed between gritted teeth.

Jenetta looked over at Lt. Commander Michaels.

"The helm is active, Captain."

Jenetta smiled sadly, sighed, and said, "That concludes tonight's game, contestants. I hope you've enjoyed your brief participation half as much as I have. I regret you won't be going home with any cash or prizes, but, as a consolation, we'll arrange for an all-expense-paid stay at the prison colony on Saquer Major as soon as we reach a Space Command base. You're welcome to rest there on the deck while we wait for word from my other teams."

Holding her broken arm to keep it from swinging, Jenetta began to pace the bridge deck slowly. It was almost a full four minutes more before the doors opened and a chubby little man in a cook's uniform entered the bridge.

"Gunny Rondell says to tell you the crew has been put to sleep and the ship is ours. Mr. Browne holds Engineering."

"Excellent, Jergen. Tell Mr. Higgiby to come aboard. Have him inform us when the cargo bay door is sealed."

"Yes, Captain, right away," the chubby little man said before hurrying out.

"Commander Michaels, prepare to take us out as soon as the cargo bay is sealed. Mr. Kellogg, send the coded message to the other ship."

"Aye, Captain," both men said.

Jenetta took a good look around the bridge for the first time. Her attention had been so focused that she hadn't consciously realized just how enormous it was. It was easily twice as large as the bridge of the *Vordoth*, which she had thought was enormous until she became comfortable with it. She could instantly identify the functions of the various workstations from the equipment panels and monitors at each, but the configurations aboard this new ship were unique. Moving to the command chair, Jenetta climbed into it. She delicately placed her broken arm on her lap and leaned back to wait.

"Mr. Higgiby reports that everyone is aboard and the cargo bay door is sealed, Captain," Mr. Kellogg said from the com station about five minutes later.

"The computer confirms the ship is sealed," Lt. Commander Michaels said as he looked at the helm display.

"Very good. Get us the hell out of here, Commander."

The current image on an enormous curved viewscreen that filled the front bulkhead wall of the bridge was a view from the bow of the ship. A small inset, presently in the upper right corner, but which the helmsman could move anywhere on the screen, showed a rear view from the stern. Lt. Commander Michaels called out the steps as they were taken.

"Depressurizing airlock seal, releasing docking clamps."

"Airlock ramp is automatically retracting. Ramp is retracted."

"Easing back with maneuvering thrusters."

The large image on the viewscreen automatically shifted with the small one so that the larger image was the view from the stern.

"Which way, Captain?" Lt. Commander Michaels asked.

"Ninety degrees to larboard."

"Aye, Captain," he said as he engaged the starboard bow thrusters. "Turning to a course two hundred seventy degrees relative, zero degrees declination.

When they were clear of the ships on either side, Lt. Commander Michaels said, "Reverse apogee achieved. Thrusters forward."

The large viewscreen image again became a view from the bow, while the small inset showed the stern view. As the ship began to glide slowly forward, Jenetta could see the other battleship beginning to back away from the dock in the stern view insert.

"Uh, Captain," Lt. Commander Michaels said. "I don't see an exit."

"Damn," Jenetta said. "The doors are closed. Newman, can you fire a couple of torpedoes?"

Hurrying over to the tactical station, Newman said, "Affirmative, Captain. What do you wish to target?"

"That flat area at the end of the tunnel dead ahead is actually two enormous doors that disguise the port entrance. I need you to blast a hole large enough for us to pass through. Fire when ready."

"Aye, Captain. Firing."

Two torpedoes raced away from the ship at an incredible velocity and entered the tunnel. Reaching the doors in just two seconds, they exploded with phenomenal fury. One door was knocked completely out of the port, the twisted hunk of metal hardly looking like a door anymore as it tumbled away into the darkness. The other door stubbornly clung to the track on its outer hinges, but only about twenty percent of it remained as an obstacle, the portion near the tunnel center area having been bent out and away. There was now almost enough open area for both battleships to exit the asteroid side by side. The habitat's outer wall had lit up with flashing red lights before the first door had even disappeared from sight.

"Hmmm, I think they might have noticed we're leaving without proper clearance," Jenetta said, grinning. "Better take us to Plus-0.05, Commander."

"But Captain, we're still in port."

"Yes, and we need to get the hell out of this port, fast."

"Aye, Captain, going to Plus-0.05."

The ship began to speed up appreciably as the forward motion was set to fifty meters per second instead of using the slowest of maneuvering speeds, the normal procedure while a ship was still in port.

"Captain," Lt. Commander Michaels said, "a line of tugs is moving to block the exit."

"Yes, I see them Commander. Ito, open up on those tugs. We can't afford to hit them with the ship. They could damage us."

Ito, sitting at a fire control station, opened fire with the bow laser weapons. One of the tugs immediately disintegrated. Space tugs, especially those designed for deep space operations, were normally built with a standard titanium outer shell, but the inner hull layer was probably only aluminum. The ship's powerful laser had most likely stuck a fuel cylinder after burning through the hull like it was tissue paper. The remaining tugs turned tail and headed for cover with their sub-light throttles cracked opened as much as they dared in the confines of the spaceport. They knew their bluff had been called.

Kellogg, manning the communication station, announced, "Everyone is awake now, Captain. They're all trying to scream orders at the same time. A number of ships are reporting that they've released their docking clamps and are preparing to back away from their airlocks."

"Time to throw caution to the wind, Commander," Jenetta said calmly. "Take us to Plus-10."

Lt. Commander Michaels twisted his head in a funny way and said, as he exhaled his breath, "Aye, Captain, Plus-10."

The entrance to the tunnel raced at the ship as the speed increased to ten kilometers per second. Because of the ship's size, the slightest miscalculation in their course could mean destruction, but not getting out of there fast also meant destruction. A second later, they rocketed through the tunnel cleanly.

"Excellent job, Commander. Now open it up. The Indians are hot on our heels."

Lt. Commander Michaels began building the envelope as he applied full power to the sub-light engines. The ship surged ahead as he said, "Time to envelope, one minute thirty-eight seconds. Did you say Indians, Captain?"

They were gaining a comfortable lead, so Jenetta smiled and said, "One of my brothers was a fan of twentieth century video dramas called 'westerns'— fictionalized accounts of encounters between Native Americans and settlers, or cowboys, in the western United States during the nineteenth century. In a number of them, Native Americans on horse-back would chase small Cavalry detachments."

"Ah, yes. I've heard about them."

Newman, still at the tactical station said, "A ship is emerging from the spaceport, Captain. It appears to be the other battleship. Confirming that, Captain, it's Captain Yates."

"Excellent. Keep an eye on the spaceport opening so we know what's coming out after us."

"Captain, it just blew up!" Newman said loudly.

"Captain Yates' ship blew up?"

"No, Captain, the spaceport blew up, the whole spaceport, the whole damn asteroid!"

Chapter Nineteen
~ August 11th, 2267 ~

"Commander, all stop!" Jenetta ordered.

"Aye, Captain, all stop."

"Mr. Kellogg, did the computer record the explosion?"

"Aye, Captain. The computer should automatically log all imaging."

"Can you replay it on the forward viewscreen?"

"I think so, Captain. Give me a minute while I figure out the process. The other ship has stopped a few kilometers off our larboard."

"Open a channel to Captain Yates, please."

At the communications station, Kellogg deftly punched a few keys. A second later, the image of Captain Yates filled the front viewscreen.

"Yates here, Captain."

"Stand by, Captain Yates. The asteroid has exploded. We've stopped to investigate. We'll send you the images since you don't have adequate crew for everything."

"Standing by, Captain."

Forty-five seconds later, Newman said, "Here it is, Captain," and the image appeared on the front viewscreen.

Everyone on the bridge watched as the second battleship emerged from the asteroid and accelerated quickly away. The hollowed out planetoid suddenly appeared to turn white and swell to ten times its size before winking out a few seconds later.

"Can you enlarge the image and play back the last few seconds frame by frame?"

"Can do, Captain."

The image of the Raider hideout filled the front screen as the individual frames changed every three seconds. They again saw the second GSC battleship emerge from the station and accelerate away just before the station went up.

A voice behind Jenetta said, "Did we do that, Captain?"

"We didn't fire on them, Gunny."

"Could it have been the eight hundred metric tons of Corplastizine we booby trapped with two torpedoes?"

Lt. Commander Michaels' eyes went wide. He swiveled in his chair and shouted, "You did *what*? *When*?"

"We brought a little present with us on our reconnaissance mission," Jenetta said calmly. "When we were caught, we tried to detonate it, but they hit us with something that killed the power on the tug and our little *present* didn't blow."

Lt. Commander Michaels exhaled a long breath. "I'm rather glad it didn't, Captain."

"So am I, right now. But back then, we expected to be killed anyway."

"Captain," Gunny said, "is there something wrong with your arm?"

"It's broken, Gunny. That lieutenant(jg) on the floor over there fired at me and I dove out of the way. It broke when I landed wrong."

"One of the guys on my team was a Space Marine corpsman. I'll get him up here to take care of it."

"Thanks, Gunny. And maybe you can take these officers down and lock them in the brig."

"Right away, Captain."

Gunny stood the three dazed officers on their feet after releasing their legs. Each was still shaking noticeably from the effect of the shocks and was incapable of offering any resistance. He herded them off the bridge while dragging the fourth by his feet. The unconscious lieutenant(jg)'s head was going to be sore from more than just the effects of the stun weapon when he woke up because Gunny wasn't being any too gentle with the man who had almost killed his captain.

"Get me Captain Yates again," Jenetta said to Mr. Kellogg.

"He's on, Captain. I've been feeding them the images of the station through the com signal. He can hear you."

"Captain Yates, hold position. We're going back to take a look and then we'll return."

"Aye, Captain. The *Chiron* will be standing by."

"*Chiron?*"

"That's the name of this ship according to the brass commissioning plate mounted on the rear bulkhead near the entrance to the bridge."

Jenetta turned around. "Yes, I see ours. We're aboard the *Prometheus*. Commander Michaels, take us back to the vicinity of the asteroid."

"Aye, Captain."

Pieces of wrecked ships and habitat continued to tumble outward from where the asteroid had been just minutes before, in addition to the large pieces of inner and outer shell from the hollowed out asteroid itself. The bridge crew aboard the *Prometheus* agreed that the destruction was all but complete.

"Okay Commander, there's nothing we can do here. Take us back to the *Chiron*," Jenetta said.

"Aye, Captain."

"Captain Yates, are you still there?"

"Here, Captain."

"We're on our way back to you. I think it'll be easier to manage our prisoners if we have them all confined on one ship so I'm going to send some shuttles over to transfer your group here to the *Prometheus*. Have the men below load up some 'oh-gee' sleds and start bringing them to the flight bay."

"Aye, Captain."

"As soon as the prisoners are transferred and secured, I'll send you some more people to assist with operations and then we'll be heading for the Periseras Cloud Formation."

"Periseras, Captain?"

"Yes, we have some friends waiting there."

"GSC?"

"No, four freighters that I was attempting to get through Raider space. We'll be able to get more crewmen there to help with the prisoners and the ships."

"Aye, Captain."

"Carry on, Captain Yates. *Prometheus* out."

"Aye, Captain. *Chiron* out."

"We've moved alongside the *Chiron* and come to a full stop, Captain," Lt. Commander Michaels said. "Uh, you did say you were a GSC officer, didn't you, ma'am?"

"Yes, I am. NHSA, class of '56."

Lt. Commander Michaels looked at her intently. "'56? You don't look old enough."

"It's a long story, Commander. I'll tell you sometime and show you my GSC ring, but right now I have to make a call. Mr. Kellogg, would you try to reach the freighter *Vordoth* on commercial frequency 25932.8?"

"Aye, Captain." After eight minutes, Mr. Kellogg said, "I have the *Vordoth*, Captain."

"Thank you. Put it on the front viewscreen."

The familiar image of the *Vordoth's* bridge appeared with Gloria sitting in the command chair. Even at the speed of IDS communications, there was a four-minute lag between send and receive.

"This is the freighter *Vordoth* responding to the GSC Battleship *Prometheus*. Over."

"*Vordoth*, this is Carver. I'm on my way back. Over."

Eight minutes later, Jenetta saw and heard, "Captain? Is it really you?" Gloria couldn't contain herself and let her emotion show as she said effusively, "I'm so happy to hear from you. I thought we'd never see you again." Realizing that people on both bridges were watching, she managed to get herself under control before adding, "Uh, we were just preparing to get underway, ma'am. The Nordakians have completed their repairs. Over."

"Lieutenant, did you carry out that last instruction I gave you? Over."

"Aye, Captain, I sent the detonate code within the past hour, as you ordered. Um— was that alright?" she asked haltingly. "Over."

"Yes, just fine. Good work. We expect to be joining you in about seven hours. Ask the Nordakians to stand down until we arrive and we'll give them an escort to Obotymot. Over."

"Aye, Captain. I'm glad to see that GSC showed up. Over."

"Uh— they haven't arrived yet. We sort of repossessed a couple of battleships from the Raiders. They owed me a ship anyway after destroying our tug. We just— traded up a bit. Over."

"What were the Raiders doing with GSC battleships, ma'am? Over."

"The Raiders stole them from a shipyard where they were under construction. Anyway, we have them now and I'll return them to GSC after we get the Nordakians safely to their destination. I'll tell you more when I see you in seven hours. *Prometheus* out."

"See you soon, Captain. *Vordoth* out."

The brief communication had taken forty minutes to complete.

"Mr. Kellogg, can you get Gunny Rondell on the com."

"Aye, Captain. I'll find him."

The crewman who had once been a Space Marine corpsman arrived on the bridge and walked directly to Jenetta. "Gunny says your arm is broken, Captain."

"Yes. Can you put a splint on it?"

"Can do, Captain. I found a med kit."

After examining the arm gently with a small sonar sensor, he wrapped an air splint around it. As he rigged an arm sling for her he said, "It's just a simple break, Captain. You're going to have to cut down on the hand-to-hand combat for a while, but you should be completely healed in a few months."

"Thank you."

"No, it's me who needs to thank you. Thanks for saving my life. The guards told me I was to be sent to the mining colony on Poqdrawk, so I never expected to see my family again. Thank you, Captain. If there's anything I can ever do for you, you have only to let me know."

"Just give my regards to your family."

"Will do, Captain Carver."

"I have Gunny Rondell on the com, Captain," Mr. Kellogg said.

"Put him on my chair's left viewscreen."

The image of Gunny Rondell filled the small viewscreen as Jenetta swung it to face her.

"You need me, Captain?" Gunny asked.

"Gunny, I'd like to consolidate all the prisoners onto this ship. Can you shuttle your team and Mr. Browne's team over to the *Chiron* and start transporting them back? We have about four hours before they start waking up so we need to be done by then. Lock them up in a couple of empty cargo bays. Put the officers and biggest bruisers in the brig, and put restraints on as many of the other large prisoners as you can. We should have at least forty-seven sets left after the six sets we've already used. All of the restrained prisoners can be put into one bay, with the others in a second. That way we can concentrate most of the guards on the second group. The restraints will keep the first group in line."

"Aye, Captain. We'll get started on it right away."

"When you're done, leave eight more men on the *Chiron* to help out. They're a little short-handed over there. We'll get everything squared away when we meet up with the *Vordoth* in a few hours."

"Aye, Captain."

"Thank you, Gunny. Carry on."

"Aye, Captain."

The com signal ended and the screen briefly changed to the GSC logo. Apparently, the Raiders had found it amusing to leave the original image in the system. Or perhaps they had intended to impersonate an SC battleship to convince commercial vessels to heave-to for inspection.

"Commander Michaels, would you turn on all larboard exterior lighting to assist the transfer operation."

"Yes ma'am."

"Mr. Kellogg, can you put up the larboard view on the front viewscreen so we can watch the shuttle operations."

"Aye, Captain."

The front viewscreen changed from an image of distant stars to show the *Chiron*, illuminated by *Prometheus'* powerful larboard lights. Without an atmosphere to diffuse the lighting, the natural bright bronze coloration of the titanium armor plating was highly contrasted against the bespeckled black background. Six shuttles moved through the spotlights on their way from the *Prometheus* to the *Chiron* about twenty minutes later. It took numerous trips to transfer all the prisoners, but in two hours the transfer was complete, with the eight additional crewmen having been left on *Chiron*.

"Captain, Gunny reports that all prisoners have been transferred and put into the cargo bays as you ordered," Mr. Kellogg said. "The ship is sealed."

"Thank you, Mr. Kellogg. Notify the *Chiron* that we're getting underway."

"Aye, Captain."

"Commander Michaels, turn off all exterior lights except for navigation lighting and take us to Periseras, please."

"Adjusting course for the Periseras Cloud Formation, Captain," Lt. Commander Michaels said. "We should arrive there in about five hours at top speed."

"The *Chiron* acknowledges and will follow to larboard and aft, Captain."

"Thank you, Mr. Kellogg." Jenetta climbed down from the command chair, saying, "I haven't had a cup of coffee in weeks. I'm going to see if I can find a food synthesizer that'll brew me a hot cup of Colombian, Commander, and maybe get a little rest. You have the ship."

"There should be a beverage synthesizer in your briefing room, Captain," Lt. Commander Michaels said.

"I'll check."

All ship's officers, upon reaching the rank of Lieutenant, are assigned quarters with attached offices of varying sizes. The captain's bridge briefing room functions as his or her second office. With doors on both sides of the bridge, Jenetta was unsure of which led to the briefing room, but she had a fifty-fifty chance so she walked to the larboard side first. The door failed to open as she reached it and she had to stop short in order to avoid crashing into it. She waited for a couple of seconds, then shifted to the left, and then to the right. Her movements were to allow the optical sensor an opportunity to get a good read on her body position so it'd know she was facing the door waiting for admittance rather than just passing it. But the doors remained closed.

Stretching out her right arm, Jenetta waved her hand near the override sensor. The doors slid noiselessly open to reveal a large, lavishly decorated office with a wooden desk that seemed large enough to serve as a landing pad for a space tug. An 'oh-gee' chair covered in deliciously soft dark brown leather floated in front of a SimWindow behind the desk and two similar overstuffed chairs faced the desk. A long, comfortable-looking sofa finished in the same soft brown leather used for the chairs sat patiently waiting for occupants against one wall. The walls themselves were paneled with real oak finished in a light honey color, not the synthetic product that only simulated wood. The light brown carpet covering the entire deck felt like it was ten centimeters thick.

"Wow!" Jenetta said to herself after the doors closed. "I wonder if this was original, or if it was modified by one of the Raider captains."

A beverage synthesizer on a sidewall caught her eye and she moved to it. Unaware of how long it had been since it was last used, Jenetta touched the 'clean' icon on the small control panel. The dispenser immediately performed a quick self-cleaning operation which included purging all the chemical lines. Jenetta waited patiently as water and liquid poured from the drip spout.

Now cleaned and ready to provide liquid refreshment, the machine waited for orders. Jenetta picked up a sixteen-ounce mug from a rack next to the dispenser and placed it into the opening.

"Colombian coffee," she said. "Black with two sugars."

"Percentage of chicory?" the machine asked.

Jenetta's right eyebrow arched. She had never been asked that before. *Must be a new program*, she thought. *Or perhaps the captain placed in command of this ship had instructed the machine to always ask about chicory if it wasn't specified when coffee was requested.*

"None," she replied, then watched as her mug was filled to within one centimeter of the top edge.

She removed it carefully, sniffed it, then took a small sip. It was delicious. It was hot, but not so hot that she couldn't take a mouthful. She closed her eyes and let it trickle gently down her throat as she savored the flavor. She had dreamt of having a good cup of coffee ever since her first day in the detention center. Drinking the weak tea they'd served with the meals had been excruciating. *Romeo might have gotten further with me if he'd offered me a good cup of Colombian instead of apple pie*, she thought flippantly, then sobered as she remembered what she'd done. She shook herself mentally to dislodge the image of his broken body from her brain.

"Computer?"

"Waiting," she heard a disembodied voice say.

"You will no longer ask if someone wants chicory."

"Accepted."

"And you will acknowledge me, Jenetta Carver, NHSA class of '56, as captain of this ship."

"CT identification recorded and accepted, Captain."

With her coffee mug in hand, Jenetta walked to the enormous wooden desk. Some people might have felt it was garish and ostentatious, but Jenetta thought it suited the ship and the almost unlimited power of the person who would ultimately command her. She placed her cup down, sat in the large, comfortable 'oh-gee' chair behind the desk, and spun herself around.

"Jenetta Carver," she said aloud to herself, "you've done it. It may not be an official posting, but for right now, *you* are the captain of the newest— fastest— biggest— baddest— battleship in the entire known Galaxy. Weeeeeeee!"

The door-chime brought Jenetta out of her reverie. She stopped spinning the chair and giggled like a schoolgirl for a few seconds before composing herself. "Who is it?" she asked.

The computer replied, "You have a visitor with an unrecorded ID, Captain."

"Admit the visitor," Jenetta said.

The computer opened the doors. Gunny Rondell walked in, his arms loaded with clothing.

"There aren't any GSC or Merchant Services uniforms in the storeroom, Captain, but I found a Raider officer uniform that should fit you a little better than the one you're wearing."

"Thank you, Gunny," she said smiling up at him. "That was very thoughtful of you."

"My pleasure, ma'am."

"Gunny, is the ship secure?"

"I believe so, Captain."

"Have you checked the list of crewmembers that had reported aboard against the identifications of the ones you locked up?"

"No, Captain. Except for the five officers from the two bridges, they're all unconscious."

"Let's at least do a head count. Perhaps the Raiders use ID bracelets or dog tags for identification. If they do, we can determine the situation while they're still unconscious. Better get a count from the *Chiron* also to make sure we found them all over there. If any are missing we'll have to start a search immediately before they can attempt to sabotage the ships."

"I'll take care of it right away, Captain."

"Thank you, Gunny. Oh, Gunny?"

"Yes, Captain."

"I've forgotten completely about the female captives. Are they still in the trucks?"

"No, Captain. I took them to a lounge on Crew Quarters Deck Fourteen where they can relax. I figured it would be better that they remain together as a group for now. They'll be fine. Jergen is with them. The young woman he helped won't let him out of her sight now that we've completed our escape. I'm amazed he managed to break loose long enough to participate in our effort to take these ships."

"You've done an incredible job, Gunny. Thank you."

"This has been the most fun I've had in years, Captain. It's been my honor to serve in your command."

Alone in the briefing room again, Jenetta gingerly removed the arm sling and then the uniform of the guard she had killed. She was happy to be rid of it for it carried the body odors of the dead jailer and it was a constant reminder of the worst thing she had ever experienced. It was one thing to fire a laser weapon and destroy a fighter craft that was trying to kill you or to fire torpedoes at ships that would destroy yours given half a chance, but killing another human in unarmed combat, so close that you can smell them and hear them gasp for their last breath, was a different matter entirely. She had only done what was absolutely necessary to save her own life, yet she feared the sight of the guard's broken and crumpled body would be with her for the rest of her days.

Donning the clean shirt and trousers Gunny had brought in, she marveled at the fit. The shoes were one size too big, but they were much better than the ones she'd been wearing. She pulled on the uniform jacket and smiled when she saw that Gunny had even found captain's bars for her. After she was dressed, she put the arm sling back on and walked to the chair behind the desk.

As she sat down, the com unit buzzed. Lifting the view-screen, it lit up with the image of the communications station operator.

"Call for you from the freighter *Jouraklihest*, Captain."

"Thank you, Mr. Kellogg. Put it through."

The image of Captain Phuth Yuixotical immediately filled the screen.

"Captain Yuixotical, it's good to see you again. I understand you've completed your repairs. Over."

"And it's good to speak to *you* again, Captain," she finally heard. "Your first officer on the *Vordoth* would only tell me that you had left on a classified mission. Now I learn that you're the captain of a GSC Battleship and a battle group commander. I'm very confused, Captain Carver. Uh, I don't recognize the uniform you're wearing. Over."

"It's the uniform used by the Raiders. My own uniform was— lost, while attempting to infiltrate a Raider base. Over."

"I see. And you're still intending to see us to Obotymot? Over."

"I am. And the chances of getting there without further attack are almost assured now. Over."

"And why do you say that? Over."

"I'm afraid that's still classified. You'll have to trust me. Over."

"I do, Captain. Implicitly. In spite of being quite confused about your true identity and mission. Have you injured your arm? Over."

"Just a simple break. I've been told I'll be fine in a few months. Over."

"I'm happy to hear that. How's your opponent? Over."

Jenetta grinned. "He's— still unconscious. Over."

Captain Yuixotical smiled widely. "I would have expected no less. Over."

"The *Prometheus* and *Chiron* will rendezvous with you in about five hours and we can depart for Obotymot two hours after I arrive. Over."

"The *Chiron*? Over."

"The *Chiron* is the other GSC battleship under my command. Over."

"I see. Very good, Captain, we'll be ready. *Jouraklihest* out."

"*Prometheus* out."

With the completion of the call, which consumed more than an hour, Jenetta sauntered over to the comfortable looking sofa and laid down. She wondered if she could grab ten minutes of uninterrupted rest. Closing her eyes, sleep overtook her within seconds.

The annoying and persistent sounds of a door-chime reached down and pulled Jenetta up from the depths of a sound sleep. Startled and confused for a few seconds by the strange surroundings, memories of the past day came flooding back as she became alert.

"Come in," Jenetta said sleepily.

Lt. Commander Michaels entered as the door opened for him. "Captain, I just wanted to inform you that we've reached Periseras and rendezvoused with the four freighters."

"WHAT!? Why didn't someone wake me up?"

"You needed the rest, Captain, both because of your injury and because of the stress that was evident on your face. You were exhausted. I would have awakened you if there had been any problems."

Jenetta sat up and rubbed her eyes with her right hand. "You're right, Commander, I did need it. Thank you for letting me sleep. How long have we been here?"

"We only just arrived. There are a number of space tugs headed this way and they're requesting permission to come aboard."

"Granted. Do we have a suitable reception room on board?"

"On a ship this large we should have a dozen conference rooms that would fit the bill."

"Please select one and show our visitors to it. Perhaps you could have someone dig up some refreshments as well. I'd like to wash up first."

"Very good, Captain. I'll take care of it."

Jenetta removed the arm sling and uniform jacket as she entered her washroom and she was gingerly washing the hand on her broken arm when the door-chime sounded again. She stuck her head out the bathroom door and said, "Come."

As the doors opened, Lieutenant Gloria Sabella entered, spotted Jenetta in the washroom, and walked to her, saying, "I brought over one of your uniforms, Captain. The one you were wearing when we talked looked terrible." Gloria hung the uniform hanger on a robe hook just inside the washroom and placed the soft-soled, ankle-high boots on the deck.

"Thanks, Gloria. It'll be great to get out of Raider clothes."

Gloria wanted nothing more than to hug her friend and welcome her back, but she didn't feel it would be appropriate behavior to hug her commanding officer. She might have succumbed to the temptation if she knew that Jenetta longed for the same thing.

"What happened to your arm?" Gloria asked.

"I broke it earlier today while I was trying to avoid being shot."

"*Shot?*" Gloria exclaimed.

"Yes, one of the Raider bridge officers objected to our taking back this ship and expressed his dissatisfaction with the business end of a lattice pistol."

"Rebecca's here in the reception room with everyone else. She can take a look at it."

"Everyone else?"

"There's an entire contingent of Nordakians, a large group from the *Vordoth*, and about two dozen scruffy-looking people dressed in uniforms similar to the one you're wearing."

Jenetta giggled. "We didn't have much time for personal grooming before our escape and most of the men do need a shave and a haircut. The uniforms are the ones used by the Raiders. I guess they're the only thing in ship's stores. We had to leave in a hurry and didn't have proper clothing when we left."

"The Raiders wear uniforms? I thought they were just a motley collection of pirates."

"They're so much more than that, Gloria; you have no idea. You should have seen their base. It rivaled any base the Galactic Alliance has."

Jenetta, in the process of changing her clothes, paused when she noticed Gloria staring open-mouthed at the markings on her chest.

"A little souvenir from my stay with the Raiders. Slavery is just one of their many illegal sidelines."

"I can't wait to hear the full story. I love the underwear, by the way."

Jenetta giggled. "Not exactly Space Command issue, is it?"

"Maybe it should be. GSC uniforms sure don't do much to make a girl feel feminine."

"You don't know how much I longed to have my non-feminine uniform a couple of weeks ago. I spent the first few weeks of captivity in just my underwear, my *original* cotton underwear. Well," Jenetta said as she finished dressing, "let's not keep everyone waiting."

Chapter Twenty

~ August 11ᵗʰ, 2267 ~

Lt. Commander Michaels had selected the large conference room on Deck Twelve for the reception and somehow scared up some simple foods and beverages, both those of Earth and Nordakia. When Jenetta made her entrance, the assemblage turned in her direction and applauded with enthusiasm. The three Nordakian captains and a dozen of their officers, all flashing pleasing shades of blue, green, and yellow, immediately approached Jenetta. When Jenetta had entered the room, there were at least half a dozen different hues represented among the Nordakians, but as they reached her, they all adopted her coloration. Hands were extended and greetings quickly exchanged.

Captain Yuixotical spoke first, saying, "The crews of all three ships in your task force have been telling us of your exploits, Captain. You've been quite busy since we last met."

"Yes, a great deal has happened."

"We've been told you destroyed a Raider spaceport that was hidden inside a giant asteroid and, with it, hundreds of large Raider fighting ships."

"So much for classified information," Jenetta said, smiling.

"Is it true, Captain?"

"I wouldn't say hundreds of *fighting* ships. It was more like sixty warships. The rest were pirated freighters and passenger liners."

"Sixty warships is a tremendous fighting force. Their destruction is very welcome. So that's how you can assure me we'll get to Obotymot without suffering attack?"

"That's not *exactly* what I said, Captain. I said the chances of getting there without attack are *almost* assured now. We don't know if there are any *other* Raider spaceports in this deca-sector. We only destroyed the one I was able to locate. There's still a potential danger, but we'll be six armed ships now, two of which are top-of-the-line GSC battleships."

"If the spaceport was as large as I've been told, and given what we suspect about their so-called 'territories,' it seems unlikely they'd have another nearby."

"That would be my first assessment as well, but this Raider organization is so massive and so well organized that I'm going to be looking over my shoulder for quite a while. Are your ships all at one hundred percent readiness, Captain?"

"Yes, all repairs have been completed and our crews are anxious to continue on to Obotymot and deliver our cargo."

"I appreciate your eagerness to be underway. I just have a few administrative details to attend to concerning personnel assignments on the *Prometheus*, *Chiron*, and *Vordoth* before we can leave. Now if you'll excuse me, there are others waiting to see me and our time is limited. I'll see you again before you return to your ship. Gentlemen, please enjoy the hospitality of the *Prometheus*."

"Of course, Captain."

Jenetta detached herself from the Nordakian contingent and moved on to greet the officers of the *Vordoth*. She shook hands with Charley and hugged Rebecca.

"Captain, it's great to see you again," Charley said. "I'd about given you up for lost when we didn't hear from you after several weeks. Gunny has told us of your captivity in the Raider detention center."

"It wasn't a very pleasant stay and there were times when I deeply regretted my decision to follow the moving cargo containers. I'm afraid the containers and cargo are lost to the company forever."

"If so, then it was a cheap price to pay for the destruction of a Raider base and dozens of Raider warships. I'll sleep a lot better at night knowing the Raiders are gone."

"We only destroyed one base, Charley. And from the way the commandant spoke, it was only one of many."

Rebecca, who had been giving Jenetta's arm a cursory examination, said, "I'm sure this ship has excellent medical facilities, Captain. Why don't we slip out and I'll take a look at your arm?"

"Just let me make the rounds and then we can go, Doc. Gloria, we have to get together after the reception is over."

"Aye, Captain."

Jenetta moved around the room exchanging greetings with everyone and spending a little time with each group. Deitrich and Higgiby had received a rousing welcome back from the *Vordoth* crew. They were telling everyone about the escape and singing Jenetta's praises to whoever would listen. Their fellow crewmembers expended just as much energy telling them of their exploits while Jenetta was captain of the *Vordoth*. Jenetta accepted congratulations from all and moved on to meet with other groups. None of the women captives had been brought to the reception and Jenetta approved of that decision. They weren't ready for such activities yet.

After asking Captain Yates to come to her briefing room following the reception, Jenetta returned to the Nordakians. They once again quickly adopted her skin hue. She spent about five more minutes in conversation before excusing herself to go to the sickbay with Rebecca.

Following a complete examination, Rebecca said to Jenetta, "I'm amazed that you're in such good shape considering your treatment over the past month. Your arm will be fine in a few months; the simple fracture of the left ulna is clean and should heal without complications. There's nothing I can do about your chest, though. As you said, it isn't a tattoo. Perhaps they have some specialists at Space Command who can remove it."

"I hope so, Doc. I'm not happy with the prospect of wearing it for the rest of my life."

"At least your uniform tunic hides it completely, Captain. Let me make you a new, solid cast for your arm and then we can return to the reception."

The thick but lightweight plasti-cast was more of a distraction than the air splint, but Jenetta knew it would keep her arm better immobilized, giving it a greater chance to heal properly. She decided to return to the bridge instead of the reception, and asked Rebecca to relay that message to Gloria.

She had just taken her seat at her desk with a fresh mug of coffee when the door-chime sounded. The doors opened to reveal Gloria standing there when she said, "Come."

"You sent for me, Captain?" Gloria said as she walked to the desk and came to attention.

"At ease. No, I asked Rebecca to request that you come up. It's Jen, Gloria."

"No ma'am. I can't call my captain by her given name."

"But I'm not your captain anymore, Gloria. *You're* the captain of the *Vordoth* now. I have this ship to handle and the convoy to protect."

"I– I'm not ready to become captain. I can't do it. I can't tell you how relieved I was when we heard from you. Not just because we knew you were safe, but also because I wouldn't have to take over for you and be both captain of the *Vordoth and* escort the Nordakians to Obotymot."

"Listen to me, Gloria," Jenetta said as she came out from behind the desk. "You're intelligent, an excellent officer, and you know your job; you just lack self-confidence. I recognize that because I've been there. And I also know you're ready to take command of the *Vordoth*. Don't you trust my judgment anymore?"

"Totally and unquestionably, Captain, but I could *never* do the things you've done."

"I sincerely hope you never have to. But I know you *can* command your ship, Captain Sabella. The threat from Raiders has been greatly reduced and you should only have to worry about normal freighter duties for the rest of this trip. And— my name is Jen."

Gloria looked at Jenetta intently for several seconds, then grinned. "Okay, Jen."

"Now, as one captain to another, I have a favor to ask."

"Anything."

"I need about eighteen of your people, including all eight of the gunners that Gunny Rondell trained. These ships are enormous and we have over nine hundred thirty prisoners. I need gunners, a relief bridge crew for each ship, and a few of your biggest cargo handlers to help with the prisoners. I'd also like to have Rebecca for a while to help me with some of the women we rescued. I realize it'll leave you a bit shorthanded, but it can't be helped."

"You've got it, Jen. We'll be accompanying you to Obotymot, so we can share personnel as needed."

"Thanks, Gloria. Two more things. Could you send over all my clothes and personal items? And I left a personal envelope on the desk in the captain's briefing room that I'd like returned. I'd also like you to erase the messages I recorded before I left the *Vordoth*, the ones that were to be sent in the event of my death."

"I'll see that the messages are erased as soon as I get back and your personal items will be returned on the next shuttle. Do you want the escape pod we found you in?"

Jenetta looked away for a second. "Wow, that seems like a hundred years ago." Lost in thought for a few seconds before looking back at Gloria again, she added, "Yes, Space Command will probably want it."

"Okay. How soon do you want to get underway?"

"Just as soon as everyone is ready. Let's plan on 2100 hours."

"Aye, Cap— Jen."

In response to the door-chime, Jenetta said, "Come."

When the doors opened, Captain Yates entered the office and walked to the desk. "You wanted to see me, Captain?"

"Yes. Captain Yates, I'd like to introduce you to Captain Sabella of the *Vordoth*."

"We already met in the conference room. Hello, Captain."

"Hello, Captain Yates."

"The *Vordoth* is going to provide us with additional crew-members for our trip. We'll each have enough for a second bridge crew and four trained gunners. If we run into trouble, I'd rather have our gunners manning the more powerful weapons on the battleships. The *Prometheus* will also get a few extra people to help with the prisoners. We'll be leaving for Obotymot as soon as the personnel transfer is complete. I estimate our departure for about 2100 hours."

"Obotymot, Captain?" Captain Yates said.

"Yes, we're going to provide escort for the three Nordakian freighters before heading for Vinnia. Obotymot is desperate for the food supplies in those freighters. They must arrive there safely."

"I see. I've heard of their problem. Well, another couple of months isn't going to make much difference and I'm enjoying my time on the *Chiron*. When I was in Space Command, I was a helmsman and fourth officer on a troop transport. I felt I might make captain one day but knew I'd never become a line officer. Being captain of a Space Command battleship is a dream come true for me, even if it is unofficial and temporary. What magnificent ships these are."

"The newest, biggest, baddest, and fastest in the fleet. I'm glad we were able to recover them for Space Command. I can only imagine how much worse things would have gotten if the Raider's plan to use them against us had materialized."

Other than the gunners, the people assigned to the *Prometheus* and *Chiron* were all volunteers and Gloria had to make the final selections since everyone on board offered to transfer over. It wasn't that they didn't wish to be on the *Vordoth*, but what serious spacefarer could pass up the opportunity for temporary assignment aboard a pride of Space Command before it even became a pride of Space Command? Jenetta made the specific assignments aboard ship once she knew who would be coming over. The relief bridge crews were instructed in the operation of the control consoles onboard the *Prometheus* and *Chiron* during the first few hours of travel to Obotymot, and thereafter there were always rested crewmen working on the bridge of both ships.

There were only two laser gunners on each watch, a far cry from the hundred-twelve two-man gunnery teams that would eventually be part of the ship's full crew complement, so hopefully they wouldn't run into any Raiders. If an emergency did occur, the off-duty gunners would race to one of the dozen weapons control centers located along the center axis of the ship. Like the bridge itself, and the Auxiliary Command & Control center, each weapons center was protected by massive bulkheads of tritanium armor and additional radiation shielding, and compartmentalized to protect the crewmen in the event that surrounding areas were breached. Once there, the gunners could control any of the ship's operational phased array lasers.

The tactical station aboard a warship functions as a mini combat information center and is always manned by three or more officers. The sizeable tactical station aboard a battleship is designed to accommodate no less than seven officers. The lead tactical officer, a Lieutenant or Lt. Commander, sits amid an almost complete circle of displays and electronic control consoles. Facing him or her on the outside of the circle are stations for the rest of the tac team. A bevy of large holo-screens hang suspended over the encircling hardware and the lead can see what each tac team member is seeing, although the image is reversed.

Once launched, torpedoes are normally guided to their targets by specialists sitting at stations in the various weapons control centers. The single crewman presently manning the tactical station can fire any of the sixteen bow torpedoes, but he can hardly continuously monitor and guide more than a few as they streak towards their targets. If the ship were to run into trouble, the crew would have to rely on the electronic intelligence built into the weapons. With no one to fire and guide torpedoes from the twenty-eight tubes located in the stern and sides of the two battleships, those weapons would most likely remain unused.

Gunny was given full responsibility for the prisoners and handled the job magnificently. An initial check of the crew records had shown that all Raider crewmen aboard the *Chiron* had been accounted for, but two men who had reported aboard the *Prometheus* were missing for the first few hours. Fearing armed resistance, Gunny had organized search parties and begun a methodical hunt for the missing Raiders, beginning in the area near their assigned posts. The two men were found in a cargo hold sleeping off the effects of a private 'last night in port' party. They hadn't even known the ship had been taken.

There had been enough restraint sets taken from the spaceport detention center to put a complete set on the largest prisoners in the cargo bays and, on the second day out from Periseras, one of Gunny's men discovered a large cache of restraints in one of the ship's holds. Every prisoner was immediately outfitted with a complete set. Observation windows into the bays were manned 24 hours a day and whenever there was a problem the guard would just activate the restraints and the problem would be over. After a few days, the prisoners became so subdued that the restraints were only activated during mealtime while food was delivered or food carts recovered. Unlike in the Raider detention cell, the prisoners were fed three times a day and crates of fresh fruit were placed in the detention hold so hunger wouldn't cause any problems.

Although Rebecca had injected surgical nano-bots to begin knitting the broken bone, Jenetta's system quickly disabled and absorbed them, then performed its own reconstruction of the arm. Before surgical nano-bots were available, the simple break would have taken nine to twelve weeks to mend in the average person. The bots usually cut that time to six weeks. Jenetta's arm healed completely during the first 12 days of the trip and she was able to begin practicing her kick boxing again using the heavy, hundred pound punching bag in the ship's gym. Rebecca declared her one of the fastest healing patients she had ever met, or even heard of. She was still talking about Jenetta's speedy recovery following her rescue from the escape pod and had even written a paper on it. For her part, Jenetta withheld the information she'd been given by Arneu about the incredible recuperative powers of her body resulting from the rewritten DNA and allowed Rebecca to believe, for now, it was a natural healing ability at work.

The small freighter convoy, flanked on either side by a magnificent new SC battleship, entered orbit around the planet Obotymot forty-eight days after departing Periseras. Not a single vessel had been DeTect'ed during the voyage. That fact in itself was normally reason for celebration, but knowledge that it was most likely owed to the destruction of almost all Raider warships operating in the deca-sector put a smile on everyone's face and an extra spring in their steps. By now every individual aboard the six ships knew the relevant facts about the destruction of Raider-One, and an expanding palisade of elaborated facts about Jenetta's role in the event was arising as the tale was expounded with every discussion.

Jenetta knew practically every square meter of the *Prometheus* by the time they reached Obotymot and really did think of it as *her* ship. During the voyage, she'd spent much of her time wandering around, exploring, solving little problems, and resolving disputes. She felt her ship could not have been more aptly named, as *Prometheus* was the Greek god in mythology known for his rebellious actions against injustice and abuse of power. According to Greek mythology, Zeus had his servants chain *Prometheus* to a rock on the mountain Caucasus after *Prometheus* gave fire to mankind, but *Chiron* the Centaur and Hercules eventually saved him. The ancient Greeks credited *Prometheus* with being mainly responsible for the survival of mankind. Jenetta saw parallels in the former imprisonment of the current crew and their freedom from the abuses perpetrated by the powerful Raider forces with the destruction of their base.

"We're in geosynchronous orbit above Vkattch, the planet's capital city, Captain," the astrogator said as the helmsman completed the maneuver. "The other ships are in line behind us with about five kilometers of separation."

"Thank you, gentlemen. Mr. Beckens, notify the *Chiron* to link up with us using our bow airlocks."

"Aye, Captain," the com operator said.

The former prisoners initially wore Raider uniforms from the ship's stores just to have clean clothes that fit properly, but after their abusive treatment at the hands of the Raiders, no one cherished wearing clothing that reminded them of the guards or the detention center. During the first few days of the journey, a former prisoner who had once been a tailor, with assistance from the former female captives, began dying and reconstructing Raider uniforms to look like Space Command issue. Except for a lack of rank insignia, the bridge appeared to be manned entirely by Space Command personnel. Only Jenetta, Captain Yates, Lt. Commander Michaels, Doctor Erikson, and Gunny wore rank insignia. The people handling duties normally handled by officers wore unadorned officer uniforms and the others wore either noncom or enlisted personnel uniforms.

"Captain, there's an entire fleet of space tugs coming up from the surface," Kilgore said.

"Put it on the front viewscreen."

The image on the monitor immediately changed from a forward-looking view of space to an image provided by sensors located on the keel of the ship. Dozens upon dozens of tugs were climbing towards the convoy. The planet far below them looked a bit like an Earth shrouded in heavy smog. Prior to the meteor strike, it had probably appeared *very* Earth-like, a beautiful blue planet with large landmasses of green and tan, and white swirling cloud formations. It should resemble Earth again one day, once the atmosphere cleared.

"They must have amassed every tug on the planet prior to our arrival," Jenetta said. "Well, we knew they were desperate for the supplies. With that fleet of tugs and the others from the freighters, they'll have all thirty kilometers of cargo sections moved down to the planet in a couple of days."

"Lt. Sabella is launching all tugs from the *Vordoth*, Captain," Beckens, said.

'*Good for Gloria*,' Jenetta thought to herself. "Let's launch our own two tugs," she said aloud. "I'm sure we have a few tug jockeys among the temporary crews in *Prometheus* and *Chiron* who will be glad to help out. Pass the word to Captain Yates and then to engineering."

"Aye, Captain," Beckens said.

Jenetta observed the freight activity for the rest of her watch. When Lt. Commander Michaels arrived for the second watch, she turned over control of the bridge and walked to her quarters to freshen up before continuing on to the mess hall.

During the infancy of space travel, tiny, cramped cylinders had been adequate for trips of fleeting duration, but for long voyages, people needed space and privacy. With each new generation of ships, larger quarters and additional creature comforts had been added, which made perfect sense when considering that people were aboard ship for months and years at a time without having an opportunity to go dirt-side or even making planet-fall. The captain's quarters aboard the *Prometheus* were the most spacious Jenetta could imagine. They contained a large bedroom with a private bath, an enormous sitting room with several sofas and half a dozen chairs, a half bath, a large office containing a desk and conference table, a dining room capable of seating twelve, and a private galley, plus attached quarters for the steward. Although true that she hadn't previously had occasion to visit the private quarters of any ship captains, she couldn't imagine that any would be larger, or even that anyone would desire larger quarters. Even the quarters intended for the most junior officers were comparatively more spacious and luxurious than her quarters aboard the *Hokyuu* had been. The quarters for the ratings were naturally the smallest. They had to share a bedroom with three other ratings, but at least they had a private half bath. Once they made petty officer, they'd rate a semi-private bedroom with a half-bath. Chief petty officers rated private quarters and full baths.

Jenetta had moved into the captain's quarters on the first day after removing all of the clothing and personal effects of the individual who had originally occupied the rooms. He hadn't been on the ship when they took control and Jenetta suspected he might have been killed when the space station blew up, but she had his personal possessions packed up and saved just in case Space Command ever found out where to send them. Lt. Commander Michaels had moved into the first officer's quarters, located right next to Jenetta's, and similarly packed up the personal possessions of Commander Pretorious that he found there.

The crew complement aboard the *Prometheus* was so small that one mess hall adequately filled their needs. Jergen, the cook from the captured freighter Nova Dawn, Captain Starnos' ship, took over the galley on the first day and made it his own. Ably assisted by Delilah and most of the other former women captives, he prepared all of the food for the mess hall. Rebecca had wholeheartedly endorsed getting the women involved and feeling useful again.

Practically everyone not on duty at 1800 was already there when Jenetta arrived for dinner. After selecting her food, she joined her usual meal companions: Rebecca, Gunny, and Leah.

"I love that red dress, Leah," Jenetta said as soon as she had taken her seat. "Is it new?"

"Thank you, Jen. Yes, it is; I just completed it today. It's Carel's favorite color."

"Carol?"

"Yes, Carel," she said, pointing to Gunny.

Jenetta looked towards Gunny, who just looked down at the table, his cheeks slightly flushed.

"It's spelled C-A-R-E-L," he said sullenly. "I was named after my great grandfather, Carel Francois Rondell."

Jenetta and Rebecca just nodded solemnly, sensitive to Gunny's discomfort and exhibiting great control by not smiling. Of course, Jenetta found it necessary to clench her jaw, not because of the name, but simply because of Gunny's obvious embarrassment.

Once the uniforms for the crewmen had been completed, the former female captives had used their free time to make clothing items for themselves, such as blouses, skirts, dresses, and undergarments. Jenetta was glad to see them busy and was happy with the progress they had made so far in recovering from the imprisonment and brainwashing. Doctor Erikson worked with the women every day, doing her best to help them adjust to life after captivity. Upon reaching a GSC base, there would be a plethora of trained specialists to continue with each of the women.

*   *   *

On the third day following their arrival at Obotymot, Jenetta traveled down to the planet's surface. She was horrified at the devastation she found. The climate had changed significantly and, although it was now summer in Vkattch, it felt like mid-winter. The leafless trees left the countryside looking bleak and naked, and the land appeared almost barren of life. The dead grasses and groundcovers were losing their grip on the soil, allowing a sort of fine-grained dust to be carried on every breeze. The loss of the topsoil would make recovery that much more difficult.

Before the meteor strike, the earth-like planet had supported a prosperous, agrarian society, but afterwards the population had gathered in vast centralized communities similar to the large cities on Earth, while the former small farming communities became virtual ghost towns. The system's sun was a G3 yellow star with a temperature of 5,580 K, but on the surface of Obotymot it was dark all the time and a filtration mask was necessary equipment. At noon, the dust still remaining in the upper atmosphere made it appear like dusk on Earth. Every process ever employed for rainmaking and weather control was being tried as they attempted to 'scrub' the atmosphere clean of airborne dirt and dust pollutants. Large ships with enormous funnels normally used in space to collect hydrogen for fuel had been converted to collect dirt and dust. They constantly dipped low into the atmosphere and crisscrossed the sky, sucking in pollution and expelling filtered air. It was difficult to believe they could make a difference given the enormity of the project, but it was estimated that the planet would have already begun to enter an ice age if not for their valiant efforts.

The planetary leaders, grateful beyond words for the arrival of the convoy, insisted on thanking Jenetta for saving their supply ships and arranged a number of special events in her honor. The sudden abundance of food supplies had put everyone in a festive mood. In obvious deference to Jenetta, everyone she met, or even saw, had adopted her skin coloration while she was on the planet. She wondered if she would ever see a Nordakian in his or her true state. She did, however, have a firsthand opportunity to observe what feelings of elation could do to Nordakians. Everywhere she went she saw the rippling of colors across the skin of happy people. And each time she was introduced at an event, the flashing became so intense that it was difficult to focus on any one individual. It was as if an entire Mardi Gras crowd dressed in brightly colored costumes was whirling as fast as they could.

After the second large State dinner over a span of a few days, Jenetta explained that she had to report to Space Command. The leaders of the colony reluctantly cancelled further activities and conveyed their goodbyes.

*　*　*

Reduced to half its former size for the final leg of its journey to Higgins Space Command base, the small convoy left orbit the following day. Although they hadn't DeTect'ed a single vessel during their trip to Obotymot, they would maintain their vigilant surveillance of surrounding space as their trip continued. Jenetta had requested that Space Command not notify her family when she first contacted them from the *Vordoth* and she debated whether to send a message to her parents now. She wanted to let them know she was alive and well, but there was still a danger. While their appearance was formidable, the ships were so understaffed that she feared they couldn't put up much of a fight if confronted by hostile forces. She decided to postpone sending the message until she was sure they were out of danger.

* * *

Sixty days out from the planet Vinnia, Jenetta finally sent another message to Space Command. It would be her first message to Higgins since the attack on the *Vordoth* and she decided to send it from the bridge of the *Prometheus* so Space Command would actually see the ship's bridge. It would take hours for the message to reach the Space Command Base and then many more hours before a reply was received.

Jenetta sat in the command chair with her back ramrod straight and said, "This is Jenetta Carver, serial number 3974A32, on the bridge of the GSC battleship *Prometheus* GSC-B368. Following a third battle with Raiders, I was able to follow them back to their base where I discovered two new SC battleships being readied for operations against Space Command and private commerce. I was captured, but managed to escape after a month in captivity. Assisted by prisoners I liberated from the Raider detention center, I seized the *Chiron* and the *Prometheus*, and successfully fled the Raider base. We're currently en route to Higgins Space Command Base at Vinnia, accompanied by the freighter *Vordoth*. Our estimated time of arrival is 60 days. Jenetta Carver, Captain of the *Prometheus*, message complete."

* * *

"Come in, Captain," Rear Admiral Brian Holt, base commander of Higgins Space Command Base, said to Captain Richard Dommler as he appeared in the doorway of the Admiral's spacious office in the headquarters section of the base. "Commander Kanes and I were just discussing the message from this person identifying herself as Jenetta Carver, Captain of the *Prometheus*. Have a seat." Even seated behind his enormous desk, Holt presented an imposing image. The seventy-one year-old admiral's once jet-black hair may have turned grey, but he was physically fit and still as sharp as they came.

"Thank you, sir," Dommler said as he eased himself down into one of two overstuffed chairs that faced the Admiral. Commander Keith Kanes of SCI occupied the other. Dommler was still breathing a little heavy, having been summoned to come to the Admiral's office immediately. Watching the Admiral, Dommler reminded himself that he had to get to the gym more often than once every couple of weeks. Of average height, he would never be the imposing figure the admiral was, but, being only fifty-seven years old, he shouldn't be breathing as laboriously as he currently was from just hurrying through the base.

"Please continue, Commander Kanes," Admiral Holt said.

Looking at Dommler with piercing steel-grey eyes, Kanes said, "I was saying that Space Command Intelligence believes this to be a ploy by the Raiders to get close enough to the base to take us out in one lightning attack while our guard is down. They went to a lot of trouble, and great risk, to steal those two ships, so they must have had this planned for some time. Those ships are the most powerful spacecraft in the known galaxy, and I don't mind telling you I've had a lot of sleepless nights thinking about them having fallen into Raider hands. If the Raiders could knock out this base, they'd have the run of this entire deca-sector. We've been the only thing keeping them even moderately in check."

"What about that message we received from Carver earlier when she was aboard the *Vordoth*?" Holt asked.

"We believe they were just priming the pump, sir. She said she'd been asked to take command of the freighter after the captain was killed. Admiral, no first officer I know of would just turn over command of his or her ship to a mere ensign, even if the first officer had no formal military training. It just doesn't wash."

"I tend to agree with you," Holt said, "but the serial number checks out. It was the one assigned to Ensign Carver and her likeness matches the file photos. She also used a valid GSC encryption code for her transmissions."

"The serial number could be obtained easily enough, sir, from records available to the general public. Ensign Carver died aboard the *Hokyuu* eleven years ago and the accident investigation files were widely distributed. I'm sure her serial number is listed in several places within official documents released to the public under disclosure laws. And the physical appearance of this woman could have been altered easily enough with modern surgical techniques. The encryption code was a valid code, but it was over ten years old. It could have been broken years ago and we just never knew it. For that matter, if Carver did get out of the *Hokyuu*, they may have found her escape pod and taken the data ring from her corpse. That's one of the reasons we retire even 'unbroken' encryption codes every year. They certainly did their homework when they prepared this operation. The Raider organization has some brilliant criminal minds.

"SCI believes the *Vordoth* was captured by Raiders and is now also crewed by members of that crime organization. It's the consensus of my section's staff that we'll be attacked as soon as the three ships get within energy weapon range of the station. The freighter alone is carrying the firepower of a Space Command light destroyer and it would be suicide to allow them close enough to Higgins for their laser arrays to become effective. According to our records, the *Vordoth* also has four torpedo tubes.

"I mean, really sir, how probable is it that such a junior officer could organize a group of escaped civilian captives into commando squads able to overpower the entire Raider crews of both stolen battleships, then command the operation of Space Command's most sophisticated vessels? Especially someone with such a poor record in command and control exercises as the real Carver had during her Academy years. Our files indicate Carver was ideally suited for a life in the service simply because it saved her from having to decide which *clothes* to wear each morning."

Admiral Holt nodded and grimaced. "Yes, I read her complete file. She was extremely intelligent but apparently equally indecisive. Well, we have our normal protection force of five warships in port. I'll issue orders to put them on alert. I'll also summon all other ships within thirty light-years to return to the base immediately. If the *Prometheus*, *Chiron*, or *Vordoth* come within a billion miles of this base, we'll show them that Space Command knows how to deal with Raiders."

"But, sir," Captain Dommler said, "what if the message is genuine? I realize it's a million to one long shot, but there is a possibility. Tests have indicated that a human in prime physical condition, as a young Space Command officer would be, could potentially survive in a stasis chamber for as long as forty-two years if the pod's power source continued to function properly. Can we just destroy them without warning?"

Holt was quiet for a few seconds while he stared down at his hands and rethought his position. "No. You're right, Captain, we shouldn't, even though the rated useful life of power cells in the *Hokyuu's* escape pods was only seven years. Send a message to the three ships informing them that they will not be allowed to approach the base as they plan. This will be their only warning and they ignore it at their peril."

"Aye, Admiral."

"I think it's a serious mistake to warn them, Admiral," Kanes said. "This might be our only opportunity to destroy the *Prometheus* and *Chiron* before the Raiders can use them against us. We should let them think we're greeting them with open arms and then strike them with everything we have. We can destroy them well before they come within range to use their laser arrays or torpedoes on the station. They'll think their plan is working and never know what hit them when a hundred torpedoes blow them apart."

"No, Commander. We must play by the rules, even if the Raiders don't. We'll warn them off first— and then blast them to space dust if they persist in their attempts to approach the station."

* * *

It took almost thirty hours for a reply to come from Space Command, about fourteen hours longer than it should have taken for a normal communication. When the message arrived, Jenetta had the com operator put it through to her briefing room. She lifted the com screen panel on her desk, pressed the 'play message' button, and watched as the screen lit up with the image of a GSC captain.

"This is Higgins Space Command Base at Vinnia calling the ship identifying itself as *Prometheus* GSC-B368. No such ship name or number is currently included in the Galactic Space Command Ship Registry. If you, the *Vordoth*, or the ship calling itself *Chiron* approaches Vinnia, you do so at your own peril. This is Captain Richard Dommler, out."

Jenetta sat back in her chair and thought about the message for a while. Then she got up and prepared a mug of coffee before plopping back down in her chair to consider the implications again. The matter would weigh heavily on her mind for the next seven weeks.

Chapter Twenty-One

~ December 24ᵗʰ, 2267 ~

Ten days before their expected arrival at Vinnia, Jenetta called Lt. Commander Michaels into her briefing room. After each of them prepared a beverage from the food synthesizer, they sat down at the desk, Jenetta behind it in her large executive chair and Michaels in one of the overstuffed visitor chairs in front.

"Hugh, I'd like you to see a message I received from Space Command."

"Space Command? I wasn't aware we had received any messages from them recently."

"This was the first and only message we've received," Jenetta said quietly. "I've devoted quite a bit of time thinking about it and decided you should be aware of its content as well." She raised the com's viewscreen panel, swiveled it towards Michaels, and pressed the 'play message' button after selecting the message from the queue.

Michaels watched without expression and then turned to Jenetta with a puzzled look. "I don't understand."

"They don't accept that we are who we say we are," Jenetta said matter-of-factly.

Michaels was quiet as he thought that over. "Who do they think we are, Captain?"

"I suspect they believe us to be Raiders and that this is a ruse to get the battleships in close enough to the spaceport so that we can destroy it. At least that might be *my* speculation, were I in their position."

Michaels looked at the floor and whistled a quiet series of notes that trailed off slowly.

"Exactly."

"What do we do, Captain? Surely you can contact the base commander and explain our situation."

"Uh, I'm afraid not. You see, to them, I've been dead for eleven years."

"I— don't understand."

"It's simple. I'm officially listed as dead in Space Command records."

"Is that so you could carry on clandestine operations? Spy stuff?"

"No, nothing like that. Did you ever hear of the *Hokyuu*?"

"The *Hokyuu*?" Michaels scrunched up his face slightly while he thought. "Isn't that the GSC quartermaster ship that exploded for unexplained causes about eleven years ago?"

"Yes. I was onboard the *Hokyuu* until a few seconds before it exploded."

Michaels chuckled. "You sure do get around, Captain. Uh— you're not telling me *you* destroyed the *Hokyuu*, are you?"

"No, of course not. Do you remember how many people were lost on the *Hokyuu*?"

"As best I can recall, all hands were recovered except one."

"Correct. That individual was one Ensign Jenetta Alicia Carver, recent graduate of NHSA, class of '56."

"You mean they rigged the explosion to fake your death?"

"No, Hugh, the explosion was real. I managed to make it into an escape pod and leave the ship just seconds before it exploded. My pod was damaged by the explosion and never fired the retrorocket intended to stop its travel near the site of the disaster. Additionally, because I was so close to the ship when it blew, I was caught in the blast. My speed was greatly accelerated when I was hit by fragments of the ship."

"How long did it take them to find you?"

"Almost eleven years."

He was quiet for a few seconds as he digested the information. "You're telling me that you spent eleven years floating in an escape pod?"

"Exactly. You're looking at the current surviving record-holder for continuous time in a stasis chamber, according to Doctor Erikson. Now you know why I look so young for a graduate of the class of '56."

Michaels was quiet for a full fifteen seconds as he worked things out in his head. "Then you're not a Space Command captain? You're only an ensign?"

"That's right."

Michaels jumped up, spilling coffee on his uniform as his mug fell to the floor. He glared at Jenetta and screamed, "You mean I've been taking orders from a goddamned *Ensign* for the past five months?"

The door-chime sounded just then, but, because of the tenseness of the situation, Jenetta tried to ignore it. It sounded again, twice. Michaels was still glaring at Jenetta when she said, "Come."

Gunny Rondell strode into the room, a concerned look on his face. As the door closed behind him, he said, "I thought I heard yelling. Is everything all right, Captain?"

"She's not a captain!" Michaels said in a booming voice. "She's only a Space Command *Ensign!*"

"Yes sir, I know," Gunny said calmly. "But that's Space Command's mistake. To me she's a captain— the best one I've ever served under. And that's saying something. How many Space Command captains do *you* know who could have engineered his or her own escape from that hell of a detention center, freed the rest of us, and seized two new battleships during the breakout."

Michaels calmed down, looked at Jenetta with a slack-jawed, quizzical look on his face, and asked, "Has *everyone* known about your real rank except me?"

"No, not *everyone*. Just the crew of the *Vordoth* and anyone else they might have told."

"And they still all call you Captain?"

"I was asked to take command of the ship after the first Raider strike. They've only called me Captain since then."

A look of thorough exasperation covered his face as Michaels plopped back down into the 'oh-gee' chair. "This is unbelievable, simply unbelievable."

Jenetta turned to Gunny Rondell while Michaels tried to come to grips with the situation. "Did you need something, Gunny?" Jenetta asked.

"That officer wants to see you, the obnoxious commander you captured on the bridge."

"I'll come down as soon as Commander Michaels and I are finished here."

"Aye, Captain, thank you. Sorry to have interrupted."

"No problem, Gunny. Dismissed."

Michaels stared at Jenetta as Gunny left. He slumped in his chair as he said morosely, "We're in a fine mess. A ship that doesn't exist with a captain who doesn't exist, traveling in hostile space and proscribed from ever making port. We're almost like a ghost ship. Perhaps we should change our name to the Flying Dutchman. No wonder Higgins is wary."

"We exist. We just have to prove it to Space Command. Do you wish to be relieved of further duty while on board?"

Michaels gripped the arms of the chair tightly and sat upright, looking at Jenetta angrily. "Of course not. I've never shirked responsibility in my life."

"I only thought you might have trouble taking orders from a captain for whom you lack respect. We still have dangerous days ahead and I need to know that everyone under my command will do what I say, when I say it. Lives could hang in the balance."

Michaels took a deep breath, relaxed into the chair, and was quiet for a few seconds. "Back in the detention cells I made a promise to obey every order you give until we clear Raider space and reach a Space Command base. I'll abide by that. Until we dock at the Vinnia base, you're the captain of this ship and I'll follow your orders."

"Even if I order you to fire on another Space Command vessel?"

"Would you order such a thing?" Michaels asked as he gave Jenetta a sidelong glance.

"I'll do whatever's necessary to protect the lives of my crew and passengers and those aboard the other ships under my command."

Michaels shook his head slowly. "I don't know, Captain. I honestly don't know if I could do that."

"I'll accept that. I know you'll do the right thing when the time comes." Standing up, Jenetta said, almost lightly, "I'm going to see what our prisoner wants."

Gunny was waiting for her when she arrived down at the cargo bay where the prisoners were being held.

"He wants a private audience," Gunny said, "so I put him over here in a utility room." Leading the way to a room not much larger than a walk-in closet, he opened the door for Jenetta. Commander Pretorious was standing in the middle of the small room with his restraints secured. His scowl and glaring look revealed his mood.

"Thank you, Gunny."

"I'll be right outside the door, Captain."

The door slid closed behind her as Jenetta approached the Raider officer.

"You wished to see me, Commander?"

"Actually, I wish that I never laid eyes on you, but that choice wasn't mine."

Jenetta grinned. "What is it you want? I'm sure you didn't ask for a private meeting only to exchange insults."

"Obviously, I want my freedom."

"I know exactly how you feel. I felt the same way while I was locked in the detention center at your spaceport." Pausing for a second, Jenetta added, "No, let me retract that. I should have said I can *imagine* how you feel. You haven't been starved, groped, and tortured as I was."

"And yet you found a way to escape," Pretorious said with narrowed eyes.

"Yes, but that way isn't open to you." Smiling she added, "I doubt you have the legs for it."

Pretorious was confused by her statement but continued with, "I think I have another way."

"Do you? I'm listening."

"I have information that I'm willing to exchange for my freedom."

Jenetta shook her head. "Not a chance."

"Don't be so hasty. You haven't heard what I'm offering."

"Very well, keep talking."

"I know what our next mission is, what target will be hit, and where."

"It's immaterial. The Raider fleet has been destroyed. You were on the bridge when that happened so I know you saw the asteroid explode. There could have been what, two or three ships that *weren't* in port for all the big meetings?"

Pretorious grinned menacingly. "Yes, you destroyed *a* fleet, but there are five other Raider space stations operating in Galactic Alliance space that have, thankfully, never even heard of Captain Jenetta Carver, and each has a fleet just as large or larger than the one you destroyed. Did you really think you wiped out our entire operation? You haven't done anything more than peck at the surface. How did you happen to become a Space Command captain, by the way? You can't be older than eighteen."

"I'm going to be thirty-three in May, if it's of any concern to you."

"It isn't. My only concern is getting out of your brig and regaining my freedom."

Jenetta arched her eyebrows. "So you can return to robbery, murder, hijacking ships, and enslaving people?"

"It's a living," Pretorious said dispassionately. "If I'm not there to do it, dozens of others are just waiting to take my place."

"Well then," Jenetta retorted with a smirking grin, "let's just say I believe in providing job opportunities to the unemployed, and that *you* shall remain off the job market."

Jenetta could tell from Pretorious' flushed face and tightened jaw muscles that he was straining to hold his temper. "You're going to be a big hero when you get back to Space Command. Wouldn't you like to be bigger still?"

"Get to the point, Commander. My coffee's getting cold."

"I'm offering you the opportunity to save hundreds, maybe thousands of lives, and you're concerned about your coffee getting cold? What kind of GSC officer *are* you?"

"The kind who's getting tired of listening to someone prattle on endlessly, never saying anything worthwhile."

"Okay, then listen to this— twenty-three of our biggest and best warships at Raider-One were designated to be part of a special attack force and our group was only *one-half* of a combined force that was scheduled to leave the day after your escape. We were supposed to meet up with an equally large force from Raider-Three and attack the target together."

"Forty-six warships? What's the target? A planet?"

"That's the question, isn't it? You want the answer and I want out of here. All I need is a space tug with ninety days of food and water on board. You have a couple on each battleship. GSC won't even know it's missing since there weren't any with the ships when we hijacked them."

"So you want me to free you and aid your escape just because you give me the name of a target that won't be attacked now that the attack fleet has lost half its ships? I'll tell you what I'll do. You give me the locations of all the Raider space stations in GA space and I'll make sure the prosecution knows how very helpful you've been. I'm sure they'll even commute the death penalty."

"Yeah, sure. I give you the locations and then I'm found dead in my cell a week later and my entire family is killed as well. You don't seem to comprehend the magnitude and power of the organization behind me. The company doesn't mess around. No deal, honey." Pretorious' control over his temper was starting to fail and he said loudly, "You really are one stupid little bitch, aren't you?"

Jenetta smiled sweetly. "Perhaps, but then I'm not the one in restraints, am I?" She turned, opened the door, and said, "I'm finished here, Gunny."

"Aye, Captain."

As she walked out of the room, Commander Pretorious finally lost all control of his temper and yelled, "You're dead, you little bitch, you're dead! You hear me? That's a promise!"

But all Jenetta really heard was the sound of a balled fist solidly striking the flesh of a face, a grunt, and the sound of a body hitting the deck. Gunny didn't like people talking to his favorite captain like that.

Returning to the bridge, Jenetta walked to her briefing room, prepared a fresh mug of coffee, and sat down at her desk while an automated housekeeping robot continued to scrub the carpet where Lt. Commander Michaels had dropped his coffee mug. She had already given a great deal of thought to what the target of the big operation might be, but having been out of touch for more than ten years made it difficult. She hadn't even heard of the Nordakians until their distress call was received. Even if she knew what was going on in the galaxy, she probably wouldn't have the inside information necessary to identify the target. It was most likely a convoy of ships the Raiders had learned about from their spy network. One thing she did believe— Pretorious would never have given her any useful information. She had practically had to melt his brain just to get the lockout codes for the ship.

* * *

One week out of Vinnia, Jenetta tried to contact the base again. This time she recorded the outgoing message from her briefing room.

"This is Jenetta Carver, captain of the GSC battleship *Prometheus* and commander of the three-ship force that includes the *Chiron* and *Vordoth*, calling Higgins Space Command Base at Vinnia. We expect to arrive there in seven days. I'm a Space Command officer who has been separated from service as the result of an explosion aboard my ship in 2256 and I'm only trying to return to duty. I'm also trying to return two recovered GSC battleships stolen by the Raiders. I have a crew comprised mainly of rescued Raider captives and I have over nine hundred thirty Raider prisoners that were functioning as crewmembers of the *Prometheus* and *Chiron* when I seized the ships. Captain Jenetta Carver, out."

Jenetta sent the message and then sat back to think. It shouldn't take more than fifty minutes for the message to reach the base, but she had no idea how long it would take for them to respond.

The reply came in six hours and Jenetta invited Lieutenant Commander Michaels into her briefing room when it arrived, having earlier informed him that she'd sent another message. Once they were seated, she raised the com screen, selected the message, and pressed the play button. The face of the captain who had previously responded appeared.

"This is Captain Richard Dommler of the Higgins Spaceport at Vinnia calling *Prometheus*. Contact us again for approach control information when you reach the fifty million kilometer outer marker, Captain. Welcome back, *Prometheus* and *Chiron*. Higgins, out."

Jenetta and Michaels turned to look at each other with quizzical looks. Jenetta had invited him into the briefing room so they could formulate a strategy, operating on the assumption that they would again be warned off.

"That's certainly a considerable change of attitude," Jenetta said.

"How should we take this, Captain?"

"I don't know. The previous message was almost like a declaration of war and this one is like welcoming home a family member."

"We *are* a family member. At least *you* are and I used to be until I retired from the service. Do you suspect a trap, Captain?"

"Do you mean, 'Will they open fire as soon as they see us?'" Jenetta shook her head. "I don't know."

"What will you do if they do open fire as soon as they see us?"

Jenetta chuckled. "Run like hell, just like any other sane person."

"You won't order us to fire on them?"

"Fire on another Space Command vessel? Never!"

"But you asked *me* if *I'd* do it if ordered to?"

"I wanted to know where you stood. Your answer told me."

Michaels stared at Jenetta for at least ten seconds before responding. "Gunny Rondell is right. You are good."

Jenetta grinned. "Thank you Commander Michaels, that means a lot coming from *you*."

"You're welcome, *Captain*."

* * *

One day before arriving at Vinnia, Jenetta ordered the convoy to halt so she could transfer all non-essential personnel to the *Vordoth*. Most balked at leaving, even after she explained she had received mixed signals from Space Command and that they were being transferred for their own safety. In the end, they followed her orders because they knew she was just looking out for their welfare. The only duty personnel left aboard the *Prometheus* and *Chiron* were the guards needed to watch the prisoners, a few people needed to prepare food, a small group in Engineering, and two shifts of bridge staff. The enormous ships really did take on the look and feel of ghost ships.

Jenetta sent two of the Raider-provided shuttles and one of the Raider tugs over to the *Vordoth* to make up for the lost tug, cargo containers, and Corplastizine. The value of the three small craft easily exceeded the value of the lost equipment and cargo.

* * *

Since Galactic Alliance regulations prohibit the use of faster-than-light speeds by any inbound ship closer than four billion kilometers to a space station, or a planet with approach control, Jenetta ordered her three ships to drop their light speed envelopes and continue on at the maximum allowable speed of Sub-Light-100 when they reached that point. Where they could have reached Higgins Space Station in less than two minutes at the *Vordoth's* maximum speed, it would instead take them eleven-point-one hours to reach the station at one hundred thousand kps. Exceptions to the rule could be requested of, and approved by, the senior officer in the GSC approach control center, but Jenetta felt that a nervous command structure would be assuaged by her maintaining strict adherence to the normal rules of traffic safety at this point.

At fifty million kilometers out, Jenetta ordered her ships to reduce speed to the required pattern maximum of Sub-Light-10. As the *Prometheus* slowed to just ten thousand kps, the com operator contacted the spaceport for approach control instructions while the *Chiron* and the *Vordoth* did the same. At this distance, communication was naturally instantaneous, and the controller gave each a precise approach vector that had them align one behind the other with the *Prometheus* in the lead, followed by the *Chiron* next, and then the *Vordoth*.

Gunny Rondell was manning the tactical station for the approach to the spaceport. "Captain, I'm picking up ten warships ahead."

"Blocking our path?"

"Negative, Captain. They're five kilometers on either side of our approach vector. The computer identifies them as a battleship, two cruisers, two frigates, and five destroyers. Aligned in staggered order, they're maintaining a ship separation of one thousand kilometers along our track just beyond the leading edge of the inner pattern at ten thousand kilometers where we're required to reduce speed again."

"Nine thousand kilometers of warships," Jenetta said thoughtfully. "Quite a welcoming committee."

Manning the helm, Lt. Commander Michaels said, "If this is a trap, they're going to have us cold. Do we proceed, or run for it now?"

Jenetta didn't respond right away.

"Captain?" Michaels said questioningly.

Jenetta still didn't answer. Her mind was racing as she weighed the options. If they ran now, the Space Command vessels would be on their six immediately. The *Prometheus* and *Chiron*, each with a top speed of Light-375, could most likely outrun every ship facing them, but Jenetta knew that running would also end any chances of returning to a Space Command base. They'd definitely be branded as Raiders because of their action, and every ship and base in Galactic Alliance space would be alerted to watch for them with orders to attack them on sight. The *Vordoth* was only capable of achieving Light-150, and a lot of innocent people aboard the freighter could be killed in the crossfire if the *Prometheus* either deviated from its approach vector or began to build an FTL envelope, actions that the Space Command vessels would interpret as hostile.

"Captain?" Michaels said again, a little louder. "What should I do?" he added, with urgency in his voice.

Chapter Twenty-Two

~ January 3rd, 2268 ~

"Proceed on course," Jenetta said soberly. "Slow to Plus-100 at the inner pattern marker— but be prepared to get us out of here fast if they open fire."

"Aye, Captain."

The bridge became deathly silent as the *Prometheus* moved closer and closer to the first warship. The bridge crew had been informed that Higgins might suspect the ship was commanded by Raiders looking for an opportunity to attack the station despite the fact that Jenetta had identified herself repeatedly. It seemed as if everyone was holding their breath and some probably were.

Time seemed to slow down immeasurably as they came within energy weapon range of the first ship, the GSC Battleship *Thor*, poised off their larboard bow. While the hatch covers over the phased array lasers and torpedo tubes of the *Prometheus* were closed and locked, the *Thor's* hatches were wide open and its arrays extended. Although the *Thor's* laser arrays were probably smaller than the hundred-gigawatt lasers of the *Prometheus* or *Chiron*, even a ten-gigawatt array could perforate reinforced tritanium armor like a micrometeor punching through two layers of ordinary one hundred mil aluminum. And one thing was certain—the *Thor's* lasers were definitely a lot more powerful than a mere ten-gigawatts.

All eyes were glued to the front monitor, watching for any sign that this was a trap. If it was, then the *Prometheus* was as good as dead. No ship practically empty of personnel would last long under the barrage this armada could unleash. Jenetta mentally castigated herself for her thoughts. She told herself that if they intended to fire they would never have let her get this close to the station. She just had to calm her nerves and ride it out.

Ten seconds later they slid silently past the *Thor* without incident. Everyone exhaled and started breathing a little easier. After passing the second ship without drawing any fire, everyone relaxed noticeably. If the GSC warships were going to open fire first, they should have done so by then.

"The battleship is falling into line behind the *Vordoth*, Captain," Gunny said from the tactical station. "There's no doubt they were waiting out there for us. I could practically feel the fingers of their gunners tightening on triggers as we passed under their guns."

"You and me both, Gunny, but I think we've passed the first test."

As they came within visual sight of the base, the ship was contacted by the docking controller and they received their dock assignment. The massive space station, floating in synchronous orbit above the planet Vinnia, dwarfed the enormous battleships. Easily visible to the naked eye from the planet below, the station resembled an oval-cut, blue opal gemstone surrounded by a sixty-kilometer silver necklace. The necklace, of course, was the docking ring, where dozens of massive ships could be docked with the station simultaneously. Roadway tunnels connecting the base to the docking ring appeared like spokes in a wheel.

Michaels, with months of practice at the helm, had a deft touch on the controls and completed the dock and lock maneuver on the first attempt. Pressurizing the airlock once the ship was securely locked in place, the port's dock master tested and certified the seal before the airlock was opened to traffic. The ten Space Command warships that followed the three ships in took up positions behind the *Prometheus* and *Chiron*, cutting off escape in case all was still not as it seemed. The *Vordoth* was assigned a spot in parking orbit where it was in full view of the station's guns. Its six-kilometer long cargo section prohibited it from docking with the station.

Jenetta, Lt. Commander Michaels, and Gunny met at the forward cargo-bay airlock entrance, and Gunny began the process that would cycle the enormous hatch. It was no more than halfway open when two platoons of Marines began pouring into the bay, weapons at the ready but not pointed as they surrounded the three. A Marine major entered the ship last and calmly walked to the group. He faced Jenetta, staring at her face and uniform intently for several seconds.

Jenetta knew from her years of training that she should immediately salute a superior officer, but an officer entering a ship is required to salute the officer of the deck first, identify himself, and ask permission to enter the ship. The fact that she was wearing insignia that indicated she was the ranking officer never entered her mind.

The Marine Major interrupted the awkward silence by saluting and then saying, "Major Ian Schoonmaker, Captain. Permission to come aboard?"

Although they were already aboard and obviously in command of the situation, Jenetta returned his salute and said, "Permission granted, Major."

"I have orders to take charge of your prisoners."

"Of course, Major. Gunny Rondell will escort your men to the cargo bays we've been using as detention centers. The majority of our prisoners are located there, but we also have prisoners in our brig."

Major Schoonmaker turned to look at Gunny, who was wearing one of the simulated Space Command noncom uniforms with Gunnery Sergeant insignia rather than a more correct Space Marine noncom uniform. Gunny immediately snapped to attention and saluted as Major Schoonmaker took in the unusual uniform configuration with narrowed eyes. Space Command did not have Gunnery Sergeants. That was strictly a Space Marine rank.

"Master Gunnery Sergeant Rondell, Major. Galactic Space Marine Corps, retired. I apologize for the confusing appearance of my uniform, sir. Our clothing choices were limited on this voyage."

Apparently deciding that he should return the salute, the major followed proper protocol before saying, "At ease, Gunny. I understand about the uniform." Turning to one of his officers, Major Schoonmaker said, "Captain Willsie, follow Gunny Rondell and take charge of his prisoners." Turning back to Jenetta and Lt. Commander Michaels, he said, "I also have orders to take charge of you and your first officer, Captain. I have a vehicle waiting. You're to come with me."

Jenetta nodded and led the way into the airlock ramp as Major Schoonmaker stepped aside. At the end of the ramp, an open-topped general-purpose military vehicle was waiting. Jenetta climbed into the right front seat of the driverless vehicle while the Major climbed into the left front and Michaels climbed into a rear seat. As soon as they were seated, the Major said, "Base hospital, depart." The driverless vehicle rose slightly, retracted its landing pads, and drove off on a cushion of 'oh-gee' waves. A second vehicle with four armed marines followed close behind.

As the gp came to a halt in front of the hospital and lowered its pads, Major Schoonmaker jumped out and waited for Jenetta and the Lt. Commander to follow him. Separated as they entered the hospital, Jenetta and Michaels were taken to different wards. Jenetta was escorted into a large examination room where a Space Command Officer, rather than a doctor, was waiting. Seated on the padded 'oh-gee' examination table, he was holding a portable viewpad. Jenetta immediately came to attention.

"At ease *Captain* Carver," the brown-haired officer with piercing steel-grey eyes said. "I'm Commander Kanes of SCI."

Jenetta had already noted the Space Command Intelligence insignia on his collar. "It's *Ensign* Carver, sir."

"I know. You've been kicking up quite a bit of space dust, Carver. Supreme Headquarters is anxious to learn how in the hell a junior officer who supposedly died eleven years ago came to be in command of two brand new, stolen GSC battleships."

"That part is fairly simple, sir. I was captured by the Raiders and commandeered the battleships during my escape."

"You just *found* the ships at a Raider base, eh? And I suppose the Raiders obligingly turned their backs while you took them out for a test flight?"

"Not quite, Commander. We had to seize control of the ships and we barely escaped with our lives. We brought back over nine hundred thirty Raider crewmembers that were manning the ships when we seized them."

Commander Kanes stared coolly at Jenetta. "And just *who* is *we*?"

"We is me, sir, and the fifty other slaves who chose to join me."

"Slaves?"

"We were all slaves, or captives, if you prefer, sir. The Raiders were sending the women to brothels once their mind-conditioning was complete, and the men were intended for hard-labor slave camps throughout the galaxy."

"So you and fifty *civilians*, including a bunch of women, just walked on board and commandeered two highly sophisticated GSC battleships and brought them back to us?"

"Essentially, sir, but your description only captures the bare essence of the action. A dozen of the Raider captives were former freighter officers or bridge crewmen, so they were fully capable of handling the duties I assigned them. We entered the *Chiron* through subterfuge in the middle of the night and then divided into the three assault groups I'd previously established. We simultaneously attacked the bridge, engineering section, and crew quarters. The takeovers only took a matter of minutes. The first assault went so well that I made a decision to take the *Prometheus* as well."

The commander raised his eyebrows in seeming disbelief and stared at Jenetta for a few seconds. She didn't sound anything like the indecisive individual her file described her to be. "Tell me about this Raider base. Where is it?"

"Well— it *was* in sector 8667-3855-1639.5273 ante-median 0196, but it doesn't exist anymore."

"Oh, they packed up and left after you escaped?"

"No sir. It sort of—," Jenetta took a deep breath and exhaled before completing her sentence, "blew up."

"Blew up? It just *sort of* blew up?"

"Well— I guess I blew it up, sir. I think the eight hundred metric tons of Corplastizine I planted in their storage depot was responsible."

Commander Kanes went wide-eyed for a few seconds and then sat up a little straighter. "Eight hundred *tons* of Corplastizine? I should say that it blew up. You could have destroyed several small moons with that much Corplastizine, Ensign."

"Well, I had to use that much because we didn't have any dithulene-35 to use as a catalyst. My chief engineer aboard the *Vordoth* synthesized a substitute, but we expected the detonation to be low yield without the proper catalytic formulation."

"But it was adequate to destroy this alleged spaceport?"

"Apparently sir. The torpedoes might have helped."

"You fired torpedoes at the station?"

"No sir. The explosion was quite sufficient."

"Wait a second. You just said that you used torpedoes."

"Oh, yes, I did. I didn't *fire* the torpedoes, sir. They were included in the cargo containers with the Corplastizine. Charley, uh, Lieutenant Moresby, the *Vordoth's* chief engineer, rigged a remote detonator to blow them. He'd told me that the synthesized catalyst would only detonate the surface material of the Corplastizine rather than commencing the normal cascading effect. I felt that by exploding the torpedoes we'd provide a much greater surface area of Corplastizine for the catalyst. But I was only expecting a diversion, sir. Since the cavern area wasn't pressurized, I never anticipated that the space station would be destroyed. However, with only a narrow tunnel available for the escape of blast-effect gases, I suppose the magnitude of the resulting explosion could have been responsible. Or possibly the explosion damaged one or more vessels and the destruction of their power systems or antimatter containment created a sort of cascading effect of its own. Each ship might have caused another ship parked nearby to explode and so on. In any event— it's gone, sir."

Commander Kanes sucked in a deep breath and exhaled it. "I see. Tell me about this space station, Ensign."

"It was constructed inside a hollowed-out asteroid with enormous doors on the entrance that could be closed if anyone came near, rendering the base effectively invisible. Before we escaped, I downloaded everything I could from the spaceport's central computer."

"And where is that information?"

Jenetta reached into her pocket and produced the tiny box of data rings. "Right here, sir. I could only find eight low-density rings in the detention center, so I was only able to save 800 Terabytes of data. But I made sure the files were from the most secure directories in the system." Jenetta handed the box to the Commander.

"Okay, Ensign, we'll see what you have here. We're also going to check the computer on the ship to see what was recorded in *its* logs."

"There should be complete image logs showing the interior of the spaceport, and I know you'll find an image log of the spaceport blowing up. It was quite spectacular, sir."

"No doubt. We'll be talking again, Ensign, I'm sure."

Commander Kanes hopped off the examination table, walked to the door, and opened it. A doctor stood waiting just outside, with the two marine guards that had followed Jenetta to the room.

"She's all yours, Doc," Kanes said as he left.

The doctor, a thin, slightly balding man of about fifty years with a friendly lopsided smile, came in, closing the door behind him.

"Good afternoon, uh, Captain. I'm Doctor Freidlander."

"Hello, Doctor Freidlander. I'm Ensign Jenetta Carver."

"But you're wearing captain's bars."

"It's a long story, sir. I'm just an ensign again now that I've left the ship."

"I see," the doctor said as he used a stylus to make notes on an electronic clipboard. "Remove your tunic, blouse, trousers, and footwear please."

Jenetta unbuttoned her tunic and turned around to hang it on a coat hook as she removed it, then stripped to her underwear. She had resumed wearing regulation-style cotton underwear the day before.

When her garments were hung up, she turned back to face the doctor, who, upon seeing the imprint on her chest for the first time, did a double take.

"What is this, Ensign, a joke?"

"No doctor, it's very real. I was captured by Raiders who intended to send me to a brothel in the Uthlaro Dominion. They imprinted this mark of ownership on me. I'd appreciate it if you could remove it."

"Uh— we'll see what we can do. You were fortunate to have been rescued by Space Command, young lady."

"Yes sir, I was *very* lucky," Jenetta said with a small grin.

The doctor spent the next hour with Jenetta, performing a myriad of tests before giving her a hospital gown and slippers to wear. The Velcro-sealed gown fully covered the imprint on her chest. A nurse showed her to her room and arranged for dinner while the two marine guards followed along and posted themselves outside her door. Jenetta spent the evening catching up on the news.

When she was taken back to the examination room again the following morning, Doctor Freidlander greeted Jenetta with, "We have to perform some of the tests over again. The results were inconclusive."

Jenetta spent the early part of the morning in the examination room, then was escorted to a conference room where Commander Kanes and six other grim-faced officers wearing SCI insignia were waiting.

"Good morning, Ensign," Commander Kanes said. "Take a seat. We have a few thousand questions for you."

Commander Kanes and the others looked exhausted. They had in fact spent every minute since the *Prometheus* and *Chiron* docked examining the ship's logs and the data Jenetta had brought back. Space Command Headquarters expected them to forward a report with their preliminary analysis by midnight tonight and they were pushing themselves hard to have as complete a picture as possible before then.

Jenetta spent the rest of the morning answering the questions thrown at her by the officers, sometimes several at once as they tried to trip her up. Kanes hadn't been kidding about them having a few thousand. At lunchtime, she was given a fifteen-minute break to have a sandwich and a cup of soup before Commander Kanes resumed the questioning. Jenetta answered every question openly and honestly, except that she chose not to volunteer Mikel Arneu's statement about her possible longevity. It was after 2100 hours when Commander Kanes and the other officers finally completed their questioning, packed up their recording equipment, and allowed her to return to her room. Her vid-screen and the holo-magazine cylinders containing current newspapers had been removed while she was out and the marine guard told Jenetta she was now limited to news that occurred prior to her arrival at the base.

* * *

"Our next topic concerns the ensign who arrived at Higgins after having been missing for eleven years," Admiral Moore said to the other nine admirals sitting around the large horseshoe-shaped table in the great hall where the Admiralty Board held their regular sessions. Aboard ship, a captain was the ultimate authority on all matters, but his or her power was infinitesimal compared to the power wielded by the ten officers around this table. Sitting dutifully behind each admiral were their aides and clerks. The galley seating was empty for this session.

The nameplate on the table in front of the speaker identified him as Richard E. Moore, Admiral of the Fleet, but it was hardly necessary. A long and distinguished career as a battleship captain and then as Earth Forces Commander preceded his ascension to one of the ten most powerful positions in Space Command. After years of dedicated service on the Admiralty Board, he'd received his fifth star and, as Admiral of the Fleet, his face was well known. If anyone needed reminding, they had merely to visit the office of any ship's captain or base commander in the service to see his image. At seventy-nine years of age, Admiral Moore was still fit and trim, without a spare ounce of fat on his five-foot, ten-inch frame. Straight silver-grey hair of regulation length still covered his head. He had always been a little vain about his hair and hated the color and texture it had adopted over the past decade, but he steadfastly refused to dye it to its original color of dark auburn, or partake of the legal drugs that would accomplish the task internally. He had the rare ability to make people understand that he wasn't to be trifled with while projecting the kindly look of a loving grandfather.

Admiral Moore's voice was soft and calm as he looked over his notes. "Normally a matter such as this wouldn't concern this board, but she claims to have destroyed a Raider base while effecting her escape, which resulted in the deaths of over 18,000 people. She also located and commandeered our two stolen battleships and returned them to our forces at Higgins."

"That was a damn sloppy business," Admiral Donald Hubera, the Director of Academy Curricula, grumbled. "Those Raider infiltrators should never have made it within a million kilometers of the Mars facility." Now in his late-seventies, the permanent scowl he had developed while an instructor at the Academy still defined the face beneath a mat of silver-white hair. Crow's-feet lines tugged mightily at his eyes and the flesh at his jowls had begun to sag slightly.

"I think we've rattled enough cages in Earth Defense Command to ensure that it will never happen again, Donald," Admiral Roger Bradlee, the Director of Intelligence, said. At seventy-six, keeping in shape was getting more difficult with each passing year. He wished that keeping his slowly spreading waistline under control was as easy as keeping the grey from consuming his hair. He had no preconceptions against taking the pharmaceuticals that kept his dark brown hair looking as full and vibrant as it had when he was twenty. "Admiral Elersey has been censured and dismissed from the service for incompetence. Captain Dumona, his flag secretary, has been charged with treason and imprisoned, along with the two other senior officers we were able to prove accepted bribes or payments from the Raiders. We've re-commissioned two destroyers from our mothballed fleet and permanently stationed them at the shipyard with orders to immediately fire a full spread of torpedoes into any ship attempting to leave the yard without proper authorization and clearance. A company of Marines will be stationed aboard any new warship once the propulsion systems are active. And all of the automated satellite platforms have been program-med to target any un-cleared ship just as they would an intruder. No one is going to steal any more ships and get away with them. The matter before us now is what to do about this young officer."

"I know her," Admiral Hubera said, running a hand over a scalp still thickly populated with short white hair as every eye in the room turned in his direction. Never one to toss away an opportunity to be center stage, Hubera sat up a little straighter and assumed a scholarly pose. "She was a student of mine when I taught at the Academy. She was bright, extremely bright, but I knew she would be a poor officer." Hubera's mouth magnified the usual scowl as he said, "She had a predilection for practical jokes. There was this one time when she…"

"So many deaths necessitate an open investigation," Admiral Shana Ressler, the Director of Budget & Account-ing, said, interrupting Hubera's reminisces before he became mired in trivia. "We'll have to convene an MIB." The seventy-two-year-old matron had begun to let her hair assume its natural grey color after the birth of her first great-great-grandchild the previous year. The new look was actually an improvement over the strawberry blonde color she had maintained for the prior seven years.

"But the Ensign was operating on her own initiative," Admiral Bradlee said, "and having been officially declared dead ten years ago, she was technically separated from the service. I don't believe the regulations permit the convention of a Military Inquiry Board in this case."

"There must be an investigation of some sort," Admiral Evelyn Platt, the Director of Fleet Operations, said. "Where has she been for the past eleven years while we believed her to be dead?" The second most powerful member of the Board, Admiral Platt had a reputation for fairness and a passion for opera. She had just celebrated her seventy-eighth birthday by flying to Rome to attend an opening night performance of Giacomo Puccini's *La Bohème,* based on the novel by impoverished writer Henry Murger.

"She claims to have been adrift in an escape pod," Admiral Moore said. "That will have to be confirmed, of course."

"Perhaps it might be best to refer this matter to Admiral Komisky in the Judge Advocate General's office before making any decisions," Admiral Bradlee suggested.

"Yes, that might be best," Admiral Moore said. "We'll discuss it again after he's had a chance to look into it and advise us of options and precedents."

*　*　*

The following morning, Jenetta was escorted back to the examination room.

"Some of the tests are still not conclusive," Doctor Freidlander said. "We'll have to run them again."

"What's the problem, doctor?"

"It seems that your retinal scans, fingerprints, and DNA don't match what we have on file for Ensign Jenetta Carver, or anyone else for that matter."

"I knew about the DNA problem, but I didn't realize the others would be altered."

"What do you mean you knew about the DNA problem?"

"While at the Raider prison I was told I was given some kind of new treatment that would, ultimately, completely alter my DNA. They wanted to change my body to make it more appealing to men. Arneu said I would grow six or more inches and that I would have the body of a goddess. His words, not mine."

"And this Doctor Arneu performed this experimental DNA testing on you?"

"No, he wasn't a doctor. He was the commandant of the base. I didn't actually see the people who performed the procedure because I was kept sedated for a week while it was done. Arneu said that at the outset the procedure was extremely painful, but he also said the procedure had been fully tested and was now proven. All I know is that when I awoke following the procedure, I felt like I had been dropped off a five-story building on Earth."

"I see. If it's true that they did something to alter your DNA, that could explain the inconsistencies. You're an inch taller than the height recorded in Jenetta Carver's medical file. And while your retinal scan is ninety-seven percent accurate and your fingerprints are a ninety-two percent match, the skin sample used for the DNA test is only a fifty-six percent match."

"Don't outer skin cells reproduce rather quickly?"

"Yes."

"So then perhaps you could take a sample from someplace where they *don't* change as quickly. Arneu said it would take a long time, years, for all my cells to be changed."

"Bone cells renew at the slowest rate. I can make a small incision in your scalp and take a minute chip from your skull. It will only take a few minutes and the pain will be minimal with the use of a local anesthetic spray."

"Please do it, Doctor."

Informed by the doctor that the incision would heal in a few days, Jenetta was allowed to return to her room after the procedure. Again, she had dinner and then read old newspapers as two Marine guards stood outside her door all night.

Doctor Freidlander, accompanied by Major Schoonmaker, visited Jenetta in her room the next morning.

"I have news," the doctor said. "You've been positively identified as Ensign Jenetta Carver."

"Well, it's nice to be recognized at last."

"Perhaps not," the Major said. He raised an electronic clipboard and read, "Ensign Jenetta Alicia Carver, serial number 3974A32, by order of the base commander I arrest you for being AWOL from your unit."

"*What?*" Jenetta shouted, jumping off the bed. "My unit was destroyed in an explosion in 2256. I spent more than ten years floating around in an escape pod stasis chamber."

"You'll have a chance to defend yourself at your hearing, Ensign. My orders are only to bring you to the brig."

"The brig? Why? Officers are normally just restricted to quarters for a minor charge like AWOL."

"I don't write the orders, Ensign. I do know that other charges are pending. The JAG attorney appointed to represent you will visit you at the detention center."

Jenetta made a face, then calmed and said, "May I have some privacy to get dressed. There aren't any other exits to this room."

"Before you leave I want to change the dressing on the incision I made yesterday," Doctor Freidlander said. "Turn around please, Ensign."

After removing the bandage on her scalp, Doctor Freidlander squinted at the area where he had made the incision. He then maneuvered Jenetta closer to the bright lights over the bed to get a better look.

"I don't understand this. The incision is healed. In fact, there's no mark to even show where I made it. It's as if I never performed the procedure."

"I'm a fast healer, Doctor."

"*Nobody* heals that fast, Ensign. I need to look into this further."

"Not today, Doctor," Major Schoonmaker said. "I have orders to bring the Ensign to the brig and that's where she'll be if you wish to examine her."

"As the attending physician, I decide when a patient can be released from my care, Major."

"You forget, Doctor, you've already declared her fit for duty and released her into my custody."

"This situation supersedes that release."

"Take it up with Commander Kanes if you have a problem, Doctor. Get dressed, Ensign."

"Yes sir, Major."

The doctor stormed out and the Major left calmly without saying another word, the door closing behind them. Jenetta dressed quickly into the uniform she had worn when entering the hospital and brushed her hair. When she was ready to leave, she opened the door. Four armed guards stood there, one of them holding a set of prisoner transport restraints.

"You're kidding, right?" Jenetta said apprehensively as she stared at the restraints.

"Sorry, ma'am," the sergeant in charge of the detail said. "Orders."

As a captive of the Raiders, Jenetta had felt like a prisoner of war and the restraints they'd used to control her had been almost like badges of courage. But to be treated like this by her own military inflicted a sense of shame and degradation that the Raiders would never have been able to impose. Her face reflected her feelings as the guard placed the belt around her waist, locked it on, and then attached her wrists to the belt. Another guard bent down and attached the composite material 'leg irons' to her ankles. With a guard holding each arm, she was escorted out of the hospital. The twenty-centimeter length of chain between the leg irons caused her to stumble constantly as the guards pulled her along faster than she could possibly move her feet, and they were half dragging her and half carrying her by the time they reached the waiting gp. A news photographer in the hospital lobby observed the action and recorded the entire event on video for posterity.

Reaching the detention center, Jenetta's restraints were removed and she was placed in a cell. The two-meter by three-meter room with stark grey plasticrete walls and floor was well lit, but still managed to impart a dismal feeling of finality. She had a wall-mounted cot, toilet, and sink, but no shower, closet, makeup table, or chair. There was nothing to read and nothing worth looking at once the solid door was closed.

"At least they didn't strip me down to my underwear," she said aloud as the cell door clanged shut behind her.

Sitting down on the cot, Jenetta contemplated her situation. After returning the two best ships in the fleet to Space Command, they had some nerve arresting her for being AWOL. She sat on the cot and stewed for about two more hours before being informed that her attorney had arrived.

Locked into full restraints again, she was taken to an interview room where a handsome Lieutenant Commander with a JAG insignia on his collar was waiting for her. As she entered the windowless, lime-green room, which contained only a small metal conference table and half a dozen collapsible chairs, her attorney grimaced at the sight of the transport restraints. He stood to greet her, immediately changing his expression to a welcoming smile. At six-foot-one with blond hair and penetrating blue-green eyes, he might have captivated Jenetta under different circumstances.

"Ensign Carver, I'm Lt. Commander Zane Spence from the Judge Advocate General's office. I've been appointed as your council for the hearing. Guard, would you remove those ridiculous restraints, please."

"Sorry, Commander. I have orders that the prisoner is to remain as she is whenever she's out of her cell."

"This is absurd," Jenetta said loudly. "Since when do officers accused of being AWOL remain restrained while *inside* the brig?"

"Sorry, Ensign," the guard said. "Those are the orders."

Spence turned to Jenetta. "Sit down, Ensign. Let's get through the preliminary stuff and then I'll look into the restraints issue."

He had to pull the chair out so Jenetta could sit down. When they were both seated, he looked at his electronic clipboard and said, "You're being charged with being AWOL. Are you guilty?"

"*Absolutely not!*" Jenetta practically screamed.

"Stay calm, Ensign. Where were you during the alleged absence?"

"Floating in space."

"Pardon me?"

"I was floating in space, at least for most of it."

"I don't understand. We're all floating in space. This entire space station is floating in space."

"It's simple, sir. My ship exploded and I escaped in a life pod. I wasn't picked up during the first three months so I climbed into a stasis chamber and went to sleep. That's where I was until I was picked up."

"And how long were you in the escape pod?"

"Since 2256. You may have heard about the explosion of the *Hokyuu*."

Spence was looking at her like she was crazy. "You're telling me you've been adrift in a life pod for eleven *years*?"

"Except for the past half year. I was picked up by a freighter and awakened."

"And where have you been for the past six months?"

"Trying to get *here*. Raiders attacked us, and then we attacked *them*, a couple of times. I snuck into a Raider base to do some reconnaissance, but I was caught. Finally, I escaped and helped the Nordakians get their cargo through Raider space. But then I came straight here."

Spence was again looking at her like she was crazy. "I see. You were caught by Raiders, but you *escaped*?"

"I can prove it, Commander."

"Can you?"

"Easily. Open up the top of my tunic and blouse. I'd do it if my hands were unfettered."

"Open your tunic and blouse? And what is that going to prove?"

"Open it and see."

Spence appeared flustered. He glanced quickly towards the guard, then returned his attention to Jenetta. "Uh— that's not appropriate behavior. I can't alter or adjust the clothing of a female prisoner in restraints."

"Commander, the guard is five meters away. He can attest to your proper behavior and that I asked you to do it."

Spence looked at Jenetta for a few seconds and then said, "Very well. Marine, you heard the ensign request that I do this?"

The guard nodded. "Yes sir, Commander. I heard the request."

Spence reached over and separated the sides of Jenetta's tunic, then unbuttoned the top three buttons of her blouse.

"Now pull the folds apart."

"My God! What is *that*?" Spence exclaimed loudly as he first saw the imprint.

The guard was straining to see without moving from his position. When he realized Jenetta was staring at him, he straightened back up quickly.

"The Raiders imprint the women they capture and intend to place in their brothels with a serial number for identification. You'll find similar identification marks on all of the female captives I brought back."

"I see. I'm sorry I doubted you."

"No problem, Commander. I hope you can have these ridiculous charges dismissed. I was not AWOL."

"I believe you, Ensign. Don't worry. Give me the names of the people you've had contact with since the escape pod was opened. I'll need to contact them so we can prepare a list of witnesses for the hearing."

Jenetta spent the next ten minutes recounting every name she could remember until Spence said, "That's enough. It brings us up to the present."

"How long do you think it will take to clear this up?"

"The hearing is scheduled for two weeks from tomorrow."

"Two *weeks*? I have to sit in a jail cell for two *weeks*?"

"I'll talk to my commanding officer at JAG and see if we can't get you simply restricted to quarters instead. It isn't as if you killed someone."

Jenetta chewed on her lower lip for a couple of seconds before responding with, "Thank you, Commander Spence."

"I'll try to stop by this afternoon to let you know how I made out."

"Thank you, Commander."

"You're welcome, Ensign. Uh— I'd suggest you remove the captain's bars from that uniform before you get into deeper trouble."

After lunch, Jenetta was informed that her attorney had returned. She was shackled hand and foot again and led to the interview room where she was greeted by a somber faced Lt. Commander Spence. Another officer, a female lieutenant about Jenetta's height, slim, with short brunette hair, appeared equally disturbed.

"Hello, Ensign. This is Lieutenant Julia Marlo. She's been assigned to assist with your case. Have a seat." Spence pulled out the chair and held it for her.

Jenetta sat down and the JAG officers took seats across from her.

"I don't understand," Jenetta said. "Why is assistance necessary on a simple AWOL case?"

"I have bad news, Ensign. It's not a hearing anymore," Spence said. "They've waived the hearing based on the evidence that you provided to Intelligence and they're going straight to a general court-martial."

Jenetta just sat there with her mouth hanging open for several seconds. "*What? A general court-martial? For being AWOL?*"

"The list of charges has been expanded. There's a lot more to this case than I was originally informed. Let me read the charges. Desertion, Impersonating a Superior Officer, Appropriation of Private Property without Space Command Authority, Torture of Prisoners you had taken into custody, and 18,231 separate counts of Murder.

Jenetta jumped to her feet, knocking her chair over backwards. "*Murder? They were Raiders.*"

The Marine guard was behind her in a second, stun baton at the ready in case she became violent.

"Sit down, Ensign, and remain calm so we can get through this preliminary stuff," Spence said.

The guard picked up the chair and Jenetta sat down slowly, shock and anger registered clearly on her face. The guard moved back to his former position near the wall.

"I think you left a few things out of the story you told me."

"I answered every one of your questions honestly, Commander."

"Perhaps, but you certainly didn't elaborate on the facts of the situation. Now what about these new charges? Are you guilty or innocent?"

"Well— well— a little of both, except Desertion. But I had good reasons for everything I did."

"But you *did* do them?"

"I guess so. I'm not sure about the number of deaths though."

"That information was extrapolated directly from the evidence you provided to Intelligence in the form of data rings. They were able to compile a roster of everyone who was reportedly in the space station when it exploded. Since you're being accused of mass murder, there's no chance of getting you out of here and all the restraints stay on whenever you're out of your cell."

Jenetta sighed and slumped in her chair, "I understand, Commander."

"Why don't we start from the beginning and you tell us everything you remember from the day of the explosion on the *Hokyuu*. Don't skip *anything*." Spence pulled a tiny vid camera from his pocket, touched the bottom with a saliva-moistened finger, and placed it on the table. Shaped like a coin and smaller than a man's wedding band, it would stick where placed until pulled up. Pulling a thin view pad from another pocket, he used it to aim the self-focusing device so Jenetta would be perfectly framed in the recorded image. As he started recording, he said, "Proceed, Ensign."

Jenetta began with the end of her last duty shift on the *Hokyuu* and related every detail she could remember. As the dinner hour approached, Spence called for an end to the session. They had only gotten as far as when Jenetta climbed into the stasis bed because Spence had constantly interrupted with questions to clarify various points.

As the JAG officers left for dinner, Jenetta was taken back to her cell where the restraints were removed and she received her dinner. Afterwards, she lay down on her cot and thought about the charges. "Eighteen thousand, two hundred thirty-one separate counts of murder," she said aloud. "They're trying to crucify me for some reason." She thought about the words of the Raider Commander on the *Prometheus*, 'You're dead, bitch, you're dead.' Before they had taken away her holo-magazine cylinders, Jenetta had read about the Space Command officers imprisoned following their convictions on charges of complicity in the theft of the two battleships. How many other officers did the Raider organization have in their pocket? In Intelligence? In JAG? Was she being railroaded to a murder conviction on orders from the Raider 'Lower Council' that Arneu had talked about?

Just how much power did the Raider organization actually wield inside Space Command?

Chapter Twenty-Three
~ January 6th, 2268 ~

Captain Quinton Carver dropped the landing pads and leapt out of the 'oh-gee' vehicle before it had even settled the final quarter-meter to the ground. He sprinted to the front door of the two-story house where he lived with his wife and pressed his hand against the palm plate, pushing open the door as he heard the lock release.

"Who's there?" he heard his wife say from the kitchen as he stepped inside the front door.

"Just me, dear," he called back excitedly.

Annette Carver noted the excitement in his voice and came to greet him, her smile widening as she saw the huge grin on his face. As her husband lowered his head, she stretched to meet him and they kissed lightly in their habitual greeting.

"You're home early, dear. Did you score a hole in one?" she asked.

"I only played five holes. I got a call from Jack McDormott at the base. He had some important news and asked me to come right over, so I found someone to finish the round for me."

"Well, don't keep me waiting. What is it?"

"It's going to be a shock. Would you rather sit down first?"

"No, I don't want to sit down, dear. What is it?" she asked anxiously. "Are you being reactivated?"

"No, it's about Jenetta."

"Jenetta?" his wife echoed in complete surprise, her face instantly becoming a blank mask. "What about Jenetta?"

"She's alive."

"Alive?" his wife mouthed silently, a look of utter shock on her face. Tears instantly formed in her eyes and began to trickle down her cheeks. She felt her throat constrict and her sinus cavities began to fill. It had been so many years. She couldn't be sure she had heard correctly. "Are you sure?" she asked shakily as her heart pounded and her chest began to heave.

"Absolutely. She's at the Higgins Space Command Base at Vinnia. She's been positively identified."

"How— how is she?" Annette Carver asked as the trickle of tears became a stream.

"I understand the base hospital has released her with a clean bill of health. She's been in stasis since the accident so she still looks almost the same as the day she left."

Annette had remained strong as long as she could. She wrapped her arms tightly around her husband and let the tears of joy pour from her eyes and dampen his shirt as she sobbed loudly. Her baby was alive. Not only alive but safe and well. Her prayers from so long ago had been answered.

*   *   *

Jenetta slept fitfully that night, at one point seeing the faces of her parents and brothers as they looked upon her with revulsion when she was marched out for execution following a speedy trial. She tried to tell them she had only done what she had to, but she couldn't talk because her mouth was filled with a gag like those used in the detention center of the Raider space station.

As she was led to the gallows, she realized she was dressed in a black leather outfit from her Raider detention cell closet, one with the arms stitched together behind her back and so tight that she couldn't raise her legs to walk up the thirteen steps. She had to be lifted to each step by the guards from the Raider detention center. They were all there, and each took his time groping her body as he raised her and turned her over to the next. Reaching the top, she found Mikel Arneu waiting to place the noose around her neck. He was wearing the large gold medal given to him by the 'Lower Council' for helping to bring Jenetta to justice.

As the trap door opened and Jenetta began to fall, she awoke suddenly and sat up on the brig cot. Soaking wet with perspiration, she rose to wash and dry her face.

"It was just a dumb nightmare," she said aloud. "They don't even execute people anymore, except for particularly depraved acts of Piracy, Treason, or Sedition. I think I've watched too many old westerns. These days they just put prisoners into a penal colony for life. But life in prison will be a very long time if Arneu was right about me living for five thousand years."

* * *

Jenetta spent every one of the next eight days working with Lt. Commander Spence and Lieutenant Marlo in the interview room while she related almost everything of importance that had happened, as well as her motivations. The only information she held back was Arneu's statements about her living for hundreds or possibly thousands of years. It sounded crazy and was best omitted from a story that already severely tested the boundaries of credulity.

On the tenth day, she wrapped up the story by talking about the Commander from Intelligence and her examinations at the hospital by the doctor.

"That's about it. I think I've covered everything," Jenetta said finally.

"I have to say, Ensign," Spence said, "that in my fourteen years in JAG I've never heard a story even one-tenth as incredible as this one, and I've heard some whoppers."

"You don't believe me?"

"I didn't say that. There's no doubt that much of what you've told us is factual and will be acknowledged by the prosecution without question. Our job will be to prove the rest of it, as well as what your intentions were. Now that we have all the facts as you know them, we'll have to construct our case."

"I don't understand the reason for the charges against me, sir. One of the things I particularly don't understand is the preference of murder charges. Those people, with the exception of Captain Starnos and his mate, whose accidental deaths I deeply regret, were all Raiders. They were the scum of the galaxy— thieves, murderers, drug dealers, and slavers."

"I admit to some confusion as well. The fact that you acted without orders would seem to be the prime motivation behind the prosecution's charges, Ensign. Headquarters doesn't like its ensigns running around killing tens of thousands of people and blowing up space stations without orders."

Jenetta grimaced. "Are they afraid I'll start a trend?" she asked facetiously. "Do they fear that ensigns everywhere will suddenly rise up and begin waging a private war against the Raiders? Oh my God— we could see the enemy dying in such great numbers that our admirals will have nothing to do."

Commander Spence scowled and said, "I sincerely hope you won't act this flippant in court, Ensign. I'm sure you understand the concerns about following the proper chain of command."

"You mean they're doing this just to teach me a lesson?"

"Not just you. By making an example of you, they'll teach all young officers not to go off on their own."

"But I didn't go off on my own, Commander. I was cut off from communication with Space Command. I had to take the actions I deemed appropriate."

"And that will be our basic defense position. You were only doing what was necessary for the survival of yourself and those under your protection while also attempting to gather intelligence that would benefit Space Command."

Jenetta leaned back in her chair and sighed. "What do you think my chances are, sir?"

"On the charge of Desertion, excellent. It's only desertion because you were gone for more than ninety days. We have a deposition from the doctor on the *Vordoth* who awoke you from the stasis bed and a video log from the sickbay that shows your extremely debilitated condition following recovery of the pod. In fact, Dr. Erikson has written a paper about the effects of long-term stasis sleep on a very physically fit individual and the rate of recovery by such a patient. Our base engineers have determined that the escape pod you brought back did come from the *Hokyuu* and that the retrorocket never fired, although an automatic command was sent, followed by multiple manual attempts. We have your daily log entries, and if the court accepts that you went into the stasis chamber when you say you did, then the most that you'll be found guilty of is AWOL. And probably only for that portion of time after you accepted command of the *Vordoth* and decided not to come straight to the nearest base."

"We had to save the Nordakians. And then we couldn't just leave them there, defenseless."

"That will be for the court to decide, but AWOL is the worst that I would expect. On the matter of Impersonating an Officer of Superior Rank, it will be entirely up to the court. By your own statements you identified yourself as Captain Carver."

"I was in command of the ship and the officer in command is always referred to as Captain. Even a lieutenant(jg) flying a single seat patrol craft is technically the captain of the ship."

"But they don't put on captain's bars, as you did."

"Uh— that's true, but we were on an extended voyage and the crew seemed to feel it was appropriate."

"What's appropriate for the merchant services and what's appropriate for the military are two entirely different things. The court will decide if your action was appropriate."

"Aye, Commander."

"In the matter of Appropriation of Private Property without Space Command Authority, it will probably depend upon how hard the owners of the freighter push and how much the service wants to back you. You don't deny that you didn't have permission to take the tug and explosives?"

"No. I couldn't contact the freight company offices for the same reason that we couldn't contact Space Command. It could have given away our position."

"In the matter of the 18,231 counts of Murder, I think the charge is absurd. We're officially at war with the Raiders. At most, I believe they'll only find you guilty of the manslaughter deaths of Captain Starnos and his first mate."

"But I didn't know the spaceport was going to explode."

"Did you not leave instructions for the *Vordoth* to send the detonation code?"

"Yes, but the charge shouldn't have destroyed the entire spaceport. It was only intended to cause a diversion. I never expected it to destroy anything beyond a kilometer's distance from the device. The detonation point was in a cargo storage area easily twenty-five kilometers from the habitat buildings."

"Regardless, wasn't the entire space station destroyed as a result of your specific orders?"

"Aye, sir. Apparently."

"On the last charge, that of Torture of a Prisoner, I think we can show just cause and that you were only inflicting the same level of pain that you and the others had been subjected to on a regular basis. Also, you had just been wounded. We'll try to convince the jury that pain affected your judgment."

"What kind of sentence do you feel I might receive for everything?"

"That's impossible to say. The two manslaughter charges alone could mean life."

"What's your best guess?"

"I never make guesses about the outcome of a general court. I just do my best to have all charges dismissed or my client found innocent. Keep your chin up, Ensign. Oh— I'll be sending over a dress uniform for you to wear in court."

"Thank you, Commander," Jenetta said dejectedly.

"Lieutenant Marlo and I will be working on this case exclusively until the court date. We'll be back if we have any more questions, but you may not see us before you're brought to the courtroom. I don't want you to feel that you've been abandoned just because we'll be devoting ourselves to talking with witnesses and planning your defense."

"I understand, Commander."

Spence looked at her appraisingly and she stared back with a rock steady gaze. "Yes, I believe you do," he said. "You're not the type of ensign I usually represent. Most are nervous and very unsure of themselves."

"As was I, but I've changed quite a bit over the past half year. The things I've done and that have been done *to* me have radically changed me and my perspective of life."

"I can see that in your eyes, Ensign. But for the trial, I want you to look soft and vulnerable. I want the judge and jury to believe you were entirely a victim of circumstances."

"I don't think I'll ever again see myself as a victim, Commander, and I hope no one else will either. That implies weakness."

"Hmmm— okay, think about this. You're facing life imprisonment. Be strong and righteous, but look feminine. Can you do *that*?"

"Aye, Sir. *That* I can do," Jenetta said as she thought about the things she had learned from Leah and from her training in the medical lab at the Raider spaceport. Not that she could, or ever would, exhibit most of that knowledge in a courtroom.

"Good," Commander Spence said.

*   *   *

Jenetta spent the next four days pacing the floor in her cell. On the evening of the fourth day, and the eve of her court-martial, Lieutenant Marlo brought her a complete dress uniform to wear for the trial.

"Here's everything you'll need," Lt. Marlo said. "Go easy on the makeup. We want you to look sweet and innocent."

Holding up the hanger and opening the tunic, Jenetta said, "There's a skirt with the tunic. I don't wear skirts."

"Tomorrow you do. The dress code permits female officers the choice between pants and skirts with dress uniforms. If it's any comfort, I'll be wearing a skirt."

Jenetta sighed and said, "Aye, lieutenant."

After the lieutenant had gone, Jenetta looked through the package that accompanied the uniform. In addition to makeup, it contained underwear, stockings, a garter belt, and dress shoes with low, squat heels.

* * *

Jenetta was taken to the courtroom the next day hobbled in full prisoner restraints. Every eye in the packed room was upon her as she was escorted to her seat from the door near the front of the courtroom, but she failed to see a single familiar face. She certainly didn't expect to see her mother since Earth was eight to ten months away by passenger ship. And her father and brothers were probably all off on active duty in various parts of Galactic Alliance space. The court-martial would be over long before any of them could get to Higgins, but she'd hoped that someone from the *Vordoth* would come to lend moral support. They couldn't possibly all have turned their backs on her, could they?

The courtroom itself was typical of most justice courts found on Space Command bases. SimWindows, projecting a scene that could have been shot outside some real courthouse in Midwestern North America, lined the sidewalls. A deep-blue cloudless sky provided the backdrop for dozens of single story buildings in a sleepy little town. All that was missing was the smell of wildflowers carried aloft in fresh air, with maybe a slight odor of manure-based fertilizer from the farmlands in the distance. The judge's bench, jury box, and counsel tables were all made from synthetic compounds that realistically simulated the oak courtroom furniture used on Earth centuries ago. The 'oh-gee' chairs in the jury box along the left wall, like the judge's high-backed chair, were deeply padded and designed for comfort, a necessity when one is expected to sit almost motionless for hours on end, but the chrome and laminate chairs at the counsel tables, like those of the audience and gallery seating, were only lightly padded.

Security cameras looked down from each corner and from the center of each wall in the large room. Although they never moved, each provided full pan, tilt, and zoom capability to their operators, ensuring that every minute of the proceedings would be preserved for posterity. Jenetta would have been shocked to learn that one floor down an entire media production room staff was already busy at work adjusting volume levels and panning the gallery for reactions to her appearance and treatment. Each of the eight wall-mounted cameras and the six discreetly hidden cameras were being controlled by a separate cameraman. A director issued instructions for zooming or panning, and continuously called out to the operator at the switcher after deciding which of the fourteen shots would go out live on the feed.

After Jenetta was seated, her four Space Marine guards took up positions along the sidewalls between the Sim-Windows. She sat quietly at the defense table between Lt. Commander Spence and Lieutenant Marlo as the court waited for the judge to come in. When he did enter, Spence and Marlo made a major production of helping Jenetta get to her feet. The judge noticed the activity and stopped momentarily to witness the sight of the petite young woman struggling to stand up while in full restraints. Jenetta actually could have gotten up easier on her own because the two JAG officers were intentionally pulling their client in different directions, although it didn't appear that way.

Once Jenetta was standing, the judge continued to his chair and sat down. The nameplate on the bench identified him as Rear Admiral (L) Chester Margolan and he certainly had the look of a career JAG officer. His hair was a shock of bright silver and his deadpan face and manner loudly proclaimed that this was his courtroom and that people best pay attention when he spoke or be prepared to experience his wrath. As soon as he was seated, everyone else in the courtroom sat down as well. The admiral immediately picked up a small silver rod and tapped three times on the silver tubular chime suspended in a small frame in front of him on the bench.

"This court is now in session on this 19th day of January, 2268," a female chief petty officer announced loudly.

"Chief, bring in the jury," the admiral said.

The jury of four male and two female officers was comprised exclusively of captains, as required in a general court-martial where an officer is charged with multiple capital offenses. Jenetta watched them closely as they filed in and took their seats in the jury box. She was sure she had never met any of them before.

As soon as the jury was settled, the judge said, "The chief petty officer will read the charges."

There was some murmuring in the courtroom as the chief petty officer started reading the official charges, but only a gasp and then stunned silence after she read the murder charge and gave the number of counts.

As the chief petty officer sat down, the admiral said, "Commander Pierce."

A forty-something commander at the prosecution table stood up and came to an easy attention. With black curly hair, there was little about him that would be described as anything but average.

"Sir?"

"If you have an opening statement, you may begin."

"Thank you, sir."

Commander Pierce looked towards the jury box. "Ladies and Gentlemen, you've heard the charges. I will prove each and every one during the course of this court-martial, most supported by testimony already offered by the defendant herself to officers from our Intelligence Section. Ensign Carver has flagrantly violated the rules that we in Space Command all live by and she must pay the price of that disregard. Thank you."

Then it was Lt. Commander Spence's turn to present his opening remarks. He turned to face the jury as he stood up. "Ladies and Gentlemen, Ensign Carver is a young officer who found herself alone and abandoned by Space Command just a few months after graduation from the Academy as the result of a tragic accident that occurred more than eleven years ago. Until just a few months ago, she was innocuously floating in space, asleep in a stasis chamber. Subsequently rescued, she awoke to a galaxy she no longer knew. While attempting to return to the Space Command family, the ship in which she was a passenger was attacked by Raiders and she was forced to take aggressive actions to protect her own life, as well as that of others who had come under her care and protection. We should be celebrating her courage and actions rather than looking for ways to punish her simply because she couldn't get advance permission to destroy the declared enemies of the Galactic Alliance. Thank you."

With the opening statements complete, Commander Pierce began his case. "I call Ensign Carver to the stand."

With the *help* of her attorneys, Jenetta rose and shuffled slowly towards the witness box. The chief petty officer had immediately come forward to swear her in, but then had to wait while Jenetta hobbled over because the restrictive chains on her ankles prevented her from taking anything greater than the smallest of steps. Cameras around the courtroom zoomed in on her legs as she shuffled along.

"Raise your right hand," the chief said when Jenetta finally reached her.

Jenetta raised her right hand as high as the restraints, which held her hands firmly at her waist, allowed. The chief petty officer turned to Admiral Margolan to see if the slight movement met the requirements of judicial proceedings.

"Just a minute, Chief," Admiral Margolan said. Looking towards the table where the prosecution attorney and Commander Kanes were sitting, he said, "Commander Pierce?"

Commander Pierce jumped up. "Sir?" he said.

"Has the defendant exhibited any sign of violent tendencies while in custody?"

"No sir. She's been a model prisoner."

"Is she being well guarded whenever she's outside the brig?"

"Yes sir. Four armed Marine guards accompany her at all times."

"Do you feel we're in any danger of being harmed by the defendant while court is in session?"

"Uh— no sir, Admiral."

"Then why is this young officer being forced to sit there shackled hand and foot."

"Uh— it's because of the nature of the charges, sir. Regulations state that prisoners charged with multiple capital crimes must be restrained at all times."

"As I recall the regulations, they only *recommend* that prisoners charged in capital crimes cases be restrained at all times, but it's mandated for those who exhibit violent behavior while being taken into custody or while in custody. In light of the prisoner's model conduct and diminutive size, I order that all restraints be removed and not be used further unless the prisoner exhibits violent behavior which, as such, justifies her restraint."

"With all due respect, Admiral, the prisoner, by her own admission, is trained in kickboxing and killed an armed guard with her feet at the Raider detention center in order to effect her escape. There is a potential danger."

"As a Space Command officer, I would use my feet, hands, teeth, or anything else I possessed to effect my own escape from Raider jailers. That doesn't mean I would do so here on a Space Command base. Release the prisoner."

One of the Marine guards immediately walked to Jenetta and removed the restraints. As soon as they were off, she tugged at her tunic to straighten it, braced to attention, smiled at the admiral and said, "Thank you, sir."

The admiral nodded soberly and said, "You'll only stay free of the restraints as long as you offer no resistance to your guards, Ensign."

"Yes sir."

"Continue chief," the admiral said.

Jenetta was sworn in, gave her name and serial number, and took her seat in the witness box.

Commander Pierce walked to where she was seated, glared at her, and asked accusingly, "Ensign, did you sabotage the engines of the *Hokyuu*?"

"No sir," Jenetta replied in complete surprise. "Were they sabotaged, sir?"

"You were the last one to exit the ship before it exploded. Why was that?"

"Somebody had to be the last one, sir. I got out as quickly as I could after the alarms woke me up and I found an available pod."

"But the escape pod you used was one from the engineering deck, not the quarters deck. And the computer in the pod shows that the ship exploded just *six* seconds after you ejected. That's cutting it rather close isn't it?"

"Way, way too close, sir, but not by choice. I couldn't find an available pod anywhere on the quarters deck, so I went down to the engineering deck to search for one. I felt that I'd have a better chance there because of the late hour."

"As a result of your tardy departure, your pod was apparently damaged by the explosion. The damage allegedly prevented the retrorocket from firing, catapulting you into deep space and ensuring you were long gone before the rescue ships arrived. Or was the retrorocket disabled before the pod even ejected?"

"Are you suggesting that I purposely disabled the retrorocket so it wouldn't function— sir?"

"It would give you a cast iron excuse for being AWOL should you ever decide to return, wouldn't it?"

"Objection, Admiral," Lt. Commander Spence called out. Rising to his feet he properly addressed his comments to Admiral Margolan. "Sir, the engineering section has already determined beyond a shadow of a doubt that the damage was caused by the explosion rather than tampering and that someone did in fact sleep in the chamber for more than ten years. Ensign Carver was alone in the pod. DNA from the hair and skin cells found in the escape pod have been identified as being exclusively that of the defendant. Ensign

Carver maintained a daily log for the three months prior to entering the stasis chamber and it has been certified as being her voice and image. We have the inspection logs and depositions and can produce the examining engineers and technicians if necessary, but Commander Pierce has already conceded in pretrial discovery that the defendant was the sole occupant of the escape pod and stasis bed for the entire ten years, eight months and seven days."

"Objection sustained," the admiral said, "move along Commander Pierce."

"Yes sir. Ensign, why didn't you contact Space Command as soon as you awoke?"

"I wanted to, but Captain Lentz refused my request, informing me they had to maintain radio silence while in Raider-controlled space."

"Raider-controlled space?" Looking at her with suddenly narrowed eyes, Commander Pierce said in a loud and angry voice, "Ensign, this is the Galactic Alliance, not a Raider hunting preserve."

"Sorry, sir. Everyone I've met refers to that sector in those terms because of the high level of Raider activity there during the past decade and the chances of attack if you're not part of a Space Command protected convoy."

Commander Pierce glared at her for a couple of seconds before asking, "Captain Lentz is the same individual you allege was the commandant of the Raider base?"

"Yes sir."

"And so you admit to taking orders from the Raider hierarchy. How long have you worked for him?"

"I've never worked for him. At the time that we first met, he was the duly appointed captain of the *Vordoth*, as far as I could know."

"And at what point did you finally decide to contact Space Command?"

"There was little point in maintaining radio silence after the Raiders attacked the *Vordoth* so we transmitted a general distress signal."

"And you immediately set course for Higgins after you destroyed the Raider fighters?"

"We changed our flight path by moving to a parallel course, but Higgins remained our destination, yes."

"And then, after assuming command of the *Vordoth*, you decided to take side trips around the galaxy instead of coming directly here."

"We were being tailed by a Raider destroyer, sir. We couldn't outrun it and we had to somehow prevent them from relaying our position to other Raider ships ahead of us. My only alternative was to go on the offensive. I formulated a battle plan and we engaged the Raider destroyer. After we destroyed it, we resumed our trip to Higgins on a parallel course well away from our previous route."

"You took a fifty-year-old freighter into battle against a modern Raider warship, risking the lives of everyone on board and the cargo?"

"I would naturally have preferred to engage them with a warship, sir, but the freighter was all I had available to me." A chuckle passed around the courtroom and Commander Pierce scowled before Jenetta continued with, "I had no choice, either of the vessel used or the action."

"But one engagement wasn't enough for you. You had to pick another fight, this time pitting your freighter against a Raider medium cruiser with *twenty* times your firepower?"

"We received an urgent distress call from a Nordakian convoy under attack by another Raider force. The officers of the *Vordoth* felt it was our duty to respond and lend assistance."

"Ensign, you were in an old freighter, not a modern battleship, and you had a duty to return here, not run around engaging hostile forces with an unarmored, lightly armed ship full of civilians. And whatever were you thinking when you took an unarmed space tug into a heavily fortified Raider camp, thereby risking the lives of the two civilians who were on board with you, not to mention risking the tug, which happened to be private property?"

"I saw an opportunity to learn the location of the Raider base and gather vital information that Space Command could use in its efforts to locate and defeat the Raiders."

"But instead of immediately returning with that information, you embarked on a dangerous adventure where you secreted *eight hundred metric tons* of Corplastizine in the Raider spaceport. Did you have authorization to plant a weapon of mass destruction in that spaceport?"

"No sir."

"And then, having *destroyed* what could have been a most valuable and useful asset to the Galactic Alliance, in addition to fifty-four large warships and dozens of valuable passenger liners and cargo ships, you began flying all over the galaxy in a Space Command battleship, wearing captain's bars and letting everyone believe you were a captain by virtue of appointment from Space Command."

"I never told anyone that I was a Space Command appointed Captain."

"Oh, you just wore the rank insignia of a captain."

"Uh, yes."

"And after you had taken prisoners during your little adventure, did you then turn around and mercilessly torture three of them on the bridge of a GSC warship, in clear view of horrified civilian witnesses."

"I had t…"

"Just answer yes or no, Ensign. Did you or did you not intentionally and repeatedly use electric shock devices on Raider prisoners in full view of civilian witnesses."

Jenetta hesitated for a couple of seconds. "Yes."

Commander Pierce nodded and turned to return to his seat. "No further questions."

Chapter Twenty-Four
~ January 19ʰ, 2268 ~

"Commander Spence, do you wish to cross-examine?" Admiral Margolan asked.

"Yes sir. Most definitely."

Walking to the witness chair in a deliberately unhurried manner, Commander Spence looked placidly at Jenetta and said, "Ensign, I think it would benefit the court to hear all the events— in the order they occurred. Would you tell us, in your own words, everything that happened from the time you awoke on the *Hokyuu* with the alarms sounding to abandon ship until you were arrested at the Higgins Base Hospital. Take your time and don't skip any details, however small."

"I object most strenuously, Admiral," Commander Pierce said, jumping up from his seat. "This could take weeks and we don't have time to listen to ridiculous tall tales, fabrications, equivocations, and prevarications."

"Objection overruled. Commander Pierce, in this court *I decide* what we do or do not have time for. As for tall tales, fabrications, equivocations, or prevarications, you will have the right to object to anything you feel is immaterial or inaccurate, and you have the right to re-cross at the end of the defendant's testimony. Proceed, Ensign."

So Jenetta began recounting her story once again, in minute detail. Her testimony took sixteen long days, owing mainly to seemingly constant objections from Commander Pierce that required Jenetta to repeatedly relate key points concerning her attacks on the Raider destroyer and cruiser, and the escape from the detention center. Then another six days were exhausted with his additional cross-examination.

The court had ordered Lt. Commander Spence to have Jenetta skip over testimony regarding her meeting with Commander Pretorious near the cargo-bay detention area, and she was restricted from even mentioning it, but there was little else that wasn't covered in excruciating detail. When Jenetta recounted events of her attacks on the Raider warships, the *Vordoth* bridge logs played on monitors in the courtroom. And when she told of the Raider base destruction, the image logs from the *Prometheus* displayed.

Pierce next questioned Kanes and the members of his intelligence section, then rested the prosecution's case.

Spence then called Doctor Rebecca Erikson, Lieutenant Gloria Sabella, and Lieutenant Charles Moresby to testify about events aboard the *Vordoth*. Gunny Rondell and Crewman Browne were called to testify about their trip in the space tug, the escape, and the taking of the *Prometheus*, and Captain Yates was called to testify about the escape and the taking of the *Chiron*. Commander Pierce seemed to grow angrier and more belligerent as each witness extolled the conduct of Ensign Carver.

Lt. Commander Michaels was the last defense witness to be called. Under cross-examination, Pierce grilled him about his knowledge of Jenetta's rank and when he had learned she was really just an ensign.

"Commander Michaels, you first met Ensign Carver on the day you escaped from the Raider detention center. Is that correct?"

"Not precisely, sir."

"Oh? Well, then when *did* you first meet her?"

"I first met Ensign Carver on the day she *rescued* me and forty-nine others from the detention center."

"I see," Commander Pierce said, scowling slightly at the correction. "And what was your understanding of her rank?"

"She identified herself as Captain Jenetta Carver."

"And you accepted that?"

"After three months of suffering at the hands of the sadistic guards in the Raider detention center, I would have accepted her as God if it got me out of there."

"Yes, I quite understand, Commander. And you agreed to follow her orders if she released you?"

"Yes sir."

"And you were present when she callously shot down Captain Starnos and his first mate, and then ordered them locked up again to await their cruel fate?"

"Uh— yes sir, I was present when the incident occurred."

"And you followed her orders because you feared she would shoot you down as well?"

"No sir. I had given my word. Unlike Starnos, I kept it."

"But you believed she held the rank of captain in Space Command?"

"No, sir."

"No?"

"She appeared much too young to be a captain, sir. Although I separated from the service a couple of years ago, I was reasonably sure I would have heard if such a young-looking officer had attained even Lt. Commander rank. But— Gunny Rondell and Crewman Browne called her 'Captain' and, without question or hesitation, immediately followed whatever orders she gave. When we rendezvoused with the *Vordoth*, the entire crew of the freighter referred to her only as 'Captain' and also followed her orders without question. All of the Nordakian officers called her 'Captain' and also did whatever she asked of them. Furthermore, she has a Space Command ring showing her to be a graduate of the NHSA class of '56, so it was— I suppose— possible that she had reached the rank of captain. I guess I came to accept her rank as genuine because of the overwhelming corroboration by— everyone around me. And I very quickly came to respect her abilities and judgment."

"But she didn't reveal to you that she was actually only an SC ensign until ten days before arriving at Higgins?"

"Yes sir."

"Thank you. No further questions."

"I have a couple of additional questions for the witness," Lt. Commander Spence said, standing. "Commander Michaels, when you *did* learn of Ensign Carver's Space Command rank, what did you do?"

"I, uh," Lt. Commander Michaels took a deep breath and sighed. Looking clearly embarrassed, he answered quickly, "I was so upset that I jumped up, spilling a mug of coffee on myself."

The courtroom erupted in laughter and the Admiral admonished them, citing the seriousness of the charges.

"No, I mean did you try to take control of the ship?"

"No, sir."

"Why not? You found yourself taking orders from a young female officer very junior to your own former Space Command rank."

"To me, she was still Captain Carver. I had promised to follow her orders until we reached a Space Command base and my word is my bond."

"But you would have tried to take control at that point if the ship was in danger?"

"Uh— no sir, I wouldn't have. Knowing Ensign Carver as I did by then, I can't imagine I could have done any better, so I would have followed whatever orders she gave. And besides, if I had tried to seize control, every other person on that ship would have voted to throw me out an airlock."

"The rest of the ship's personnel respected her?"

"*Respected her?*" Lt. Commander Michaels echoed, his voice rising substantially in pitch. "That would be a *gross* understatement. Sir, in my twenty years in Space Command, I never saw such unfeigned respect afforded to any captain, or even any admiral. She had saved every last one of them from death or worse, and they *knew* it. I've heard some of the *Vordoth* crew call her the Ice Queen, but that's strictly a reference to her professional demeanor on the bridge during combat operations. They all knew of her competence, her compassion, her personal warmth, and her genuine concern for their safety and wellbeing. They would have done *anything* she asked of them. Anything!"

"Thank you, Commander, that's all."

Lt. Commander Spence turned away, then turned back.

"Oh, one last thing, Commander. Did you concur with Ensign Carver's action when she *temporarily incapacitated* Captain Starnos and his first mate with a stun pistol?"

"Absolutely. If she had let him go off on his own, he might have destroyed all our chances for escape. We were deep in the bowels of a Raider stronghold with 18,000 Raiders between us and freedom. A second escape party doubled the likelihood someone would be detected. Once an alarm sounded, the station would go on alert and be locked down. Nobody would have gotten out."

"That's all, Commander, thank you. Admiral, the defense rests."

Jenetta locked eyes with Lt. Commander Michaels and gave him a hint of a smile as he stepped down and passed the defense table on his way to the back of the courtroom.

"Commander Pierce," Admiral Margolan said, "do you have any rebuttal witnesses to call?"

"No sir."

"Then you may begin your closing arguments, gentlemen. Commander Pierce?"

Commander Pierce stood and approached the jury. "Ladies and Gentlemen, you've sat here patiently, day after day, and listened to witnesses laud the virtues of Ensign Carver. She has apparently made a great many friends during the past few months. But this case isn't about friendship; it's about the *rules* that form the basis for our service. Ensign Carver has repeatedly chosen to disregard those rules and we cannot allow this to become an example that others will imitate.

"Rather than proceeding directly to this base when she had the opportunity, she willfully chose to remain away. That constitutes desertion according to the regulations that all Space Command officers, noncoms, and enlisted personnel live by.

"She blatantly impersonated a superior officer by wearing the rank insignia of a Captain and, while she may never have stated it outright, she certainly allowed people to believe it was her official rank by virtue of Space Command appointment.

"She appropriated private property and then caused it to be destroyed when she intentionally detonated an explosive device of incredible power inside the Raider space station.

"By her direct actions, she is responsible for the deaths of 18,231 citizens. It makes no difference what their occupation; they were alive before Ensign Carver caused their deaths inside the spaceport. She was acting independently and without authorization when she carried out this mass execution.

"Lastly, this— this— Ice Queen— *willfully* tortured three fettered prisoners on the bridge of a Space Command vessel in plain sight of others. This can*not* be tolerated in this day and age.

"You must find her guilty of all charges so others won't consider following her example by ignoring the military regulations that we in Space Command live by. Thank you."

"Commander Spence?" the admiral said.

"Yes sir, I'm ready."

Lt. Commander Spence stood and approached the jury. "Ladies and Gentlemen, I thank you for your patience with this case. It's not the usual type of case heard in this courtroom. In fact, it's not the usual type of case heard in *any* courtroom. Why do *you* think that is? *I* think it's because cases like this are not usually prosecuted. When someone displays the courage, strength, and intelligence that Ensign Carver has exhibited, they're hailed as heroes and parades are given in their honor. They aren't shackled hand and foot and thrown into a tiny, dark prison cell, left to wonder and worry in solitude about their fate as has been done to Ensign Carver since she was taken into custody.

"Let's examine each of the charges carefully. First, Desertion. There is simply no basis for this charge. Ensign Carver was the victim of an explosion aboard a ship soon after she graduated from the Academy. She was just beginning her career when, all of a sudden, she's flung out into space and *lost*." Lt. Commander Spence paused for effect. "She was extremely lucky to be found and awakened ten years and eight months later, and has since that time been trying to get to a Space Command base. Every witness that has testified has spoken of her intense desire to return to Space Command. There was never any intention on her part to either leave Space Command originally or remain away one minute longer than necessary. Her deviations were for good and valid reasons and strictly followed the oath that she took when becoming a Space Command officer.

"Second, Impersonating a Superior Officer. Again, there is no basis for this charge. Ensign Carver was *asked* to take command of the *Vordoth*. She didn't demand, or even request, to become its captain. And the uniforms she wore, which were not even Space Command issue, were altered without her consent by a second-in-command who felt that the insignia of rank was appropriate aboard a freighter to help the crew identify with her new position. You've all had an opportunity to examine the uniforms, marked as defense exhibits C through F, and seen that the buttons are clearly stamped with the merchant services logo. When she referred to herself as captain, it was as the Captain of the *Vordoth*, and later of the *Prometheus*. In the detention center, it was necessary for her to quickly gain the acceptance and support of the captives if she was to successfully lead them to freedom and safety. She *never* said that 'Captain' was a Space Command rank, and she *was* the *legitimate* Captain of the *Vordoth* at that time.

"Third, Appropriation of Private Property without Space Command Authority. There isn't any basis for this charge because Ensign Carver was the duly recognized Captain of the *Vordoth*. By accepting the temporary position of Captain, she accepted responsibility for the assets of the freighter company and was duly authorized on that basis *under Galactic Law* to use the assets as she saw fit to preserve and protect the remaining assets. The freight company has not pursued any legal remedies, indicating that they are happy with the situation and, in fact, most appreciative of Ensign Carver's assistance in saving the ship, crew, and most of the cargo.

"Fourth, The Murder of 18,231 Galactic Citizens. These were not galactic citizens; they were Raiders. They were murderers— rapists— drug dealers— slavers— thieves— and criminals of every sort. In a word, *scum*. If any Space Command ship had encountered them, its captain would not have hesitated to blow them out of existence. Ensign Carver simply saved the Space Command lives that might have been lost in future encounters and engagements with these Raiders and their *fifty-four destroyed warships*.

"Fifth and last, Torturing a Prisoner. Ensign Carver had just minutes to get the *Prometheus* moving or all on board would be lost. They desperately needed the lockout command override code, and she got it in the only way possible. She only used the same shock techniques that had been repeatedly used on her and the others in the detention center and stopped as soon as the senior officer supplied the code. There was no lasting damage to any of the Raider officers. And you heard Lt. Commander Michaels clearly state that the nickname Ice Queen was used as a sign of utmost respect, not disparagement, as Commander Pierce would have you believe.

"Ensign Carver deserves to be acquitted of all charges, and she deserves the respect and gratitude of all the citizens of the Galactic Alliance for what she has accomplished. It's an incontrovertible fact that there has not been a *single* attack by a Raider ship in this entire deca-sector of space since the spaceport was destroyed four months ago. We can thank Ensign Carver for that. I ask that you do what is right and just, and acquit her of all charges. Thank you."

As Lt. Commander Spence returned to his seat, everyone could hear the soft tread of his shoes on the carpeted deck. Not a single sound came from the gallery. They seemed to have stopped breathing.

After Admiral Margolan had given instructions to the jurors, and they had filed out, he addressed the courtroom.

"Ladies and Gentlemen, the proceedings are in recess until the jury reaches its decision."

Everyone in the courtroom rose as the Admiral left. Jenetta turned to Lt. Commander Spence and said, "Whatever the outcome, thank you, Commander."

"It's been my honor, Ensign. I mean that, just as I meant everything I said in my closing arguments. I don't know how long it will take the jury to reach a decision, but Lt. Marlo and I will meet you back here when they return."

Jenetta was escorted back to her cell to await the verdict. She hadn't worn the restraints since the Admiral had ordered them removed, but her four guards were never more than an arm's length away whenever she was outside the courtroom or the cell.

Chapter Twenty-Five

~ February 13th, 2268 ~

Jenetta paced nervously around her cell for three days before being informed the jury had reached a decision. After changing into her dress uniform, she was escorted to the courtroom. Lt. Commander Spence and Lieutenant Marlo were already waiting.

"Three days for their deliberations," Jenetta said as she took her seat. "Is that good or bad, Commander?"

"Impossible to say, Ensign. I've seen the verdict go both ways in that time."

Before Jenetta could say anything else, Admiral Margolan entered the court from his chambers door. Everyone rose to their feet until he had climbed to the bench and taken his seat. After the usual taps on the chime signifying the court was in session, the Admiral told the chief petty officer to bring the jury in.

When they were seated, Admiral Margolan said to the jury, "Ladies and Gentlemen, have you reached a verdict?"

The captain who had led the way into the room stood and said, "We have, sir."

Jenetta, Lt. Commander Spence, and Lieutenant Marlo stood up and came to attention. Jenetta was so scared that she had to clench her teeth to keep them from chattering and remind herself to breathe. Lt. Commander Spence, aware of her anxiety, reached down and held her right hand. His simple action seemed to have the desired calming effect.

"Please read your decisions," Admiral Margolan said.

The captain depressed the power button on a holo-tube and began reading from the display as the first page emerged along the length of the viewer. "To the first charge, Desertion, we find the defendant, Ensign Jenetta Carver, not guilty.

"To the second charge, Impersonating a Superior Officer, we find the defendant, Ensign Jenetta Carver, not guilty.

"To the third charge, Appropriation of Private Property without Space Command Authority, we find the defendant, Ensign Jenetta Carver, not guilty.

"To the fourth charge, The Murder of 18,231 Galactic Citizens, we find the defendant, Ensign Jenetta Carver..." The captain paused as his eyes left the display and traveled to Jenetta's face before he announced, "...*not* guilty."

That had been the big one, and Jenetta squeezed Lt. Commander Spence's hand tightly and let out a sigh of relief but remained at attention.

Returning his eyes to the holo-tube, the captain said, "To the fifth charge, Torturing a Prisoner, we find the defendant, Ensign Jenetta Carver, not guilty."

The captain switched off the holo-tube and handed it to the chief petty officer before retaking his seat. The chief petty officer then carried it to the Admiral.

Admiral Margolan addressed the jury with, "Thank you, Ladies and Gentlemen." To Jenetta he said, "Ensign Carver, having been found not guilty on all charges and specifications, you are immediately released from custody and are ordered to report for active duty three days hence." To the courtroom in general he said, "This proceeding is now closed."

As the admiral rose, everyone in the courtroom rose and waited until he was out of the room, but where courtrooms usually clear out fairly quickly after the proceedings are over, the attendees remained standing at their seats. Jenetta didn't notice that everyone in the courtroom was still watching her, grim-faced and with rapt attention, as she turned first to Lt. Commander Spence to thank him again for all he'd done, and then turned to Lieutenant Marlo to thank her for all her efforts as well. As she turned to leave, Jenetta became aware that every pair of eyes in the courtroom appeared focused on her. She hesitated for a second, clenched her jaw muscles, then moved with purpose to the aisle from her place behind the defense table. The trek to the doors at the rear of the room, like the path of a prisoner treading a gauntlet of old, seemed infinitely long, but she hadn't taken more than two steps before the courtroom erupted in thunderous applause. Hands reached out to grip hers or pat her on the arm or shoulder as she continued towards the door, and she smiled and nodded to the people, shaking hands like a stumping politician as she went. The cameras followed her movements until she disappeared out the doors. In the media center below, an official spokesperson then recapped the entire trial and verdict on live feed and closed the production.

Unsure of where she was going, Jenetta didn't even care. She just wanted to get away from the courtroom and feel free again as quickly as possible. Exiting the courthouse, she was immediately besieged by media people who began shouting questions at her. Her only response was, "No comment," as she pushed her way through the newsies with the assistance of Marines posted outside the entrance. As she neared the outer periphery of the crowd, she saw her closest friends in this part of the galaxy. She felt tears form at her eyes and trickle down her cheeks as first Gloria reached her, then Rebecca, Charley, and Leah. Even Gunny Rondell managed to reach Jenetta and received a hug and a kiss on his cheek. The photographers never stopped taking pictures.

"Let's get away from here," Charley said as he and Gunny blocked the newsies from Jenetta. Moving as a group to a nearby lift, they stepped into an empty car while Gunny prevented anyone else from joining them.

"I knew they'd have to release you," Gloria said as the doors closed.

"That makes *one* of us," Jenetta said. "I was scared witless."

"You're way too famous for them to do anything else."

"Famous?"

"Of course. The story is all over the news. Didn't you know?"

"No, I was being held incommunicado and couldn't watch the news or read the papers."

"I didn't understand that. We all tried to visit you but they wouldn't let any of us in."

"You did?" Jenetta said tearfully. "I thought everyone had forgotten about me. You know, out-of-sight..."

"Like that could happen," Gloria said, stretching out her arms to hug her. "Either that we'd forget about you or that you were out of sight."

"I guess I was being silly, but I was *so* scared. You have no idea what it's like when you begin to think the entire galaxy has turned their back on you. I guess the isolation was more of the over-application of regulations in capital crimes cases. A prisoner needn't be allowed contact with anyone except his or her attorney until after the adjudication process has been completed. At least I wasn't chained hand and foot every time I left the cell once the admiral ordered them to stop."

"We're going to celebrate," Gloria said. "Can you leave the base?"

"Yes. I don't have to report back for three days."

"Great, as soon as we heard that a verdict had been reached, Rebecca made reservations for dinner at a restaurant on the civilian concourse level."

"Before you knew the verdict?"

"We knew they wouldn't put you in prison. At worst it would have been some kind of administrative censure."

"And just how did you know that? I thought I might be spending the rest of my life in a jail cell."

"I already told you, you're way too famous. The Raider attacks in this deca-sector have totally ceased since you destroyed their base. Freighters are starting to operate openly again without waiting for convoys and Space Command is recommending that all vessels in this deca-sector activate their AutoTect systems. It's all because of you and what you did. We can't go *anywhere* without seeing your face in the news or on newspapers and magazines. If they'd put you in jail, the Galactic Alliance Council would have had their heads, or the population of every planet would have *theirs*. There were images of you being dragged from the hospital in shackles when you were arrested that made every newspaper, magazine, and news broadcast in the entire galaxy. The headlines read, 'Heroine Humbled Hobbled and Held.'"

Jenetta groaned. "That means my folks saw it. I didn't have any idea the news of the court-martial had even been released."

"There wasn't any way you could stop it. Those of us subpoenaed to appear at the court-martial were restricted from talking about the case until it was over, but the rest of the *Vordoth* crew, along with most of the fifty captives you freed, have been interviewed by every news service in the galaxy. Also, every captive and every member of the *Vordoth*'s crew sent a personal message to the Galactic Alliance Council demanding your immediate release and the Nordakians have sent messages to both the Council and Space Command."

"The Nordakians?"

"Yes. They've officially petitioned the Galactic Alliance Council to have you brought to Nordakia so they can honor you formally. They were also responsible for our ships being welcomed at Higgins Spaceport. The royal family themselves contacted the Galactic Alliance Council and Space Command Headquarters after we left Obotymot to praise your actions and thank the GSC for ensuring that the emergency supplies got through."

"What?"

"They told Space Command that the arrival of the food and medicine at Obotymot saved thousands of lives. You're to be the first Space Command officer ever honored by their planet. Space Command couldn't very well convict you of actions that the entire Nordakian and Terran civilizations are praising you for. It would make them look pretty damn stupid."

"I'm speechless."

"Let's head for the restaurant and we'll fill you in on everything else that's been going on since you were jailed."

"I have to send a vidMail to my family first."

"Okay, there's a GaMPS across from the restaurant. We'll drop you off and wait in the restaurant for you."

"Great."

Fifteen minutes later, Jenetta was sitting in an enclosed com booth in the Galactic Message & Parcel Service center thinking about what she was going to say. When she was ready, she pressed the 'Start Recording' button and the red light started flashing.

"Hi Mom. Hi Dad. Hi Billy, Richie, Andy and Jimmy, if you happen to be there. I can imagine what a shock it was to learn I'm still alive. It was a shock for me too. I never really expected to be rescued from the escape pod. I've been unable to contact you during the court-martial, but I've been told that it's been in the news so I guess you know all about it. I'm sorry to have put all of you through so much, but I have good news. I've just been acquitted of all charges and I'm free again, but the bad news is I don't know when I'll be able to get back to Earth. I have to report for duty in three days and then I'll learn where I'm going to be posted. I guess I'm the oldest ensign in Space Command now, or at least I've had the rank longer than anybody else. It seems I've had a lot of firsts lately. I..."

Jenetta paused to take a deep breath and said in a more subdued voice, "I've changed a lot since I last saw you. Not physically; I only look about a year older that way. I'm talking about growing up. I've seen and learned a great deal since I was awakened from stasis sleep, and I've been forced to do some things that I'm— not really proud of. But I don't want to talk about them right now. I'll explain more when I see you. For now just know that I love all of you and that I miss you terribly. I can't wait to see you and hug you. All my love."

Jenetta pressed the 'End Recording' button and took a breath. Realizing that a tear was running down her cheek, she wiped it away and composed herself, then stood up and left the booth.

"How much do I owe you?" she asked of the young male clerk at the counter as she held out Gloria's credits card.

"No charge, Ensign. This one's on the house. I'm glad you were acquitted."

"Thank you. Thank you very much."

"You're welcome, and good luck."

Jenetta left the shop and walked across to the restaurant, where Gloria, Rebecca, Charley, Gunny, and Leah were waiting. Gregory's had the subdued but elegant look of expensive restaurants from the twentieth century. A lot of real wood had been brought to the station for the construction of the interior and then stained to a red walnut color. The earth tones of red, yellow, and brown were pervasive throughout and there was none of the glitzy chrome and bright neon currently in vogue and general use throughout the concourse.

As Jenetta sat down, she held out the credits card to Gloria. "The clerk wouldn't let me pay."

"Okay, Jen."

"I'll have to look into the back pay situation. I'm going to need a few things."

"You'll have quite a payday coming up with eleven years of back pay," Gloria said.

"I may not. They've had me listed as being dead for a lot of years."

"But they must have updated the records by now. They couldn't court-martial a dead person."

"If you think that, you don't know the JAG section or the service, Lieutenant," Gunny quipped.

"There's also the matter of being in stasis," Jenetta said. "They normally adjust the pay for crews traveling long distances while in stasis. You only get about one quarter pay while asleep."

"That's still not too bad," Charley said, "you practically don't age and you get paid twenty-five percent."

"It's not all good. Your family and friends continue to age and may be gone when you get back from a long trip with multiple sleeps. Then there's the physical recovery required after a long stasis sleep. Anyway, the service will determine the amount I'll get."

"Do you have a place to stay tonight?" Rebecca asked.

"Not yet, but I'll arrange for a room at the Bachelor Officers Quarters until I get posted."

"You could stay aboard the *Vordoth* for now," Gloria offered. "We'll be in port for several more weeks and it would keep the damned newsies from leaching onto you when you leave your quarters for meals and such."

"Thanks, Gloria. That would be great. I'll stay with you for the weekend at least."

After placing their food orders, they talked about the court-martial until their cuisine was delivered. The aroma was fantastic and Jenetta wasted no time digging in and savoring every bite, delighted to be eating real food again. The brig only served synthesized meals of indeterminate fare.

Once everyone had finished eating and they were enjoying a final cup of coffee or tea, Rebecca asked for the check. Nodding amiably, the waiter gestured to a short, dark-haired man standing next to the maitre d'hotel.

"Hello, I'm Gregory, the proprietor of this restaurant," he said as he reached the table. "Did you enjoy your meals?" he asked, to which everyone at the table praised the food and service in the most enthusiastic of terms.

"I'm glad you enjoyed it; the cook made an extra special effort for you. We're happy to have served Ensign Carver and her friends from the *Vordoth* in celebration of her acquittal today. Today's meal is courtesy of the restaurant. I hope you'll all come back again."

Jenetta was amazed the proprietor recognized them, but dismissed it and said, "I'll certainly be back again if I'm posted here for a while. Thank you very much, Gregory."

"You're welcome, Ensign. Good luck at your new posting and I'll look forward to serving you again." There was something in the way that he said it that made Jenetta wonder if he knew where she was to be posted. She was tempted to ask but resisted the urge because a restaurateur couldn't possibly have such information.

As they left the restaurant, the cheerful party turned towards the shopping concourse, but they hadn't gone more than a dozen steps before the mob of newsies that had been scouring the station for them converged on their group from every direction. They hurried to another lift tube as Charley and Gunny again blocked the shouting nuisances from getting to Jenetta.

Inside the lift, they enjoyed a respite from the yelling while the car dropped to the transport level where a shuttle from the *Vordoth* waited. Twenty minutes later they were all on their way to the ship, now barren of any cargo container link-sections. The laser array sections were still attached to the main ship though, easily making it the meanest looking civilian ship in the port.

"The company has given us special permission," Gloria said, "to leave the array sections in the configuration you set up, and we'll keep them as long as there's a threat from Raiders or Space Command again restricts private ships from mounting exterior weapons. They're delighted with the tug and shuttles you gave us, by the way, and they're even letting us keep one of the shuttles. They've sold the other one to replace the containers and cargo. Charley picked the best one for us. It's neither the biggest, nor the newest, but it's in the best condition."

"How about you? Are you to be the new captain?"

"No, a new captain will be joining us before we leave here, but I'm not unhappy about that since I still have a lot to learn. And they've promoted me to Lieutenant Commander effective with the beginning of the new month, so I'll probably be the first officer on our next trip. We shouldn't have any trouble filling out the crew with the Raiders gone."

"Congratulations, Commander."

"Thank you, Captain."

"Ensign."

"Captain. It'll always be Captain to me, Jen. At least until you make Admiral."

Jenetta laughed. "That won't be for a very, very, very long time."

"But it will happen. I just know it."

"Thanks, Gloria. And thanks for being such a great friend."

"Likewise, Jen."

* * *

"I trust all of you have been watching the Ensign Jenetta Carver court-martial with the same high degree of interest as myself," Admiral Richard Moore said to the other members of the Admiralty Board during a regularly scheduled meeting in the Admiralty Hall at Supreme Headquarters on Earth. "I understand it's been the most popular live event broadcast in the history of military vid broadcasts, playing to SRO audiences in all locations."

"*I've* certainly been watching," Admiral Evelyn Platt said. "The details of her battle tactics, enemy base infiltration, capture, treatment, and escape have been fascinating. I haven't missed a minute of the broadcasts, recording any parts I couldn't watch live so I could view them later."

"I've heard that activity aboard every ship, and on almost every base, has practically ground to a standstill whenever the daily broadcast signal was received until the broadcast ended," Admiral Roger Bradlee said.

"The audacity and successes of this young girl have been awe-inspiring to an officer corps too long without significant victory against the Raiders," Admiral Raihana Ahmed said.

"Not just the officer corps," Admiral Raymond Burke said. "The ratings and noncoms have been rooting and cheering for her since the first minute the court-martial began. You'd think she was fighting to have all ship and base messes roll back the clock to the days when the British Empire ruled the seas and provided free beer with every meal."

"The court-martial seems to have had a significantly greater impact than we foresaw," Admiral Loretta Plimley said.

"I believe the issue of the 18,000 deaths aboard the Raider base and the destruction of the destroyer and cruiser she fought have been adequately explained— and accepted," Admiral Arnold Hillaire commented.

"We certainly can't be accused of being too soft on our own in *this* case," Admiral Bradlee said. "In fact, many people have privately commented to me that we were being far too severe with the girl."

"Carver certainly garnered a lot of sympathy among the media," Admiral Lon Woo said, "but I think most everyone is satisfied with the outcome of the court-martial."

"Of course they were sympathetic," Admiral Donald Hubera said. "They saw us as bullying a young, pretty, defenseless girl who we had missed finding when we looked for *Hokyuu* survivors. They felt we screwed up and were only trying to shift attention away from our failings."

"We did screw up by not finding her," Admiral Plimley said. "On that point, they're absolutely correct. As a result of our examination of her pod, certain modifications in design and retrofit are being discussed that will prevent such problems in the future. We want to ensure that we *never* lose another officer or crewmember in such a manner.

"We're left with the thorny issue of what to do with this young ensign now," Admiral Moore said.

"Not so young," Admiral Shana Ressler said. "She looks young because we failed to find her escape pod after the explosion of the *Hokyuu*, but she's been left seriously behind by her classmates, most of whom have advanced to Lieutenant during the past eleven years, and one has made Lieutenant Commander."

"Ensign Carver has had a great deal of attention turned her way as a result of the court-martial," Admiral Raymond Burke said. "It seems to me that we must either reward her substantially, or bury her so deep in some totally obscure job that her name, face, and actions will be quickly forgotten and rarely, if ever, mentioned again."

* * *

Jenetta was delighted to be able to spend two days with her friends on the *Vordoth*. It was a wonderfully relaxing time and she was able to totally unwind and temporarily forget both the depression of being closeted in the station's brig and the despair of possible consequences from the general court-martial. Rebecca was rarely seen without Charley when they weren't on duty and Gunny seemed thoroughly infatuated with Leah. It appeared that Leah had finally developed a mutual attraction with a man taller than herself and she couldn't stop staring at him with adoring eyes. The group of friends dined together each night and then talked or listened to music in the officer's lounge. Now that Jenetta was just an ensign again and free of all command responsibilities, she longed to take a few wide-open throttle rides on a maglev sled, but without a cargo there was no tunnel through which to travel. Life was just so unfair at times.

On the morning of the third day, Gloria dropped Jenetta off at the orbiting Space Command station so she could report for duty. Jenetta was directed first to the paymaster's office where she spent about an hour while records were checked and updated. Before she left, her Space Command credits card was adjusted with back pay and compensation for the personal items she had lost when the *Hokyuu* was destroyed. She received a full year's pay for the months she'd been awake before and since the stasis sleep, and almost three years pay for the ten and a half years she had spent in the stasis chamber. She felt rich. Next, she was directed to personnel where she filled out more forms and picked up her new orders before being redirected to housing. The housing officer arranged for quarters in the BOQ and told her to report next to the hospital, but before leaving the housing office she was permitted to use a com station so she could check her orders.

Touching the data ring to a media drawer spindle, she learned she'd been assigned to the base's science office. She'd been hoping for an assignment to a ship— *any* ship. As a sickly feeling developed in the pit of her stomach, extreme depression set in. Her adventure was over. Her days of traveling through space at faster-than-light speeds were over. Other than a biennial trip home, she might never again set foot inside a ship from now until her retirement from Space Command unless she resigned her commission and sought a position with a freight company. "And no one even thanked me for returning the two battleships," she said aloud to herself. "Maybe I *should* resign."

Although she'd received only four and a half years pay for the eleven and a half years of time since her graduation from NHSA, her service records indicated that she was being credited with the full term for seniority and retirement purposes. That should mean that the Academy's 'ten years of service' requirement for her education was officially satisfied. If true, she could resign her commission at any time, but she would have to confirm that before she applied for separation.

Chapter Twenty-Six
~ February 13th, 2268 ~

Aware that her facial expression probably mirrored her mood, Jenetta set her jaw and tried to wipe away all sign of melancholy before leaving the housing office.

At the hospital, she was told to wait until Doctor Freidlander was free. She took a seat and waited for about twenty minutes until a nurse came to escort her to the examination room where the doctor was waiting.

"More testing, doctor?"

"I want to see if there have been any further changes during the past few weeks."

Doctor Freidlander spent about an hour performing various tests before sharing his findings with Jenetta.

"You've grown half an inch since you first reported here. That's extraordinary. I can't doubt any longer that you were subjected to some medical procedure that's causing you to change. Furthermore, your body seems to be working over-time to complete the changes, as well as repairing any damage at an unprecedented rate. Are you eating well?"

"Yes. I always seem to be hungry, though."

"That will probably change once your body stops growing. Right now, it needs the nourishment to fuel the rapid changes, so you should have the appetite of a teenager. Enjoy it while it lasts."

"Enjoy hunger?"

Dr. Freidlander gave her a lopsided smile. "Enjoy being able to eat like a teenager again without worrying about the food winding up on your hips."

"Do you think my face will change very much? Arneu said that in a couple of years even my own mother may not recognize me."

"Your appearance is changing, but we don't believe the changes will be so extreme that people who have known you won't recognize you once they understand the reason for the change. And as a result of the court-martial, it's unlikely that anyone won't be aware of those reasons. Your height will be the most radical of the alterations, but we have your new DNA on file now so we'll be able to identify you should your retinal images and fingerprints change further."

"That's comforting, but can't you do something to stop the changes?"

"No, nothing I'm afraid. First, I don't know what process was used, and second, all that research was ended long ago. We still use DNA information for identification and as part of the health diagnosis procedure, but no DNA alteration testing is permitted. I'd *love* to know how your body has been programmed to repair itself so remarkably, but even that kind of research is forbidden."

"So I'm stuck with whatever they've programmed me to become?"

"I'm afraid so. I can show you what our computer thinks you'll look like when the changes are complete based on the DNA in your new cells. Would you like to see that?"

"Very much."

The doctor keyed in a few commands and the viewscreen displayed the naked, three-dimensional representation of a woman, revolving slowly so it could be seen from all views. The height lines behind the body showed it to be just over five-foot eleven-inches tall. The body was perfectly proportional for the height, and the skin appeared flawless, without so much as a single freckle or blemish.

"Is that me?"

"As we believe you'll appear when the changes are complete."

"It's terrible! Look at the size of my breasts! They're at least a full cup size larger. How will I be able to run with a chest like that? And the size of my hips makes me look like a freak. The face isn't too bad. It still sorta looks like me, but why do you show it with makeup?"

"That's not makeup. It's the natural pigmentation programmed into the DNA. You won't have to use makeup unless you want to highlight the effect, or reduce it."

"So this is Arneu's idea of a goddess?"

"Not just him. The men in the genetics lab have all fallen in love with the image."

"I don't think I'm going to like being changed to look like that. Can I be surgically altered to reduce the size of my breasts and hips?"

"Of course, once the changes are complete."

"How long will that take."

"As you're aware, all the cells in the body, even bone cells, eventually die and are replaced. That takes about eight to ten years. So once the DNA is completely rewritten, you can be altered."

"Ten years? Well I guess that's not much when compared to five thousand."

"Ensign?"

"Nothing sir, just a little inside joke. What about my chest."

"Did you notice the model?"

"I saw that you included the imprint on the model. Extremely accurate detailing, but when can I get it removed."

"You can't. It's been permanently imprinted into the pigmentation of your chest as programmed in your DNA. We can kill the pigmentation, leaving a white sign instead of a magenta one, but we think your body will just replace it again because of the changes that are still occurring. We might try grafting new skin over the top."

"I wouldn't want a new white sign to replace the old magenta one anyway, so I'll go with the skin graft."

"We'll start growing the new skin immediately. It should be ready to transfer in about four to six weeks. We just need to get a small sample of your skin before you leave so we can start the culture."

"Okay, doctor."

"I'm still amazed at how quickly your scalp healed where we removed the bone cell sample. There's not a single mark that indicates the procedure was ever performed. Remarkable."

"Yes, thank you doctor. That was excellent work."

"Don't thank me; your body did all the healing. I'm just amazed at how quickly it did it."

"I'm a fast healer. As I told you, my arm knitted in a week and was completely healed in twelve days."

"Yes, I read Doctor Erikson's report. That was amazing also."

"I'm just a fast healer."

"Even for a fast healer, that's really amazing. With surgical nano-bot assistance, it should have taken at least six to seven weeks for that bone to knit completely. And there's absolutely no evidence that the bone was ever broken. *That's* unheard of."

"Arneu said that the procedure they used on me would make me heal ten times faster than average people. It was important for the new life they intended for me. I guess whip marks would heal overnight."

"Whip marks?" the doctor said in surprise.

"I was slated to be a pleasure slave in one of the kinkier resorts, a submissive who loved masochism. You know, the 'whip me, beat me' crowd."

"I can see where a speedy rate of recovery would be beneficial in that kind of occupation."

"Yes, well, my programming was useful when we took over the *Prometheus*. My arm was broken during the assault and the pain just made me stronger, so instead of being down for the count I was able to continue on and do what had to be done."

"I see," the doctor said with a strange expression on his face. "I think you should be interviewed by the Psych Department this week. You would have been called in anyway during the next couple of months for your annual evaluation when a time could be scheduled, but I think what you've just told me makes it a priority."

"Okay, doctor."

After removing a skin sample from the underside of Jenetta's arm, the doctor sprayed on a bandage. "There, Ensign," he said, "you're all set. You can report to your new duty posting now. The Psych Department will call with your appointment information. Stop back here every couple of days to have the dressing under your arm changed until it heals."

"Thank you, doctor."

Jenetta's first stop upon leaving the hospital was the officer's mess hall. It was noon and she wanted the fortification of a full stomach before reporting for duty in the science section. She picked up a tray and silverware before walking along the food self-service counters where she chose a large chef's salad, both hot entrées of chicken and meatloaf, and heaping sides of corn on the cob, mashed potatoes, green beans, rice pilaf, potato salad cup, and two Golden Delicious apples. The food was fresh here. There were food synthesizers available for anyone who might want to use them, but during meal service hours they were normally only used to make rich, creamy deserts that looked and tasted like the real thing but which contained no more than a half dozen calories. Looking around, she spotted an empty table and headed for it. As she prepared to eat, she took out a printed transcript of her orders and read it over thoroughly.

"Excuse me, is that seat available?" a familiar voice asked from behind.

"Yes, it is," Jenetta said without turning around. "Please join me, Commander."

Spence walked around the table and put his tray down so he'd be facing Jenetta.

Jenetta followed his eyes down to the food arrayed before her and smiled. "I'm still a growing girl and I'm a little hungry today."

He nodded and grinned, saying, "I thought you might be expecting two or three other people. How have you been doing, Ensign?"

Jenetta looked up into his penetrating cobalt-blue eyes and said, "Very well, sir, thanks to you."

"I'm happy I could help. You didn't deserve to be treated like that and I still can't fathom why they went after you in that way. The evidence against a conviction seemed so over-whelming to me, although I didn't want to give you false hope in case I was wrong."

"Well, it's all behind us now and I can get on with my life."

"What ship have you been assigned to?"

"No ship," Jenetta said dejectedly. "I've been assigned to the Science Section on the base."

"I take it that's far from what you were hoping for."

"It's not even close. I was hoping to be assigned to a ship, even if it was only another supply ship and even if I was again the only science officer aboard."

"Don't give up hope; it could still happen. Maybe they just don't have any posts open right now."

"Maybe," Jenetta said in a kind of sigh.

Jenetta and Spence spent the rest of the meal talking about the court-martial and the verdict. As the time approached 1230, Spence announced he had to leave for an appointment. Before going he asked, "Do you think you'd like to have dinner with me sometime this week?"

"Sure, I'll probably be here every night around 1730 hours."

"No, I mean at a real restaurant," Spence said as he placed his large hand on hers and squeezed lightly.

It felt as if a current of electricity had run up Jenetta's arm, but she kept her voice under control. "Oh— sure. When?"

"How about Friday?"

"Great. What time, Commander?"

"1900 hours?"

"Okay. I'll meet you in the lobby of the BOQ at 1900 hours, four days from now."

"I'll be looking forward to it, Ensign. See you then."

She watched Spence's tall figure as he walked away, expecting him to look back, but he never did. She raised her eyebrows and wrinkled her brow as she thought about running her fingers through his blond hair, then polished off her lunch and left to report to her new posting.

The Science Section occupied a significant portion of the office space in the wing where it was located, and Jenetta walked through a dozen corridors before finding the room referenced in her orders. She took a deep breath, then stepped into the area where the computer would acknowledge her desire to enter and activate the door-opening mechanism. An officer, whom she estimated to be in his late fifties or early sixties, sat working alone at a long table filled with papers and graphs.

"Ensign Jenetta Carver reporting for duty, Commander," she said as she came to attention in front of him.

Lt. Commander Wilfred Davis stopped what he was doing and looked up. "Welcome, Ensign," he said. He had the look of an academician who was more at home in a sea of books or charts, or standing before a class of unlearned students, than performing the duties of a commanding officer of Space Command personnel, even if this was just the Science Section. "Your orders, please?" he said.

Jenetta handed over the data ring and waited while Lt. Commander Davis viewed and verified the message.

"Alright, Ensign. Welcome to Higgins Space Station by the way."

"Thank you, sir."

"You've been away from astrophysics for a while so you'll have quite a bit of catching up to do. We've collected a tremendous amount of new data since you graduated from the Academy. It's been a wonderfully exciting eleven years!"

"Yes sir. I'm looking forward to catching up on everything I missed," Jenetta said, with as much enthusiasm as she could possibly muster.

"Marvelous. I'm going to assign you to my most dedicated researcher. You'll have remarkable opportunities to help advance our knowledge of the universe under her expert direction. Follow me."

With Jenetta following, Davis led the way to an astrophysics lab down the corridor from his office where an auburn-haired officer was working intently on her computer. The nameplate on the desk identified her as Lieutenant Margaret Kesliski.

"Lieutenant, this is Ensign Carver. I'm assigning her to your section." Turning to Jenetta, Davis said, "Carry on, Ensign."

"Yes sir."

Kesliski, whom Jenetta estimated to be between twenty-eight and thirty, stood up and said icily, "Follow me, Carver."

Jenetta fell in behind the thin, five-foot eight-inch Science Officer who looked and acted every inch the part of a researcher who preferred to do her own work and never be bothered by other people. As they reached a science console near the back of the room, Kesliski said, "This will be your station. I'll get your computer access set up and then you can begin."

"Er— begin what, Lieutenant?"

Kesliski let out a quick breath, finally showing her displeasure with having been disturbed. "Whatever you're assigned, Ensign. To start with, we have a lot of new data on a globular cluster that has to be analyzed. A couple of the stars seem to have intensified significantly of late."

"Okay, Lieutenant," Jenetta said, less than enthusiastically.

Kesliski, picking up on the subtle tone of dejection in Jenetta's voice, said, "I know it isn't as exciting as fighting Raiders, but it's important work. I would hope that you can muster a little more enthusiasm in the months and years ahead."

"No doubt, Lieutenant."

Kesliski grimaced ever so slightly in response to a remark that could be interpreted a couple of different ways. As she walked away, she said, "Carry on, Ensign."

"Aye, Lieutenant."

Jenetta glanced around the room before taking a seat at her new desk. She recognized the ultimate in dead-end jobs when she saw it. Maybe in twenty-five or thirty years she would be promoted to replace Lieutenant Kesliski when Kesliski moved up to replace a retiring Lt. Commander Davis. Kesliski would probably remain at that rank until she reached mandatory retirement age of eighty-five, and she would be perfectly content as long as she had her work.

Arriving at her new quarters in the BOQ that evening, Jenetta found her personal possessions already there. They had been delivered from wherever SCI had stored them while she was in the brig. Perhaps they had simply been left on the *Prometheus*, but most likely Space Command Intelligence had examined every last item under an electron microscope. She wondered what they thought when they played her personal log ring. She didn't doubt for a second that they would have been able to get past the encryption technique she had used, but it had probably taken them more than a few days to crack. The simple encryption block was of her own design and the password required appending the date of the most recent entry in reverse order.

When her things had been stowed and the picture of her family resided prominently on her dresser, she logged into the base-net and discovered she had a message from home waiting. It was just what she needed to help her forget the disappointments of the day. She touched the 'Play' button and watched as the screen lit up with an image of her Mom's face.

"Hi Sweetheart. I can't begin to tell you how wonderful it was to get word that you were alive and safe. When I learned of your survival, I couldn't stop crying for days. I cried almost as much as when you were lost, but these were tears of joy. I want so much to throw my arms around you and hug you as hard as I can, but— that will have to wait until you come home. I tried to get in touch with you immediately, but they told me you couldn't receive messages. Then, when we learned about the court-martial, we became worried again. You haven't been out of the news here in weeks. I can't go anywhere without seeing your face, but— it's kind of nice; it tells me that you're still safe. I'm glad you were acquitted of all those charges; I knew you would be. We raised you right and you certainly couldn't have done any of the terrible things they accused you of.

"You probably want to know what's been happening for the past eleven years, so I'll try to squeeze in as much as I can while time permits. Your brothers are all off-world right now. Billy just made Commander last month, Richie is a Lieutenant Commander as of two years ago, and Andy and Jimmy are Lieutenants, hoping for promotions to Lieutenant Commander. They're all doing well and they'll probably be sending their own messages because I sent them a copy of the message you sent me. You missed Daddy's retirement party last year. He was the captain of a frigate when he reached mandatory 'shipboard' retirement age of sixty-five. They offered him a desk job and he could have stayed on for another twenty years and possibly made admiral, but he didn't want to be in the service if he couldn't be in space. His ship had a chance encounter with a Raider cruiser the year before he retired, but the Raiders managed to get away after they exchanged a few shots.

"The timer just went off so I have to sign off. Daddy is going to compose his own message to you and send it tomorrow. We love you, honey. Take care of yourself."

The message ended and Jenetta played it three more times. It made her both happy and sad—happy because she was so delighted to hear from her mother, but sad because her mother looked so old. She could never recapture those eleven years, even if she lived to be five thousand. Where the receipt of the message had originally lifted her spirits, this reflection left her feeling more depressed than ever. Almost as depressing was the news that her brothers were doing so well. While they were moving up in rank and position, she was stuck at ensign with little likelihood of advancement anytime soon.

*　*　*

On Tuesday morning, Jenetta received a call from the Psych Department at the hospital informing her that she had an appointment for Wednesday morning. As soon as she was off the com link, she went to Lieutenant Kesliski to notify her that she would be late the following morning.

"They probably want to learn how you could slaughter more than 18,000 people. I'm surprised they've waited until now to look inside your head."

"I was acquitted on that charge, Lieutenant," Jenetta said defensively. She bit her tongue to avoid saying anything more on the subject.

"It still happened and you're still responsible for their deaths, even if they're not going to lock you up and throw away the key for doing it. I'm opposed to killing of any sort. You should have just reported back to Space Command instead of trying to be a big hero."

Jenetta continued to repress her resentment and simply replied, "Yes, Lieutenant. Whatever you say, ma'am."

Aware that Jenetta wasn't going to take the bait and become insubordinate, Lieutenant Kesliski scowled at her. "Carry on, Ensign."

Jenetta had another message waiting when she got back to the BOQ that evening. This one was from her dad.

"Hi Honey. Gee, it was *great* to hear from you. It's so wonderful that you're alive, and I'm so proud of you that I could bust. I've been spending every minute possible watching the news on the vid since most of it has been about you for the past four weeks. I pulled some strings and got into the theater on the base while they were broadcasting the court-martial here. It was only being shown live to senior officers since so many wanted to attend, but they recorded it and ran replays around the clock for junior officers and enlisted personnel. It's replaying again, in its entirety, for those who couldn't get in before. It hasn't been released to the general public yet, but your brothers have seen it because it was transmitted on an encrypted military channel that was picked up by their ships and then rebroadcast throughout the vessel."

Jenetta sat up straighter, her eyes wide and mouth agape. They had broadcast the entire court-martial? To everyone in the military? Everywhere?

"I was plenty disturbed hearing about the things they put you through in the Raider detention center and I'm glad you made the bastards pay. I loved watching the *Vordoth* image log records of your attacks on the two Raider warships. Congratulations on two stunning victories. And you should have heard the cheers in the theater when they showed the *Prometheus'* image log of the Raider spaceport blowing up. I was screaming at the top of my lungs, trying to get them to shut up so I could hear every word of testimony. They finally calmed down and I discovered that we didn't miss anything. I know how proud you must have felt, having conceived the plan, planted the explosives, and actually been there when it happened.

"Oops, there's the timer. I have to go for now, honey. Take care of yourself and give'em hell. I love you."

Jenetta was too disturbed to replay the message right away. She'd never suspected for a second that every military ship and base in Galactic Alliance space had seen the entire court-martial. Every armchair quarterback in Space Command would now be critiquing her tactics as if she'd been commanding a warship instead of a freighter. Thank God she'd been acquitted of all charges. She wondered if they had been broadcasting when she was led into the courtroom wearing the prisoner transport restraints. Even worse, Commander Pierce had grilled her repeatedly when she testified about being suspended from the holding bar in the anteroom while clad only in her underwear. That would be an image everyone would carry in their head for years. She suddenly felt sick to her stomach. It would take years, decades perhaps, to live that down. As for the rest, she certainly wasn't going to have much of an opportunity to 'give'em hell' while flying a desk in a back office of the Science Section.

Reporting to the hospital the next morning as ordered, Jenetta was immediately escorted into the office of Doctor Praeges. Though decorated with contemporary office furniture, the walls were lined with art from the cosmic grab bag of an eclectic collector. Every major period seemed to be represented.

"Sit down, Ensign," the short, thin psychiatrist said before smiling warmly and gesturing towards a comfortable chair opposite his desk.

"Yes sir."

"Doctor Freidlander has talked with me about you. Of course I know of your exploits, as do most other people, but I hadn't heard that you'd been programmed. What do you remember about that?"

"Not much, sir. I was just taken to a section of the medical facility and put into a special chair like a recliner. Straps were used on my arms to hold me there and an adhesive strip with a number of wires attached to it was put on my forehead. All I remember after that is hearing soothing music."

"No injections?"

"There could have been; I don't know. The next thing I remember is being awakened and taken back to my cell."

The doctor looked at Jenetta thoughtfully for several minutes. Jenetta was starting to squirm a little under his dispassionate stare when he asked, "What music were they playing?"

"It sounded like Vivaldi's Four Seasons, the Summer movement."

The doctor turned to his computer and typed a few commands. A few seconds later, the Summer movement started playing through a speaker in the ceiling. "Like this?"

"Yes, this is it, sir."

The doctor nodded thoughtfully. "Okay, Ensign. Let's take a walk."

Jenetta followed the doctor down the corridor to another room where there was a recliner similar to the one she'd been placed into at the Raider medical lab.

"Take a seat, Ensign."

Jenetta sat down as instructed, but when the doctor attempted to put a strap on her right arm, she recoiled away from him.

"Simulating the exact situation you experienced will help your mind recreate the event. It will assist our efforts in finding out what they did to you."

"Oh— okay, doctor."

Secured to the chair as she'd been secured in the detention center medical lab, the doctor put a plastic adhesive strip with attached wires on her forehead. He tapped a couple of keys on a command console and she heard the Summer movement playing. She didn't remember anything after that until the plastic strip was being peeled off. The wall clock indicated that it was almost noon. More than three hours had passed since she climbed into the chair.

"What happened?"

"I simulated the conditions you told me about and then used our equipment to put you under. It's a fairly simple and common procedure. I gambled that it was the same one used on you. They never expected you to escape from their control, so they didn't make it very elaborate."

"What did you learn?"

"I found out they fed you a lot of instructions about pleasing men and women sexually. Fortunately, nothing that would violate Space Command security. They really did intend for you to become a pleasure slave and so never attempted to affect your loyalties. I neutralized as much as I could and you probably won't beg anyone to beat or whip you when you get sexually aroused, unless you wanted that before. And you won't feel any lesbian urges unless you leaned towards that. I only attempted to neutralize what they added; I didn't try to modify your original behavior."

"Then I'm finished here?"

"For now. I want you to come back and see me if you begin to experience any strange dreams, fantasies, or desires, especially of a sexual nature. The mind is a complex instrument and, although I instructed you to forget their programming, the mind doesn't really forget, it just sort of— bypasses it. Some of it could resurface again in time if it's triggered by some special memory or activity."

"Okay, doctor. Thank you."

After leaving the Psych Department offices, Jenetta went to see about having the dressing under her arm changed. A nurse escorted her to an examination room where she was asked to remove her tunic and blouse. As she disrobed, the slave imprint received no more than a cursory glance from the nurse. *By now, the entire hospital has probably seen pictures of it'* Jenetta thought sardonically. *In fact, they're probably selling 20x30 centimeter color glossies in the hospital gift store, or perhaps giving one away with every purchase over five credits.*

Removing the old bandage, the nurse said, "What is this? There's no open wound under this gauze."

Jenetta felt the area and discovered there wasn't any tenderness at all. Holding up a hand mirror, all she saw was a slightly red area. "I guess it healed. Doctor Freidlander took a small skin sample the other day."

"Well you certainly don't need further dressings, Ensign. The redness should disappear in a few days. You won't need to come back for it."

"Okay, Lieutenant, thanks," Jenetta said, smiling. She left the base hospital after getting dressed.

By now, Jenetta was getting used to all the attention. As an ensign, it was her duty to salute senior officers she encounter-ed and hold that salute until they returned it or passed her by. But she found herself in the unique situation of being saluted by the senior officers first and returning their salute. Many noncoms and ratings she encountered would actually stop, step aside, and snap to attention, holding their salute until she returned it, as if she was an admiral. Her face was still being splashed across the media constantly, but it was beginning to be a bit irksome. It only served to remind her that her adventures were over and how much she was going to miss her time aboard the *Prometheus*.

It was close to noon so she decided to have lunch at the officer's mess before reporting to work. Despite the smiles and admiring looks she received from everyone, no one invited her to join them at their table. She ate alone, then carried her dessert, two enormous navel oranges, back to the Science Section with the intention of eating them later in the afternoon when the hunger got so bad she couldn't wait for dinner.

The rest of the week dragged by as Jenetta spent hour after boring hour plotting star positions in the globular cluster and examining the anomalous readings. The high points in her week occurred when she received messages from her four brothers, all happy and excited to learn that she was still alive and hopeful of seeing her soon. They had frequently been at each other's throats as siblings, but once grown they had become as close-knit as a family could be. Being a total military family gave them a common bond that would sustain them for the rest of their years, but Jenetta had begun to seriously consider tendering her resignation. Her first month aboard the *Vordoth* before she had accepted command had been so wonderful. Perhaps she could get a berth on a freighter, possibly even the *Vordoth*. Any berth on any ship would be better than working in the Science Section with Kesliski. But resigning from the service was a major career move. She had worked all her life to become a Space Command officer. She would have to think it over for a couple more weeks before making a decision, or even making inquires about the satisfaction of her educational obligation.

* * *

On Friday morning, Jenetta was working on computations related to the globular cluster anomalies when Lieutenant Kesliski approached her workstation.

"Carver," Kesliski said, "drop whatever you're working on and get over to headquarters."

"What's up, Lieutenant?"

"How should I know? They just called and ordered me to send you over immediately. Maybe they've come to their senses and have new charges to file against you. Get yourself in gear, Ensign."

"Aye, Lieutenant."

Jenetta stood up, straightened her tunic, and walked to the door. She hoped Lieutenant Kesliski didn't have telepathic powers, but— it would be okay if she did. They couldn't put someone in the brig for what they thought of a superior officer, as long as they didn't actually vocalize their feelings or record them where others could find them.

Chapter Twenty-Seven
~ February 20th, 2268 ~

A sense of extreme uneasiness began to grow in Jenetta as she hurried to the headquarters section of the space station and Lieutenant Kesliski's speculation was probably responsible in no small part. Having just been released from the brig a week earlier, she had no desire to relive that experience.

Redirected three times after reporting to the HQ administrative office, she ultimately wound up in the outer offices of Admiral Holt, the base commander. The admiral's aide told her to have a seat and she would be called shortly. As she sat there waiting, Commander Kanes of SCI arrived and was sent immediately into the admiral's office. He had looked at her, nodded, and said, "Ensign," as Jenetta had jumped to her feet. A few minutes later, Commander Pierce, the JAG officer who had prosecuted her at the court-martial, arrived, and was also sent directly in. He also acknowledged her, as Kanes had, when Jenetta again jumped up.

Getting more nervous by the minute, Jenetta fidgeted in the chair. Could it really be as Kesliski had speculated? Were they preparing to bring new charges against her? She didn't think she could be tried again for the original charges, so it must be something new. Sabotage of the *Hokyuu*? That seemed to be the *only* thing she hadn't been charged with yet, unless she was to be charged with exceeding the ten-kilometer allowable length when she had towed the Nordakian freighter with the *Vordoth*. Or was there something Doctor Praeges found while rummaging around in her mind? Had he discovered that Arneu told her she might live a substantially prolonged life? Was she going to become a lab rat while they experimented on her to find out the secret of near immortality, if that was even true? So far, she'd only had Arneu's statements to that effect. Would they send her to a special hospital where she would never again know freedom? She knew that while she was on the space station there was nowhere to run to, nowhere to hide. She shouldn't have delayed submitting her resignation. Once she was detached from active duty, their ability to commit her would be seriously diminished. For now she would simply have to play along and watch for an opportunity for escape. If she could get to the *Vordoth*, perhaps she could stow away until it left orbit. There were plenty of planets in the Frontier Zone where one could get lost.

The com panel on the aide's desk sounded just then and the aide looked at the message. "You may go in now, Ensign," he said.

Jenetta stood up, straightened her tunic, and arched her back. *Well, here goes*, she said to herself. Walking to the doors that led to the admiral's office, she took a deep breath and released it slowly before moving into the sensor area that would announce her readiness to enter.

The doors opened to reveal an enormous, lavishly decorated office filled with senior GSC officers. Jenetta's eyes widened. It seemed as if everyone on the base with the rank of Commander and above was there. Everyone stopped talking and turned to stare at her as she entered. Jenetta took two steps into the room and came to attention as the doors closed behind her. With everyone staring at her, her concern was growing with each passing microsecond. Her only consolation was that she felt sure they wouldn't have assembled a group like this if their intention was to commit her to a hospital, but she couldn't fathom why else she'd been summoned.

Admiral Holt, sitting at his desk in front of a SimWindow currently displaying a view of the enormous GSC Space Command base in Nebraska, said loudly, "Come in, Ensign, all the way."

Jenetta advanced to about two meters from his desk and again came stiffly to attention. The admiral rose, came out from behind an ornately carved desk that appeared to come from a different era, and confronted her. At six-foot two-inches and over two-hundred pounds, the still fit seventy-one-year-old admiral cast an imposing figure as he stood in front of her, unsmiling.

"For such a small officer," the admiral boomed as he towered over Jenetta, "you throw a mighty big shadow, Ensign. I've done little except talk to people about *you* for the past four weeks. I've been fielding calls from the Galactic Alliance Council, Space Command Supreme Headquarters, the Admiralty Board, the Nordakian Palace, the Nordakian Space Force, and every damned news organization in the galaxy."

"I'm sorry for causing you so much trouble, Admiral."

"Trouble? Did I say anything about trouble?"

"Uh— no sir. I thought that was what you meant."

Admiral Holt smiled and said in his booming voice, "Hell no! I've been having the time of my life! It's the most excitement we've had around here in years!" Lowering his voice to a more normal speaking level, he added, "That yarn you spun at the trial was one of the best stories I've heard since I was a small boy sitting on my grandfather's lap as he read C.S. Forester's epic tales about his fictional seafaring officer, Horatio Hornblower."

"Fictional? I *assure* the Admiral that every word of my testimony at the court-martial was true."

"Oh, I believe you, Ensign. Your story's been put through the wringer and checked every which way from Sunday to Saturday, and back again. Commander Kanes' boys and girls in Intelligence haven't been able to find a single statement they could disprove— or even doubt. In fact, most of it has been verified by as many as fifty witnesses. If anything, the witnesses unanimously say you understate your own participation and heroism in the events that transpired."

"I only did what I felt was fitting and proper for a Space Command officer, sir."

"It's our considered opinion that you went well above and beyond 'fitting and proper.' You showed initiative and daring, properly coupled with superior intelligence and training. Those are qualities we prize highly in our officers. Your escape from the detention center enthralled me the most. That was all guts and glory, from the moment you killed your guard in unarmed combat and then single-handedly took out all the other guards, until the space station blew up. It's unfortunate you had to leave Captain Starnos and his first mate behind, but, confidentially, in your place I would have done exactly the same thing. You must be hell on wheels with a pistol, Ensign. The witnesses unanimously state that you drew your side arm so fast they didn't see your hand move and that you had shot Starnos' mate before Starnos had even started to fall."

"I anticipated trouble from someone, Admiral, so I was ready. I'd had a couple of weeks to plan every phase of the escape."

"But you couldn't know who would challenge your authority for command, or what the situation would be like once you got out of the detention center?"

"The situation was a bit fluid, sir, but aren't all military operations? I calculated that if the command issue was raised, it would likely come from someone not accustomed to following orders, such as a freighter captain or senior officer. I regret that I had to leave Starnos and his first mate behind, but a second escape group would have significantly reduced the odds of anyone attaining freedom. I knew I was never going to be shipped off to a pleasure resort in the Uthlaro Dominion to live out my life as a mindless sex slave, so I was prepared to do whatever was necessary. And I'll make no apologies for the destruction of the station."

"And you shouldn't. We're not upset about the loss of that spaceport. Hell, we would have blown it to Hades ourselves if we had known of it. We're also extremely grateful that you were able to bring back both the *Prometheus* and the *Chiron*."

"Thank you, sir. It's nice that someone has acknowledged *that little fact—* at last."

Admiral Holt chuckled and said, "Been feeling a little unappreciated, Ensign?"

"Yes sir, a little."

"Well, don't be. We *had* to do what we did."

"Sir?"

"We had no choice but to put you through the hell of a general court-martial. You killed, on your own initiative and virtually single-handedly, over eighteen thousand Raiders in the spaceport and another thousand or two in the ships you engaged while acting as captain of the *Vordoth*. That's more Raiders than all of Space Command has captured or killed in the past decade. There's no way in this universe that could just be swept out the airlock. There would have been a formal inquiry even if an authorized task force had destroyed the base.

"Supreme HQ believed that some of the more radical members of the press might try to propagandize the annihilation of the Raider Base as an example of military excess, so we decided to give them a different rallying position. They all love underdogs, so we gave them one they could really get behind—you. Commander Kanes, who by the way has been one of your staunchest supporters since your identity was confirmed, assured us you could hold up through the rigors of the court-martial. After the things you accomplished, we all knew you were made of stern stuff. The trial itself was planned down to the smallest detail, even to eliciting sympathy for you by hobbling you with prisoner transport chains during the early stages. I hear that fact alone brought people over to your side in droves before the trial even began."

Jenetta was stunned by the revelation. "You mean it was all rigged, sir?"

"Oh, no, it was a real court-martial. The six jurors, who, by the way, are all in this room right now, weren't a party to discussions about the case until after the court-martial was over. We just knew in advance that the overwhelming evidence would lead to your acquittal. In fact, we made the charges as preposterous as possible so that acquittal was the only sane response. You see, this way people can't say the military is trying to hide anything. Occasionally, situations do occur which the public is far better off not knowing about, but this was much too big to keep under wraps so we had to bring it out into the open. Now everything has been bared and inspected under a microscope from every possible angle. You've been acquitted and it's over. There are no dirty little secrets for reporters to dig out. Is that clear?"

"As crystal, sir."

"Good. And there won't be any further discussion of what I've just said outside of this room?"

"Did you say something, sir?"

Admiral Holt grinned. "You'll go far, Ensign." He looked over at Commanders Kanes and Pierce and said, "Gentlemen?"

At that invitation, both officers came over to face Jenetta.

"Ensign," Pierce said, "we very much regret the way we had to treat you, but we had difficult roles to play. We had to suppress our respect and appreciation for the incredible things you've done while appearing cold and angry, and we needed your reactions to appear genuine. The fear and anguish you had to be feeling after serving Space Command so heroically must have been horrendous. I know nothing I say can ever erase that memory, but you should know I admire you more than I can adequately express."

"Ditto from the Intelligence section, Ensign," Kanes said, "but after what you did, and from the time I spent interviewing you, I knew that you could take the heat without cracking. You're one tough little customer. Well done, Ensign. Very well done!"

Jenetta wondered what they'd say if they knew just how close she'd come to resigning her commission and separating from the service. Understanding the reason for the unfair treatment didn't erase the resentment she felt for being used so badly, but it began the process of healing the hurt. She swallowed the words that she'd like to hurl in their faces and instead said, in diplomatic fashion, "Thank you, gentlemen. I admit that I was feeling a little down, but you've completely restored my faith in the service."

"The reason we've called you here today," Admiral Holt said, as Pierce and Kanes returned to where they had been standing before coming over to face Jenetta, "is to thank you for what you've done and let you know that all of us here support your actions one hundred percent. Most of us are even a little envious of the excitement you had for a few months. The worst thing in the universe, for a command officer, is to be stuck behind a desk, as many of us here today can testify."

"Yes sir. I know *exactly* what you mean."

Admiral Holt chuckled. "Not happy over in the Science Section? I can understand that. The work performed there is important, but it's not for everyone. Posting you there temporarily was just another part of the plan. We've all come to realize that you can best serve the Galactic Alliance in another role, but until we'd had a chance to perform a full psych exam, we couldn't possibly appoint you to any position that required more than a basic security clearance. You were in the hands of the Raiders for a full month, after all. Dr. Friedlander's call to the Psych Department was just a coincidence. You were already scheduled for a complete exam. Dr. Praeges has restored your security clearances and your service classification has officially been changed from science officer to something more befitting your abilities and desires.

"Next week," Admiral Holt continued, "you'll report to your new ship. You'll be back in space again and this time you'll be in a command position on the bridge. I wish I was going as well, but my job is riding that desk back there now."

If Jenetta received nothing else for everything she had done, transfer to a command position as a helmsman or astrogator would be reward enough. She hoped the position would be aboard a research ship instead of a quartermaster ship or reclamation vessel, but she would be immensely satisfied with any command slot.

"*However*," the admiral continued, "one of the best parts of this job is what I get to do now. The room shall come to attention."

The officers in the room formed several lines and adopted the appropriate rigid stance while the admiral took a holo-tube from his desk, activated it, and read the page that popped up.

"Ensign Jenetta Alicia Carver, by special order from Space Command Supreme Headquarters, with unanimous confirmation by the Galactic Alliance Council, you are immediately advanced to the rank of Lieutenant Command-er." Lowering the holo-tube, he said, "Congratulations, Com-mander."

Jenetta had immediately realized she was being promoted when the admiral began reading, but she expected to hear 'Lieutenant(jg).' When the Admiral said 'Lieutenant Commander,' her jaw dropped and she just stood there with her eyes wide and her mouth hanging open.

Admiral Holt chuckled. "This is the first time I've seen you at a loss for words, Commander."

"Li— Lieutenant Commander? Surely you meant to say Lieutenant(jg), sir."

"No— I meant to say Lieutenant Commander."

With narrowing eyes, Jenetta asked, "Is this a joke, sir?"

Admiral Holt grinned. "Supreme Headquarters is not in the habit of making jokes, Commander."

"Uh, no sir. But isn't that— rather an unusual promotion? I mean, from Ensign to Lieutenant Commander? That's three grades, sir."

"Advancement from ensign to lieutenant(jg) is not really a promotion in the normal sense, but rather an upgrade at the discretion of a commanding officer when he or she feels the new officer is deserving. If not for all this brouhaha with the court-martial, you would have received that immediately upon your arrival here. So it's really just a two-grade promotion. And yes, even that is a bit unusual, although in Earth's history there have been battlefield promotions that far surpass it. I prefer to think of this advancement as simply being— overdue. You were repeatedly skipped over at promotion time because we, um— temporarily misplaced you, so Space Command is merely placing you where someone of your demonstrated talents and ability would no doubt be after eleven years in Space Command. Most of your classmates who have remained in the service have reached Lieutenant and one recently made Lieutenant Commander. After what you've done for the people of the Galactic Alliance, we can't have you being junior to any of your former classmates. And Commander?"

"Sir?"

"I've made a small wager that you'll be the first of your graduating class to reach the rank of captain— officially. Don't let me down."

"No sir. I mean, yes sir. Thank you, sir."

"Here's your first set of three bars to replace the single that you're currently wearing. Admiral Margolan, would you assist me, please."

"I would be most honored, sir," Admiral Margolan said.

Jenetta stood at attention as the two admirals replaced the ensign insignia on each epaulet with new insignia that showed her rank to be lieutenant commander. When they were done, both stood facing Jenetta and saluted her. She immediately returned their salute.

"Since we're officially at war with the Raiders, I'm also pleased to award this Purple Heart in recognition of the broken arm that you suffered while retaking the *Prometheus*," Admiral Holt said, holding out a medal case. "I'm as glad as you are that you were able to avoid those lattice shots."

"Yes sir. Thank you, sir."

"It's also my pleasure to give you the Space Command Star you were awarded following the explosion of the *Hokyuu*. It was awarded posthumously, but the records have been amended so you're entitled to wear it. I know it won't make up for the many years you lost, but it's the best we can do."

"Thank you, sir."

"And here's your new service classification insignia." Smiling widely, Admiral Holt held out a small jeweler's case and raised the snap-open lid. The case contained the two new gold insignia for her collar.

Jenetta started to reach for the box and then froze as she saw the insignia. All command officers wear gold collar insignia in the shape of an inverted 'V,' meant to be symbolic of an early spaceship blasting off from a planet. But the insignia that Admiral Holt was holding also contained a red garnet inset at the widest part of the 'V.' Intended to represent the flames from the ignition of liquid fuel, only the collar insignia of a line officer contained that red inset.

"I don't understand, sir," she said.

With smiling eyes the admiral said, "You were expecting to be posted maybe to a research ship, quartermaster ship, or possibly a reclamation vessel? Something like that?"

"Uh, yes sir."

"Because of the regulation that requires all line officers to be graduates of the Warship Command Institute?"

"Yes sir."

"The Admiralty Board endorsed your advance registration for the next class of WCI students."

"They did?" Jenetta said, her face lighting up.

"But then they withdrew it," he said, his face reflecting sadness.

Her smile immediately faded. Crestfallen, she said, "They did?"

"They decided that it would be— awkward— to have a Lt. Commander who had seen such action as you have, and been the subject of so much attention, in a class with a bunch of inexperienced ensigns. They felt the other officers would be in such awe of you that it could affect their performance. Besides which, during these difficult times we can't have an

officer with your abilities and experiences sitting in a classroom for two years while a professor tells you things you
already know, and possibly even know better. Or worse,
wasting those talents by posting you to a Quartermaster ship
or Research vessel, as vital as those services are. So the
Admiralty Board has decided to waive the regulation in this
instance and allow you to assume your new post aboard ship
immediately.

"I fully endorse their decision. I've had an opportunity to
review the bridge logs of your time as captain of the
Vordoth— not just the logs recorded immediately prior to and
during the attacks, but the normal watch logs as well. I
recognize command ability when I see it. You belong on the
bridge of a warship."

Jen returned her gaze to the small case and reached out
with trembling hands to accept the insignia, a lump material-
izing in her throat as tears welled up in her eyes. It was her
lifelong dream come true, a command posting to a warship.

"The room shall be at ease," Admiral Holt said and everyone relaxed. Handing Jenetta a data ring, the Admiral said,
"Here are your orders to report to the captain of the Prometheus two days from now by 0700 hours. You are now the
second officer of that ship. As second, you'll be back in the
command chair for part of each day, although it will be the
third watch."

Jenetta was dazed anew as she stared at the Admiral
through moist eyes. "The *Prometheus*, sir?"

"One of the two best warships in the fleet, as you well
know."

"Yes sir, but..." Jenetta took a deep breath and shook her
head slightly to clear it. "Thank you, sir. It's more than I ever
dared hope for."

"The *Prometheus* and *Chiron* are returning to Earth for
their official launching ceremonies, but the *Prometheus* has
been commissioned effective on the date you took it back
from the Raiders. As such, the logs and the ship's identification plaque on the bridge will forever show that the first
captain of the ship was one Ensign Jenetta Alicia Carver.

You're also entitled to wear a golden pip on your collar. There's one in the case with the new collar insignia."

Jenetta's jaw dropped again. As far as she knew, no other currently serving officer had been permitted to wear a pip before attaining the official Space Command rank of Captain, the rank required for appointment to warship command. Although Space Command and the Space Marine Corps have many different ship configurations for warfare operations and support, only Space Command's destroyers, frigates, cruisers, and battleships are included under the umbrella term, 'warship.' A golden pip represents a previous warship command, while a red pip represents a current appointment. Admiral Holt wore five golden pips on his collar.

"You're the only ensign in the history of Space Command to be officially recognized as the captain of an active duty GSC battleship. In fact, I don't believe any officer below the rank of Commander has ever been acknowledged as the captain of any warship. It's a great honor, Commander."

"I know, sir," Jenetta said, as she wiped at the tears that had trickled down her cheeks. "I'm feeling a little light-headed."

"Stay with us, Commander, there's more. Following the official launching of the *Prometheus*, the ship will take you and a delegation of Galactic Alliance Council members to Nordakia where you will be awarded the Tawroolee Medal of Valor."

"Nordakia? I don't know what to say, sir."

"Then don't say anything until you've heard it all," Admiral Holt said.

"There's more?"

"The Galactic Alliance Council has voted to award you the Medal of Honor for your infiltration of an enemy base, your successful destruction of the Raider spaceport, and the return of the two stolen battleships. The ceremony will be held on Earth preceding the official launching of the *Prometheus*."

"Medal of Honor? Me?"

"Yes, you, Commander."

Jenetta took another deep breath. "Is that all, sir?"

The admiral chuckled. "Isn't that enough?"

"Oh, yes sir. Yes sir, definitely. I just want to pinch myself now and wake up. This has to be the best dream ever and I want to record it on my personal log ring so I don't forget a bit of it."

The admiral laughed robustly and the officers in the room joined in. "It's not a dream, Commander. It's better than that. It's real."

Jenetta pinched her leg hard, just to be sure. "Yes sir. It certainly seems to be."

The ceremonies over, the attendees began to introduce themselves and personally congratulate Jenetta. She smiled, shook hands, and did her best to remember all the names. Officers began to filter out after congratulating her and the room was almost cleared when Jenetta thanked the admirals and was dismissed.

The morning had brought a rollercoaster of emotions, beginning with the fears that she might either be re-arrested or bundled off to a research lab somewhere for endless experimentation. The revelation that the court-martial had been a sham, of sorts, had both shocked her deeply and temporarily filled her with resentment, but she understood why she hadn't been informed beforehand. She probably couldn't have emoted the necessary reactions if she'd known in advance that she'd be cleared of all charges. Then to be promoted three grades and have numerous honors heaped upon her had been both exhilarating and numbing. Lastly, to learn that she was now the second officer aboard the *Prometheus* carried her to a dizzying height. Her elation was almost too much to suppress. She wanted to scream, as she had when she'd learned of her posting to the *Hokyuu*, but as the newest Lt. Commander in Space command, it just wouldn't be decorous.

She still had an hour until lunch so she walked back to the Science Section to get the few personal things she had in her desk. On the way, she stopped just long enough to replace the science officer insignia on her collar with the new line officer insignia and single pip. Using her reflection in a thick polycarbonate door at the entrance to the Science Section, she ensured they were properly positioned and then admired their appearance on her collar.

Immediately spotting the new Lieutenant Commander rank insignia on her epaulets, Lieutenant Kesliski accosted Jenetta before she was ten steps into the room.

"Are you insane? They just finished court-martialing you for wearing captain's bars and now you show up wearing the rank insignia of a Lt. Commander." Kesliski grinned slightly. "I can't let this slip, Ensign. I'll have to report this breach of conduct to Base Security."

"It's *Lt. Commander* Carver, *Lieutenant* Kesliski. I've been promoted and reassigned as second officer aboard the battle-ship *Prometheus*, leaving shortly for Earth. If you have any questions, you're welcome to call Admiral Holt's aide and verify my promotion and posting. But if you call Base Security *without* first checking, I'll have you slapped in the brig for making false accusations against a superior officer. Now get out of my way, *Lieutenant!*"

Lieutenant Kesliski practically jumped aside at the crisply spoken command, her eyes wide and her mouth hanging open. Jenetta walked calmly to her desk, retrieved her personal items, and then headed for the door, stopping where a shocked Lieutenant Kesliski was still standing.

"Close your mouth, Lieutenant; you look exceedingly foolish like that. I know you haven't approved of me and intended to make my life as miserable as possible while you were my supervising officer, so it's a real pleasure for me to say farewell." Reaching into her tunic pocket, she produced the science officer insignia she had just replaced on her collar. "Here," she said, holding out the insignia to the lieutenant and depositing them in Kesliski's hand when it was extended, "perhaps you'll find some use for these. As you were."

Jenetta turned and walked from the room. Telling Kesliski off had been the best few seconds she'd had in that office.

Lt. Kesliski looked down at the collar insignia in her hand as the door slid closed. Her surprised facial expression changing to show the frustration and anger that was beginning to boil over inside her, she screamed loud and long before throwing the insignia against the nearest wall with all the strength she possessed.

As she walked down the corridor, Jenetta heard Lt. Kesliski's emotional outburst. A smile momentarily lit up her face before being replaced by the staid expression she felt was expected of a senior officer on duty.

~ The End of the Beginning ~

*** *Jenetta's exciting adventures continue in:* ***
# Valor at Vauzlee

Appendix A

The existence of hyperspace had been hypothesized since the twentieth century. Certain scientists and mathematicians claimed to be able to prove 'mathematically' that it existed, but discovering a means of transitioning matter into or out of hyperspace continued to evade researchers. Once generally propagandized as the only practical avenue to faster-than-light travel, research all but ceased in that regard when a small cadre of scientists, working under a government research grant at a U.S. university, chanced upon a naturally occurring phenomena they immediately named Dis-Associative Temporal Field Anomalies. Their original objecttive of finding new methods to more accurately predict the formation of tornados using lidar measurement was quickly set aside as excitement over the new phenomena gripped the team. DATFA research was later credited with pounding the final nail into the hyperspace FTL coffin.

Rather than simply being a different dimension in space, DATFAs exist *outside* space. Or at least outside the currently accepted physical laws and scientific definitions for three-dimensional normal-space and hyperspace, not the standard plebeian dictionary definition of 'the unlimited expanse in which everything is located.' As word of the discovery leaked, scientists who had long theorized the existence of wormholes, though none had yet been identified, immediately announced that wormholes were simply naturally occurring DATFA interchanges with certain unique properties of stability and ingress. More pragmatic scientists preferred to engage in research with a proven scientific fundament, so the number of scientists working to develop the field of DATFA expanded rapidly. Within a decade, under the tight security of the U.S. military, the theorems had been developed into practical mechanics and the door to galactic adventure was about to be flung wide open. Miniscule formations of DATFA could be coalesced, then expanded to completely surround a physical entity. By 'constructing' this temporal field anomaly around its entire length and breadth, an entity effectively disassociates itself from the physical bonds of normal space and time. When viewed against development of life on Earth, the current inhabitants of the planet moved from an intrastellar civilization to interstellar explorers overnight.

A ship outfitted with a temporal field generator can first build its envelope, then advance by building another envelope, slightly ahead of, but overlapping, the first. The ship is then 'absorbed' into the new envelope as the older envelope dissolves. In this way, the ship goes along for the ride like a surfer catching a wave, but being disassociated from the mechanics of the surrounding space and time means there's no sensation of movement. To change direction, the shape of the next envelope is altered slightly with the forefront aimed more in line with the direction the ship wishes to travel. To speed up or slow down, the ship simply alters the rate at which new envelopes are created. When the temporal field generator is disengaged and the envelope dissolves, the ship is in a new place, still just as stationary as it had been when the initial envelope was built. Time does not slow down as the ship approaches and then exceeds the speed of light. It's as if no such relative barrier exists in normal space. Nor does time stop for the travelers in the envelope. It simply continues as it had before. Inside the envelope a new space and time exists. A trip takes only as long as it takes to create the full series of temporal envelopes from starting point to destination.

By disassociating a spacecraft from space and time, Einstein's Theory of Special Relativity was marginalized for space travelers. In fairness to an incredibly brilliant mind, he had himself already admitted something was missing from his calculations that prevented him from developing a single, unified theory of relativity. His theories about a repulsive form of gravity that emanates from empty space, and which was later named dark energy, would have benefited greatly from knowledge of temporal anomalies.

Earth's first successful faster-than-light spaceship put the United States at the forefront of galactic exploration, and it continued to press that advantage by producing a series of ever faster spaceships, capable of generating new envelopes at ever greater speeds, as it explored the cosmos. Along the way, it naturally laid claim to planets capable of supporting human life, and immediately established colonies as evidence of ownership. While international treaties governing ownership rights on Earth's moon had been signed, none that referred to territories outside Earth's gravitational influence had been officially inked. For decades, the issue was cause for great debate, anger, and hostility among the more fanatical elements in the nations on Earth technologically unable to send their own explorers into space, because it allegedly denied them the opportunity to spread their religions and cultures among the stars. Naturally, the 'godless' United States was blamed by them as the party most responsible for their almost total inability to compete in space exploration. One senator, with tongue firmly planted in cheek while on the floor of the U.S. Senate, agreed to accept personal responsibility for the fact that camel dung cannot properly be synthesized into spacecraft fuel. He added that it's difficult to conquer the stars while you're doing your damndest to remain rooted in the eighth century.

*   *   *

As established interstellar colonies grew, their citizenry demanded a home rule government not subject to martial law except in times of obvious crisis. These first stirrings of independence were recognized in the U.S., whose own struggle for independence from distant colonial rule in the late eighteenth century is still celebrated each year. In a magnanimous gesture, the U.S. Government guaranteed complete independence to all its colonies once they reached a certain population density, subject to the proviso that areas where previously established business interests existed be designated as permanent U.S. Enterprises Zones. This en- sured that certain so-called independence efforts were not just a precursor to planned nationalization of valuable and pros- perous business assets. Within all Enterprise Zones, planetary governments were required to observe the business rights spelled out in the Off-World Colonization Act of 2035. Other spacefaring nations soon followed the U.S. lead and granted independence to their larger colonies.

A further legacy of the U.S. lead in the early exploration of the galaxy was the adoption of Amer as the defacto standard language in most off-world colonies, just as American had long been the official language of international business, shipping, and aviation on Earth. Amer was a more business oriented, less stylized version of the American language, still with all the colloquialisms and nuances that had crept into the English-based language over the centuries. Even so, scattered enclaves, and eventually even entire colonies, were established where zealous individuals kept alive their ancient languages and cultures.

* * *

As the decades passed, and space travel became almost commonplace, the need for laws governing space, an agency to enforce those laws, and courts to adjudicate issues and violations, became obvious to everyone. The solution, arrived at by a committee composed of representatives of earth and the fifteen largest planetary governments, was the formation of the Galactic Alliance. Established as a confederation of member planets, the purpose of the GA was to promote the general welfare by providing extra-world security to all member planets. From the start, it was decided the GA would, within specific boundaries, regulate interstellar transportation, establish policies for peaceful trade between planets, create a galactic monetary system, and establish a military arm that would enforce the laws and protect the established territories of the GA. No control of planetary governments was ever planned for or desired. Initially composed of sixteen original signatories to the charter, it was clearly recognized that the number would grow as populations grew in both established colonies and colonies that hadn't yet been envisioned.

Representatives from the home worlds that signed the initial accords worked for eight years to develop and ratify a constitution, then delineate the territory to be included. Galactic Alliance space originally encompassed a cylindrical area of space with a diameter of five hundred light-years, that stretched to five hundred light-years on either side of a median line extending through the center plane of the galaxy. At the beginning of the twenty-third century, the Alliance amended the territorial delineation to include all galactic space above and below the cylindrical diameter, and added a one hundred parsec wide band around their territory, except where parts of that space had already been claimed by another nation. Although officially GA space, the newly claimed area was far too vast for proper enforcement of laws, and that part of the GA became known as the Frontier Zone. The expansion immediately created a common border with two nations, the Clidepp Empire and the Aguspod. A third nation, the Kweedee Aggregate, expanded their territory shortly thereafter, extending their border up to the territorial border of space now claimed by the GA. With that expansion, slightly more than one-half of Galactic Alliance territory shared common boundaries with other nations, while the remainder bordered on unclaimed space.

From the beginning, it was decided that not all planetary governments within the claimed territory need become active members of the GA, but that all space outside every planet's sensible atmosphere (one hundred kilometers above the planet's mean surface), would be subject to all the laws of the Alliance. Any attempt to create an extra-planetary ruling government within GA space would be treated as sedition, or invasion. True to its charter, the GA maintained an official 'hands off' policy with both member worlds and non-member worlds. What happened on their planet was their own business, with four notable exceptions. One was in the area of sentient life rights. Absolutely no slavery involving sentient life forms would be permitted anywhere in GA space. The manufacture of illegal substances, intended for export off-world, was prohibited. The development of certain technologies, whether for export or not, were outlawed. And lastly, counterfeiting and other attempts to affect the economical stability of the Alliance Monetary Fund would be dealt with quickly, severely, and decisively.

If civil unrest or violence on a planet threatened to expand beyond a planet's borders, then the GA had not only the authority to step in, but also the mandate to do so. That included the authority to arrest individuals traveling to another planet for the purpose of sowing the seeds of revolution. If a legally recognized planetary government requested assistance, the GA might send in help to restore order. But each intervention had to first be approved by the GA Council. And there was no guarantee that the government calling for assistance would be allowed to remain in power once they arrived. The forces of Space Command and the Space Marine Corps would not be used to prop up unpopular or puppet governments.

Finally, as a further incentive to join the GA as a participating and voting member, all non-member worlds were prohibited from trading with or interacting with business interests on member worlds. The benefits of membership were immediately apparent to everyone who had goods to export, or desired the importation of goods from member worlds. Member worlds were also free to withdraw from GA membership and again trade with non-member worlds, but withdrawal mandated a full ten-year waiting period before an application to rejoin the GA was considered, during which time there could be no trade with member worlds. To ensure that illegal trade was not conducted, an outpost was established in orbit around every inhabited, non-member planet. All ships were required to submit to a full inspection when arriving or leaving the planet. It didn't stop smuggling, but it severely retarded its growth.

Contact with any world containing sentient life, which had not yet achieved space flight capability on their own, was strictly forbidden. A heretofore un-colonized planet that was found to contain native sentient life could not be colonized, or even occupied until approved by the Galactic Alliance Bureau of Alien Affairs. Where a planet with sentient life had already been colonized, the GABAA was charged with working out a reasonable settlement of claims.

Any violation of the rule of law, or any attempts to subvert the regulations, carried the strictest of penalties. Space Command was charged with watching for such interference, authorized to take whatever steps it deemed proper to prevent such abuse, and under mandate to arrest the perpetrators. The ships and cargo of convicted violators were seized and sold to support Space Command operations.

The Galactic Alliance Headquarters, sited at the former SAC HQ in Nebraska on Earth because the planet seemed to offer the best security during the early years of the GA, was the official home of a body comprised of democratically elected galactic officials. Earth was not at the center of Alliance space, but it was over five hundred light years from the borders of the Alliance's nearest neighboring nation. Regardless of the form of government on the home world to be represented, only GA officials that had been freely elected in a planetary referendum under the supervision of GA monitors, could take their seats in the Alliance Senate. Each planetary delegation would then elect a single member to a committee of directors known as the Galactic Alliance Council. Each councilor's vote was weighted by a complex formula designed to ensure the fairest representation for both large and small planetary populations. A council member could be recalled at any time by a majority vote in his or her delegation, and a new council member seated. The size of the council would only grow as the number of member worlds grew.

* * *

The Galactic Space Command was developed as the enforcement arm of the Galactic Alliance. With no desire to totally reinvent the wheel, it was decided to use the navies of Earth as models in its creation. Its final form seemed to represent the navy of the U.S. more than others, but that might have arisen more from convenience than anything else. The committee started with the U.S. Navy as its foundation, and only altered the structure where it felt another nation's service branch provided a more enlightened solution to specific concerns. It was fully recognized that the final form would change as practical application met Utopian ideals.

A Space Marine Corps was created to provide ground forces for special situations, and to perform as security personnel aboard all SC warships, bases, and space stations. The Corps had no interstellar fleet of its own, but all SC warships carried detachments of Space Marines, landing craft, and fighters. SC troop transports would be used for deployments when larger forces were involved.

The Supreme Headquarters for Space Command was also located on Earth, and upon enactment of its charter by the Galactic Alliance Council, it immediately assumed command of all colonial military bases off-world. While owing its creation, funding, and continued existence to the Galactic Alliance Council, Space Command would for the most part operate independent of that body as it enforced interstellar adherence to GA laws.

The chief governing body within Space Command is the Admiralty Board. Comprised initially often members, all of whom have attained or surpassed the rank of Rear Admiral (Lower), the board meets several times a week to settle the pressing issues of the service. Presided over by the Admiral of the Fleet, decisions are decided by a two-thirds majority vote, although certain veto powers always remain with the AF and GA Council. The meetings are usually conducted in private, but always take place in the Admiralty Board Hall. A gallery area is available when the Board wishes to invite interested parties to view its proceedings.

Appendix B

This chart is offered to assist readers who may be unfamiliar with military rank and the reporting structure. Newly commissioned officers begin at either ensign or second lieutenant rank.

Space Command	Space Marine Corps
Admiral of the Fleet	
Admiral	General
Vice-Admiral	Lieutenant General
Rear Admiral - Upper	Major General
Rear Admiral - Lower	Brigadier General
Captain	Colonel
Commander	Lieutenant Colonel
Lieutenant Commander	Major
Lieutenant	Captain
Lieutenant(jg) "Junior Grade"	First Lieutenant
Ensign	Second Lieutenant

The commanding officer on a ship is always referred to as Captain, regardless of his or her official military rank. Even an Ensign could be a Captain of the Ship, although that would only occur as the result of an unusual situation or emergency where no senior officers survive.

On Space Command ships and bases, time is measured according to a twenty-four clock, normally referred to as military time. For example, 8:42 PM would be referred to as 2042 hours. Chronometers are set to always agree with the date and time at Space Command Supreme Headquarters on Earth. This is known as GST, or Galactic System Time.

Admiralty Board:

Moore, Richard E.	Admiral of the Fleet
Platt, Evelyn S.	Admiral - Director of Fleet Operations
Bradlee, Roger T.	Admiral - Director of Intelligence (SCI)
Ressler, Shana E.	Admiral - Director of Budget & Accounting
Hillaire, Arnold H.	Admiral - Director of Academies
Burke, Raymond A.	Vice-Admiral - Director of GSC Base Management
Ahmed, Raihana L.	Vice-Admiral - Dir. of Quartermaster Supply
Woo, Lon C.	Vice-Admiral - Dir. of Scientific & Expeditionary Forces
Plimley, Loretta J.	Rear-Admiral, (U) - Dir. of Weapons R&D
Hubera, Donald M.	Rear-Admiral, (U) - Dir. of Academy Curricula

Ship Speed Terminology	*Speed*
Plus-1	1 kps
Sub-Light-1	1,000 kps
Light-1 (c) (speed of light in a vacuum)	299,792.458 kps
Light-150 or **150 c**	150 times the speed of light

Hyper-Space Factors	
IDS Communications Band	.0513 light years each minute (8.09 billion kps)
DeTect Range	4 billion kilometers

Sample Distances

Earth to Mars (Mean)	78 million kilometers
Nearest star to our Sun	4 light-years (Proxima Centauri)
Milky Way Galaxy diameter	100,000 light-years
Thickness of M'Way at Sun	2,000 light-years
Stars in Milky Way	200 billion (est.)
Nearest galaxy (Andromeda)	2 million light-years from M'Way
A light-year (in a vacuum)	9,460,730,472,580.8 kilometers
A light-second (in vacuum)	299,792.458 km
Grid Unit	1,000 Light Yrs^2 (1,000,000 Sq. LY)
Deca-Sector	100 Light Years^2 (10,000 Sq. LY)
Sector	10 Light Years^2 (100 Sq. LY)
Section	94,607,304,725 km^2
Sub-section	946,073,047 km^2

The following two-dimensional representation is offered to provide the reader with a feel for the spatial relationships between bases, systems, and celestial events referenced in the first three novels of this series. The mean distance from Earth to Higgins Space Command Base has been calculated as 90.1538 light-years. The thousands of stars, planets, and moons in this small part of G.A. space would only confuse, and therefore have been omitted from the image.

Should the following map be unreadable, or should you desire additional imagery, .jpg and .pdf versions of all maps are available for free downloading at:

www.deprima.com/ancillary/agu.html

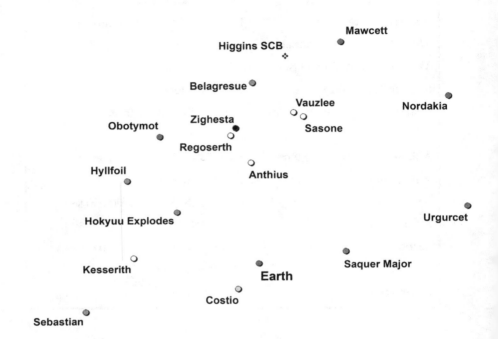

Lazziter

Mawcett

Higgins SCB

Belagresue

Vauzlee

Nordakia

Obotymot

Zighesta

Sasone

Regoserth

Hyllfoil

Anthius

Hokyuu Explodes

Urgurcet

Kesserith

Saquer Major

Earth

Costio

Sebastian

Ethridge SCB

CPSIA information can be obtained
at www.ICGtesting.com
Printed in the USA
BVHW040511070422
633568BV00005B/369